MEN·ON·MEN
4
·BEST·NEW·GAY·FICTION·

EDITED BY
GEORGE STAMBOLIAN

INTRODUCTION BY
FELICE PICANO

AFTERWORD BY
ANDREW HOLLERAN

A PLUME BOOK

PLUME
Published by the Penguin Group
Penguin Books USA Inc., 375 Hudson Street,
New York, New York 10014, U.S.A.
Penguin Books Ltd, 27 Wrights Lane,
London W8 5TZ, England
Penguin Books Australia Ltd, Ringwood,
Victoria, Australia
Penguin Books Canada Ltd, 10 Alcorn Avenue,
Toronto, Ontario, Canada M4V 3B2
Penguin Books (N.Z.) Ltd, 182–190 Wairau Road,
Auckland 10, New Zealand

Penguin Books Ltd, Registered Offices:
Harmondsworth, Middlesex, England

First published by Plume, an imprint of New American Library,
a division of Penguin Books USA Inc.
Simultaneously published in a Dutton hardcover edition.

First Printing, October, 1992
10 9 8 7 6 5 4

Acknowledgments

"Pico-Union" by Luis Alfaro. Copyright © 1992 by Luis Alfaro. Published by permission of the author.
"If a Man Answers" by David B. Feinberg. First published in *The Ten Commandments*. Copyright © 1992 by David B. Feinberg. Published by permission of the author.
"Everyman" by Robert Glück. Copyright © 1992 by Robert Glück. Published by permission of the author.
"The Magistrate's Monkey" by Richard House. Copyright © 1992 by Richard House. Published by permission of the author.
"The Little Trooper" by Manuel Igrejas. Copyright © 1992 by Manuel Igrejas. Published by permission of the author.
"The Valentine" by Greg Johnson. First published in *The Southwest Review*. Copyright © 1991 by Greg Johnson. Published by permission of the author.
"Ten Reasons Why Michael and Geoff Never Got It On" by Raymond Luczak. Copyright © 1992 by Raymond Luczak. Published by permission of the author.
"Fucking Martin" by Dale Peck. Copyright © 1992 by Dale Peck. Published by permission of the author.
"Love in the Backrooms" by John Rechy. Copyright © 1992 by John Rechy. Published by permission of the author.
"Opening the Door" by Paul Russell. Copyright © 1992 by Paul Russell. Published by permission of the author.
"Sacred Lips of the Bronx" by Douglas Sadownick. Copyright © 1992 by Douglas Sadownick. Published by permission of the author.
"Bone" by Randy Sanderson. Copyright © 1992 by Randy Sanderson. Published by permission of the author.
"The Fiancé" by Michael Wade Simpson. First published in *The Crescent Review*. Copyright © 1991 by Michael Wade Simpson. Published by permission of the author.
"New Year" by Jack Slater. Copyright © 1992 by Jack Slater. Published by permission of the author.

The following page constitutes an extension of this copyright page.

REGISTERED TRADEMARK—MARCA REGISTRADA

Library of Congress Cataloging-in-Publication Data

Men on men 4 : best new gay fiction / edited by George Stambolian.
   p.   cm.
   ISBN 0-452-26856-7
   1. Gay men—Fiction.   2. Gays' writings, American.   3. American fiction—
Men authors.   4. American fiction—20th century.
I. Stambolian, George.   II. Title: Men on men four.
PS648.H57M473   1992
813′.0108353—dc20   92–53547
                                                                              CIP

Printed in the United States of America
Set in Janson
Designed by Leonard Telesca

TO THE
PUBLISHING TRIANGLE

CONTENTS

INTRODUCTION   1
FELICE PICANO

LOVE IN THE BACKROOMS   10
JOHN RECHY

FUCKING MARTIN   23
DALE PECK

THE FIANCÉ   40
MICHAEL WADE SIMPSON

SACRED LIPS OF THE BRONX   48
DOUGLAS SADOWNICK

THE LITTLE TROOPER   66
MANUEL IGREJAS

CULTURAL REVOLUTION   92
NORMAN WONG

THE MAGISTRATE'S MONKEY   111
RICHARD HOUSE

TEN REASONS WHY MICHAEL AND
GEOFF NEVER GOT IT ON   147
RAYMOND LUCZAK

THE GREEK HEAD   162
PETER WELTNER

THE VALENTINE 202
GREG JOHNSON

NEW YEAR 216
JACK SLATER

INSIDE 245
DAVID VERNON

IF A MAN ANSWERS 253
DAVID B. FEINBERG

PICO-UNION 268
LUIS ALFARO

THE SEX OFFENDER 284
MATTHEW STADLER

OPENING THE DOOR 316
PAUL RUSSELL

BONE 336
RANDY SANDERSON

EVERYMAN 359
ROBERT GLÜCK

AFTERWORD 391
ANDREW HOLLERAN

ABOUT THE AUTHORS 398
PUBLICATIONS OF INTEREST 404

INTRODUCTION

• FELICE PICANO •

"THIS FOURTH VOLUME won't be dedicated to anyone's memory," George Stambolian declared in the spring of 1991. He was at the point where he'd selected many of the stories and the book was coming together for him. "There've been enough dedications to the dead, enough of AIDS for that matter, in the series," he said.

Instead, George chose to dedicate the book to an organization—the Publishing Triangle—only a few years old but, as he realized, already active in the community, rapidly growing, and an important factor in gay literary life. The irony, of course, is that this fourth volume of the distinguished, bestselling *Men on Men* series is, despite George's wishes, in memory of George Stambolian himself.

As first an acquaintance, then a friend over the past decade, I'd found myself alternately flattered and frustrated by George as he gathered material and formulated concepts for each volume; pondered, agonized over, then at last wrote out each introduction; went out "on the road" with each book as it was published, doing all he could to publicize the work, the authors—and gay male fiction.

I was flattered, because who wouldn't be when someone as bright and cultivated and thoughtful as George selected them to bounce ideas off of, on occasion to consult with, and sometimes merely to listen to when he needed to complain about those critics of the series who he was certain were going out of their way not to understand what was being written and published—and what he and the series signified.

I was frustrated because as one of those authors and myself a publisher of gay literature, I had more experience with the cold reality of the world and I knew that for all the success of the three previous volumes, in a sense George would always be butting his head against a wall: None of us—not the writers, not the critics—would ever attain the high standards of behavior, subtlety, or intelligence George required.

In the last few months of his life, and even with some neuropathy from the HIV virus, George spoke with emphasis and at length not only about this fourth volume and the stories within it, but about the entire series: what it represented to him and what he hoped it would come to represent, what he believed it ultimately would come to stand for in American literature. He also re-voiced his strongly held opinions about the short-sightedness, the provinciality, the intolerance, and sometimes the outright bias of many reviewers both within and outside of the gay community. He left no doubts that he regarded the *Men on Men* series—even more than the other popular, scholarly books he had authored—as the keystone of his legacy.

The mental journey George Stambolian made to become editor of this series was critical—yet also unusual in gay men of his generation. For those of us a few years younger, for whom the Stonewall Riot and the resulting Gay Liberation movement seemed natural, indeed inevitable, many of our conservative gay elders turned out to be as much "the enemy" as those straights who openly oppressed us and denied us what we felt were our inalienable rights. Enemies, because closeted gays seemed to wield great power and influence in many areas of life: politics, business, the arts, and especially in the University. For every Paul Goodman and Martin Duberman who chose to come out and support Gay Liberation, there were a dozen powerful, entrenched gay men who remained closeted, sometimes sulking, often actively working against us. Given their power to influence youth at its most impressionable, they represented the single greatest hurdle—and possible channel—for wider tolerance and the growth of gay rights.

George Stambolian was a respected, tenured professor of French Literature at Wellesley College, author of *Marcel Proust and the Creative Encounter* (1972), when he turned his attention to the gay scene as it was being lived and written about in New York City and its environs in the late seventies. This is critical because it determined both the course George took and the influence he was to wield. His first step "out" was to join with Elaine Marks in collecting and contributing to an important anthology of critical texts: *Homosexualities in French Literature* (1979), a volume that spoke mainly to his academic peers, utilizing academic methods and terminology. At the same time, George helped to form the Division of Gay Studies at the Modern Language Association, which has since become a major revitalizing influence within the MLA.

Only then did he begin tentatively to write nonacademic work: short pieces for the *New York Native*, book reviews for *The Advocate*. His growing interest in and knowledge of the visual arts led him into the burgeoning gay painting, sculpture, and photography scene, centering upon the Robert Samuel Gallery, which first showed the work of Robert Mapplethorpe, Duane Michaels, George Platt Lynes, *et al.*, and where George first met gay writers, specifically the members of the Violet Quill Club. He'd already begun interviewing gay men—for *Christopher Street*, "A Beautiful Man," "A Diva," "A Self-Made Man," etc.—in which men were granted total anonymity and became utterly self-revealing. The interviews later appeared as a book, *Male Fantasies/Gay Realities* (1984).

By this time George had become aware of the publication of the first group of openly gay novels that had grown out of the post-Stonewall community: *Dancer From the Dance, Faggots, Confessions of Danny Slocum, The Lure, Nocturnes for the King of Naples*. George read those books correctly with vision rare for the time and saw them not only as pure outgrowths of that community but also as urtexts of what was to become Gay Male Fiction: the theme and style and standard-setters for what would follow, utterly different from the work of any preceding writers who happened to also be homosexual or who happened to write about homosexual life.

The existence of a club of authors like Whitmore and Ferro and Holleran etc. actually meeting over a period of months to read their works and discuss them with one another—in effect giving birth and shape and character to this new literature—struck the professorial, the critical, and the romantic strains in George; he saw all of us as "present at the creation." Although he didn't come to know the members of the Violet Quill Club until after it had stopped meeting, George had noticed us, seen us all around. He told me he'd recognized me years before. While walking his dog early one Sunday morning, he'd watched as I and two(!) companions walked past, obviously after an all-nighter at Flamingo.

Imagine then how petty and off-the-beam George considered those critics of the first volume in the *Men on Men* series who carped that he had merely put together a book of pieces by his "friends," with insufficient geographical or thematic diversity. George believed that he was doing nothing less than establishing an entire "canon" of work (as F. R. Leavis and E. M. Forster established a canon of great English novels, and Edmund Wilson one of great American authors) that he believed was as indigenous and important as those other American literary movements that have enriched literature in our century: Southern Regionalism, Urban Jewish Writing, African-American and Feminist Fiction.

Looking back on the first three volumes of *Men on Men*, one can make out both a history and a hagiography of gay male fiction in America, yet one also detects a strong reaching out from New York, toward the South and West—especially to younger writers from Los Angeles and the Bay Area.

George's aims in selecting work for this fourth volume seem clear: an even greater branching out to encompass those ethnic and racial variations not yet written about, to further enrich our lives with the even greater diversity possible in gay life. Yet as always, George made it clear that he was choosing the best stories currently being written. If African-American gays and Asian-American gays and Latino gays were now writing good enough fiction for him to present, George insisted that was because of the explosive growth of the gay male culture in this country, reflected and perhaps even stimulated by the previous three volumes of *Men on Men*. He wondered if the new work would have been written without the strong example, or even simply the existence, of the corpus he'd presented and, professorially, helped codify.

One writer already established in that corpus was John Rechy. From *City of Night*, through *Numbers* and *Bodies and Souls*, Rechy has staked out his authorial turf in the netherworld of gay life: those shadowy, sometimes violent, always ritualized, raw areas where men meet for anonymous sex. Rechy's own slang and terminology have become welded into our speech patterns, his understanding and description of our behavior has been frighteningly accurate. In the story "Love in the Backrooms," Rechy returns us to a specific time and place, those now-demolished, once-decaying piers on the Hudson River in Greenwich Village in New York City. But his purpose is to tell a timeless tale: of innocence taken and at the last minute left unspoiled by what might be interpreted as either the untrammeled egotism or the almost Medieval gallantry of a more experienced man.

Michael Wade Simpson's "The Fiancé" is in sharp contrast to Rechy's story, with its indirectness, its gentility. Yet it, too, is a story about that seldom discussed and very manly attribute of gay men: grace under duress, with its picture of the "arrived" older writer living in the past but drawn into the now by the presence of the beautiful intended of his favorite niece.

"Fucking Martin" is another double story—indeed, this volume is filled with double and triple stories. Here the narrator tells the fairly straightforward tale of the impossible, betrayal-filled love, and eventual death, of a lover—Martin—yet he reveals an even deeper and longer-lasting relationship between himself and Susan, his discreet, perfect, omnipresent female friend.

A different kind of double-vision and another kind of betrayal imbue Douglas Sadownick's haunting "Sacred Lips of the Bronx." Here, the story is of the decline of the older, traditional, Jewish Bronx, embodied in the seventeen-year-old narrator's grandmother Frieda, an almost saintlike woman. Yet it's via his regular Saturday trips accompanying (read "protecting") Frieda to the synagogue that Michael encounters the "new" Bronx: Latino, vital, different—embodied in the free, obscene, sexually alluring Puerto Rican basketball players—

especially one, Hector. When Michael and Hector finally have sex, it is a verbal as well as a physical bout. Like those hours of lay-ups on the court, it is totally athletic yet laced with a continuous, almost necessary thread of mocking (and ethnic) insult.

The violence that John Rechy shows ritualized almost out of existence and which Sadownick shows simmering below and only rarely rising to the surface, informs every page of Manuel Igrejas's disturbing "The Little Trooper." In almost documentary-fashion we are taken on a fascinating, grim trip into the unfulfilled, disconnected lives of a group of ordinary, lower-middle-class, suburban gay men in northern New Jersey, one of whom happens to be a policeman. Igrejas is unflinching and unrelenting in showing us the strong emotions, yet also the banality behind the headlines we read in local tabloids.

Two past stories texture Norman Wong's ironically titled "Cultural Revolution": one is the story of a forbidden sexual alliance that an American traveler, Alex, tells to Michael, the Chinese-American narrator. It's unclear whether this story is true or fabrication, yet it's designed to add "exoticism" and eroticism to their accidental and not completely fulfilling sexual liaison. The second story—almost legendary to Michael as he was growing up—is the story of his father's ancestors, of how and why they left their hometown in China when the Japanese invaded. As Michael and his father visit their home, this legend alters, becomes more real and more moving—adding new solidity to the difficult father/gay son relationship.

Another kind of story-telling as plot device occurs in Richard House's baroquely inventive "The Magistrate's Monkey." The "outer" story in this tale-within-a-tale is of an older businessman keeping a pretty, young boy in the rooms of a residential hotel in an unnamed foreign city. To distract the boy from boredom and growing fears of illness, the lover begins a story, as Scheherazade kept her husband (and her head) in *Thousand and One Nights* by telling stories. House uses this double-vision effectively, showing how as the death anxieties grow, threatening to separate the two men, it deepens and colors the tale one of them tells, embellishing it with sex and embroidering it with violence until it becomes the objective correlative of their crumbling relationship.

Both Raymond Luczak and best-selling novelist David Feinberg use the dual-story format in similar yet inventive ways to show how even our greatest human ability—communication—can become sidetracked by love and sex and indeed fall victim to them. Luczak's icily told story is about the failed relationship between a deaf man and a hearing man; and how inertia often works more than prejudice against the disabled. The originality in Luczak's story is the unbiased point of view; both men, deaf and hearing, are equally guilty for not following through, for being proud, egotistical, ultimately unrealistic.

David B. Feinberg (author of the novels *Eighty-Sixed* and *Spontaneous Combustion*) uses humor like a Swiss Army knife—it can be a barometer, stiletto, rasp, or spade. His cautionary narrative is about that very contemporary phenomenon in gay life—telephone sex—and two apparent strangers' single, utterly ritualized, and patently fake conversation. Feinberg tells the story from first one, then the other's point of view, to drive home the glaring divide between the men, then caps off the tale by showing how the call changes not only the men's attitudes but also their lives.

As in all previous volumes of the series, illness and death cast a long shadow over the work: AIDS itself plays a part in David Vernon's smartly titled "Inside." A bravely funny "inside narrative" told from the point of view of an ill gay man, "Inside" manages to amuse and move us and also to address the many-sided, always-loaded question of how the contemporary mind can and should view the human body.

In Paul Russell's "Opening the Door," the survivor is the narrator; the dying character a youth, almost a stranger, only briefly and quite imperfectly known. Russell's up-to-date tale shows how fatal illness has returned to our everyday lives. Until AIDS, such illness and death were distanced for most of us, sanitized, almost reified, by happening mostly to the quite aged and usually in hospital wards, where victims of chronic illness lay for months, sometimes years. With so many young dying, with hospitals so crowded many are left out in hallways or sent home to die, illness and death have been given back to us, made more immediate and thus more horrible, yet ironically rendered less life-shockingly frightening because it has become so common.

In Peter Weltner's "The Greek Head," the death happens "off-stage," before the story begins, and it sets into motion an entire pavane of past and present relationships among two gay couples sharing a building in San Francisco. When one member of the older couple dies of a stroke, the surprising terms of his will brings into question how well he was known to his lover, and exactly what his relationship was to one of the younger couple; in fact, it calls into question how well we can ever really know another.

As does Jack Slater's moving "New Year," where the death of a strong, often absent, ambivalently loved father finally "brings home" an African-American gay man living abroad. While portraying the personal and familial forces behind that gay man's exile, Slater also shows us those apparently immutable forces shaping African-American life which can be partly escaped by being gay.

Robert Glück's moving and surprisingly straightforward "Everyman" explores the approach of death in several stories woven together: that of Ed, an ambiguously considered previous lover; Mac, an elderly heterosexual "character" in their neighborhood of San Francisco; and even that of Lily, a beloved pet dog. Glück is known as a "New Narrative" author, one of that formidable group including Kathy Acker, Dennis Cooper, and Kevin Killian among others, but seldom has this new style been used with such ease, grace, and fine-tuned control of some rather complicated emotions.

In complete contrast to the previous theme is the other eternal theme of gay life: youth coming out. Virtually all of us grow up in a heterosexual, not a homosexual, society and we usually begin adolescence feeling different and alienated. Even when we do discover other gays, we're still untaught in how gay society works. Though we sense it is somewhat different than what we've experienced, we don't know specific manners or customs expected of us, or how to react to the behavior of others. We need to learn what to expect, how to behave, what certain slang means, which hopes and fears we may have are irrelevant and which realistic. We need heroes and role-models, confirmation of our deepest unspoken feelings, a sense of really belonging.

It's not such a crisis in Greg Johnson's laid-back, autumnal story, "The Valentine," where the older man is a "retarded" high-school handyman. In fact, coming out happens easily, almost naturally. But it can also occur unnaturally, even violently, as it does in Randy Sanderson's "Bone," where a teenager's coming out evokes his father's deepest prejudices and hatred, requiring a gay couple's physical presence, example, and eventually even their complicity in getting the boy away from the locus of such homophobia. What makes Sanderson's well-wrought fable even more affecting is that it contains a second growing up and coming out—that of the narrator, a peaceful, previously unactive gay man who is "radicalized" by the father's bigotry and who, by helping the boy, himself becomes an "activist." It's a lesson that AIDS and intolerance have taught many gay men lately.

Finally, as though to point to even newer directions and still barely tried themes and ideas possible in gay male fiction, George has included two pieces that seem to fit no previous categories; except that both are (like many Conrad and James stories) "inside narratives." Luis Alfaro's "Pico-Union" authentically paints a bold yet subtle picture of what it's like to be a young Latino gay in Southern California as it's daily lived. And Matthew Stadler's strangely calm yet Kafkalike "The Sex Offender" is similar to his recent novel *Landscape: Memory* in that it seems to be as much about the hidden potentials of language and written style as it is about being a lover of boys who must face the strangeness of being gently "reformed" by and for society.

When, years—decades—from now, those new directions in gay male fiction have become known, solidified, themselves the new corpus of accepted work and authors, we will still have to look back to the *Men on Men* anthologies to see our origin, and our growth. George Stambolian made the discovery that all pioneers make: He had to build a bridge so that we—so that even he himself—could cross it.

LOVE IN THE BACKROOMS

• JOHN RECHY •

LOS ANGELES, 1992. In this time of daily dying and grieving, there are memories that emerge constantly of a former time, memories of intimate strangers glimpsed only briefly, most often within shadows. They rise almost spectrally, those memories, because they belong so fully to our distant yesterdays. Out of those yesterdays, some memories persevere. Among them for me, there's one of a young stranger who didn't know he changed my life. I wonder how he survived the years that were still to come. I will not allow myself to consider that he did not survive. This is an account of that encounter in another time, another world.

New York, 1978. During the day, trucks haul in the denuded carcasses of cattle, to be cut up in wholesale butcher shops along Washington Street. At night, slaughtered animal meat will be replaced in the abandoned trucks by human flesh involved till dawn in sporadic male-sex on the bloodied floors. In the backrooms of bars squeezed in between the meat stores, sex orgies will be performed with the ritualism of a mass.

Just beyond and along West Street, dead buildings face skeletal warehouses, deserted piers. There, throughout the day and into the night and dawn, gay men roam for sex in burnt-out rooms, amid the rubble of crushed glass, metal pipes, tangled wire. Among the male clusters, deep at night, stray female prostitutes and transvestites lure straight men to fuck on the rotting boards of the dock. Near garbage piled into modern sculptures, hoboes sleep under newspapers. Tattered men and shaggy women band about fires illuminating pocked walls. Gaunt young marauders also stalk the piers.

I have returned to explore New York after almost ten years away, living largely in the seasonless and therefore timeless city of Los Angeles, the city of lost angels. This warm fall day, I have already surveyed the periphery of the area I've come to hunt in, have explored the gay ghetto of Christopher Street, the twisting, circling streets, have paused to touch the building that was the Stonewall Inn, where we rioted on the eve of Judy Garland's funeral. As I cruise among the afternoon sex-hunters in this gay ghetto, why is it that I sense a mood of euphoric despair in the streets, of a troubled paradise? Why is the recurring laughter forced so low, the men so self-consciously masculine? "Lumberjacks," "motorcyclists," "cowboys" lounge about, stroll, even tend chic antique stores, pretty flower shops. With my gym-pumped body, I belong to one flank of this new rigid breed, and I sense a posed defiance like mine among them, feel very much—in them and myself, too— a pressurized hostility, charging the cruising. Is this attire the new drag of anger turned inward, a sissy-hating imitation of our bully oppressors?

I stand on Washington Street and face the trucks bringing in that day's meat, the raw flesh of cattle hangs on savage racks. Brutal pornography, blood smears the white coats of the butchers snatching at the meat with hairy hands.

I walk to West Street, and into the midst of violent sexturf. On a truck ramp before an empty warehouse across the street, two women sit dangling their legs, signaling drivers. A giant transvestite on stilted heels lolls nearby, peroxide, sequins, colored flesh challenging the murky afternoon.

Fire and vandalism have battered two abandoned warehouses along this stretch of piers, gutting the rooms within them. I pass a scorched door. I hear the grinding of footsteps on shattered glass. Inside—its original function a mystery now—thick grilled wire creates a large cage. Within it four men bunch into one carnivorous form. I walk along a connecting lot. Separated from it by a tin wall—slashed with yellow, green, red paint as if someone has tried urgently to decorate the hard ugliness—a wharf juts from it into the gray water. I move toward the other vacant warehouse, where I have seen male figures gathering. To enter this scarred building, you stoop under an oxidized gate, like the blade of a jagged guillotine lowered midway.

Inside, piles of scrap iron form dead-animal shapes on the left. The building extends the equivalent of two blocks onto the Hudson River. Within the enormous room, its ceiling higher than two stories, are other rooms, once perhaps offices; blackened frames cling to each other for support. Rubble accumulates in layers, heaped thickest against the corners of the fire-blasted rooms.

Random stairways lead to other bony rooms within the main one. One stairway ends without connection, seared. As it rises to a second landing, the largest stairway is devoured midway by total darkness. Inside a gutted inner room within the main building, wires dangle from a lower ceiling. One creates a rigid noose. Pipes protrude from under the debris, metal bolts a dirty orange. Through patches in the building's walls, the unmoving water has a metallic sheen. Barges float dead.

Sexhunting men roaming the abandoned hollows are swallowed by deep pools of shadows. The sound of footsteps is disembodied but realer in this isolation than the now alien roar of traffic outside. Dangerous holes sear the wooden floor. An erect iron column thrust out of a shaft in the middle of the room is tangled by pipes and wires.

Ready to join the silent hunt, I remove my shirt. I pass other cruising men. I wait in the torn shaft. A man slides down before me. Others glide by, fuse with each other.

Against a patch of light a slender figure is hiding, watching. The nerve of vagrant sexuality aroused hotly now, I move to another man, to another, and as quickly away, toward the knot of darkness beyond two converging stairways.

The slender figure against the light begins to follow, stops.

The boards on the stairs are loose, you feel out the solid patches. Past the bolted darkness you emerge into another large room. Splinters of glass from broken windows shine in sequins out of the rubbish. Within the frames of smaller rooms, men fuse. The floor exudes the odor of urine and dried semen. At the end of this room a hole gapes into another partition of the building. You stoop to enter a farther room. Cinders and burned wood turn the spoilage ashen. Five men fuck, suck, kiss. On a glassless window sill in another of the smaller wall-less cubicles, a bearded man sits smoking, staring out toward the river. His legs are spread indifferently to a man groveling soundlessly at his crotch. Near me, a man squats, mouth open, crushed cans at his ankles. After moments, I move away from him.

A heap of rubbish stirs nearby. Awakened momentarily, a dirt-caked tramp shifts his position on the floor.

In the backroom of my mind, memories stir. When I was a child, hoboes on their way to California would spill out of freightcars to ask for food in El Paso, where we lived. By then, my Scottish father, once so grand in the music world, was reduced to a janitor in a hospital. Haunted by memories of gentility, my beautiful Mexican mother fought to survive his angered pain, to protect me from it. We, too, were poor. Still, she fed the hoboes on plates reserved for them, and they sat eating on the ground in our grassless backyard. I remember that distinctly, and then remember sweet moments of tranquility: when as a little boy I would lie on my mother's lap while she curled my eyelashes with a saliva-moistened finger.

Now on the piers in New York, I flee into the thick blackness of the stairs, down them, back to the main floor.

A man is blowing me when I notice again the following presence, now clearer in a diagonal slash of light by the entrance. A youngman. He looks incongruous—his clothes are careless, not yet self-conscious in revealing tightness like mine. I feel more than see his intense eyes.

I ease away the man squatting before me. He glances toward the youngman. The sound of words an intrusion, the man says to me, "That kid's a beauty, huh?—but he won't make it with anyone, and he's been here all afternoon, he looks scared shitless, like it's his first time and he's about to cry." He shakes his head, perhaps at his own evoked first time. "I think he's following you."

The implication of the youngman's confusion—only that, I tell myself—goads me to do what I have never done before, approach first.

He's tightly slender, with flawless skin, wavy black hair. I stand next to him. "Hi."

He looks up. "Why did you let just anybody do that to you? All afternoon." He looks down at his scuffed tennis shoes. "Why?" He looks up.

"It's none of—" The anger dissipates as I study the hurt face. Large, dark eyes, long, thick eyelashes. "Why the hell did *you* come here?" I blurt in defense.

His words tumble out: "My brother was bragging about how him and his friends come here and beat up queers, so I knew this is where I'd find someone like me—"

"Jesus." I touch his shoulder, slightly. The surrounding rubble—I feel it ensnaring us. The props of decay loom more sharply now within this devastated graveyard. An area at the end of the pier and by the water looks cleaner. "Let's go over there," I point.

A smile jumps on his face—that quickly he moves from sadness to joy. It's as if I've seen two distinct photographs of him, and both reveal the careless beauty that only those who are unaware of it can have.

"I bet you come here a lot, the way you—"

I block his accusation. "It's my first time." Then I add quickly, "My first time here. I'm from Los Angeles."

"Hey! You know any movie stars?"

I mention some names, but he hasn't heard of them. We've reached the end of the pier. Only distance had purified this area. The ubiquitous rubbish has invaded it, too. Dank boards slant dangerously toward the licking water. On a stairway, missing boards leave gaps like blackened teeth. We stand within the frame of what was once a room. I push the debris away with my feet. The youngman's face burrows on my bare chest. I can feel his eyelashes as he begins to slide down awkwardly.

No. I raise him by the shoulders. I hold his face. He hugs me, and my arms respond. Our lips touch. I feel his natural muscles against my iron-pumped ones. His groin grows large against mine. His fingers outline the curve of my pectorals, my shoulders, biceps. I touch the creaseless flesh of his chest, the firm ridges of his flat stomach. He opens my fly. I begin to open his. He pulls back.

"I'm embarrassed because my prick isn't too big," he says.

"That doesn't matter," I tell him. He holds my cock and I

hold his. It's large, thick, hard. "You're not small at all," I tell him.

With obvious pleasure he leans back, looking down in surprise at his own cock. Now he studies my body slowly. Automatically, I flex. Our cocks touch.

We move farther into the frame of the pillaged room, away from the shifting forms.

"Can we go where you're staying?" he asks me.

"I'm staying at a hotel. It's too far. Gramercy Park, and I'd have to leave right away," I say with regret.

"There's nobody where I live," he tells me. "Let's go there. My mother's working and my brother's never there."

He lives only a few blocks away. In a surviving building. His room. Two beds. Right that we should come here, to affront his brother's violence. We lie naked on the white sheets of his unmade bed. His sinewy body fits into mine. His furry crotch, the hairless chest, the surprisingly hairy legs, the eager cock press tightly against my crotch, chest, legs, cock. "This is the most beautiful I've ever felt," he says, and I force myself not to echo him because it's like a first time for me, too, almost like a first time. I open my lips on his, our eyes remain open. Our hands slide up and down on each other's cocks. My cum spills on his cock, his on mine. Joined, it drips onto the white sheets, cum thick and white and clean on his bed.

But it did not happen like that. I only wish it had.

We did not go to his home. His brother might be there. We stayed on the pier.

We move farther into the frame of the pillaged room, away from the shifting male forms. To match my shirtless body, he removes his shirt. He unbuckles my pants and I unbuckle his. Under our feet, the crumbled pier filth stirs. His sinewy body fits into mine. His furry crotch, the hairless chest, the surprisingly hairy legs, the eager cock press tightly against my crotch, chest, legs, cock. "This is the most beautiful I've ever felt," he says, and I force myself not to echo him. I shove away a tangled wire coiling at our feet. I close his eyes, shutting out the rubble. A piece of oxidized metal falls into the rusty water. I look at his long eyelashes. This is like a first time for me, too, almost like a first time. Among the blinded decay, I open my lips on his.

Our hands slide up and down on each other's cocks. My cum spills on his cock, his on mine. Joined, it drips onto the encroaching waste, cum thick and white and clean among the spillage. Still holding each other, "I'll see you again," he says assertively.

"No—I'm leaving Sunday," I tell him, releasing him.

The sad photograph of his face.

"Look," I say quickly, "don't come here again." My words surprise me. Am I betraying my outlaw world? I hear myself: "You're very goodlooking, and you're so young."

"And you're goodlooking, with your muscles and—"

"And if you keep coming here—" I look at the battleground. I think of the edge of despair I court within the beloved excitement of the sexhunt. "There are better places to meet people. For you," I add, faithful to my life. With astonishment I realize I'm speaking to him as if he were my child. And in a very real sense, isn't he?—to lead away from the imposed guilt and ugliness that I—we, homosexuals of my generation—survived, though scarred by those turbulent times.

"I found *you* here," he reminds me.

Yes, and I found him, too. But I don't say that.

Outside on the dimming street, we put on our shirts. The roar of traffic is real again.

"My name's Bobby—" He goes on to tell me his last name, that's how new he is to the world of anonymity. "Yours?"

For the first time in a lifetime of thousands of furtive encounters, I give my real name.

I signal a cab and hurry across the street. I turn to wave at Bobby.

Scuffed tennis shoes rising and falling rapidly, he rushes—I see him as I look back through the cab's rear window—away from the devastated pier.

Past midnight. I return to the area of piers. A goodlooking man follows me as I walk along the truck parked for the night near the first warehouse. Behind one, we lick each other's body, cocks.

Separating, I move along the piers. Forms—five men—enter the caged darkened room. A shabby youngwoman, in black, eyes outlined starkly, follows them into the cage. In the dark will she become a sexless orifice among the men? In a parked car, the head of a female prostitute disappears—the driver of the car leans back. Sorting them out from the few men hunting women or transvestites here, other women walk past the homosexual men cruising the dangerous cadavers of the piers.

Behind the tin wall, against it, a row of shadows squats, another stands. I lean against the wall, connecting with two men for seconds. Then I walk onto the muddy dark of the wharf. On the wooden pier a man fucks a woman among the dark outlines of glued male bodies. A dazed man asks me if I have any 'ludes.

In the lot, cars cruise the area. The light from across the street is ashen orange, creating a mist like embers. Men lean against car windows. Others surrender to the caverns of the warehouses.

The electric orange mist is darker on Washington Street. I move into the maze formed by parked trucks. The sound of feet on discarded beer cans jangles the darkness. In the aisles between the trucks outlines wait for a sexual connection. A man has followed me. We jump into the back of one of the trucks abandoned for the night. Sighs stir its heavy darkness. We move into another truck. We go through the motions of sex without coming.

Out on the street, I face an apartment building, walls blackened with wordless graffiti. From a few lighted rooms, men signal to those on the street. From a window a man motions me to the entrance. The buzzer releases the door. Ripped tile has left black gouges in the lobby. I walk up squeezed corridors to an open door. The muscular man stands naked in a desperately elegant room, an incongruous isle. I take off my clothes. On the floor we make it with each other.

Outside again, figures straggle like deserters in neutral turf. In the declined entrance to a darkened building, I fuck a blond youngman. The plaster pulverizes like ashes where his hands push against the wall.

*   *   *

Another night. I stand outside the hotel waiting for a cab. The woman I am going to the theater with is making a hurried call inside. I see scuffed tennis shoes, quickening.

"Hey!"

Bobby approaches me. "I knew if I kept hanging around Gramercy I'd see you. I've been back and forth all day for two days."

I feel a mixture of pleasure and apprehension, apprehension at the implication of his waiting for me for two days. I tell him I'm going to the theater, to call me at midnight. My friend comes out. Bobby looks at the beautiful woman, frowns. "Okay," he says, squares his shoulders, walks away.

When he calls at midnight, I agree to meet him at 14th and Seventh. I want to avoid the immediate intimacy of being in the hotel room with him. In the cab paranoia brushes me. I remember his gay-hating brother. What if Bobby told him?

I see him waiting at the corner and all apprehension disappears. He's not wearing a jacket, just a loose shirt. His face is intense, his hands are deep in his pockets. He sees the cab stop, he smiles, runs toward me. "Hey!"

We walk along surviving buildings. A chilly wind gathers the city's loose trash. We pass a phone booth. He jumps in, dials without inserting any coins. "Just wanted to say hello," he says into the phone.

I realize anew how young he is.

"Who was the girl you were with?" he asks me softly.

"A friend," I tell him.

"Oh." He stops. "I'm going to L.A. with you," he announces. "Not now. But when I save enough." He thrusts his chin determinedly downward. "I love you."

I *feel* his words. They pry open locked chambers within me, spuriously sealed wounds. At the same time I recognize in his words the clear tone of threatening obsession.

He's telling me he'll get a job in Los Angeles, "in a gas station." Then he says: "And we'll be lovers and live together." Cold, he huddles close to me as we walk. "And while you're away and I'm here, I'll never have sex with anyone else—and I'm going to swear that on my mother's picture."

I carry my own mother's photograph in my wallet with me always. "No," I say.

"Never with anyone else." To seal the promise, he closes his eyes tightly. We sit on a bench in a small park. The wind shoves dead leaves against the refuse at the edges of the park. He shivers close to me. His head turns, and he kisses me on the cheek.

The huge impossibility. But I kiss him back. "Bobby, you're just a kid," I say finally.

"So what?"

So what? I stand up. We begin walking again. Plastic bags overflowing with packed trash lie on street curbs. Even in the chill air there's the miasma of decay, a psychic poison.

"You can't come with me to California," I tell him.

"Why?" His face is lowered.

"Because I'm married, I have a kid." The lie hurts me, but I tell him what I think will release him most quickly and with the least pain from his shaping obsession.

This time when he looks up, there's anger. "I thought you were the greatest person I ever met. But you're fucked up, like my goddamn brother! Fuck you!" he shouts at me. Shoulders straight, he walks away from me along the cold street.

I will cling to the memory of that proud swagger. He didn't whimper. He won't grovel.

Later, I will imagine that I said this to him and that he understood: If you were older, a veteran of the same wars, or at least more experienced, maybe then. But I have too many open wounds from battles in the sexjungle, and I'm too tired to be your guide past or through that jungle I love and hate. But in exploring it deeply, perhaps even my contribution to its worst—and I hope I've been courageous—maybe I can purge some of it for you.

And still later, I will imagine that instead of lying to him, I said I loved him.

Almost three a.m. I enter one of New York's backroom orgy bars in the rotting west end of the city. A posted "dress code"—"only leather, uniforms, Western allowed"—and nominal "membership" keep out gay "undesirables," the unattractive, the old, the effeminate discarded abruptly by two men guarding the door.

A huge American flag covers one of the walls of the front

bar. Men lean against counters. Laughter is roughened. Beers are clutched as if in protection against an effeminate move. Spit is thrust onto the floor in rehearsed contempt. I walk past the bar and into the backrooms.

In a cold red light like dim fire, I see a large room and red-shadowed figures. The odor of urine, amyl, dead cum saturate the rancid air. In cubicles throughout, forms bend as if in an arcane ritual. Almost before I can see them fully, two naked men—chains dangling loosely from their wrists, studded belts crisscrossed on their torsos, genitals squeezed by black cock-rings—crawl on the dirty wooden floor to lick my boots, moving on to another's, then another's.

Nearby, a naked man is strapped against a wall, bound outstretched hands and feet creating an *X*. Another man holds a vial of amyl to the nose of the strapped man. Beard-shaded and wearing black chaps, black boots, black shirt, black gloves, black cap, dark sunglasses, another man leans back, a black belt in his hand, arches his body, and lashes the belt across the ass of the tied man, who growls in pained pleasure. Others gather to watch or take turns whipping the naked man. A man wearing only a tangle of sequined leather belts licks my crotch through the cloth of my jeans. Red shadows form into men fucking, kissing, sucking, rimming.

Figures meld, separate, reshape, some naked, others in jock straps, a few in cop uniforms, most in leather, others in studded straps and harnesses.

Garbage has been allowed to accumulate in places—or, is it possible?—has it been brought in, in homage to rot? Crushed newspapers, smashed cans, shreds of torn underwear.

Several cubicles contain toilets, props in the decay of fantasy, each toilet is occupied by crouching men, blowing whoever stands before them.

The only sounds are those of moist mouths on flesh, the crunching of feet through the imported litter, the punctuated *whack!* of a lashing belt. And moans.

Later—yes, later, I will feel outrage at this live monument to heterosexual oppression, the imitation of the places their hatred has pushed us into, imposed guilt shaping this performance, a black mass to that oppression. I will think that later. Now I move with icy excitement through this ravished fantasy, from body to body, to crawling figures, mouths. I float shirtless through this red dusk of mangled sex, orifices, organs.

In the center of the large room a wooden ladder leads down into a farther depth. I descend. More dark red silhouettes, imported garbage, shackles, chains on walls. In a dirty tub a man lies naked. Men urinate, spit, masturbate on him. A man twists his nipples. Sweat mixes with piss and cum and spittle. The looks are of dazed numbness.

I move from body to body in this crushed fantasy, from orifice to orifice, without reciprocating—no, not here.

The wrists of a goodlooking man—naked except for his boots—are bound to straps hanging from the ceiling. The heels of his boots lodged into two propped metal sockets, the man's legs are spread wide. A man in leather and wearing a cowboy hat holds his fist to them. The fist gleams in the light which is the color of blood. Face expressionless, the "cowboy" pushes his fingers into the open ass. The strapped man's cock is soft. Others—being sucked, rimmed, fucking—watch. The strapped man's body shines with red sweat.

Sounds of pain and pleasure merge. Mounted by another man, a naked man crawls toward me on the floor. As he sucks me, the sharp slap of the mounted man's hand flails the naked ass.

Caught in the terrible current—and feeling a gathering scream in my throat—I push the gnawing head down, down, to my boots. With my hand, I cover my eyes and mouth to shut out the carnage and to stifle my scream.

A growing cluster of men—five at first, seven, more—fuses into a throbbing, grinding mass of flesh moaning like a great wounded beast devouring itself or licking its own wounds.

Outside the bar now and back in the cold electric orange drizzle on the streets, I see a car stop abruptly, motor left running. Five skinny young bodies hurl themselves into the maze of parked trucks. "Faggots! Queers!" I hear the clash of sticks on flesh. The five rush back into the car and speed away.

Several dazed men stagger bleeding from behind the trucks. One man falls on the littered pavement. His blood falls into the filthy rain.

*   *   *

Today I am returning to Los Angeles. The drizzle has turned into heavy rain in New York. I wait—my luggage beside me under the awning of the hotel—before I signal a cab. I look to one side of the street, to the other. I remember scuffed tennis shoes, long eyelashes. I search the street again. I wait longer. Finally, I wave for a cab.

In a few hours I will be back in Los Angeles, amid the smoggy palm trees and the tanned violence.

FUCKING MARTIN

• DALE PECK •

I HATE THE empty moment before emotion clarifies itself. I hate sitting on Susan's couch and staring at her living room, which feels unfamiliar, even though nothing about it has changed. When she comes from the kitchen, carrying a platter of crackers that ring a smooth brown mound, she says, "Hummus," and dips a finger into the speckled-green paste. "I think they put parsley in it or something." Hummus. Parsley. The world revolves around this opposition for a moment and then, when I've accepted it, I realize that I'm afraid. Susan sits on the couch, looks at me. I can see the curve of her breast through a gap between two open buttons of her shirt. It rises and falls with her breathing. I notice the dimmed lights, the hush, the new sound of wordless music, and into this heady air I breathe my first words of the night. "Susan," I say, "you have to risk AIDS in order to get pregnant." I wonder then, as her hands rush to her chest, if she undid the buttons deliberately.

Seduction was Martin's art. Sometimes on a Sunday morning, the light in the tiny rooms of our apartment softened by closed curtains, he told me old stories. In the living room, sprawled on a futon, or in the kitchen, as he fried bacon or made omelettes and I sat at the table. How loosely I held him in that small space, one hand around my coffee, the other tracing the waistband of his underwear, the smell of both—coffee, underwear—mixing in my nose. For a while the only sound would be his metal spatula scraping the pot, but when he started speaking it was like a catalog, a litany, was unrolling from his mind. Martin had a great memory for names, places, dates, for technique, though soon I realized he wasn't bragging, or trying to make me jealous, or being nostalgic. He wasn't trying to recapture his past—merely to validate its existence. The remains of those mornings are mental pictures that I've drawn from his words: Martin, in the Ramble, lowering his glasses, slowly undoing the buttons of his shirt. I remember how carefully he chose his words, as carefully as, in days past, he must have chosen his method. He didn't unbutton his shirt: he undid the buttons one by one, his fingers working down his chest, a V of skin spreading behind his passing hand like the wake of a boat. And he knew me, too, knew that my own backward-looking eyes would revel in this knowledge of his past, that my mind would take it in like liquor, until the whole of his experience would become inseparable from my own, and it would seem that the words which had been mouthed in his ears had been whispered to me, and the hands which had run across his body had passed over mine. I don't remember, I *am* Martin: in a club, sliding a beer down the nearly empty gutter of a bar, coins tinkling to the floor as the bottle passes; in an alley, standing in shadow, listening to approaching footsteps, striking a match at just the right time. Though I'm sure he told me about the men he picked up, I don't remember their looks, why they attracted him, even if his seductions were successful. I did realize, even then, that he presented himself as an object, played roles out of movies and books; but he knew this too. You could in those days, John, he said. This was strange to me—not that he knew about roles, but that he had ever assumed them. I had played the pursuer in our relationship, had, on seeing him at Susan's old piano at one of her parties, pulled a rose from a jade vase and placed the half-open flower in his lapel buttonhole as he sat at the piano. I wonder though: If I had possessed the ability to see him differently, would his piano playing have seemed a pose, a facade even more romantic than the one I'd assumed? But knowing that would require a different set of eyes, now, and in the past as well, and as I'm no longer skilled at pretending to be who I'm not, I . . . never mind. Just know that what I remember is Martin—my lover Martin, the object Martin—posing himself for sex, for it is only that object which I now possess.

Memories pollute a planned atmosphere of seduction. Nothing will happen until the past has been dispelled. Susan's apartment, if pared down to uneven wooden floors, cracked walls, and paint-smothered moldings, could be the one I once shared with Martin. I try to focus on her, but she pulls aside her hair and, beyond her shoulder, the ancient piano falls into view. Nostalgia traps us—the food, the music, everything, chosen according to past times. "My friend who likes hummus," Susan has called me—what, about that, is sexy? She speaks now in a careful voice. "Do you remember—?" she starts. She stops when she sees what I look at. She knows that I—that we both—remember. It seems all we *can* do is remember, and that is why she doesn't finish her sentence. Attached to everything we say are twenty years' worth of words—our history together. Tonight that chain seems especially heavy, perhaps because another link is about to be added to it. When Susan suddenly closes the windows, I think at first that she does so to foster the nostalgia, but when she sits down again there is more space between us than had existed previously. We both look at the new space, but neither of us move into it.

I've been with a girl before—once, when I was eighteen, a long time ago. She and I had just finished our first years in separate colleges and were home for the summer. We'd known each other for years, had even been close friends in high school, but it took nine months apart and, that summer, the absence of most of our friends to force us together. Still, I think it's safe to claim we were experimenting—not with sex, for, though neither of us knew it about the other, neither of us was a virgin. No, we were experimenting with love, and we failed. And it's not that I *didn't* love her, nor she me. Who knows, without love it might have been easier—certainly, less painful. But even people so young have pasts—I'm thinking of my year at school, of three boys, three experiences, that I didn't understand. I'm thinking of my past, not hers, but in the end, both got in the way.

We drove to the river one night in my father's old pickup. It was late June, early July. Already there was something between us: movies in the evenings after work, weekends in stores trying on expensive clothes that we never bought, long goodnights on her front porch that left me alone in bed with a hardon. We did a lot of things, I realize, that created their own conversations, or made words unnecessary. We never talked about ourselves. On the way to the river, I sped down rutted dirt roads and the cab was filled with engine noises and music that screeched out of the single-speaker AM radio. We sang along and laughed and cursed at the more vicious bumps. At the river we rolled our socks into our shoes and waded into the shallow, slick-like-oil water. We held hands. It was night, the sky clear, and I invest the stars now with great significance because you don't really see them in the city and they have for so long been a symbol of romantic love. Ten feet away from the water the air had been hot and still, but in it we were cool, and laughed quietly at little jokes, and skittered on stones hidden in the sand. Though we hadn't talked about it, we both knew what was going to happen.

It was on a sandbar, surrounded by water, that we spread an old holey blanket through which the sand penetrated so easily that soon she suggested we abandon it and stretch out directly on the ground. I said no, the ground was damp, and besides, it wasn't really ground but sand, it would get all over us. A stupid argument followed—we didn't fight, but we became paralyzed by an inability to agree and eventually we fell silent, I half-on, she half-off the blanket. I remember lying there looking up at the stars and feeling the effort of not speaking grow harder and harder when suddenly her face interrupted my view and she kissed me. The kiss went on for a long time, and then extended itself, as the rest of our bodies became part of it and our clothes came off. Then all at once she rolled off me, and even as I noticed that the blanket had become a wadded mass between us she said, John, do you remember Hank? and after I'd said yes, she said, I had a baby in April. His.

All at once, things expanded: my mouth, my eyes, my mind,

my arms and legs even, flung wide in an effort to catch the sky that seemed to be falling on me. Only one part of me shrunk. It's unfair to say that her sudden revelation did us in; really, she merely provided an excuse I'd been looking for. What she said didn't repel me, but just then—when I was wondering if I should put on a condom, wondering if this would feel as good as, or better or worse than it did with boys—just then she made sex seem unerotic, less like fantasy, more like life.

She started to talk then; she told me about hiding in her dorm room because when she left it for meals or classes people pointed at her. Her friends advised her to abort. That was okay for other women, she said, but not for her. Counselors, her parents, people calling themselves her friends, told her to drop out and raise the baby; if possible, marry the father. That, too, was okay for other women but not for her. She had plans, and besides, who knew where he'd run away to? She told me about back pains and stomach cramps. She described an adoption agency that paid the medical bills and allowed her to screen parent profiles and name her baby. She held Stephanie in her arms once, and her mother snapped some pictures before the nurse came. She told me how Stephanie had turned her face to her breast and sucked the hospital gown. It made her think that humans should be marsupials, that we should have a pouch where we could grow in warmth and darkness, that nothing that fragile should have to face the world without the opportunity for retreat. When she's eighteen, she told me, they'll give her my name, she can look me up if she wants. Well, I said—I could think of nothing else to say—now I know why your mother flashes the porch light on and off.

We laughed too long at that—plainly, neither of us knew what to say. Then something made me mention the boys I'd had in college, and it was her turn to be beside me, silent. I told her that my problem seemed trivial compared to hers, but at least I understood it. I told her that I enjoyed anal intercourse but when a boy pulled his penis out of me it felt like defecation (I really used these words—they seemed safely clinical). She told me that a woman she knew, on her fifth baby, said giving birth felt the same way: like taking a good shit. I felt she was offering me some kind of connection, but only a ladder's, and no matter how far I climbed, she would always be ahead of me.

After that we were beyond shyness, and we rolled close to hold each other for warmth. She pointed at a jagged line where a few river-fed trees met the sky in a beautiful pattern of shadows. She'd discovered abstract art in college, she told me— Once I was in the library I didn't want to leave it, and I spent hours in the stacks leafing through books—and it seemed to her that the world should be as simple as squares, triangles, circles, squiggly lines. All you need to do, she said, is border off the tips of those trees and the sky with a frame, and you'd have something, an image, no longer just trees or sky. The figure is dead, she proclaimed. Centuries of reproduction have destroyed it. The trees seemed fine to me but, looking at them, I realized I couldn't distinguish them from all the other trees I'd seen in my life. I realized that they *were* dead, for they had been obscured by a thousand other trees from my past—some real, some created, some that existed only in my mind. I didn't want to accept that, but I couldn't deny it, so I kept silent. But the only thing I really understood that night was that she and I would never be lovers, and the strongest emotion I felt was relief. And I should tell you that that girl, of course, was Susan. But on the river that night, I didn't know what that would mean today, which is why I didn't reveal it before. Because knowing this, knowing the future, changes things, changes the past.

Susan's laughter coils like smoke through the air before reaching my ears. Bent over so that her shirt falls open, she rolls a second joint. "They make machines for that," I say. "Rolling joints?" she asks, laughing again. "Well, cigarettes I suppose. But like most things, it does things it wasn't intended to." Her droll "Really?" seems exaggerated; her follow up— "like assholes?"—surprises me. Trying to joke it off, I take the knife from the hummus. Susan's shoulder rubs mine as I bend next to her. "Like this," I say, and fake a stab. Her smile vanishes. She takes the knife and sets it on the table; the heavy clunk of metal on wood startles me. It's too easy, how the meanings of once-familiar actions change. Susan slips the joint in my mouth; "Such things are for people with clumsy fingers," she says as she lights it, and maybe it's because I've almost forgotten about the rolling machine, but when I've exhaled, and she is still holding smoke in her lungs, I say, "There's nothing wrong with my fingers," and run them along her arm. Susan's eyes lock on the space beyond my right shoulder. She exhales slowly. I've touched her a thousand times before; I do nothing to make this touch sexual. But the confusing blend of friendship and sexuality is inevitable. It is, after all, why we're here.

There was a time when I'd wanted to be powerless, and have sex. I wanted to lose control. I went to the Spike.

I met Henry. About forty then, defined by a decade of discos, gyms, and steroids, Henry wore leather pants and an unbuttoned button-down blue plaid shirt with the sleeves ripped off. A man's name, Lou, was tattooed on his shoulder, and his mustache was speckled gray. When he shook my hand my knuckles cracked. He bought me a beer, I bought him a beer, I told him what I wanted, he said, eventually, Do you have any limits? It was a Friday night; I said, I have to work Monday afternoon. And it's not enough to say he hurt me, to say that for two days and three nights he controlled me: I asked for that. He gave me something else, something I didn't understand until much later.

It was not, I think, in Henry's nature to hurt anyone. When I stroked his slick-leathered thigh in the taxi, he moaned; there was nothing dominant about it. If he'd had his way, we probably would have had sex normally, with perhaps a few accoutrements: a leather harness, latex gloves. But I insisted, and he knew what to do. We both did, we *all* did, we'd been taught, by people now mostly dead. So I submitted to his kissing, stripped for him, called him Master; on his order, I licked his boots. He collared me, attached a leash, led me on my knees to his bedroom. I was drawn but not quartered, tied to the four bedposts. My ass gripped his sheets and pulled them into my crack. The red rubber ball gag started out egg-sized, but soon became an orange in my mouth. He stuffed wax in my ears and I heard my breath come fast and shallow. He hooded me. And he knew, Henry. Before zipping the eye slits, he pulled a mirror from the wall and held it above me. I saw what

I'd wanted to see: not myself, but a picture from a magazine. I was powerless, if not ridiculous. But I hadn't lost control. Then he closed the eye slits. They didn't seal completely, and I could see, if I shut one eye or the other, the jagged outline of the zipper and Henry's shadow as he moved about the room. Still, I was close enough to blind and nearly deaf from the wax. Bound, gagged, unable to do anything else, I waited.

S/M, if you let it, or if you can't stop it, delivers what it promises: pain that transforms. At first I understood things. I felt him handle my cock and balls; I could see, without looking, the thong stretching my balls away from my body and separating them from each other. It hurt, and my hips rocked a little in protest. The nipple clamps were two sharp pains that translated into two useless pulls against my bindings. When he twisted the clamps, I tensed, trying not to resist, trying to be above the pain, but I realized that my head was rolling from side to side. And then I didn't know what was happening. Later I found he'd been pouring hot wax over my chest, stomach, balls, but then it just felt like my skin was on fire. I couldn't help myself, I struggled. The gag hadn't been a gag until the first time I tried to scream against it, and then it was. But even though I knew I couldn't speak, I continued to try, tried to force the gag from my mouth by the power of my breath alone.

It went on like this, until eventually I was just struggling. The pain ceased to have meaning in any real way. I simply wanted to be released, but I had no control over that. In realizing this, and accepting it, a wave of heat washed through me and seemed to separate my inner body from my skin, and the pain, and the fighting, were outside me, and inside I was still. I barely noticed when Henry cut off my head and held it above my body so I could look at myself again. My skin, inflated like a balloon, was held to earth only by thin ties at the wrists and ankles. I smiled to think of my real self bouncing around freely inside, painless, weightless, like children in the Moon Walk at the fair. My mind bounced too, from memory to memory, and all of them seemed somehow transformed into visions that, no matter how painful they might have been once, were now ecstatic, and it was wonderful, a kind of freedom from the past—it was what I wanted. And then he made me come. I felt his hand on my cock vaguely at first, not knowing what he was doing. But as he pumped I grew hard, the wax cooled, I forgot the tit clamps and cock-and-ball harness, and he kept pumping until eventually, inevitably, I came. And it was just like any other too-long-delayed orgasm: anticlimactic and tiring. I lay in my bonds, bored. And for two more days and two more nights I was bored, as Henry tried to think of ever more exciting things to torment and arouse me. Oh, it was amazing what he could do, and not draw blood.

And I remember asking him a totally inappropriate question once, when the gag was out of my mouth. Lou, I said, is he still alive? Henry scratched the tattoo as if he wished it would come off. Louise, he said, my ex-wife. Yes.

(These words circle their subject, I know. Understand, it's not that *I'm* trying to be coy, vague, or ambiguous—it's just that John's and Susan's actions are guilty of the same indirection. Though both know what's happening—and rereading this, the situation seems clear—they still act as though, without acknowledging what's going on, it will happen anyway.) Susan bats at smoke, goes to open the windows. Worming my toes into the warm space where she'd sat, I close my eyes and lean back, only to jump forward when Susan sits on my feet. "My violet!" she says, pointing at my hands, immersed in a pot in her lap. "My feet!" I respond. She raises herself so I can move them, and I pull my fingers from her plant, a withered African violet. Brown-edged leaves hang from an aged, thick stem; dead ones line the pot. "I told him I'm no good with plants," she says, and when I realize she means Martin I grab the pot again. "Maybe you should take it home." "Maybe I should." Sometimes I only understand people through objects, and in the solid unerotic shape of this plant I see Susan: were she truly trying to seduce me, she wouldn't have brought Martin into the room more than he already is. Already she's sliding across the couch. "I'd feel bad if it died." There's a hush after I say this; it's an old rule and now I've broken it: Don't mention death around people who have lost someone. "Jesus, John," Susan says then, taking my hand, forcing me to look up from Martin's plant. "When you make love to me, please, don't think of him." Quiet after that, broken only by the sound of the plant being set on the table. What's truly remarkable, I suppose, isn't that it's dying, but that it lived this long. We stare at each other in silence. And it's like the first time: When the silence becomes uncomfortable, we kiss, and then, for just a moment, I hear water running somewhere close by.

Sometimes sex is perfect. I remember my fourth time with Martin, the first time we fucked. I remember the fourth time because that's when I fell for him. Something held us back our first three times; our minds were elsewhere, our hands could have been tied. There we were: Martin's place, Martin's old couch, the one he sold to Susan when he moved into my apartment. Not the couch that Susan and I sit on now—she got rid of that one years ago—but still, a connection exists, a tie to the past, to Martin, a—

There we were: Martin and John. The two of us, three a.m., empty bottles on the coffee table. We had exhausted conversation, wine had exhausted us, we stared at the TV. It was turned off. How did he do it? I mean, I know what he did: He put his hand on my leg. He didn't look at me when he did it, just lifted his right hand off his right leg and set it down on my left one, just above my knee. Just above my knee, and then it slid up my thigh, slowly, but not wasting time. That's what he did. But how did he make my diaphragm contract so tightly that I couldn't take one breath for the entire minute it took his hand to move to my belt? My stomach was so tight a penny would have bounced off it. His fingers found the belt buckle, worked it, a small sound of metal on metal, a sudden release, a rush of air—my lungs' air—and my pants were open and I was gasping for breath.

Martin put his hand back in his lap. His words, when they came, were even. He could have been talking about the weather. You could slip a condom on your cock, he said, and twirl me on it like a globe on its axis. The words took shape in the room; they made sex seem as understandable as pornography. On the blank TV screen I imagined I saw Martin and myself, fucking. I looked down at my open pants, at my underwear, white as a sheet of paper. Or I could do you, he said. Still I hesitated, not because I didn't want him but because the very thought of fucking Martin added so many possibilities to

my life that I grew dizzy contemplating them. Just do what
you want to do, Martin said, but do it now. I kissed him. I
pulled open the buttons of his shirt, pushed down his pants. I
bent over him and ran my tongue over his chest, into his navel,
down to his cock and balls. When I got there I swabbed the
shaft until it glistened. I rolled his balls around my mouth the
way a child rolls marbles in his hand. And it's important to
know that I didn't do this because I suddenly loved him. I just
wanted to fuck. Do it, I whispered. Do it.

And he did, lying on the floor, on a rug, though I didn't
twirl as easily as those globes in high school, and, in fact, after
one revolution, I didn't twirl at all, but sat astride him and
rocked up and down. And he pumped, pumped like anyone in
any skinflick ever made, though I didn't think of that then, but
only of the amazing sensation of having this man inside me. A
funny thing happened then. He pumped and I rocked, and I
rocked and he pumped, and eventually our rhythm must have
been just right, for the rug, a small Persian carpet–type thing
patterned in tangled growing vines, came out from under us as
if it had been pulled. I fell over, he slipped out of me, we
ended up on our sides, side by side, laughing. We lay on the
floor for a long time, mouths open, our stomachs heaving as
we sucked in air. We touched each other only with our fingertips, and then only slightly, and we lay on the floor for a long
time, laughing.

We finished on his bed. I don't remember going there, just
a point at which the world returned like a shadow and I saw
my cum splashed on his stomach and legs, and his splashed on
mine, and below us was a white sheet instead of the rug. Then
for a moment I wanted to take everything a step further. I
wanted to run my finger through Martin's cum and lick the
finger clean. But Martin smiled at me. He kissed me. When
my hands went for his body, he caught them halfway and held
them. In a light voice he said, In my experience, there are two
kinds of men in the world: those who play with their lover's
hair when they're getting a blowjob, and those who play with
their own. Though I tried, I couldn't remember what I'd done.
Which type am I? I asked. You, he said, and showed me as
he told me, put one hand on my head, and one on yours. And
which are you? Martin looked at my hair. If there was a mirror

handy, he said, you wouldn't have to ask that question. His words didn't really *mean* anything, but they accomplished what I think he meant them to: I forgot my desire to taste his cum. He lifted the sheet then and fluffed it with his arms, like wings, then let it settle on our shoulders, and I didn't realize we were standing up until I awoke hours later.

After that he could have asked me to do anything. A caress from Martin had more strength than any punch Henry would ever land. But he rarely used this power. And I suppose I had the same control over him—didn't he, as well, sleep standing in my arms? We shut the windows, turned off the phone, unplugged the clock. We wore no clothes for days, and used our time to make love, to eat and sleep. What I remember from that time, the time we shut out the world, is sweating on his bed as he dove into me, and someone somewhere flushing a toilet and the wall behind Martin's bed rattling as water rushed through pipes concealed within it. The headboard shook the wall as well, creaked and chipped paint in time with our grind, and water ran through the pipes.

It occurs to me now that just after that time I asked Susan what pregnancy was like. She'd been talking, vaguely, about having a baby, though she said she couldn't name five straight men in the world that she'd want to father it. If you've ever had a cock moving deep inside you, you know that it can feel like a part of you, even as you realize that it belongs to him. Can you imagine this staying in you after he pulls out, staying, growing, moving around eventually, making its presence, its separate life, known? This is how I imagined pregnancy. I asked Susan if this was reasonable. She sighed and smiled. Not even close, she said. Not even close.

When her shirt comes off, I'm struck by the strength in Susan's shoulders. Instead of unbuttoning it, she pulls it over her head, and her hair falls back audibly to surround her thin neck. Sometimes I think it's Susan, and not Martin, who is the love of my life. I don't know why I believe in such a concept— perhaps because thinking it distracts me from the larger fact: that I can have neither of them. Except for Susan, except for tonight. And that other night: I remember the river, both of us tenderly helping the other off with clothes. Tonight we kiss for a while, then stop, come to the bedroom. In here, candles instead of electric light or darkness, windows open but curtains drawn, so that they move in the breeze. Incense. The music from the other room. Susan busies herself with setting the stage, and then we pull our clothes off alone and pretend to ignore each other. But Susan, folding her bra in half, catches my eye. "There's an extra toothbrush if you want to brush your teeth," she says, and looks away. I have to fight back laughter. I know the kind of laughter it would be, cynical laughter, sad laughter, having more to do with things outside this room than in it. I feel like something's been stolen from me. I want to compliment her, tell her I think she's beautiful. At the river, I could have done so—I did, because the sex we had then was, we thought, just between the two of us. And it's not that Susan is no longer beautiful, no longer sexual. But her sexuality exists apart from me. Her apartment, these trappings, are one thing; she'll play with them. But not with herself. Not tonight. Tonight I'm not her lover. I'm just helping her to have her baby.

When she first came to us, only Martin and I knew he was sick. We'd known for months, but were still unwilling to give his illness the legitimacy, the finality, of a name, a word. (I know that too much of this story takes place in the past. But that's what I would say to Susan if I could speak to her, if I weren't writing about John, who nuzzles her breasts and compares them to, imagines they are, Martin's. I would say, "Too much of this story takes place in the past," and, without speaking, Susan would nod. She knows that too.) She presented her plan: She would have a baby and raise it alone. Perhaps one day she would marry, but she didn't foresee it and she didn't particularly care. She was happy fucking around: She wanted a baby, not a husband. But she didn't want anonymous sperm or the hassle of a turkey baster, and she couldn't afford artificial insemination. She wanted to do it the old-fashioned way. And she wanted to make love to me. I asked what she expected of me, besides sperm. Uncle John, she said. You will be Uncle John, and this one here will be Uncle Martin. She didn't understand why she laughed alone at her joke.

Before she left she asked him if he'd lost weight. After she left he said he was cold. In the bedroom I curled up with him under the blanket. Then he was hot and wanted to throw the blanket off but I suggested we take our clothes off instead. And then he was cold again and I took him in my arms and rolled us in the blanket and when I'd finished we were pressed together front to front and I opened my mouth and closed it over his and tickled his lips with my tongue until he let me in. And then he pulled back and said, You shouldn't, and I looked into his face, so pale that it seemed almost greenish, and I said, I should, and kissed him again.

Wrapped in the blanket, stretched out on the bed, we could have been suspended in space. By our feet, by our heads, by our cocks, suspended in time. I reached down and pushed my cock between his sweating thin legs and pulled his between mine. Sometimes when we did it that way I imagined that I was inside him but that night I imagined I was inside a woman. That was the only way he'd let us do it anymore, he said my health has got to be protected, said he loves me too much to kill me, said anything to keep me away from him because now, now that he's sick, he's afraid of what he wants because he's afraid of what he wanted because he thinks that what he wanted not what he did is why he's going to die.

When at last we unrolled the blanket, it seemed that buckets of salty-sweet water rolled off the bed as the last fold parted. Though untouched, the sheets were soaked, and I remade the bed before joining Martin in the shower. His thin back was bent over a fern he kept on the deep window ledge; his fingers pulled a few brown leaves from the pot and let them fall in the tub. Because you love me, he said. And because you love her. I said, What? He said, I think you should, if you can, if you stay healthy, you should help Susan. After I'm dead.

After he said that I didn't do laundry for two weeks, didn't do anything, and when I came across those sheets again they were wet as if we'd used them just minutes ago, and covered in places with a thin green layer of mold. I held them in my hand and felt their green sliminess stick to my fingers and I didn't know what to think: if this was the product of fucking Martin, or if this was the product of nothing, or worst of all, if this, the product of fucking Martin, was nothing.

After he died I didn't tell anyone for fifteen hours. I left his body in the hospital bed in the living room through the day, pulled back the covers once and looked at it, and then pulled them up to cover what was there. From seven in the morning until ten at night. I might have left him like that forever but Susan came over to check on us. I brought her into the apartment and sat her down and then I walked over to Martin and kissed him on the lips. They didn't taste like him. Nothing happened. I looked at Susan. She was crying; I remembered that she'd known him longer than I had, that she'd introduced us. I said, I wanted to do that in front of someone, so that when he didn't wake up, I'd know he was dead. And after Martin's body was gone and his bed sat there empty because they pick up bodies any time but they only pick up beds between nine and five, weekdays, I sent Susan away and then I went out myself. The air was hot and dry, the only moisture spat by air-conditioners. I didn't want to be alone with my grief, I wanted to give it to someone, to the whole city. I stopped a man on the street, put my hand right on his chest. Martin, I started, but the man ran away. Didn't he know I could never hurt him? I walked a long time, until I had no place else to go, and I went, for the first time, to the Spike, where I met Henry.

Two years have passed.

In this world, Susan says, there's as much nihilism in having a baby as in having one by me. I can't argue with that.

Science says I have nothing to protect her from. But still.

Part of the arrangement with the adoption agency was that every year, on Stephanie's birthday, Susan received an update on her daughter's life. The letters, addressed "Dear Birth Mother" and signed "The Adopted Parents," were always short, and came with two or three severely cropped Polaroids of Stephanie. Only fragments of bodies—hands, the side of a leg—indicated that she didn't live alone. When Susan moved from Kansas, she didn't leave a forwarding address with the agency.

The situation presses against me like—like how? Like trampling feet? Like uplifting hands? We weren't prepared for this—any of this. In our childhoods, in the heartland, we were taught that education equals a job, a job creates security. Marriage is the natural product of maturity, and happiness—and children—stem from that. And though there are times when the past overwhelms the present, and nothing will happen, there are also times when the present overwhelms the past, and nothing that happens makes sense. Here, today, the equations are changed: Silence equals death, they teach us, and action equals life. And though I no longer question these anymore, I sometimes wonder: Whose death? Whose life?

Martin's life resided in his right hand. He pointed it out to me with his left; his right hand rested on my thigh and he said, Look. I looked for a long time and then, just when I was about to ask what I was looking for I saw it, his pulse, visibly beating in the blue trace of a vein in the patch of skin where his thumb and forefinger met. For a moment I considered pressing my own finger on it, as a joke—I don't remember if this was before or after we knew he had AIDS—but I didn't, I—

I don't remember what I did. Mouth open, teeth resting against Susan's inner thigh just above her knee, I stop what I'm doing as I realize I'm crying. My body trembles slightly. I feel, don't see, Susan's head lift up. "Dale?" she whispers.

Then he puts his hand on her pussy where soon he will insert his dick and for all intents and purposes plant his seed; he runs fingers through her bush and teases her clit and her head sinks to the pillow. She can't see his face or the tears streaming down it. He remembers suddenly what he wanted to tell that man on the street: Martin, he would have said, Martin is dead. Martin is *so* dead. And he remembers a piece of sado-babble that Henry had whispered to him. You will never be free of me, Henry had said, and John realizes that, though this isn't true of Henry, it is true of Martin. And Susan. Even more than he fears what he's doing now, he fears what will happen when Susan finds someone else, falls in love, leaves him. He admits something to himself that he's always known but never accepted: that he wasn't her first lover—just as she wasn't his—and that they won't be each other's last, as well. That, even as his passion for Martin has become this lament, his grief, too, will pass away, and Martin will be even more dead. And whatever else happens, the person that may or may not have been conceived tonight will not be Martin.

It's not that things fall apart in the end, but they break down—if not for you, then for me. The sum of life isn't experience, I realize, isn't something that can be captured with words. Inevitably, things have been left out. Perhaps they appear in others' stories. Perhaps they were here once and John's forgotten them. Perhaps some things he remembers didn't really occur. But none of that matters now, for even as Susan takes John inside her he knows that this baby means something, though I've fought against that; and even Martin has become something abstract, a symbol, like the rose John once put in Martin's lapel, like Susan's African violet, like the fern in the shower. But after tonight, Martin's face will be inseparable from Susan's, from John's own, which is just a mask for mine. How can this story give Martin immortality when it can't even give him life? Now I wonder, has this story liberated anything but tears—*my* tears? And is that enough? I want to ask. To which I can only answer: Isn't that enough?

I thought I'd controlled everything so well—the plants, Martin, John, Susan. Even the semen.

In this story, I'd intended semen to be the water of life.

But, in order to live, I've only ever tasted mine.

THE FIANCÉ

• MICHAEL WADE SIMPSON •

THEY STILL CALL me when they can't think of the right words for Rambo to say before sex. I always know. Hollywood loves me.

My niece is out from Boston. She brings a friend. It is one of those days God must have called up for filming—flash flooding, then rainbow, Los Angeles is suddenly crystalline, deep breaths take on orgasmic power, you say *Have a nice day* to a telephone solicitor and mean it. Brigadoon. It's so easy to hate LA—the smog, the cars. I say, *See it today.*

She stands by the taxi, thin, poised, purse and coat, allowing her friend, a man, and the driver, a woman, to move before her, chivalry and luggage, the hill of stairs, my door. Then she sees me, laughs, runs ahead of them, the little girl again, into my arms. We are each other's favorite. She wears perfume now. It becomes her.

The young man smiles and grips: he is well trained, too. They are a study in khaki. They are here for a week. He is stunning.

He sips wine and looks, she chatters. I watch. My house is small but well placed. At night the city is an incandescent plain laid out beneath me, more starry than the sky. I love a view. I love my house. It may be boxy, ticky-tacky, a bungalow built before the talkies, but I think of it as a temple. I belong to the place as the hill and the lights and the smog all belong around me.

I play the High Priest—barefoot, in caftan. I rarely go out. Hollywood is used to recluses. Everything and anything can be delivered for a price. The problem is, I'm too tired to place an order. It was bound to happen—all the wicked things I did that I can't even remember now. So I stay home. All there is left to do is sit on my Marie Antoinette recliner and wait for my heart to go. I used to call myself *Writer*.

I love the musty smell in here, especially after the rain. As a decorator once exclaimed to me, *Memorabilia is always in!* I hope so: there's no taking this crap down. My walls are covered with framed glossies, caricatures, movie posters, erotica. I don't dust very often. I have cobwebby male statuary, vase after vase filled with matchbooks, a disco turntable and tiny dance floor, and an old mirror-ball, not spinning on the ceiling. I save menus, undershorts worn by so-and-so, marked-up scripts, broken props—and there, on my mantle, are my favorites: three gold-plated statuettes dressed up in Barbie clothes. All named Oscar. My life has had moments.

My niece has been here often. The young man is sipping his wine and moving from wall to wall.

She helps me set the table. I ask in the kitchen, "Is he any sort of vegetarian?" We're having crown roast and velvet potatoes.

"Mmmm. Winter food," she says. "He'll love it."

"Are you two, uh," choice of titles boggles the mind nowadays, "lovers?"

"*Lovers!*" She giggles. "Uncle Robert, he wants to marry me."

Oh my. He is beautiful. Watch him look out at the view. What is he thinking? There is a hint of smile. I can see the corners of his mouth move under his moustache. It is the bushy kind that makes straight men look more masculine, and, therefore, more gay. Maybe that's why my niece likes him. He doesn't say much. He looks like a god and lets her do the talking. I can see her point. There is something to be said for the still-harbors type.

I don't usually care for straight men. In my movies, the

women talk and the men fight. I'm convinced it's what they do best. And there are always gay actors to play the trickier roles. Straight men are like sports. They need their uniforms, they need their teams and their rules. And they need to knock the shit out of one another. It's a basic truth. They pray to Hemingway. If I ever had to talk to one, on the set or at a party, I'd stick to the Dodgers and the Rams. Or scare him away with my eyes. Size him up. Let him see.

At dinner, my niece, who is in her twenties, begins to tell a story. She recalls every visit she has ever made to California, from childhood on, with individual scenes, usually involving me. I give her a blank diary every birthday. Perhaps there will be a book someday.

He eats slowly, half her pace and without talking. He has ice-blue eyes and the kind of hair that falls into place on its own. His cheeks seem to color occasionally as he listens (it may be just the candlelight). She is one of those brutally honest people who never needed EST. Now she is telling exactly how she misbehaved. It is true, I suppose. It was easy for her here. I didn't try to father her or mother her. It was all sex and love and parties, and it was every weekend and then some. Embarrassed, he smiles, nods, leans over his food.

Does he know this already? Does he love her? Why, as the two of us eat and listen, do I feel his eyes on me?

She has just finished the *Ride in the Mercedes to the Desert at Sunrise* chapter when he finally puts his fork down. She smiles at me and continues as I begin to clear dishes. My niece knows I don't care to talk, and he seems to be listening with interest; indeed, I catch the corners of his mouth, the smile and the frown switching on and off beneath his moustache. I hear the beginning of the next chapter, *Funeral of a Friend*, and I stay in the kitchen.

I miss Fritz every day. His picture is on the mantle by the Oscars. His motorcycle rusts away in the driveway. I use his ties to belt my caftans. I tend his roses. His absence is pain— pain that I cherish now, as mine, as him. It's been over six years. He was one of the first to go.

She is describing Fritz's funeral, which I considered fitting— a few close friends and a boys' choir in our backyard, scattering the ashes into the wind and then going swimming. She loved

Fritz and flew out from Boston, the only one from my family. I remember her, crying in the Jacuzzi. His death. That plague. It changed everything.

I am whipping cream and crying when I hear the fiancé speak. It is a private question—he assumes I can't hear over the electric beaters. But I can. His voice is grainy-edged. His question is short.

"Why didn't you tell me?"

It is practically the first thing he has said all evening. One sentence. I don't hear her reply. *Why didn't you tell me?* What didn't he know? About Fritz? About me? *Why didn't you tell me?*

Something in his tone gives me pause.

I re-enter with the coffee tray, and they are both silent. She is looking at him, and he, almost apologetically, at her. That is, until I set the coffee down.

They turn, both of them, to stare at me.

"Where are we now?" I say, and she quickly responds, now directing her story to me.

"Last time I was here, I'd been dumped by some asshole, I'd dropped out of school, everything was bad, and I stayed for nearly a month. You were writing every day. Remember? One day I decided to learn how to cook. I went out with your gold card and came back with cookbooks and food, stayed in the kitchen, and cooked and cried and ate and didn't leave for weeks."

I remember. She brought me back to life. "I wrote and you fed me. We'd sit at the table by the pool and watch the lights. What food! We ate ourselves silly."

"We talked about love," she said.

"I wrote a movie for Fritz."

"And the rest is history." She smiles at my dolls on the mantle, then gets up to hug me.

"Welcome back," and I mean it. I love her more than she knows.

"I love you, Uncle Robert."

That night they are both in my dreams. A church. Daytime. *Long shot*. Red carpet, white walls. Long, open windows. Streaming sunlight. *Close-up*: She looks radiant in her bridal veil, he is wearing white too, they are shining, glowing white. *Long shot*: I am at the back of the church. *Medium shot*: They turn and smile to me. I walk down the aisle to join them.

"Uncle," she says, close up, through her veil, "I'm so happy for you."

She places his hand over mine. The ice-blue eyes meet mine and his mouth is electric, ecstatic. I am receiving a miracle. He is giving me love.

"Do you take this man?" she asks.

His voice, "I do."

He is lying by the pool. I like their Eastern pale. I sit behind my typewriter with a new idea. Later, I am interrupted by my niece.

"I'd like to get some groceries and things. Is it all right if I borrow your car?"

"Yes, the tank should be full."

"He likes it here," she says.

"He seems very nice."

"Yes," she says, kissing my neck.

Perfume suits her.

I go out after a while and he is swimming laps. Fritz had the pool built long and narrow, not oval or kidney-shaped, just for that purpose. I insisted on a curvy Jacuzzi off to the side. I could sit there Sunday mornings in the churning, bubbly warmth, with a cocktail and sunglasses, as he swam his laps. Now the fiancé switches from crawl to breaststroke and pushes off the far wall, swimming toward me, then stopping. He dog-paddles in the middle of the pool.

"I hope you don't mind," he says. "Skinny-dipping."

I realize his suit is on the cement by my feet.

"Of course not," I say, pointing to the sign on the cabaña: NUDE LIFEGUARD WANTED.

"Jump in," he says, sending a splash my way. "It's wonderful."

"Oh, no, thanks, this is my winter."

He laughs a surprising laugh—a baritone giggle—now swimming close, coming to the wall, by my feet, white skin in aqua, dark patches, curves. The water bleeds off his arms onto the hot cement and pools under my feet. I look down at them. And at him.

Then I can't stay that close. "You can jump into the shower in the cabaña when you're ready. There should be towels and shampoo."

"Oh, thanks," he says, watching me leave, pushing off the wall with his legs, making a blue wave. Flutter kick. The backstroke.

Sunbeams block the doorway to the cabaña, steam billows by me, then disappears. I move into the shadow. He is soaping himself, a mysterious shape through curtain, water, steam. The Spanish tiles echo like a drumroll or an engine. He wears a suit of bubbles. He hums Rodgers and Hammerstein.

He will open the curtain and step out, into my arms. Or he will lift my caftan over my head and draw me into the steam with him. I know exactly what he wants. I will kiss his neck and pull his hair, I'll gulp hot water and breathe steam and pin him to the wall. I will massage him and he will moan. I know exactly what he wants. I've seen him look at me. He wants me. I want him.

The humming stops.

"Are you there?"

"Yes."

The shower goes off. The steam begins to lift.

After a moment the curtain opens. He stands there. I see. *I know who he is.*

The next day the two of them head for a museum. I plead illness and send them off to a restaurant for dinner. I lie in bed drinking coffee. They return. I get up and stand next to the wall that separates the two bedrooms and wait for sounds. They talk for a few minutes. Then there is nothing.

She says she loves him.

In the hours before dawn I talk to Fritz. I fix a cup of tea and sit in my robe and slippers on a lawn chair, beside the roses. He grew only white roses. He hated the others. I like red roses, pink roses, scarlet, yellow, amber, mauve. I begged for colors until the day he died. Now, I watch the white roses in the dark.

In the cabaña he would have his hustlers: young, high, dirty kids off the street. First he would bathe them. He would wash their clothes and dry them, he would lay them down and kiss them, he would feed them, let them swim, give them money, drive them home. He loved his boys.

He loved parties. There were pool parties with starlets and orgies with stars. One party someone drowned. We called the police, but no one could find the dead man's clothes. No one had seen him arrive. No one knew him. They took him away, and no one ever claimed him.

Today I wait until the first hint of gray and the rise of the petals. That is when I feel closest to Fritz. It is when I would always awaken and ask him questions in his sleep, and he would tell the truth.

"Do you really love her?" I ask. Out loud.

"It's you, isn't it? Why have you come back?"

"Why did you leave in the first place?"

"Where have you been since you left here?"

"Do you love me too?"

I watch the sun rise and wait for any answers.

On their last day, my niece begs me to leave the house with them. I say no, I need to write. She proposes lunch, a long ride, a walk on the beach, shopping. No, I say, I must write.

He is standing behind her, fondling her hair. His swimming routine has worked away his pale Boston ghost color. He looks California now, he looks as if he's staying. She is determined to get me out of the house, but it is his idea that works.

"Why don't we go see a movie?" he says.

I laugh, but she doesn't.

"What movie? Where?"

"Your uncle's movie. The latest, greatest one. It's playing tonight at a theater in Santa Monica. I saw it listed."

My niece's eyes go wide. She knows I've never seen it.

"That is an incredible idea," she says. She also knows how to bully me.

She makes dinner, and I decide to get drunk, in order to lessen the terror. I am afraid to leave my hill. I am not the man I was. Fritz is gone. I no longer act before I think. I only think. I write. I no longer live.

*   *   *

We have salmon steaks. She has heated a loaf of French bread and made a salad. I am filling my glass again, shivering under the table, thinking up excuses, too drunk to come up with anything convincing. He knows. He looks at me across the table, and for the first time since the cabaña, I look back. The ice-blue eyes and the smile meet with a leg touching mine, under the table. It is not erotic in the least. It is friendship. I can smile.

My niece will drive the Mercedes with the top down, fast, like I used to. We will go see the movie that means the most to me, as we mean the most to each other. I am standing in my livingroom, alone again with the man she loves. Fritz is slowly giving me answers.

The fiancé turns to me.

"May I call you Uncle?"

Fritz. Is it you? Are you there?

My niece comes bursting through the door, catching my dismay.

"Come on, we'll be late."

I start to stall.

"You're not getting out of this."

I'm looking at the mantel. Falling. I see Fritz smile, and I catch myself.

The fiancé speaks softly. "Everything will be all right."

Fritz also had ice-blue eyes. I know, and my niece knows.

I reach for Oscar in the blue velvet gown and hand it to her.

"Here, this is yours."

I hand the go-go boot and miniskirted statuette, my favorite, to the fiancé.

"You get to have this guy."

I pick up the red gingham number.

"So," I say. "If I go, they go."

We go.

SACRED LIPS OF THE BRONX

• DOUGLAS SADOWNICK •

THE YEAR I began escorting my grandmother to synagogue was the year I began dreaming of another boy's lips.

Even my parents noticed.

"It's not the Sabbath, Michael," my mother said, as I changed from a Patti Smith T-shirt to a double-breasted, aqua blue sports coat I had picked up at the Salvation Army. "What does a boy your age want with an old lady?"

My grandmother Frieda was said to be going through some kind of "breakdown" at the age of seventy-eight, so they all worried. Frieda had always been pious—and ignored. But when my grandfather Isaac died, she grew lax in following some of their more firmly cherished Jewish commandments. That's when she became the talk of our Bronx neighborhood.

If a butter dish touched a piece of roasted meat in the refrigerator, she didn't go overboard scouring the plate three times in scalding salt water. When the Day of Atonement came around during the first of the fall breezes, and she felt lightheaded from a morning of fasting, she helped herself to a piece of carrot boiled in onion broth. Then she downed a mug of buttermilk in three or four dense gulps. "God doesn't want me to die from hunger," she said, patting away a coating of creamy saliva from her old-lady's moustache. She used the corner of her white cotton tablecloth as if it were a napkin.

This behavior confused family members.

"I hated some of those customs," my father confessed to me one Saturday afternoon when he spied his mother-in-law waiting for a bus to Fordham Road on the holy Day of Rest. She was wearing her one fancy outfit: a black, gaberdine dress and shawl. "But it's a crime to see them *all* go."

There were other infractions. On the afternoons during which Frieda was growing more and more lonely and forgotten, she could be found chatting with six or seven black ladies in her cluttered living room. Thelma, Mildred, Lecretia—I knew their names. They were engaged in making Frieda into a Jehovah's Witness, and spread their *Watch-Tower* journals all over Frieda's 1940s coffee table like vacation brochures. My grandmother nodded over tea with them for hours, stringing them along about Jesus, just for the company. "Stupid *schwartzes*," she'd mutter the moment they'd leave.

And once, I spotted her frail form sitting off to the side in a local coffee shop, ordering a BLT in her thick Polish accent. "Holt da mayo, please," she said to a doll-faced, Italian waiter. I watched her for a half-hour from the L-shaped counter where you got your salt pretzels and malteds. When her lunch arrived, she peeled a slice of bacon from the triple-decker and regarded it as if it were a dollar bill she had discovered in her sandwich.

But, with all this, she never stopped going to synagogue. In fact, she began visiting the one-story, brown brick building as much as three times a day, usually after meals. Hung above the brass-lined doors, in reddish-gray clay, was the synagogue's official name: B'nai El. Once you stepped inside, the pine floors, brick walls, and dusty, stained-glass windows made you feel as if you had barged into an old lady's living room. Mostly everyone called this synagogue "the Jerome Avenue shul." You were supposed to feel at home here.

I remember entering the sanctuary with Frieda for the first time that year. There was a sudden brush with nostalgia. Four years before, I had been the shul's last Bar Mitzvah triumph. I sang; the Rabbi lifted the Torah scrolls; the crowd stood; Frieda and Isaac held hands. After that day, like most kids, I stopped attending services. What had happened? Now I was seventeen. The inescapable awkwardness of my bent posture, light olive skin, crooked nose, and fleshy cheeks had made me into an object of interest to those who were either lighter or darker than me. I had what guys from New Jersey or lower Manhattan called "a Bronx look." I didn't have to be in a room of half-blind Jews. But it was so tranquil inside, and I now felt a loyalty to that.

It was a below freezing day in January, and many streets were trapped under intricate layers of ice, slush, salt, and animal waste. (Frieda, who had refused to remain at home, took toddler steps. I held her by her tiny elbows wrapped in thick layers of wool.) I got a shock touching the brass knobs to the mahogany doors leading into the shul. I got another jolt once inside when I touched the metal bar holding the prayer shawls. "Such a pretty boy," the old congregants said when they saw me flinch. I heard whispers: "A *gootn yid*." "A good Jew." "God bless . . ." They beamed wide-eyed, like the well-dressed relations in *Rosemary's Baby*. As if pain was your sacred initiation here.

"Sit down, and pray to God, Mickey," my grandmother told me, her blood-shot gaze shifting from the smiles of her friends to the scene of screaming fire engines outside on a nearby Bronx street. "Before the whole world burns down."

Something was burning down.

You could smell the soot in the crisp air on the way to worship. The shul was located a block or two from Yankee Stadium, a few steps from the elevated IRT train on Jerome Avenue, the Lexington Avenue Line to be exact. It also was across the street from what was reputed to be one of the Bronx's finest network of basketball courts. That winter, only a lone crew of five or six Puerto Rican athletes dared challenge the bracing Bronx winds to shoot hoops. They burned newspapers, coffee cups, and milk cartons in New York City garbage cans to keep their hands warm.

"Hey, it's the chump . . ."

"The one from high school . . ."

"Hey, brain . . . !"

I was the youngest person at the Jerome Avenue shul. At first I would find myself disdainful of the archaic Yiddish that hung in the air like Havana cigar smoke, Old Spice aftershave, and hair-nets. But Frieda had picked something up about me that no one else had. My high school life was crowded with yearbook associates, theater rehearsals, and honor roll wannabes. My family was heaped high with aunts who spied on each other from nearby beauty parlors and uncles who owned Bronx automotive stores and talked business whenever you walked by. But it wasn't enough. "It's in your face," Frieda once said. "Come sit with me in the shul. It will ease you."

"Okay," I said.

I told myself that I would accompany her because it gave me an excuse to walk past those Puerto Rican b-ball players. Their improvised lay-ups, schizo dribbles, and psyched-out passes impressed even Frieda, who winced at them. On the first hint of a thaw, they removed their windbreakers and sweated hard. When I closed my eyes in the shul during the passages in which the old Rabbi muttered himself into a trance, I'd see their curvy backs and wild forearms spiraling up and down in the air, and my breath would quicken, dart-like. "Mikey, you have so much feeling for God," Frieda would say, seeing this.

I had seen these guys even before Frieda began taking me to shul. Sometimes they killed time over at Jerome Avenue, near the stores underneath the El. They leaned against the green, iron-girded pillars that held up the tracks iced with pigeon shit. They had just moved to our neighborhood and didn't know anyone. My father would curse them out from our kitchen window: "Goddam spics" or "Go to goddam hell."

I'd sit in English class, answering a question about Shakespeare, and imagine myself having been raised with a tight, washboard stomach and thin, purple lips. I secretly took up smoking just to see how the thickened, yellow puffs would trail out of my lips when I licked them wet. I felt a little as if I were going crazy, like Frieda. I began talking to myself in the pidjin Spanish I picked up on the streets.

It got so bad that I'd leave chess club early and hang around the dilapidated Jerome Avenue newsstands waiting for the roving teenagers to show up so that I could act like I didn't know them. They always showed up, too. Their gold and black Giants T-shirts, damp from basketball sweat and Gatorade, sticking to their flat bodies. I'd page through the *Village Voice* and catch a glimpse of them talking, and I'd feel lonely. It was a little like going to the movies by yourself. Here's one scene:

Two of the more hyper guys run into a bodega and buy 7-Ups and exotic coconut drinks, before heading home, a mere stop or two from here. And another: I stare down at the asphalt, and then lift my head up fast, catching sight of an angled, quivering muscle on the back of a shirtless teenager—he's turning away from the wind to light a cigarette. Meanwhile, another boy—the quiet one—listens for the distant sound of an oncoming train.

Then: All five scamper up the forty or so stairs to the train platform, running into an open car door just as it's ready to shimmy close. They kick each other in the ass like Latino Harpos. Thump a basketball in front of a black lady's sleeping face. Scream out the train window. Collapse into graffiti-covered seats. They were bound for neighborhoods where they spoke only Spanish. Seeing them go, I'd feel lonely.

I picked up the quiet one's name: Hector.

"Hey, Hector! can't you play no basketball . . . ?"

"Hey, Hector! where'd you learn how to dribble, from your sister?"

"Hey, Hector! don't you eat, man . . . ?"

Hector was so thin. Sometimes I thought he was inhumanly two-dimensional. That one day he would turn to one side or the other and disappear off into the sky, like one of Frieda's secret demons. That he felt good about being empty inside, so that he could run around the basketball court and feel both feather-light and numb in case he made a mistake. He had green-veiny skin that was discolored in snowflake designs near his shoulders. You could see the beige polka dots trailing up from his biceps because he cut his T-shirts into shreds, making them into ragged tank tops. Maybe he liked showing off his disfigurement. Maybe he liked the way it was laid over his musculature like a doily. He was such an eccentric beauty, who knows? I couldn't keep my eyes off him.

"Whatcha looking at?" his pal, a heavy-set black Puerto Rican guy, once barked at me after their basketball game.

"I'm not looking at nobody."

"Shit . . ."

It must have been obvious. Hector turned around, slowly—ghosted. It was the first time I saw his entire face. It was oval-shaped, like a teaspoon, with a caffeine stain at his lips. He looked at me like I was a detraction from his full-time job, which was sweating and heading home. And being thin. He turned away.

The whole group of six knew a chump when they saw one and occasionally yelled, "Hey, whitey," or "Yo, faggot," or "Bitch," or "Kiss my pinga," when they saw one of us Jewish kids on the street. I always wanted to say something, but words stuck in my throat like they do in a dream. I felt terrible. I worried that Mrs. Minelli or Mr. McPhee, walking home from the butcher with brown paper bundles of chopped meat, had witnessed me being called a girl. "Move out the way, Sonny," I remember Mr. McPhee saying. To him, it was just noise. Goyim. Niggers. Kikes. Eyetalians. He hated us all. We all made noise.

Once, I ducked into a card and tobacco store when Hector caught me looking at him under the train tracks; a moment later, I saw him buying his mother an oversized birthday card. Another time, I stared at him when he was alone in front of a mailbox, and he looked right through me, blowing his nose in his fingers and then shaking the snot out on the street.

One afternoon after school, just as the late spring humidity came like a blast furnace to the Bronx, he and his friends saw me and yelled, "Hey you." My humiliation was a kind of jump start past my shyness, and I shouted back: "Hey you." A few Italian ladies, walking home from the fish market, stared at me like they had heard a terrible joke. The Puerto Ricans were laughing. "Hey you?" one of those guys said, his hysterics claiming something inside me, like a forceps or a fishing hook or a secret shot of my father's Seagram's Seven: "hey you! Hey You!! HEY YOU!!!" Hector just looked. Everyone's sweat was evaporating from his body; I thought I saw a mirage through the smoky city heat: Hector walking over to me—his thin arms and legs filling up my entire vision. But he was just standing still.

"Hey you!!! Hey you!!! Hey you!!!"

Eventually, a couple of friends from calculus class spotted me alone. They came over and yelled.

"Hey you, Puerto Ricans!!!"

"Hey you, Jews!!!"

One of the most irritating things you could do in the Bronx

in those days was to call someone by his ethnic identity. It hurt, but not enough to cause a riot. It was at this very moment that Frieda appeared, as if from nowhere. I didn't see her approach, but I felt her warm, pulpy fingers on my hand.

"Hey . . . you . . ."

"Grandma!"

"You are becoming a hoodlum?"

I shook my head no, but her mind was already off somewhere. I took her hand, and we walked towards the synagogue. In the distance, I heard the guttural cries and the assorted Bronx accents: "Heee yyyyyoooo." I wanted to tell her something—that I was lonely, that those boys had called me names, but she shook her head. "Pray to God," she said. "You have the fire of the Evil One in your eyes."

So I went with her.

As a child I paid special attention to Frieda's tales of the Evil One. ("He is quiet like an angel," she'd whisper, "but swoops down at night—and gets you, and hits you on the face . . . !!!") The way she held me in her arms and kissed me!—I'll never forget that. It seemed to unhinge my mother, who made a point of calling Frieda into the kitchen: "Ma, help me with the brisket, will ya?" And as I grew older—eleven, twelve, thirteen—I went to synagogue with Frieda and Isaac and watched the old man weep during the mediational standing prayer. "Your grandpa is a good Jew," Philip, the Rabbi's son, said as I began preparations for my Bar Mitzvah. "The best." Like Frieda, the Rabbi was getting infirm and a little crazy, so Philip began taking over. And when I was rehearsing the ancient tunes, I made Philip cry with emotion. Philip: he was a revered basketball player on Sundays, a seminary student every other day. He'd teach me the singsong chants in cutoffs, smelling like the asphalt. The aloof Rabbi—a German refugee—seemed stirred by the progress I made in my renditions.

But one's parents saw it as a sign of imbalance to keep up such practices after the Bar Mitzvah was over. "Are you normal?" my mother asked me as I persisted in praying in synagogue on the Sabbath. "Normal kids play ball on the weekends." The Rabbi's son whispered in my ear, "Keep with it. It's in your blood." But it was not healthy. "There's no future in this," my mother said. "When you get married, then you can go and pray like an old man."

These were the days when the Bronx was changing, and the change was having a strange effect on all of us.

Frieda and Isaac moved here in 1946. It's where they raised a family of five boys, four girls, and twenty grandchildren. She spoke a Polish Yiddish and went to market on 167th Street, a full day's experience back then, considering how many Jewish stores (bookstores, dairy markets, religious books and clothing retailers, butchers, bakeries, pawn shops—never mind Frieda's and Isaac's tailor shop) you had to browse through. Now those places were either burnt up or selling food we weren't allowed to eat. That's where my parents, brother, aunts, uncles, and cousins lived in fear and resentment. In five years, our neighborhood shifted from blue-collar Jewish, Italian, and Irish old-timers to poor Puerto Ricans and blacks. In our little courtyard you could hear the melodies: Zero Mostel from Mrs. Kaffel's kitchen, Machito from Mr. Candelario's. Barbra Streisand from me.

The competing sounds drove me crazy. In my dreams I would hear the mambo and see Hector's pencil-thin lips. He'd be dancing with his basketball in one hand and a Coca-Cola in the other. I would wake up in the middle of a hot summer night with an erection, unable to go back to sleep, the bed sheets soaked through. Murmuring "bitch," or "pinga," I'd relieve myself, thinking of Hector and the way the soda-pop made his lips shine like shellac.

One Saturday afternoon, the daydreams got very bad. I wished I could go to synagogue, but that was out of the question. My parents, seeing some profound but quiet change in me, had prohibited too many visits with Frieda. "She's a witch," my mother would say of her own mother. "I always suspected it, and now I know it." Playing baseball with friends was suicidal; I couldn't catch the ball. So I just turned on a metal fan in the bedroom I shared with my brother and read. But my mother played the Broadway recording of *Fiddler on the Roof* so many times that the album began to skip. Next door, a kid was blasting Santana's "You Got to Change Your Evil Ways." I ran out of the house—"I'll be back for dinner"—

and reached Jerome Avenue. I took the subway down to Times Square, as I had many times that year.

I know now that the scenes in those theaters were no different from the shadows I saw in my head when I sat alone in synagogue and closed my eyes. Truth be told, I saw many of the same things in my mind's eye: men who smelled like my father's Chesterfields and whiskey; the reflection from a switchblade I once saw in the dark; the Puerto Rican kids who zoomed in on my nose like I was a long lost Mediterranean; the Italian boys who called out "Mamma" as they came on your sneakers; the cigarettes I was too fearful to inhale; the hours in the dark away from my father's golf games and my mother's voice—"Turn off the golf game!"; the heavyset men who hunted me down like I was a stupid, starved animal who didn't know how to say no (I did not know how to say no).

I had memories of hours spent sitting alone in a broken seat watching anal intercourse on the torn-up movie screen. These memories came easily to me as I sat on a velvet-covered bench in synagogue listening to the monotonous singsong of the Rabbi. Both places were stuffy, half-empty, and secretive. In the theater, I'd wash the crusts of dried cum off my jeans and stomach hairs; in the shul, I'd scrub the stink of saliva-heavy kisses off my cheek and forehead. Neither place had soap. In the theater, I'd sleep and recall being held by Frieda when both she and I were younger. In the shul, I'd dream, too; Torah scrolls opening up, the words becoming big, human lips—both Philip's and Hector's. (They both said very sacrilegious things).

Now that I think of it, there are a hundred other similarities. A few years later, they would renovate the porn theater with neon lights and new carpets and make it feel like Saks Fifth Avenue, but it would get so popular with the punkers and AIDS activists that they shut it down right away. At about the same time, the city tore down Frieda's synagogue after the last refugee had died. There was an analogy of addictions, too. The hugs, kisses, grunts, and simple lifts of a skintight nylon T-shirt—never mind the leaden weight of skin and flesh in an Irish kid's corduroys—brought me closer and closer to the truth about my family and me. In a similar way, the pats on the head by Frieda's friends, the delicate crinkle of the yellowed pages in old prayer books, the scent of urine in the ladies'

dresses, transported me to an invisible city where feeling close
to God was your passport. Holding that passport in the rooms
of my Bronx household was almost impossible.

At home, in my parents' bathroom, I read *Portnoy's Complaint*
and thought "How odd." Sure, I knew I had to be very careful.
I feared bumping into my mother or one of her sisters on my
way out of the theater. I wore a Yankees cap over my face. It
was all a tense experiment. But there was more, too. These
secrets were buried in me like a stripper's sense of self-respect.
I knew I wanted love. And a boy's lips. Things you couldn't
find in Times Square or synagogue.

Frieda was becoming all love, which was why she was so
dangerous to my parents and their world. "I wake up in the
morning," she confided in me, "and see the Angel of Death.
And Michael, he has your face." But she was not frightened.
So I decided not to be, either. I kept a change of shul clothes
at her house. I'd lie to my mother, running out of the house
with a catcher's mitt or a hockey stick or a basketball or a
bathing suit or a soccer ball, screaming: "Um, see ya. . . ." But
I was really bound for Frieda's house. We'd walk under the
Jerome Avenue El to get to the shul, and see those basketball
players.

"Hey, Hector," they yelled. "Here's your girlfriend walking
by."

But, after a time, they stopped yelling. The sight of a young
man helping an older woman conjured up something familial
in them. They respected respect, it seemed.

"*Mira*, there's that *hombre* again."

"That old lady—she's a witch, man."

"No, man, that's his *abuela*!"

"Shalom," they screamed. "Shalomy."

Frieda would just smile, and hold my hand.

I began to know Frieda for real when I walked with her
through the decaying Bronx streets to shul; the folds of flesh
near her palm, so loosely wrinkled you could almost feel direct
bone; the quiet sighs she took when we waited for the 168th
Street light to turn green; the memories she entertained of her
mother, now dead, whom she had left behind sixty years ago
in Poland, and who taught her to listen to her own heart; the
secret potions, amulets, and incantations she picked up from

superstitious Poles and now resorted to more and more. Just like I began to know Hector and Hector's guys for real; their odd loneliness among each other as they traveled two miles from their ghettoes to play at our more well-appointed basketball courts; the fear of the Jews and their holidays I saw in their eyes; the boredom that sometimes overtook them in the midst of an endless game.

Men cannot sit with women in Orthodox synagogues; so Frieda and I parted ways once we entered the little shul. The Rabbi was immobile and stick-thin, but his voice still shook the chandeliers. It blasted: "God, O Merciful One, Holy, Holy, Holy!" The old men who were already seated would gesture "come, sit down," and they'd wrestle each other to be the ones to show me the place in the prayer book. "Here." "No, here!" Frieda had many friends herself, but she preferred listening alone. From the laced, wrought-iron partition that kept the aging men from the aging women, I watched my old grandmother shake softly in her seat, her droopy eyes closed, her lipsticked lips mouthing the ancient words by heart.

It was on a fall Saturday afternoon—a year since I had been escorting Frieda to shul—that I understood why I thought so much of Hector here.

On cold afternoons, I'd see him. When the weather got warmer, I saw him. When I began going to shul with Frieda on Saturday mornings, and then on weekday evenings, I'd cross paths with him. That summer, I worked in a deli, cooking kosher franks on a grill full-time to make money for college. If I was energetic, I'd get up early and walk with Frieda to the morning service. I'd only linger in the hushed sanctuary for a few minutes; I needed coffee and some time to get ready for work. It would be very early—7 A.M. to be exact. (It wasn't uncommon to see the basketball courts start filling up by then. If you were an athlete during a New York City summer, you had to get up very early to get your practice in. By noon, you'd fry.) As my morning routine with Frieda became a pattern, I'd see Hector on the Jerome Avenue streets at the crack of dawn, too.

Sometimes he'd be dribbling a lone basketball. Other times, he'd be paging through a *Playboy* or *Sports Illustrated* or *Redbook* magazine near the very newsstand I used to watch him from. As the weeks and then months passed, our eyes would meet, then bolt away. By the time the October breezes began turning the leaves on the city's oak and birch trees purple, orange, and red, we were on Bronx speaking terms.

"Yo."

"Yo."

I might have kept walking, but I slowed down, as if it occurred to me that it was finally time to buy a magazine. It was cool and dewy still, a morning breeze sending the smell of percolating coffee and toast from the greasy spoon across the street. I felt lonely and acutely hungry looking at Hector as his eyes trailed across words on a page. I could smell the scent of Dial soap from his body which seemed less sculpted than I had imagined from viewing him from afar. It was just a body, sharply carved and unpredictably pitched to one side or the other, depending on how his feet were planted on the concrete. I had looked at him so many times in so many different ways over the past year—sometimes in clandestine glimpses with Frieda; other times in defiant fast stares—that I had forgotten the difference between secrecy and reckless boldness. They both seemed the same, when it came to watching Hector.

When he turned to me, I saw his lips, framed by little flairs of peach-fuzz, quivering. Then he picked up another magazine.

"You a Jew boy?"

I stared at him.

"You go with your old grandmother to church?"

"It's not church . . ."

"Jew boy," he said, smiling.

"Puerto Rican," I said back.

He nodded, matter-of-factly.

"Right . . ." he said.

". . . Right," I added.

He snorted. I opened my mouth, as if about to laugh (a Bronx gesture if there ever was one). "Yeah," I said. That seemed a little stupid, or even ill-mannered, but it came out of my mouth like a prayer and felt good. I said it again: "Yeah." It was a big step. I think I moved my hand, as if to acknowledge this. He held his small, brown fist to his side, like I'd better be careful. What was amazing? That we were talking.

That he could both act dangerous and be dangerous, could act vulnerable and be vulnerable. These four directions played on his lips.

"Jew," he said, dispassionately. He gave me a look, as if to say: We have these lines.

"PR," I said.

I looked at his magazine: On the cover was a famous Puerto Rican pitcher.

He saw me looking.

"I got a subscription," he said. A few beats of silence. Then: ". . . a stack at home."

Cautious signals played on his eyes. My hands shook a little in the morning breeze.

Upstairs at his three-room apartment, two subway stops away, his mother looked a lot like mine. She balanced an unlit cigarette in her tight, cracked lips. She was a compact woman, with a youthful urgency and light brown, discolored skin, like Hector's. Hector and I sat at the orange and white Formica kitchen table, covered with peach-colored, plastic place mats. She served us espresso, and little cubes of sugar-iced yellow cake on a paper plate.

"He goes with his *abuela* to church," he told his mother, who nodded. Then she left the kitchen.

"Jew."

"PR."

We both drank our coffees.

In his room, a few minutes later. The plaster-cracked walls were covered with pictures of Jesus and Joe Namath and Roger Daltry and some Latin-looking keyboard player I didn't recognize. There were Catholic comic books, and neatly written homework assignments on white loose-leaf paper piled near eleventh grade textbooks, and ratty spiral notebooks. He showed me some drawings and then his homework, pieces of paper on which bold *A*'s and *B*'s had been inscribed in red ink. I was conscious of him watching me. There were more tours. I was conscious of Hector clicking his bedroom door with the help of his back. After some additional tours around stacks of *Sports Illustrated* and assorted seashells collected from "the clean beaches of Puerto Rico," he pushed me. By accident, I fell onto his linoleum floor, which smelled of Mr. Clean. By accident, he did too. He lay his thin, marionette arms casually over mine. It was more of a slow, motionless cascade than anything else. I was conscious of his fingertips searching for skin, like the feet of an upside down insect, scrambling for the ground.

"What did you call me?" he asked, making believe he was holding me down against my will, locking fingers into mine.

"What did you call me?" I asked back, making believe I was getting aggressive. He held my fingers too tightly.

And although I felt the breath from his scant mouth pressing on my neck, and though I heard the words, "I called you a Jew, Jew," I didn't dare let myself give in to him for fear that he would tell his friends. I stayed still, in one rigid place, my body unable to rest itself on the floor and take in this curious spot. Instead, I focused on the shock of a wish that was no longer just deferred, and the sense that Hector's incantory breath on my neck may have meant one thing to me and a different thing to him.

It was a new place, just as shul and the theater had once been new, and sensing this, I felt my neck release itself fully into the gravity of his small, little room. This is what it had all been for, hadn't it? We lay there for a few minutes. Some strands of black, oily hair rested in my face. It made my nose itch, but I didn't dare move to scratch. Nothing happened. The world of men had before been a mix of tactile boredom leading up to shattering appetites. Now: the smell of skin and a hint of mutual loneliness. Had all this been ordained by the forces of a Bronx in flux: the thud of a basketball, the cracked voice of a rabbi? I heard the thud in my head, and it hurt. It was a way of staying focused on the immediate problem: Now what? To my right I saw his bed frame and the dust balls beneath it. To my left was the bedroom door, against which his sneakered feet were jimmied.

I saw a look of wild despair in his eyes. "You like it?" he asked, his voice shaking, his eyes dark with shame.

"I don't know," I whispered, amazed to find myself unable to talk. The lips moved, but no words came out. I found myself uncontrollably—imperceptibly—caressing the skin in between his T-shirt and the black, leather belt holding up his shorts. I felt goose bumps trailing up and down his side, where my fingers were.

"What do you do in that church?" he asked me, speaking into my neck through sweaty tangles of black split ends.

"The same thing you do in yours."

"Nah," he said, starting to stir. He shifted his weight and pushed his face away from my neck in a jolting arc heading upwards. He propped his left elbow up on the floor and balanced the left side of his face on it. It was clumsy, but fast—like the way he dribbled a basketball. When he was done, his lips were positioned maybe a foot and a half from mine.

"What do you do in there?" he asked, staring.

I understood that he thought I carried magic amulets in my pocket, that I drummed up spells to make him follow me. He thought I was a demon, just as Frieda taught me to believe that he was one. "We pray for you PRs to go away."

He smacked my face.

"Well, we ain't going away."

The blow was not expected. My face stung in a million places, even though he had not hit me hard. His soft palm really just dusted the right side of my profile. I had never been slapped like that, a dusting. I would have wrested myself from his grasp, except that suddenly my hands had been freed. You learn things sometimes by learning and not thinking. Like a witch sensing her magic in old age. Or a rabbi closing his eyes and seeing the end of his history. I smacked him back, mimicking the action of the palm touching his right profile, much in the way you pat a dog's back. He clenched his lips when I said: "We pray for you PRs to drop dead."

He smacked me again, saying nothing.

I hit him again—not too hard but hard enough. He made believe he lost balance and fell a little to his side. "Whew," he said, scratching an eye. When he regained his position, he made a scrambling motion with his bony legs that said with a certain unspoken insolence: move your legs. I did, making a "V" shape. I felt his crotch sink into mine.

"We want you Jews to drop dead," he said. This time he used a lighter touch, more of a brush than a smack.

"Then this place would really be a dump," I said, copying

his style, but hitting the opposite side of his face, with a differ-ent hand. I had two hands free; he had only one.

His breath began to deepen. His eyes moved about in their sockets: little bloodshot marbles inset in Indian bones. "*Coño*," he said. The way he bit his lip, and allowed himself to slide into this new person now, made him seem superreal. As I had seen Frieda in the street after synagogue. I was aroused. I moved myself away from my sharp zipper, inserting a quick hand in my pants. I knew that he knew. He lifted his weight up and allowed his eyes to scan down to my crotch, seemingly blasé, the way he would look when a basketball circled around the hoop a dozen times before it eventually shook itself through.

Then he buried his face again in my neck so that I couldn't see his lips. His voice was muffled. He was afraid to say it: "faggot."

There had been moments in synagogue when I would feel tortured—out of place. Mr. Bluestein was incontinent. Mrs. Levine gave me the Evil Eye. At such times, a prayer would seize up on my lips, and I would find myself entertaining a strong impulse to murder Mrs. Levine or Mr. Bluestein. If I really went with the prayer to the next step—a repetition; a deep-throated tremor—a humble love of my people might flood over me. Strange, a simple prayer calling up a river like this.

"I hate the way you Jews pray."

"I hate the way you PRs ruin our neighborhoods."

And then: a blackout. His crotch swirling in place above mine like a flapping of wings—was it the Angel of Death? And then when the light came back, a bucking of youthful abandon. A few hidden muscles but no hidden moves. A curl in the torso, the necks ready to crack out of line. Pants stayed on; shirts shriveled upwards. A spinning by the lips, some saliva sputtering. Salty and strange tasting the sweat produced by despairing rapture. We lay, frozen.

When I heard Hector's father come home and lumber into the toilet, I left the house. (How did I know it was his father? The banging of the doors, the drunken belching, the deep-throated cursing—that's how many Bronx fathers acted when they came home from work in those days.) My heart pounded numbly in my chest as I took the subway home.

When I got off the train, late for work, I spotted Frieda walking back from synagogue. Her shuffled gait looked more strained than ever. I felt ashamed to see her. She touched her fingers to my forehead and said, "God bless you." I walked her home. Her black leather shoes left a trail of marks on the concrete.

The next day, when I called on her to go to synagogue, she was dead, her little form curled up in the dirty cotton sheets.

I have tried to remember the scene in different ways over the years, but the only real memory I have is of holding her hand. Then dropping it, suddenly. It was cold and hard. Then a certain cloying shame. Could I not be more courageous with my grandmother? I was frightened to look out the window, for fear of seeing the Angel of Death flapping its huge black wings like a monster. For the first time in a year, I felt defenseless. I would have to call my mother, a thought that made me even more clenched and wary. She'd take over. "What were you doing over there?" she'd ask. I thought I should take my outfits and Frieda's stones and amulets—things she had shown me in secret—and toss them into the incinerator. But I was afraid to leave the body alone.

I walked towards the window and looked out. I still felt confused about what had happened with Hector, and now more confused by a thought that occurred to me as Frieda's body got colder and colder: For one year, I was a true Jew. I had lived as Frieda's people had lived for centuries in forests and slums, their darkened lives turning around and around because the passion of love kept them alive. Now it would all be a memory. The faculties of my heart were ebbing as Frieda's soul sailed up to the Master of the Universe. I had no will to pursue this course alone. It would take me ten years to remember what she had taught.

Outside, a million people populated our streets, and most of them were not white. Out from their mouths you could hear so many languages, even with the window closed: Spanish, Spanglish, Italian, blue-collar white ethnic English, Black English, Sicilian, Armenian, Greek, Creole, Pentecostal ravings. Buses lumbered by—destined for points further south of us. Mothers were calling after their kids. Jilted lovers sat on car hoods, waiting for dates, mouthing their own quiet prayers of brokenheartedness. Drunken husbands screamed at their wives in front of the children. It was a cloudy day.

I wanted to say a prayer over the body. Anything. Frieda's name. Or Hector's. It would have been something I would have done yesterday. Now I silenced myself. I looked at the filthy glass and saw a reflection of my face, the place where Hector had hit. In a minute, it'd be time to call my mother. For now, I looked out the window. I saw two different Bronxes: the scene outside Frieda's window and the spot on my face Hector had dusted with his hand. At one point, if I squinted hard, I could see both at once. Then all I could see was an image of myself squinting. I looked like a little, lost child.

THE LITTLE TROOPER

• MANUEL IGREJAS •

"GET MAD, BLUE Team!" Ed shouted at the sweaty tangle of elbows and kneecaps. The game was volleyball and Ed had grouped all his problem kids into the Blue Team, hoping the pressure of keeping the ball aloft might spark them into a little body English. The Blues were all precocious and chubby and probably stayed glued to their computers at night. And they were well mannered. Not wishing to step on anyone's toes, they politely let the ball bounce past them. The Reds, tall, tough, and bony, were slaughtering them. Just then the ball bounced off Shelly Arbogast's curly blond head and back over the net into Red no-man's-land. This surprise point unified the Blues, and "Use your head, Shelly!" became their battle cry.

Ed laughed and ran his hands over his chest. He was proud of his chest. He folded his arms tight before him and flexed his pecs. Whenever Shelly and his pals imitated Mr. Horvath they puffed up like peacocks and hugged themselves. Ed was thirty-six and in peak condition again. He ran every morning and was at the Y three times a week. Dark haired and dark eyed, of average height, he was always being told he reminded someone of someone. He looked like a man in an ad for a tie in the *Sunday Times Magazine*. The Blues scored four more points.

A squad car pulled into the playground. A solitary cop emerged, rubbing his forehead. Tall and pudgy, with thinning blond hair and a round, sweet face, he entered the school through a side door. A janitor was swabbing the stairs with disinfectant. "Watch your step, Frank," he called. No reply, as the cop strode past. He entered the gym, saw the game in progress and hesitated. Ed was at the sidelines shouting, "Crank it up!" The cop's big footsteps went unheard in the din. He was a few feet away before Ed noticed him, looking at him with no surprise and some displeasure. His face suddenly weary, he started to say something when the cop aimed his revolver with both hands and shot Ed between the eyes. The game ended immediately.

"Thank you, Uncle Frank," Kimberly screeched at her mother's insistence. Instead of kissing Frank as ordered, she grabbed her doll and ran into the kitchen.

"Who's ready for more?" Frank's mother asked, eliciting groans from anyone who heard her. The adults were clustered around the dining room table drinking coffee and brandy, the kids sprawled around a huge silver tree. *King Kong vs. Godzilla*, which had become a holiday tradition, was blasting from two television sets.

Mrs. Antolino tried again. "More coffee?" She was a round, chirpy champagne blonde who neither looked nor acted her age. To her question there were equal yesses and nos. Husband looked to wife and Frank knew that within an hour he and his mother would be alone in the house.

"Where are you going?" she asked.

"Crespo's having a party. I promised I'd stop by."

"Be careful. The roads are slippery, and you've been drinking."

"Yes, Ma." He went to his room, took a flask of cognac and a bottle of poppers from the bottom dresser drawer, grabbed his coat. He kissed his sisters and nieces, shook the hands of husbands and nephews and drove to The Male Box.

It was early, the roads icy, the place half full. Frank scanned the room and saw men much like himself, decent guys in their thirties who could stand to lose a few pounds, men who had fled the arms of familial bliss for arms less familiar and more particular. He wanted to connect with someone lean and mean tonight. Someone he could rouse to gruff, if fleeting, affection through application of sheer goodwill. That man hadn't shown yet and when he did he was sure to be pounced on by the other goodwill wishers in the joint.

For them, sincerity ranked next to beauty in the scheme of things. If Lean and Mean never showed they would turn to each other and wade into conversation loaded with common touchstones. Then they would stumble out together and drive to a spotless apartment with a tiny, blinking tree. In good faith they would tend to each other's bodies, warding off disappointment until the last possible moment and, parting amicably, would break the dinner date set for Thursday night.

John buzzed him into The Tubs and gave him a peck on the cheek. "Merry Christmas, honey. The gang's all here tonight, so if you don't get laid it's your own damn fault." The lobby looked warm and homey with a real sparkling tree next to the cigarette machine, fruit and cider set up on the snack bar.

A handful of men, sprawled across carpeted tiers watching *It's a Wonderful Life*, held their positions so intently it looked as if they meant to live or die there. Frank walked past them to the back, and the film's stringy soundtrack gave way to a slithery, seductive jazz tape. The place was hopping. Men darted from the orgy room to the steam room, from the showers to the dorm, and the door of every cubicle was open. He walked past decent shadowy forms and melting, betowelled Buddhas. He took a shower and stood next to a short, curly-haired boy with a tiny, sleeping cock and a big round ass. The boy gave him big, blank eyes as he rinsed, then followed him to his room. Frank positioned him every possible way, gobbling up the blankness as the kid watched impassively. After twenty minutes he released his silent partner and tried to move in on a sloppy-sounding tangle in the orgy room.

He sat in his room swigging cognac, sniffing poppers, feeling like an unassembled robot, parts scattered across the cot, a wildly ticking motor lost somewhere in the debris.

A short, handsome black man walked by, stopped and looked intently at Frank. He tried to collect a smile but it cracked into a grimace and the man moved on, settling in the next room for a noisy, lip-smacking session. Frank closed his door, lay back and listened until someone in the next room climaxed, thumping and cursing. He fell asleep.

An hour later he opened his door and a dark-haired, well-built man walked by, giving Frank the barest nod. Frank came to attention and waited for the man's return. No sign of him. He went to the upstairs dorm where he found the kid from the shower locked in a passionate embrace with a fat old man. A pretty young black man with a huge cock stood in a corner while four guys worked on him.

He found the dark-haired man downstairs, watching the tail end of *It's a Wonderful Life*, smiling to himself. He looked like a well-preserved professional, probably married, the kind of guy you'd see in a beer commercial. He wasn't really handsome but his self-possession shone. This is the man I want, Frank thought. He went back to his room and waited. The man walked by and nodded. The next time around he smiled and his teeth looked perfect. The next time he stopped.

"Come in." Frank's voice, strong and clear, startled both of them. The dark-haired man entered and Frank jumped him. The session was long, jumpy, silent. They parted with a handshake, satisfied, then met again ten minutes later checking out. The dark-haired man, Ed, said, How about coffee?

They sat in a booth at the Cedar Crescent. Ed had just moved to New Jersey from Illinois. He used to be a gym teacher but now he sold shirts at an NBO outlet on Route 46.

"I could use some shirts," Frank said.

"Come by anytime."

Frank studied Ed's face. The eyes were dark and lively, with a melancholy downslant to them the liveliness sought to overcome. Looking at him gave Frank a beneficent hard-on. "I don't want to talk anymore. I want to fuck."

Ed's apartment was spartan and low-tech, everything brown and white, including the sheets. Frank had never been with anyone so delighted in his own skin. Ed fell asleep and he stayed up listening to hail hit the frosted windows.

Ed called his mother on Christmas Eve. "Jingle Bell Rock" was on the radio and a *Cheers* repeat was on the tube.

"Do you have company, dear?" she asked.

"Yes, some friends stopped by." He was drinking vodka on the rocks after running out of tonic and limes.

"Do you have a cold, Ed?"

"I'm fine, Mom, fine." He cleared his throat.

"And Nick?"

"Nick's fine, too." He was losing it. "Gotta go, Mom. Merry Christmas." He stared at the television. Someone said "pond scum" and the audience roared. Pond scum. Was it funny? He flipped the dials and stared at a glitzy remake of *Miracle on 34th Street*. He stared at the tube through the bottom of his glass, holding it up like a monocle, thinking, This is very sad. He pictured the drama of blowing his brains out with a shotgun. Or pills, which he didn't have.

He thought about a suicide call to Wendell, the ugly driver at the store. Wendell always muttered "homo" as he walked by. "Wendell, this is Ed Horvath. I want your big, black dick." Where did he live? East Orange? Wendell Nebbins, Nevins? Yeah, getting fucked to death by Wendell, by a dozen hairy, mean truck drivers. He found a Wendell Nevins in the phone book. He called Randy instead. Not home. He was out of vodka.

He drove to the McDonald's off the parkway, a place he equated with hell. Randy first took him there in the summer, right after Nick split. It was a steamy night and a lot of men were draped around their sparkling cars. Among the anxious trolls there were a lot of cuties looking defiant and abashed.

"See?" Randy said. "There's a whole world of men waiting to be had. In Jersey, the parking lot is ground zero. Everybody can play Miss Thing in the bars with sprayed-on attitude, but that snooty number who sniffed at you on the dance floor is sitting in her Honda fingering her fly."

"Is there some gay handbook you get this crap from? I did all this stuff years ago, and I don't want to do it again. All I want is Nick back. Once he gets this garbage out of his system, he'll be back. We have a history together; he can't turn his back on that. I'll give him a month. It hurts now but we'll be stronger for it."

"You're dreaming."

"I don't want this. Please take me home."

He went back twice. Once he came home with a stacked little football player who wouldn't look him in the eye. The kid popped out of sheer terror and was gone in fifteen minutes. The next time was a rainy, killer Sunday afternoon. It was

hard to figure the action in the parking lot, so he went to the
tea room. The stalls had doors hung so low, anyone over five-
nine could gape into them. Two geeks sat in side-by-side stalls,
stroking their meat and giving any passerby the bright eye.
While Ed washed and washed his hands, a father and son hurried in. The daddy, about Ed's age, hustled the kid, who was
maybe seven, into the only free stall. The kid tinkled leisurely,
asking if he could have a strawberry shake. The daddy didn't
answer and zoomed the kid out without washing his hands,
glancing at Ed as he passed. The hysterical glint in the father's
eye made Ed feel like a lowlife child molester. He ran to his
car. The station wagon next to him contained the rest of the
family unit. A blond mommy and Melissa waited patiently for
their burgers and fries.

Never again. Until tonight. He pulled into the parking lot.
Only one car there. He saw gray hair, the glint of glasses.
"Blowjob?" the occupant asked. He drove down deserted Cedar
Boulevard. The whole world was huddled in cozy bunches
drinking eggnog.

He had a drink at Rah Rah's. There were seven other people
there including Carol, the barmaid and a straight, sloshed Hispanic couple. And Al, who was everywhere with his bulldog
face and insinuating voice. Ed sat a bar-length away from him,
but Al joined him anyway, bought him drinks unasked, and
told his amazing stories of tricks with delivery boys, plumbers,
toll collectors. The punchline was always Al's hand on your
knee, no matter how many times you said no.

He drove into New York. Trilogy's tables were empty, and
the bar was lined with pale, thin leather queens with busy
white hair. He weaved uptown to the trusty Everard Baths
with its endless, nondenominational marchers. A small, beefy
blond man wearing a jockstrap sat in the next room. His eyes
widened as Ed stumbled in. Up close the guy was in his forties,
with a foreign sailor's tattoo on his bicep. Ed smiled loopily at
him, sat down, rubbed the tidy bulge the man motioned to,
and aimed to kiss him. The little man turned his head away.
Ed lifted an eyebrow and sat back. The man turned to him in
great distress.

"You are beautiful man," he whispered in broken English,
"but I am not want this."

"That's fair," Ed said, too drunk to care. He went to his room, lay down, and passed out. He woke at 7:40 in a cold sweat and drove shakily home.

At 4:30 the phone rang and woke him up.

"What's up?" It was Nick.

Ed was immediately alert. "You call me after all this time and you ask me what's up? You don't even start out with Merry Christmas?"

"Merr—"

"Don't even bother. So this is the plan, huh? I should expect to hear from you on Christmas and my birthday?"

"Come on, Ed. I just wanted to see how you were. I still care about you."

"If you care about me, then you get your ass over here and live with me. I don't want you caring about me and fucking somebody else. Look, why are you calling me? Where is babykins?"

"Can you try being normal for once in your life?"

"Where is he?"

"At his folks'."

"And how is the little darling?" Ed's grim smile collapsed, and he burst into tears. "I don't want this. I don't want it like this, Nicky. I mean, nothing makes sense. I'm losing it. I don't know what the hell I'm doing anymore. I want to see you so bad, Nicky. I thought this would be all settled by now, and we'd be back together. Why did this happen? I'll never understand it. Never."

"Please, Eddie . . ."

"What did I do wrong, Nick? It's Christmas and you're not here. It just keeps getting worse and worse . . ."

"Shhh. You'll pull through. I know you will. You're my little trooper."

"I am? Still?"

"Always, always, always."

Ed blew his nose on the bedspread. "Let me go now, before I make a bigger fool of myself." He hung up and roamed around the apartment before he settled on the cold bathroom floor, his favorite hiding place.

He showed up drunk and a couple of hours late for Randy's Christmas bash. With pretty George at his side, he downed everything handed to him, including half a 'lude. Randy kept pulling him into the bedroom for long, boring pep talks. Ed looked for George and found him sitting in Al's lap.

"Oh honey, don't sit there. You'll get worms," he said, or so George told him the next day.

He was in his car, driving up Route 1. A gray shadow swelled up in the rearview mirror. Ed knew that the shadow was everything. Everything had followed him to the car. It was him and everything alone on the road. He stealthily switched off the radio. He hit the power buttons and brought down all the windows. The shadow was being sucked out the window but it held on to something, a seat belt strap or coat hook. Ed stepped on the gas. The shadow flew out the window. He watched it in the mirror as it bounced along the empty highway. It was his coat.

He was sitting in The Tubs, surrounded by chubby geeks all transfixed by black and white shadows of Christmas past flickering on the huge screen. He had spent a long time in the steam room and took a cold shower. He avoided looking at anyone and removed any hands placed upon him. He felt better. Christmas was over. This kind of flat-out wretchedness was good for the soul, he hoped, in the long run. This old movie had never seemed so interesting before. I am just going to sit here. It's better than sitting home alone. He felt a tiny tug of emotion as a teary-eyed Donna Reed kissed James Stewart. He decided it was time to walk around.

Frank got an apartment in Newark, a twelfth floor studio in one of a row of highrises on a once prestigious street. The neighborhood was in transition: well-to-do old white ladies, young Hispanic families, and white gay professionals stood in the checkout line at the Foodtown. Frank had tricked in this building and a couple of others on the strip and saw some familiar faces.

He didn't like living alone. The apartment was furnished with his sisters' leftovers. When he wasn't working or with Ed, he watched TV or looked out the window. The apartment rang with the hollow sounds of his slow movements. An empty glass placed on the kitchen counter reverberated for minutes afterward with no sound to take its place. When the phone rang it startled him as an alarm might; answering, he heard his voice bounce off the white walls, politely and earnestly. Most nights he fell asleep on the couch.

Then there was the window. In the morning he could see Boystown on the hill across the river and beyond it Manhattan's golden needles. At night the high-intensity lights gave the street a grisly purplish cast. One night he watched a crouching man break into a car from the passenger side and ransack the glove compartment. After dark the squatty hills to the east looked like a backyard barbecue haphazardly strung with lights, and behind them Manhattan glowed like some great unquenchable fire.

Being a cop in Cedar Chips was neither exciting nor dangerous. His beat was days in Cedar Center where he filed reports on fender benders and chased crowds of kids away from the video arcade. Frank was a cop because his father was a cop, a fat cop who died of a heart attack while snoozing in his squad car on Election Day, 1977.

Ed asked him to go to a Valentine's Day party. Frank was nervous on the way down. He'd never been to a gay party before. It was a huge garden complex near the Woodbridge mall. He could tell Ed was nervous, telling some long boring story about a driver at the store whom he called King Kong.

They walked into a crowded, noisy room done up in silver and black with pink trim. Black hearts dangled from the ceiling. A tall, bearded man with frizzy beige hair rushed up to Ed and gave him a big kiss. He squeezed Frank's hand.

"This is Randy, my oldest friend," Ed said.

"He means I've known him the longest," Randy said, still squeezing. He looked about forty with too bright eyes surrounded by worn-out skin. "Do you love the black hearts?"

"But yes. I adore them," Ed said in a new voice. "Where's the booze?"

Randy led the way. He was a history teacher at the middle school down the road and worked weekends as a deejay at a singles barn on Route 35. This explained the state-of-the-art sound. Jennifer Holliday wailed from four speakers, and when some of the guests joined in Randy ran to a closet to turn down the sound. Ed got swallowed up in a kissy circle on the way to the bar but Frank pushed ahead to the kitchen counter set up with half gallons of Shop Rite booze and mixers. Some men were sitting around a pink modular couch in the living room doing lines on a marble coffee table. Frank, surrounded by strangers, downed three stiff gin and tonics.

"I used to think the idea of safe sex was boring," he heard someone say, "but now I'll settle for it. Puleeze, I'll settle for anything. Have you been out there lately? The bars are filled with these . . . these children and the whole scene is gossip and clothes. The last time I walked into The Male Box I looked around and said to myself, 'Class dismissed.' It's pathetic. There is no place to go for the horny mature queen." The speaker, a short, beefy man, turned in Frank's direction and growled.

"Got my drink?" It was Ed with his arm around a slim, intense young man Frank recognized. "Thanks. Frank, George. George, Frank."

Frank smiled and George looked away. They met last winter at Feather's. George sent his friends home and hitched a ride with Frank. They stopped in the middle of South Mountain Reservation and fucked in the car in the bitter cold.

Ed took his drink and walked away with George whispering in his ear. Fuck you, Frank whispered. He followed them with his eyes and noticed a poodle-haired blond smiling at him.

"Is this your private stock or can anybody get to it?" a voice said at his shoulder.

"Sorry," Frank said and stepped aside for the man who had growled at him. He was wearing a lumpy yellow velour pull-over and tight designer jeans with a big swirly label on the rear end.

"Could you slide it over a bit, tiger?" the man said, pinning Frank against the counter. "Oh, did I say tiger? I meant bear. You look like a big grouchy bear." He offered a hand. "Al." His other hand rested on Frank's shoulder.

Frank pulled his hand away and tried to move back. Finding nowhere to turn, he fumbled sideways and fixed himself another drink. Al had a big swarthy face that started melting below the eyes. His mud-colored hair looked wet and squashed. Frank imagined him getting ready for tonight, carefully picking out his outfit, brushing and rebrushing his hair, clipping nose hairs. Making one mistake after another as he dressed and primped, he probably blew himself a kiss in the mirror on the way out.

"I have to tell you this," Al said. "I'm not the kind of person who throws himself at another person, but I am sincerely attracted to you and hope you will consider coming home with me tonight."

"Um, I've got a ride. I mean a date."

"Oh, forgive me. I would never stand in the way of true love, unless of course he would like to join us. Really I wouldn't mind being smothered by you, if you know what I mean." Tufts of wiry hair puffed out of his pullover. He looked like someone who would have hair on his palms. They were evenly matched weightwise, so as far as who got smothered it was a toss-up.

"No," Frank said. "Are you in some kind of new religion or something?"

"No, my darling. Why?"

"It's just hard to believe somebody could be so obnoxious on their own."

"So you're a vicious bear," Al said. "So, who's the lucky date?"

"See that guy in the red shirt? By the couch? Him."

Al's face flattened. "Oh, her? Edwina Horvath? She must be practicing witchcraft again. Did she make you drink anything?"

"Hey!"

"Oh, it's a nice package, I guess. Lord knows *everybody's* seen it. Well, Our Lady of the Vapors strikes again."

"Knock it off."

"Believe me, honey, beneath those pecs beats the heart of a dizzy queen."

"Shut up!" Frank said, startling everyone within earshot. He pushed past Al and headed toward the bathroom where a line had formed. He went into an all-white bedroom. The poodle-haired blond was sprawled across the enormous bed giggling into the phone. A group sat respectfully around a wide-screen TV watching a grimacing Jack Wrangler, got up as a sheriff, stuff his sausage into a prisoner's mouth.

Frank walked onto the terrace and shivered. He decided to call a cab and go home.

"Hang up," he said to the blond on the bed, who obeyed.

The dispatcher told him it might be an hour or more. He hung up and sat on the bed. The blond stared at the back of his head. On the screen two men slurped tasty-looking cocks by firelight. He got up.

"Is it okay if I use the phone again?" the blond asked.

"Knock yourself out."

In the living room, Ed was part of a little circle formed around two men who had just made an entrance. "Yo, Frank. Over here. I want you to meet somebody."

He was introduced to Nick and Danny. Nick was short and dark with a bushy mustache and sleek black hair streaked with gray. Danny was young, a little taller, tawny haired. He looked pretty and pampered, his full lips stuck in a nervous centerfold pout. The two men conspired to look as if they'd just come from the gym, muscles pumped and bursting out of identical black tees that read THE WORKS and might have said across the back, WE'RE LOVERS.

Ed seemed determined to make small talk with these two, though no one involved made eye contact. Frank figured Nick was some old flame and Danny his consort. The kid seemed very uncomfortable and broke loose to get a drink. Frank bolted too—the bathroom was free. Then he went to the bar and found Al leaning into the kid. He dropped his pitch when Frank reached for the gin and Danny ran away.

"A little drink to ease the pain? Are you jealous, my darling?" Al said.

"Get lost."

"I see Liz and Dick are at it again. Those two are so dreary. Ed usually has a hissy fit and leaves. Maybe tonight she'll behave herself because you're here."

"What's your problem? Is the man bothering you?"

"He's boring," Al said. "I find that unforgivable. I'd much rather talk about you. They tell me you're a cop."

"Yeah."

"Fabulous. Did you ever kill anybody?"

"Not yet."

He didn't see Ed anywhere. Nick and Danny sat stiffly on the couch with Al hovering nearby. Frank smoked a joint on the terrace with the phone blond. His name was Kip; he was a child psychologist who lived in Hawaii.

"And you come to Jersey for the parties, right?" Frank said.

"You're a real bastard, aren't you?"

Frank zoned out while Kip talked about his miserable childhood. His father was a junkie, his mother an alkie, or vice versa. "So all my life I've been an enabler."

"A neighbor of who?"

"Am I boring you?"

"A little."

"I love it." He slipped Frank his card with his mother's phone number penciled in. "I'll be there until Thursday."

Randy made coffee. Frank helped him set out some styrofoam cups and bring out a sheet cake. He finished off the rest of the chicken wings and ate about ten deviled eggs.

"Having fun?" Randy said.

"Oh, I'm having a fucking blast," Frank said, his mouth full.

Randy divided the cake. "You have to be patient with Ed. He's had a rough time. He used to live with Nick. We're all from the same town in Illinois. Nick got transferred out here— he's in computers—and Ed followed him. It was okay for a month or so, but once Nick hit the Jersey streets, it's bam! The bitch is in heat. Here you've got all these humpy Italians strutting around, and Nick feels right at home. He didn't want to play Mr. and Mr. with Ed anymore, and Ed took it hard."

"So where do you fit in?" Frank said.

"I don't fit in." Randy licked frosting off his fingers. "I knew Ed first and went after him. But he doesn't see me that way. So I'm his dear, dear friend. All through the thing with Nick. I even up and moved out here because I knew it wouldn't last and he'd need a friendly face. I was a port in the storm for a minute there, but stand here as I might, Ed looks right through me. And what does he see? Somebody like you."

"Yeah?"

"You're a nice guy, I'm sure, but you're not what Ed needs right now. He doesn't need another, um, nonverbal Italian."

"Thanks," Frank said. "I guess you believe what you're saying. And I guess you think you mean it for the best, but me and Ed are big boys, and what goes on between us is our own business."

They didn't talk on the way home. Frank got out and walked up the scrubby path, past an ancient white lady walking two tottering poodles. He closed the door to his apartment and the buzzer sounded.

"Look, I'm sorry," Ed said. Frank pulled him into the bedroom. Later he said, "Now talk."

Ed jumped out of bed and started pacing. "See, the idea was I was going to walk into that room with you, so proud. I knew Nick was going to be there with babykins and I was going to rub your nose in his face, or something. Then I walked in and saw those faces and they're saying, 'Oh, what's she up to now,' and I knew I couldn't do it."

"I know."

"Oh, it wasn't noble," Ed said. "It wasn't like I couldn't do that to you, that it wasn't fair to you. I just didn't have the balls to pull it off. So I started acting up."

"I know that."

"And then I thought, do I want to start this all over again? I mean, so far it's been like something out of Colt Studios, two big goons cavorting picturesquely, no muss, no fuss. Right now I don't want to feel any particular way except good. I am very fucked up." He slumped on the edge of the bed.

Frank pulled up behind him and held on to him. "I don't care where you came from or what you did. All I want is, when you're with me, you're with me."

"Yes."

"You can do what you want on your own time, but I don't want to hear about anybody else. And if I catch you screwing around, I'll cut your balls off."

"Yes."

And at that moment they were in love.

They were running in Branchbrook Park. It was early, before the hordes of Orientals with cameras and picnic baskets came to wander among the cherry blossoms. Ed was in a good mood, he was teaching again and trying to get back in shape.

"Are you still with me?"

"Right behind you," Frank said. "Stop showing off."

Frank caught up to him. "You do this every fucking day?"

"Just about."

"Christ!"

"Come on," Ed said. "It's good for you. Besides, you're a

public servant. You should be able to chase down a purse snatcher."

"Hell, I'll just shoot him."

"Stop complaining. You could stand to lose a few pounds. Nobody likes a fat cop."

Frank stopped. Ed turned and saw his face. He jogged back to him. "What's the matter?"

"You think I'm fat," Frank mumbled.

"No I don't. You're always complaining that you're getting fat. I just want you to be happy. I want you to be as happy as I am. With you, I mean." Ed looked around, then patted Frank on the rump. "Come on. Don't mope. Be my little trooper."

"I really hate it when you say that," Frank said.

Ed lay in bed. Frank came out of the bathroom with a warm washcloth and towel. He tenderly wiped Ed down, then dried him.

"What are you thinking about?" Frank asked.

"Nothing."

"What's wrong?"

"Nothing. I just worry sometimes."

"You never have to worry about me," Frank said.

"Maybe not right now. But you've never been—involved before. You don't know what it's like out there."

"I know enough."

"It's like we're in this cave, sealed off from the rest of the world. We might be the only two faggots left on the face of the earth, for all we know."

Frank said, "I hate that word. Why do you always say it."

"It's just a word," Ed said.

"There's other words."

"Whenever somebody whispered 'faggot' to me, I used to freeze with terror. I hate anyone, any passing idiot, having that kind of power over me. Then I realized, hey, I am—of the alternate persuasion, I am a faggot, God bless me. And so are most of my friends. We are faggots, Mr. Stranger, Mr. Pinhead, and what are you going to do about it?"

"It means a different kind of person, not you and me."

"It's you and me *and* them. It has to be all of us or it doesn't mean anything."

"I don't like it," Frank said. "I don't want to be that."

"So what are we?"

"We're two guys, that's all. Two guys."

"Frank, I'm afraid I'm going to be laying here one night and you're going to stand over me and say, 'I don't want this any-more.' And I'm just going to crumble up and die. You Italians are so temperamental. When the feeling's with you, it's terrific, but when it's gone, it's gone."

"I love you," Frank said.

Ed was silent for a moment. "Then I had just better shut up."

Frank and Gene Crespo were in the locker room at the end of their shift. Crespo was pulling on his sweat pants. He jogged home every day. He was married and had two small kids. He was short, dark, and wiry with an antsy gleam in his eye. If he played his cards right he'd be Cedar Chips' next chief of police. Somebody told him once he looked like Al Pacino in *Serpico*, so for the last ten years he was always carefully bearded and tousled. Frank and Gene went through school together but were never really tight. He thought Frank was lazy.

"So, are you gay or what?" Crespo said.

"Why?" Frank said.

"What do you mean 'why'? Does that mean yes?"

Frank didn't answer.

"Frank, this is a small town. People talk."

"So what?"

"Look, it doesn't matter to me, but you just kissed any pro-motions goodbye."

Frank didn't know what to say. He looked up at Crespo and shrugged.

"This ain't New York with all them groups. You're all alone out here, man." Crespo appeared to give up. He laced up his sneakers, put on his knapsack. "Why, Frank? Can you tell me that?"

Frank met Crespo's therapeutic, condescending gaze. Even as a kid Crespo was always pushing it, sticking his big nose into things, playing Mr. By-the-Book. He didn't really give a damn about anybody else, he just had to separate himself from the herd. Frank stood up. He was a foot taller than Crespo.

"The way you worry about me gets me right here." Frank pounded his chest. "But I don't want you to worry about me, pal. I do my job, and my private life is my business. I don't wear no buttons or make speeches. I don't put my business in the street. I don't ask no questions and I don't want none. I'm happy with my life. Are you? Good."

Crespo didn't answer. He started running in place. He turned and ran out of the locker room.

Trilogy on Christopher Street was Ed's favorite New York hangout. It was a Tuesday night in May. They were having dinner. Frank was quiet.

"Back home when I used to think about New York," Ed said, "this is the kind of place I used to imagine. You know, good-looking upscale guys, sophistication, ambiance . . ."

"Um." Frank cleared his throat.

"It means atmosphere."

"I know what the fuck it means."

"Sorry. Why are you so quiet?"

"Why are you so wired tonight?"

"It's a beautiful night. I'm out on the town with my handsome boyfriend. All's right with the world."

"Oh," Frank said.

They were silent until the dinner plates were cleared.

"Are we going to get a place together or what?" Frank said suddenly.

"What? Where did that come from?"

"My ass is on the line here, and you're dancing around . . ."

"Slow up, big boy. Did I miss something? Did we talk about this?"

"Where the hell is that kid?" Frank downed his drink. He stood up and waved at the waiter.

"Calm down," Ed said. "Whoa. I like the idea of sharing a place, but I don't want to be rushed into anything. I'm just starting to get on my feet again."

The waiter brought Frank's drink. They were silent.

"Why don't you want to live with me?" Frank said.

"Look, if you do anything, do it because you're thirty-five years old and it's time to get off your ass. Don't do anything because of me. You got out of your mother's house, and that was good, but you need to spend some time on your own. Then you think about settling down. I don't want all that responsibility."

"What does that mean? Yes or no?"

"Oh, today's the deadline?" Ed said. "You're amazing. I'll never understand how you think. You let everything bubble inside you and then you come out with three clear sentences—bim, bam, boom—and now it's the law. I've been through this before and I'm not rushing."

"I don't want to hear about it."

"Things are good right now. That's all I know."

That night Ed said, "Stop. Get up a minute. I can't breathe."

Frank jumped out of bed. "Can you breathe now?"

"Yes. You were just too heavy on me."

"Excuse me. I'll just take my fat self to the couch."

Ed heard the TV click on. He imagined Frank's puss as he sat on the couch. He couldn't bring himself to go in after him and fell asleep. He woke as, step by step, Frank made love to him. Two, three, four, Ed counted off in his head as Frank worked his way up to his neck.

"Can we just go to sleep? I'm pretty tired," Ed said.

Frank plopped down with a big sigh and turned his back.

"Nothing's wrong. Don't be upset," Ed said. "We'll talk in the morning. Come on, where's my little trooper?"

"Here I is," Frank said into his pillow.

Frank was on his beat, where Grand Avenue intersected with Cedar Boulevard. It was the early morning rush, and traffic sped down the hill to Newark. He stood in front of a store where a row of upside down legs sported the latest panty hose. His presence discouraged running the light and there was a lot of apologetic backing up. Gangs of girls in neon clothes smoked cigarettes on their way to the high school a block away. Boys with gym bags followed them calling out names. Frank didn't want to move. He wanted to be home, on the couch with a pillow over his head. If a car swerved out of control and headed toward the disconnected legs, he might jump out the way. Might.

Ed wanted to take a week off—"a little breathing time" was the way he put it. Oh, nothing was wrong, he just wanted to "rethink his position." Ed really acted like a teacher sometimes. What am I going to do tonight and the next night? And the next? Don't call, he said. Be a little trooper. What did that mean anyway?

Ed ran around straightening up the apartment. He changed clothes three times: sweatpants, jeans, shorts. He was listening to love songs on the radio, switched it off and cued up Vivaldi. Nick was on his way over, and Ed wasn't sure in which attitude he wanted to be found. It should be tasteful and reserved. Oh, hello, just another night with the classics. Do come in. He'd had a couple of belts of vodka but they weren't working.

In the middle of balancing his checkbook he called Nick, an impulse he instantly regretted. He was surprised to find Nick low and mopey. Danny was gone. It was quick—"I don't want this anymore" out of the blue, and he was off to Florida with kids his age. Ed tried to keep the delight out of his voice. He liked Nick best when he was mopey: he was much more malleable. There were some glib expressions of sympathy, then accusations, then reminiscences in their long conversation. There were also long pauses that felt familiar and erotic. Finally Nick asked, "Are you busy tonight?"

"No," Ed said as casually as he could.

When the bell rang he realized he was barefoot. Nick liked his feet. He pulled on socks and stumbled to the door. Nick walked past him and set a six-pack of lite beer in the refrigerator. He emptied his pockets, putting two fat joints on the kitchen table, a gold coke kit, a bottle of poppers.

"Where's the KY?" Ed said, putting his arms around him. Nick shuddered in his embrace. He looked terrible, his face gray and unshaven, eyes bleary, his hair cut gruesomely short. He was dressed in black, which made him look both sinister and fragile.

"You didn't have to bring the goodies," Ed said, "I can stand you sober."

They got undressed. Nick was wearing his lucky jockstrap and a studded cock ring.

"You make me feel naked," Ed said.

"You are naked, stupid."

They started on the couch and wound up on the floor, each working off his grudges. The coke made them speedy, and they were at it a long time. Nick straddled Ed's chest, mechanically pulling at his exhausted cock, his face dark and blank. Ed ran his hands over the sculpted stone of Nick's ass, felt the birthmark at the base of his spine.

"I really hate your guts," he said.

Frank dreaded walking into his apartment. All day on the street he tried but couldn't keep his mind off Ed. It was worse at home, where his imagination bounced off the shiny white walls. He had never felt the power of the phone before. It always seemed to be in the corner of his eye, like some *Twilight Zone* terror with a life of its own. He thought if he primed it, it might ring. He called his mother.

"Hi, Ma?"

"Who is this?"

Around eight Thursday night it did ring and his heart pounded. A woman's voice asked for Mr. Anto-line.

"Yes?"

"Mr. Anto-line, I'm Sherry from Major Marketing. May I ask you some questions about diet soft drinks?"

He answered all her questions, each of which triggered a series of subquestions. He found himself thinking about the sweetening and consumption of soft drinks. He imagined Sherry as a young bleached blond sitting alone in a dismal green office while her mother watched the baby. She had trouble following her script, and he was patient with her.

"And may I ask how old you are, Mr. Anto-line?" Was that in the script?

"Thirty-four."

"Oh, you sound much younger. May I ask your first name, Mr. Anto-line?"

He liked being Mr. Anto-line. Sherry was thanking him for his time and seemed reluctant to let him go. He wanted to ask her if she needed a ride. She sounded like someone who needed a ride. He wanted to say *Wait!*, when she told him to expect some coupons in the mail. When he hung up he was out of breath.

He called Ed. Not home. He drove to his apartment and sat in the car looking at the dark windows. He went to The Male Box. It was very crowded, Dollar Night. It was hard to get to the bar. A short, humpy dancer spread his pink cheeks to the crowd, pulling off his jockstrap in one motion. Frank wedged himself into a corner and stayed for an hour. He called Ed. No answer.

"Hi, stranger," John said, buzzing him into The Tubs. "There's only a few stragglers here. You sure you want to come in? Yes? Well, there's always me. I get off at two and every half hour after that."

Frank sat in his room with the door open and heard heavy footsteps upstairs. He took off his towel and lay back with his eyes closed. You made me do this, he thought. I don't care what happens. He started to fall asleep. Cold hands ran up his leg. He opened his eyes and saw a large, hairy shadow.

"Hi there. Are you awake? What a surprise to find you here." It was Al. He started to snuggle in beside Frank.

"So—" Al said.

"I don't want to talk," Frank said, sitting up.

"What do you want, darling? What do you want?" Al said, sinking to his knees.

He called Ed on Saturday morning. Ed sounded surprised.

"Why are you surprised?" Frank said.

"I'm not. I was thinking about you."

"And I was thinking about you. When am I going to see you?"

"Soon."

"What the fuck does that mean? What about tonight?"

"I think it's too soon. I haven't cleared out all the cobwebs yet."

"You said a week. It's been a week."

Ed was silent.

"You'd better fucking talk to me, Ed. You'd better start talking."

There was a long silence.

"I need a little more time," Ed said.

"What happened? What did I do?" Frank said in a strange voice.

Ed got scared. "Nothing. It's nothing you did. It's just that I'm so messed up. I don't want to drag you down too."

"I can help you," Frank said. "Please."

"Let me go now. I will call you this week. We can go out and do some talking. Let me go now, please." He hung up.

Ed didn't call. Sherry from Major Marketing didn't call. The phone rang once that week. It was his mother.

"So when are you coming down?" she asked.

"I don't know."

"When?"

"I don't fucking know, Ma."

"Call me when you're normal." She hung up.

He lay on the couch and stared at the ceiling. There was a water stain that came to look like an Indian's profile or a Volkswagen Beetle. He had the phone on his chest and fingered the buttons of Ed's number. How can he not care about me? Something must be very wrong. He would never do this. No answer. He tried every ten minutes, letting it ring ten times, fifteen times, twenty. He drove to Ed's apartment. Lights out. He rang the bell. He sat in his car and waited. It was nearly 3:00 A.M.

He woke up in his car at 7:30 and drove straight to work. After the morning rush he drove the squad car to the middle school and went to the gym. A young black man led the boys in jumping jacks. Frank waited politely by the bleachers. There was a break while boys pulled mats off the wall for wrestling.

"Excuse me," Frank said to the teacher, "I'm looking for Ed Horvath."

"He's off this week. He'll be back Monday."

He stumbled through the week, drinking himself to sleep, feeling, still, every second tick by. Saturday he found himself in Trilogy, unwashed and unshaven, drinking himself into a state of nervelessness. He stood, swaying, in the center of a bookstore back room with his hand on his wallet.

He plowed across Seventh Avenue, swept along on the piss

foam tide of his own misery, the path was magically cleared for him by streetwise strollers. "I'm a cop," he said, laughing, to a pretty girl with frightened eyes who conscientiously didn't see him when he lurched into her shopping bag.

An old woman wearing a blue winter coat and blue babushka stood by Cooper Union pleading with passersby in a thin, pullstring voice, "Please help me, I'm hungry. Please help me." She kept a huge white hand extended. Frank got close enough to be spun around by the big hand and found himself looking into her pale, myopic eyes. She gave him a one-on-one version of her pitch, putting extra schmaltz into it.

"Lady, you got the wrong number."

"Gimme some money, you fucking asshole. I know you got it," she said in a new voice.

"What?"

"Gimme some money, you fucking asshole. I know you got it." She was clamped onto his arm.

"I'm crazier than you are, lady," Frank said, "so you better let me go. I could kill you right now and nobody would stop me."

"And you're a fucking asshole," she said, releasing him. She wandered up the street and resumed her litany with lunatic calm.

He passed the St. Mark's Baths and doubled back. Inside, he stood before a black marble and gilt check-in counter. The snippy bald concierge's brief glance made him feel as if he'd flunked the entrance physical. It seemed many dark flights up before he met his attendant, Angel, who led him past dim red rooms carrying two towels and a small cup of goop.

His big flat feet resounded in the hall as he bumped into walls and beautiful men. Every room he passed contained a living centerfold, perfectly lighted and posed. Beautiful men with blank faces and big cocks roamed the halls, sticking their noses and cocks into rooms and pulling out instantly. He gaped at cover boy faces that looked through him. A deeply tanned boy in a jockstrap lay on his stomach. Frank walked into his room. "Just resting." A voluptuous hairy man sat placid and naked in his room, his balls drooping off the cot: "Just resting." A mock construction worker, his face shadowed by a hard hat, stroked his big pink cock. Frank stepped in and the hard hat shook vehemently. In the ersatz moonlight of the dormitory he saw muscular shadows that stared straight ahead. He walked through and back again slowly. No one stirred.

Maybe he was dreaming. He might have passed out on the couch and burped up this morbid fantasy filled with desirable, untouchable men. A tall shadow brushed past him heading out of the dorm. This chance touch sent a shiver through him and stung him back into consciousness. He followed the shadow, a spectacularly built cowboy, downstairs to the showers and watched, dry-mouthed, as the cowboy lathered the length of his pink skin. He kept the Stetson on in the shower, which meant he must be bald or almost. The guy's face was pinched and mean, and his weak chin was covered with corrective stubble. Frank stood alongside under a cold drizzle, and the cowboy's eyes met his for a full second. Frank followed him up three flights of stairs, unable to catch his eye again. He watched the cowboy offer his hard, uncircumcised cock at open doors and pull back when a hand reached out. The cowboy turned a corner and he lost him. Grunts and moans of pleasure drifted into the hall from unidentified rooms, and he imagined they might be piped in over the loudspeaker.

He circled the third floor again and saw his dream man propped on a cot, stroking himself. Frank stepped into the room and the cowboy gave him a mean eye. His ears pounded as he reached for him with a cold hand.

"Just resting."

Frank closed the door behind him. "Just let me touch you."

"No," the cowboy said.

Frank grabbed his cock. "Please."

The cowboy jumped up. "Get out." He awkwardly reached past Frank to open the door, keeping the towel modestly before him. Frank stumbled out and bumped into a thin, middle-aged black man. The black man stepped into the room and slammed the door behind him. Frank heard the cowboy say, "Yes! Give it to me, daddy! Give it to me!" He stared at the number on the door: 303.

He fled to his room and threw himself on the cot. He buried his face in the pillow. He gasped for air, tears came out of his nose. He fell asleep with his head under the pillow. A pounding on the wall woke him up. Someone was getting plowed in the next room. Frank sat up. "Go home," he said to himself and immediately followed his own advice.

He had a headache but it was wonderful to be on the street. The Village was filled with lovers eating ice cream cones. It was wonderful to be in his car with the radio playing love songs. At the end of the Holland Tunnel what wafted through the windows felt like fresh air.

He scrambled four eggs, fried up a half a pound of bacon, drank three glasses of apple juice. He took a megavitamin and stretched out on the couch. He fell asleep watching a Burt Reynolds movie.

He got up early the next morning and ran in the park. He took almost all his clothes to the basement laundromat. He vacuumed the whole apartment and washed the floors with pine soap. He bought the *Star Ledger* and read the sports section, the comics, *Parade* magazine. His mother was surprised when he stopped by with a strawberry shortcake. He took his nephew to see *Return of the Jedi* for the second time.

His momentum evaporated the moment he was unsafely inside the apartment again. He played hide-and-seek with the phone all evening, then stood by the window watching for Ed's car. This helps me, he thought, this is my life. "This is my life," he said to the window, "and I don't like it."

Ed jumped when the phone rang. He let it ring five times before he picked up. He realized he sounded sleepy.

"Yes? Um. Hello?"

"Ed? How are you doing? It's Frank."

"Great. What's up?"

"Where you been. I haven't talked to you for a while."

"See my mom. You know."

"Oh."

"And how are you?" Ed chirped.

There was a long silence. Ed listened to Frank breathe.

"I'm fucked in the head, man. I'm completely fucked in the head. When can I see you?"

"Give me a minute, okay? I just got back. I've got to get my bearings."

"Can I come over now?"

"Um. No."

"I got to see you, Ed. It's so bad. It feels like I'm going to die or something. Nothing makes sense. What did I do wrong? What did I do?"

"Shhh. Shhhhh. Take some deep breaths. You'll be okay, sweetheart. I have to talk to you too. Tuesday. I'll talk to you Tuesday."

"I won't make it. I know it. Tonight—"

"I can't," Ed said. "Not tonight. My mom's here." Nick jumped off the couch and ran into the bathroom, shutting the door.

"Oh."

"Keep taking deep breaths. You sound bad."

"Yes." Frank took deep breaths. He unrolled some paper towels, wiped his eyes, blew his nose. "I really miss you."

"Will you be okay until Tuesday? We can clear the air then."

"What does that mean?"

"It means . . . look, I'll talk to you Tuesday. I got to go. It's late and I'm beat."

"Ed?"

"Tuesday. Okay, sweetie? You get some rest now. Goodnight."

Ed put down the phone, walked into the kitchen and made himself a drink. "You can come out now."

"That really sucked," Nick said.

"What was I supposed to do?"

"You should talk to him. Call him back. I'm going."

"No."

"You should talk to him," Nick said.

"I think it's too late."

CULTURAL REVOLUTION

• NORMAN WONG •

MICHAEL FELT TOO nauseated to look for the muffled laughter on the bus, more like an American school bus than a Greyhound. It rode slowly without shock absorbers to Xi'an from Macau, sixty miles past the Communist border. He brushed away his father's breath from his arm as he inched toward the window. Outside was a monotonous field of short rice plants, jutting out of a mirror of water. Occasionally there stood a half-naked Chinese farmer under an oversize straw hat.

"American school has taught him to forget all of his Chinese," Michael's father had said repeatedly to relatives in Hong Kong, with notes of shame and pride in his voice. When they arrived there two weeks before, Michael had found his relatives' accents difficult to understand; but he always understood his father, even though sometimes he pretended not to. And by the end of the first week he found himself deciphering his relatives' conversations, though he still could not readily contribute to them.

Father and son had spent eight days in Hong Kong with uncles, aunts, and countless cousins. Every meal was spent at a round table with a lazy-suzy, spinning Chinese delicacies around: dim sum, roast suckling pig, shark fin soup, sautéed frog legs. In large restaurants, noisy family parties were partitioned off in sections, each complete with a color TV and a Mah-Jongg set. The city's noise and its muggy heat, unlike

Hawaii's drier heat, made Michael ill. A doctor gave him a prescription for antibiotics and told him to drink bottled water to clear out his system. Then they took a ferry to Macau, where they stayed with his grandmother. She lived in a second-floor apartment, cluttered with porcelain statuettes and smelling of incense, along with another old woman, her maid and companion, whom one of Michael's uncles had imported from the mainland.

On the bus to Xi'an, his father's home village, Michael complained about stomach cramps. His father answered, "If it's not one thing, it's another. It was a waste of money to bring you here in the first place." August was the only time that this trip to the homeland would have been possible. Michael was going off to college in two weeks, to the U.S. mainland. He could hardly wait. It was five thousand miles from Hawaii and his family to Chicago, white man's land. Michael again turned to the window, only to discover there a reflection of a white man's face staring at his reflection and laughing.

This was the real China. In high school Michael had learned about Sun Yat-sen, the Japanese invasion, and the Cultural Revolution. He had pieced these facts together with the few stories that he had milked from his father for an oral report in the eighth grade. Back then Michael had found these stories unsatisfying. He had written in his mind his own version of his father's life in China. When his father was just a baby, the Japanese had invaded his village. Michael remembered the story of his grandmother fleeing, fearless, with his infant father in her arms to hide in the rice fields. But on this trip he cared little for the real bits of his father's past which he discovered along the way. It was already too late; he wanted to be on his way to Chicago, writing his own future.

As his father led the way out of the bus, Michael turned around to look at the man in the front seat. He looked like an American college student, with short blond hair, white skin, a thick neck like a rugby player, a few strands of chest hair pushing up between his shirt's collar. His hand searched in his backpack, pulling a camera out of the pouch. He looked up at Michael.

The hotel was an ugly square building, six stories high, the tallest around. The lobby was decorated in fifties style, a green and white tile floor speckled with black dots, a simulated wood counter for a reception area, and a matching freestanding backboard. Off to one side of the lobby a pair of glass doors led to a restaurant where tables were covered with stained red cloth. Chinese men and women, uncomfortably dressed in black polyester trousers and wrinkled white shirts buttoned to their necks, lazily carried trays of water glasses and standard Chinese dishes.

After signing for their room, Michael's father insisted that they deposit their bags behind the counter and begin an immediate search for the old home. "I don't know if it's even still there. It's out by the rice fields. I can't believe it all looks the same as twenty-five years ago." Michael hated seeing his father so excited. The white man from the bus walked in the lobby, his backpack sealed, the camera heavy in his hands. He walked past Michael to the front desk. "We shouldn't just leave the bags behind the counter," Michael said. "They won't be safe."

He watched his father examining the receptionist behind the counter. She signed the white man into the guest book. Thick black-framed glasses accentuated the roundness of the young woman's face. The line of her bangs was uneven, and a noticeable strand of black hair stayed behind the lens of her glasses, though her own eyes were blind to it. She smiled with buckteeth. The white man showed her his American passport. "You go ahead, Dad," Michael said. "I want to go upstairs with the bags and lie down for just a little while. I'll catch up with you later. It must've been something I ate at dim sum this morning."

He and the white man rode the elevator together up to the same floor. Michael said how horrible the bus ride had been. They looked at each other once more before going to their separate rooms. Michael loved air-conditioning. He lay down on one of the two twin beds. He was glad that he and his father would be sleeping separately tonight. He rolled on the bed and then jumped up, giving it the appearance of being slept in. He then left the room and proceeded down the hallway, to the white man's room; the door was open a crack. He stepped in and closed it behind him.

"Quiet. We better not talk," the white man said. "Thin walls. My name's Alex." He moved closer. He was twice Michael's width, but the top of his head came to Michael's eyes. Michael was thin like a typical Cantonese man, like his father. But he had grown tall. "All that milk and white bread has made him so tall," his father had explained to the Hong Kong relatives.

His feet hit the footboard of the bed. "Damn," he called out. "This bed is too short."

"We should try to be a little quieter."

Michael liked the feel of Alex's thick flesh. They held each other tightly, and turned their bodies sideways. Alex ran his hand down Michael's knobby spine to the thin flesh of his buttocks and slowly patted him there, lulling him. When Michael was little, he had slept in the same bed with his father, while his sister had been in the other room with his mother. His father would pat him on the butt to sleep.

After sex, Alex began to doze off beside him. Michael avoided touching him by leaning to one side of the bed, almost falling off. He did not want to sleep here, but neither did he want to get up to look for his father. This trip to the homeland had already gone on for too long, in Michael's opinion. His feet knocked against the footboard again. "This is ridiculous."

Alex opened his eyes. "What, me?"

"No, the footboard."

Alex sat up in bed and massaged Michael's feet. "Is that better, baby?" Alex braced himself over Michael, pinning him down at the shoulders. Michael closed his eyes as Alex kissed him on his pressed lips and then on his neck, where he lingered wet and long.

"You're going to get me in trouble," Michael said. "Let me go."

"Too late."

Michael jumped out of bed and stood in front of the mirror on the wall. A red spot darkened on his neck.

"If I spoke Chinese to you, would you be able to understand me?" Alex asked.

"If you do, I'll ignore you like I do my father." He wanted to remind his pickup that they had met less than an hour ago and that he did not even find him that attractive. He had only looked at Alex on the bus because he was the first white man he had seen in a long time.

*   *   *

Michael did not say no when Alex asked to come along to look for his father. Alex would serve as a buffer between him and his father. Outside the hotel Alex immediately began to photograph everything around. "Everything is so simple," he said. "It's like the 1950s. A village, a country where time stood still. I bet this place is exactly the way your father remembers it." Michael stood by silently as Alex bargained with an old ricksha driver. His accent and diction were perfect. He asked the old man how far the rice fields were. The old man's legs were dark and wrinkled like beef jerky; lines divided his face. He laughed, showing a single rotten tooth, as Alex took his picture while he mounted the rusty bicycle.

"This white man knows how to speak Chinese," the old man shouted to another driver. The black hood overhead focused their view to the back of the driver and road ahead. The old man stood on the pedals, pushed downward, and started the bike in motion.

"I'm surprised that he's able to drive this thing," Michael said.

"I was in Beijing in the spring," Alex stated. "It's a wonderful place. Even more exciting than here. Canton and the South have been influenced and spoiled by Hong Kong."

Alex told Michael that he was studying in Hong Kong, where gay life was much more in the open. He made occasional trips to the mainland. Michael said that he was going to college in Chicago the following month. "The Midwest is culturally dead. It's white mall country," Alex said.

People scurried out of the ricksha's way. A thin sheet of dust hovered above the dirt road. Shops—groceries, bakeries, drug stores—occupied the first floor of the buildings. Above, families were crowded in two-room apartments; children hung out of windows, while their laundry blew lifelessly on the line, bleached shirts and trousers. The ricksha drove between the buildings, down an alleyway. Wooden stands sold local delicacies: wilted greens, hanging roasted ducks and dogs, and frogs in straw baskets, climbing on top of each other. An old woman sat on a stool, twisting a live chicken's neck.

"Did you meet anyone in Beijing?" Michael asked.

"Any gay men? Yes."

"That's pretty amazing. Chinese gay men. Chinese men gay in Beijing."

"And what about yourself?"

"I've been corrupted by America," Michael said. "You are the *bok gwei*, the white devil. First the man you corrupted in Beijing, and now me."

"I don't think I could've corrupted you any more."

"There weren't any gay men in China before the white man came along," Michael laughed. "Except perhaps the drag-queen opera singers. Every culture has their transvestites. But they were not real men; they were aberrations."

"You're being silly," Alex said. "Did you meet anyone in Hong Kong?"

"Are you serious? I've been with my father for the entire two weeks. We even had to sleep in the same bed at my grand-mother's. It was such a small place. One of the bathrooms was just a dark room with a hole in the ground."

The ricksha drove out of the village and into a quieter coun-tryside along the rice fields. Ahead was a small group of houses. Michael knocked Alex's hand off his lap. "We're almost there," he said. He began to wonder whether bringing Alex along was such a good idea. What if Alex told his father what had happened in the hotel room—but his father was too naive to understand, even if told. And besides, he was doing the white tourist a favor by bringing him along to visit a real Chi-nese home. "So tell me about the man you met in Beijing."

Alex again placed his hand on Michael's knee. "We met under the big Mao picture in Tiananmen Square, near the entrance of the Forbidden City. That's where you hang out if you want to pick up a local man. They're especially interested in white men. But they're very careful; it's a severe crime in China."

"Who did you meet?"

"He was a little older than me. Ming Tim. Very serious looking. Dark-skinned and lanky. I saw him. He saw me. We looked at each other for about fifteen minutes, and then as I walked away, he followed. After a while he joined me, and we continued walking without speaking. Then he told me that he had to leave. He had to pick up his *wife* at the factory. In China, they won't give you your own apartment unless you're married. The other alternative is to live with your parents for the rest of your life. As he walked, he said, 'I want to see you again. Tomorrow I'll meet you in front of your hotel.' Then he ran off around a corner."

"Did you spend your entire time in Beijing under the Mao picture?" Michael asked.

"No. Do you want to hear the rest of the story?"

"Yes, but hold off. Here's the old home. Now no gay stuff, or I'll drown you in the rice fields."

"Oh, that could be fun."

The ricksha slowed and stopped. On one side of the road stood a row of five brick houses, attached to each other, all alike, and on the other side, the rice fields. Up close, Michael could see that they were parallel rows of weedlike plants, rows and rows nestled in soft, dark mud; extending to the mountains beyond shrouded by clouds. A farmer stood in ankle-high water, his face hidden by his straw hat. He held up a plant to the sun. His skin, dark like leather, stretched over his protruding ribs.

"He's beautiful," Alex said.

"Rice queen," Michael scowled.

"I like the Chinese culture, and its men."

Out of the center house, Michael's father emerged, looking out of place in his polo shirt and belted trousers. "Nothing has changed," he said.

Michael and Alex walked towards him. "I used to live here," he said. "A few of the old neighbors are even still here."

Alex walked up to Michael's father. Michael froze. "Hello, I'm Alex. I'm staying at your hotel, where I met your son." Alex shook Michael's father's hand. "He told me that he was going to look for his father's old home. What a wonderful idea. I had to invite myself along. I'm a student at the University of Hong Kong. Modern Chinese history. Michael told me all about your visit back to the homeland. It's great that you can come back after all these years."

"Hello." Michael's father gave the stranger a lipless smile, and then walked directly over to his son. "Are you still sick? It took you a long time to get here. I was already planning to go back to the hotel. It's too hot. Is the hotel room air-conditioned? I'm feeling a little sick myself."

Michael was relieved by his father's cool reception of Alex, though he was disappointed that the only white man around did not pique his father's curiosity.

"They only have outhouses in back," his father continued. "The same ones that were here when I used to live here."

From behind his father, two old women emerged from the green doorway. Sticks, stones, weeds, and bricks littered the front yard.

"This isn't your son, is it?" said the younger of the two, pointing to the white man. Her hair was silver and uncombed, and she smiled a gold tooth. Beside her was a much older woman, hunched over like an insect. She looked only at the garbage on the ground. She was blind. Behind surviving white strands of hair, her hard white scalp was dotted with dark moles.

"No, this is my son. Michael, show your respect to Wu Tai Tai and her daughter, Mai Lee."

Michael held Mai Lee's hand. He could only feel bones. Her thin smile grew, and her eyes strained to open wider. He did not dare to shake the blind mother's hand.

"They lived next door when my mother and I lived here. Now they live here. The house is exactly the way that I remembered it. Nothing's changed."

Alex held his camera to the group. "I want a picture of this moment." The camera clicked. Michael turned and stared at him with contempt.

"Your son is tall," the old daughter said. She held her hand above her eyes to block the sun as she looked Michael up and down.

Inside, the old blind mother poured glasses of hot tea from an aluminum thermos and passed them to her daughter to hand to Michael and his father. Michael passed his glass to Alex. The men sat in large uncomfortable wooden chairs decorated with carvings of flowers on the arms and a Chinese character on the back. The door stood open, letting in a warm breeze and a view of the constant rice fields.

"Do you know what this means?" Alex whispered to Michael, pointing to the character on the chair.

Michael did not respond.

"Peaceful."

Michael turned away. The old women spoke in heavy local accents. He strained his eyes to follow their conversation. His head began to ache.

"They're talking about you," Alex said. "Your father says you're going to college in Chicago. The old daughter said, 'Such a foreign, faraway-sounding place.' "

He began to regret the moment on the bus when he had given Alex that first look. He hated Alex for explaining the writing on the chair, for hiring the ricksha, for interpreting his father's conversation. He wanted to be away from all of this. But he did like the adventure of having sex in Communist China. He found Alex's preference for Chinese men odd because he himself had never been attracted to them. They would seem too much like his father: bony and without any body hair. He looked out at the farmer. He wanted to know the rest of Alex's pickup story. It seemed dangerous and perverse. If he could only get him alone again for a little while, he could hear the rest of the story and then tell him to leave.

"Not much has changed since you left," said the old daughter. "The old school is still there. If I remember correctly, you were such a bad boy, Mr. Lau. Crying all the way to school every day. A new house went up farther down the road, maybe ten years ago. America must be so exciting compared to all of this. All the furniture is still here. You didn't come back for anything? Did you?" Her eyes widened. "We haven't thrown anything out. It's all still here. We weren't sure whether or not you were coming back. Why would you want to? America sounds like a dream."

Hawaii is not America, Michael thought. Chicago, the mainland.

He looked out the door at the rice fields again. The Japanese had invaded this village—a long time ago, before the Mao picture on the wall, the color TV, before Peking was renamed Beijing. Slowly and patiently, the farmer examined his crop. His grandmother had been a brave woman. But could even the small body of a Chinese woman safely hide among those short plants, in all that water?

Michael was tired of listening to Chinese. "Let's look around." He led the way past the old mother.

"What a big boy," she said, looking at the wooden floor.

*　　*　　*

The ceiling of the adjacent room was two stories high, but still the room was dark. There were no windows, just an open doorway in the far corner, letting in some light. Against the left wall a wooden staircase led to a small platform and closed door. On the right, a bed neatly made up with white sheets and a red embroidered quilt. A sewing machine sat in the center of the room. Yards of olive green cloth unraveled from the tabletop onto the floor.

"I bet the real bedroom's upstairs," Alex surmised.

"Finish your story," Michael said. "I want to know what happened."

"You want me to tell you now? Here?"

"Yeah, while they're in the other room." Michael sat down on top of the bed.

"All right. Where was I? The next day Ming Tim was waiting for me outside my hotel. 'I've got it all figured out,' he said. 'My wife's spending the night at her mother's tonight. Forty miles away from here. I'll take her to the bus station and make sure she gets on the right bus. I'll meet you here again, tonight, at nine o'clock.' I agreed, and he hurried away again."

"This bed is hard as a rock." Michael moved his hand across the floral pattern of the quilt. "Sorry for interrupting. Go on."

"You sure you don't want to listen to them out there instead? I'll translate for you. You can hear my story later tonight—in my room. Your father and those two old women are talking about the real China. I want to know why the old mother is blind. She wasn't born that way, you know. The part of her face around her eyes seemed pushed in. But I can't really tell. She won't look up. I guess she doesn't have a reason to. They say that if you weren't born blind and become blind, you would always remember the last thing you saw."

"I don't care about her. Just tell me the rest of your story." Michael began to relish depriving Alex of a real Chinese conversation.

"All right. You're the Chinese emperor." Alex stood in between Michael's opened legs and began to stroke his hair.

"Stop it." Michael pushed him in the stomach. "Finish your story."

"At nine o'clock Ming Tim stood outside my hotel. His cap was pulled low over his face. He led me to a darkened alleyway and handed me a Mao jacket. I wore it over my own jacket. He pushed another cap on my head. The way I was dressed, I almost looked Chinese.

"At the mouth of the courtyard of an apartment complex, Ming Tim pulled me aside again. 'Look to the ground,' he said. 'Don't look up until you are inside my apartment. We'll be walking to the entrance now. There may be people around. When you see a light, put your sleeve over your mouth. Stoop over a little. If anyone sees you they'll think that you're a sick relative of my wife. Keep your eyes down. Don't look up.

" 'If you can't walk straight, watch my feet. Don't walk too close to me. And don't ever touch me. At least not until we are inside.' He laughed for the first time.

"First I saw the dirt courtyard floor for about a hundred yards, then I almost tripped up a short flight of stairs at the entrance of the building. Speckled tiles in the lobby. Fluorescent bulbs humming overhead. I kept looking for Ming's feet. We stopped at the beginning of a flight of stairs.

" 'Keep one hand on the wall, the other over your mouth,' he said. 'Let's go.' My Chinese was not as good back then. I was afraid that I had misunderstood him. I was sweating under all those clothes. He pushed me against the wall. 'Someone is coming.' "

Just then, Michael's father entered the room, the old daughter following behind.

Michael stood up from the bed. "What's upstairs, Dad?"

His father looked at him and then at the wrinkled quilt. "Don't lie on someone else's bed," he said in English. "Are you still sick?"

"No. What's upstairs?"

Alex took a picture of the sewing machine and the green cloth. The flash shocked the room to life. The old daughter jumped back.

"Don't do that anymore," Michael said.

"Upstairs is my mother's old bedroom, your grandmother's room."

"We don't ever go up there," Mai Lee said. "We sleep down here." She pointed to the bed.

Michael's father walked up the creaking stairs, followed by Michael and Alex.

"Take another picture, and I'll break your camera," Michael said.

Halfway up the stairs, his father turned to him. "I may have to use that outhouse after all. I don't think that I can wait until we get back to the hotel."

Michael rolled his eyes.

His father looked down at his neck. "What's that?"

Michael knew that he was referring to the hickey. He pulled up his collar. "It's nothing. I think it's a rash." He heard muffled laughter from behind.

"I hope you don't have to see another doctor. If it's not one thing, it's another."

As they continued up the stairs, Michael wondered if Alex would be joining them for dinner, further intruding on him and his father. If he did not have dinner with them, Alex would wander to the marketplace and sit by himself at a noodle stand. The soup would smell of freshly chopped scallions. A native farmer would sit with him, amazed by his Chinese, and talk to him, telling him about his family, life in China, the rice fields. Afterwards, they would walk around town, slowly veering off to the abandoned schoolyard for sex. Meanwhile, Michael and his father would have their dinner in the hotel restaurant. The food off the streets of China was too dangerous. In Macau, he and his father had ordered bowls of steamed mussels from a street vendor. He had vomited all night into a plastic bucket beside the bed. His father climbed over him out of bed and woke up the old maidservant who was sleeping on the rattan sofa in the living room. Querulously, he had ordered her to brew some roots. When she entered the bedroom, Michael saw that her blouse was half-unbuttoned; she had pulled it on before coming in. He could see the shadows of her jugular veins, as she set the bowl down beside the bed and picked up the bucket. She drained it out in the squat toilet, rinsed it in the kitchen sink, and brought it back to him.

"You're spoiling this entire trip," his father muttered from his side of the bed.

"Leave me alone." Michael held his breath and drank the bitter tea in one tasteless swallow.

"Here, put this on your chest," his father said to him.

"What is it?"

"Tiger balm."

"No." Michael felt his father's hand, spreading the greasy sweet ointment on his chest.

"You're so skinny."

"Just like you."

Michael looked past Alex on the stairway at the old daughter standing frozen below. She looked up at the three of them, each appearing less Chinese from top to bottom. The wood of the stairs squeaked painfully with the weight of human bodies for the first time in so many years. The old daughter clutched the railing; her foot mounted the first step and then stopped.

In the bedroom, a large bed, draped with a canopy of cobwebs and dusty silk sheets, sprawled out from the center. The mattress was full of rat holes. The engravings of the headboard told a tale of court life in ancient China. Facing the foot of the bed was a matching bureau, and on the wall above it, a white rectangle, lighter than the rest of the wall, where something used to hang, perhaps a mirror. Closed wooden shutters trapped a musty odor. They would open onto a panoramic view of the rice fields. Carved on the wood were more characters and floral scenes.

"I slept here with my mother after my father went off to work in the coal mines of South America," Michael's father said.

Michael remembered his father telling him that his grandfather had died in the mines there.

"Why haven't the old women come up here?" Alex said. "Do you believe them?"

"This is still my mother's house," Mr. Lau stated. "They only live here."

"Will she come back, your mother?"

"She told me she would never come back."

Again Michael wondered why his grandmother was so adamant about staying away. He stood at the doorway, ready to go back downstairs. He looked back in the bedroom to see Alex and his father read the writing on the shutters together. The perfect son-and-father team. Below, at the foot of the staircase, the old daughter was joined by her mother. The old daughter looked upwards, while her blind mother looked down at the steps. Maybe they were afraid that they would have to leave. His father would discover things missing, accuse them of theft. Michael surmised that the old daughter had sold the mirror which had originally hung on the wall above the bureau in order to buy the sewing machine—so that she would not need to leave her mother home alone all day. His father stood close to Alex, their fingers touching the shutters.

"I can't read this," Alex said. "It's faded away too much." He tried to pull them open.

Michael's father hit away his hands. "Don't. They've never been opened. My mother never opened them."

In the kitchen, the old daughter explained to Alex how the gas canister was hooked up to the stone stove. "We refill it once a month," she said. "I don't do much cooking. Only for my mother and me. We don't eat much." The old mother poured more glasses of hot tea. Michael sat on a stool in the kitchen, holding up Alex's camera, looking out the back door through the viewfinder. His father ventured to the outhouse with a few sheets of tissue in his hand. The chickens scurried out of his way. Once he was safely inside, under the thatched roof of the small stone closet, Michael snapped the picture.

"Come away from that wok," Michael called to Alex, "and tell me the end of your story. Tell me the juicy bits once you get inside Mao's apartment."

"Ming's. Now? In front of these two women?" Alex asked.

"They won't understand. Let these two old relics hear. Nothing else exciting happens here. Imagine living your entire life in this house, in this village. Tell me the end of your story before my father gets back from his reunion with the outhouse."

Alex took a glass of hot tea from the old mother's offering hands and pulled up a stool next to Michael. With wide eyes the old daughter stood over them, listening to the foreign words. "Once we were in the apartment, Ming locked the door. Then I heard another man's laughter. 'It's okay,' Ming said. Another Chinese man was sitting in front of the TV. He was younger, my age. I don't remember his name. I took off the

Mao jacket and cap, and Ming and his friend took everything else off for me. They were so excited. They ran their hands through my chest hair, pulling it with their fingers. Then they cupped their small hands all over me, as if they were measuring me up: my hands, my chest, my nipples, my head.

"We took a shower together. It wasn't a regular shower, like what you're used to. It was a small square room, a single window way up high, a drain in the center of the white tiled floor. They sat on a bench across from me, huddled delicately, their fingers pointing as I poured warm buckets of water between my legs. We talked about the weather, America, China. They told me that they wanted to visit America. That nearly killed me, sitting there naked listening to them say that. We can visit them and see how they live, but they can't do the same—if they could even afford it in the first place, of course. And to think how dangerous it was to have me there.

"Later on, we did just about everything together, and then we fell asleep."

"What do you mean everything?" Michael asked.

"I'll show you later," Alex teased. "Let me finish my story. But sometime before morning, someone pushed me out of bed and told me to get dressed quickly. When I reached for the Mao jacket, Ming held it down. He wouldn't let me have it. 'It's very late,' he said. 'No one will see you leaving.' Now I could clearly see the way that I had come in: the stairs, the cracks on the wall, the entire width of the entrance's tiled floor, and then the darkened courtyard. We walked maybe a hundred yards beyond the entrance way of the complex before he said, 'You go back alone now.' I reached out for him, but he had already turned around. There was no moon out. I strained my eyes to look for him. I felt so lonely that night, walking back to my hotel room."

"Here comes my father."

"Let's go back to the hotel now," said Michael's father as he stepped over the threshold. "The outhouse is disgusting. There are bugs all over the place, and the smell. Lucky that old woman's blind."

In the front yard, they shook hands with the two old women, and Michael's father handed them each several Hong Kong dollars. They humbly thanked him, shaking their heads from side to side, proclaiming, "No, no. This is too much." Through the viewfinder of the camera Michael looked at the rice fields. Still only one lonely farmer. He looked up from beneath his hat but was still too far away for Michael to see his face, to discover his age. He could have been eighteen or as old as his father.

"Go out there and pick up that farmer," Michael said to Alex. "You *bok gwei*, bringing your evil ways to China, ruining simple people's lives."

"Homosexuality is not exclusively a white thing."

"But you think you're our savior, don't you," Michael retorted. "We all want to sleep with you. Every Chinese man wants a white man. No? Because we ultimately want to be like you. The beauty of the imperialist."

"There are a billion people in China, and there are bound to be a few fags," Alex said, "like you."

"I don't want to be like you."

"Here, give me the camera and let me get a picture of you, of you and your father in front of the ancestral home."

"No."

"I told you my story, now give me my camera and get in the picture, *baby*."

"No." Michael pulled the camera away from Alex's reach. It fell onto the ground. The back flipped open.

"I don't believe you," Alex said. "You're a fuckin' baby."

"Shut up," Michael said. "It's been fun. I'll be seeing you around sometime."

Alex stared at him with annoyance. For a moment Michael feared that he would say something to his father and the two old women. But would they even understand? The three of them stood, smiling and nodding. His father fidgeted back and forth. He still had not gone to the bathroom. Alex bent down to pick up the camera. His father was having the perfect ending to his reunion. Alex began to walk alongside the field, a lonely tourist heading back to this hotel; he kept watch over the farmer in the field. Michael imagined Alex making love to the farmer, and then saw himself with the farmer. The farmer's body would be skinny like his own. With each movement their elbows, knees, bones would knock painfully together.

His father continued to pace the ground. "Hurry, hurry," Michael thought. He wondered if his father even suspected that his son had turned out so different from himself. His father had said to his mother, "If I don't take him to China now, he'll forget that he was ever Chinese." "Take him," his mother had added, "and find him a Chinese wife." His father should have never left China: Would he have turned out straight then? *I'm different from all your Chinese ways, Dad. I'm an aberration. This is your homeland. Not mine.*

"I'll always remember these rice fields," his father said to the old women. "It's so peaceful out here. What a green land of comfort. I remember the story my mother told me about how the rice fields saved our lives. How she ran out there when the Japanese came marching through. How she lay low in the mud with me wrapped in her arms."

The old blind mother looked up from the ground. Her eyes ached to open. "Is that what she told you?" she asked; her voice rose in the heat.

"No, Mother," the old daughter gasped. "Not now."

"You were in town that day, Mai Lee, when they came through. You did not see firsthand the horror they brought to us. You did not see what happened to these people here. *I* was standing in this field with your father that day, Mr. Lau."

"My father was in South America," he replied nervously. "You must be mistaken."

"I'll never forget," she continued. "Your father couldn't see that Japanese soldier approaching him from behind. When the soldier called over to him it was already too late. Your father started to run. You can't run in mud even if your life depends on it. And besides, where was he running to? The mountains? The soldier took aim. I jumped on that Jap's back and knocked him to the ground. He pushed me over, got up, and shot your father down."

"Enough!" the old daughter cried.

"My father was not here when the Japanese came. He died in the South American coal mines."

"Your mother was probably too angry and upset to bother to tell a little boy the truth." The old mother continued: "From the fields I could see all the brick houses. The killings, the rapes, the looting. But I could not hear a single cry for help.

It's so quiet out there. You can see these houses from miles away.

"I saw your mother, looking down at me from her bedroom window, her face framed by the open shutters. She had witnessed the execution of her own husband. I was told that it was then that she ran off with you in her arms and hid in the outhouse. She stayed there in that darkened, stinking closet, until we found her there two days later. That outhouse saved your life."

"No," Michael's father said. He stood cold in his place.

"Believe me, Mr. Lau," the old mother pleaded. "He was shot down." She brought her hand to her face, the knocking of bones. "It was the last thing that I *saw* before the soldier bashed out my eyes with the handle of his rifle."

Michael reached out to steady his shaking father. He patted him on the shoulder, then on the back. His father moved away. He looked as if he wanted to vomit. He turned and walked off alone down the road.

Michael looked back at the mother and daughter, carefully framed in the green mouth of the door. Dollars stuck out of the open collars of their blouses, as if they were ancient prostitutes. Bricks and planks littered the ground. Slowly, his father's old home would crumble away. He turned down the road after him.

That evening they ate an early dinner in the hotel restaurant. "She's a crazy old woman. She doesn't know what she's talking about," his father said and then remained silent for the remainder of the meal. Lying in bed, Michael could not sleep; his feet knocked against the footboard. He turned to see the quiet face of his sleeping father. His father could only remember the past one way: the way it was told to him. This thought choked Michael. His father would never be able to accept his son's future as a gay man. Michael felt a pain in his stomach again. The air-conditioner hummed softly.

The next morning they passed over the dim sum breakfast downstairs and settled for packaged biscuits and boiled water. It was still early when they boarded the bus. They were heading back to Macau for a couple of days and then to Hong Kong; from there they would fly back to Hawaii. Michael would leave for Chicago soon after. His father dozed off beside him, their arms touching as the bus rocked on the dirt road. Michael was afraid that the rest of the trip would be as quiet as this.

He looked at his own reflection in the window and then outside. Beyond the fields, the sun was coming up over the peaks of the faraway mountains; the light slowly erased his reflection from the glass. The farmer in the field took off his straw hat. His face was gaunt, tired, resigned: an old man's face. The voices and the laughter on the bus melded into a single violent hum. Michael squinted his eyes. The farmer, upright and unmoving, began to sink. Michael ran toward him. His sneakers moved sluggishly in the mud. The glassy water took hold of the farmer's trousered legs, embraced his naked stomach and chest—the same color as the mud, and swallowed the bulging veins of his neck. The Chinese man's eyes turned into his head. Michael fell onto the rice field expanding out forever around him.

THE MAGISTRATE'S MONKEY

• RICHARD HOUSE •

TO JOHN W. PLOOF

"He is as beautiful as an angel!"

—Gilles de Rais

ADRIAN COMES OUT with some fairly stupid things; this morning I find him stretching his mouth in front of the bedroom mirror, waggling his tongue, apparently looking for mouth ulcers.

I ask him what is wrong. He says that he thinks he has trench mouth. I begin to wash; Adrian continues his search. I ask him if he thinks he has much longer.

"What longer?" he replies, pulling at his mouth.

"Many more days. How much longer do you think you'll live?"

Adrian is taking his health very seriously, or as seriously as a fourteen year old can.

"It was a joke," I say.

"Very funny," he replies.

I walk through the bedroom drying my face with a hand towel. He sits on my pressed white shirt, and with both hands grubs through his pubes, inspecting himself. All day long he lounges on the bed, watching TV and reading magazines, with a "do not disturb" sign on the door so that the maid will not interrupt him.

"You could do a few more useful things with yourself."

"Such as?" he asks.

I ask for my shirt. Adrian tuts and rises from the bed. He stands naked at the window, watching the traffic below, playing with his finger in his mouth.

"If you're that worried, I could cut it out here and now," I offer.

"It isn't funny," he argues. "It happens to be very sore."

The boy sticks out his tongue, stretching his mouth as wide as he can manage. There is a small rash running along the side of his tongue.

"You have bitten yourself."

He shakes his head. He can't remember when.

"Then it must have been in your sleep." I point out of the window. "There are people in those flats, you know."

The boy flops backward onto the bed.

"Why don't you have a house or an apartment like everyone else?" he asks.

"What use would a house be?" I ask. "The hotel is just fine. Besides, I don't pay."

"Who does?"

"Harris and Barker's." I am looking for my tie. "Ultimately the American taxpayer."

Adrian rolls over, laughing.

"I'm a subsidized butt-hole. A teenage tax scam for a chocolate salesman."

"I'm not a salesman," I correct him.

"What's the difference?" He turns onto his stomach, baring a naked ass at me. "I am."

"Aren't you going to dress today?" I reply. The tail of my tie sticks out from under the boy's stomach.

"Are you going to make it worth my while?" he asks.

I zip the tie out from under him.

Each morning before breakfast, Adrian and I barter over his day's expenses. It is this quiet and private deal which, to his delight, defines him as a whore.

"What do you need today?" I ask him.

"Eighty," he replies. "Is this your money or the taxpayer's?"

"All mine," I assure him.

I offer him fifty but he keeps his hand outstretched.

"Sixty?"

He crumples the notes into his hand.

"And bring me back some of those chocolates," he asks.

"I have nothing to do with the chocolates. I'm nothing more than a family name."

I kiss him on the lips. "I am a piece of tradition, and tradition sells itself—every good prostitute knows that. Call me today," I say. "Remember to call me."

After two poor harvests my parents could meet neither their taxes nor their tithe. Fearful that they would forfeit their lease, they agreed to sell me to the magistrate. I suspect that I was drugged, as I have no memory of the long, hot journey across the plains. I awoke, roused by a fragrant early morning breeze bearing a sweet trace of lemons from the orchards below, as we descended into the cool, lush valley of the magistrate's estate. Smooth sandstone walls rose and widened beside the road; the village, the aqueduct, the orchards and villa, everything lay hidden between the butter-smooth walls of the gorge.

At a place agreed between the parties we waited for the magistrate's merchant, who would conduct the exchange. My parents secured a rope around my waist and stood discreetly at a distance beside the road. Blossoms from the citrus groves blew across the track, and the air was filled with their heavy scent. From a distance we watched the merchant marching boldly up the track, a swarthy figure wavering in the haze, dust rising from his footsteps. He wore a large, stiff, black felt hat to protect his face from the sun. Stopping several yards ahead of me, he paused in the shade of the tall cypress trees with his hands on his hips, catching his breath. After a moment he summoned me forward and my parents loosened their hold of the rope. The merchant considered me, sucking on his tongue and playing with his hands in his pockets. He was not as handsome as I had first imagined, for his face was bright red, as if scalded, its features sharp and shrewish and crossed with many deep scars, and he stank as if he had slept with animals.

Resting one hand upon my shoulder he instructed me to unbutton my shirt. Turning me slowly about he pulled open the garment and pinched at my skin. The merchant carefully inspected my eyes, teeth, and mouth, and picked at my hair searching for lice.

"Open your trousers," he demanded.

I did as the merchant asked and produced my penis for him.

He handled it carefully, drawing back the skin to see if there were any infections. Satisfied, he then weighed each testicle in his hand.

"Is he still a virgin?" the merchant asked my parents. "Has anybody had him?"

My parents assured him that I was pure and had not been had or touched by anyone. Content with the reply the merchant bowed forward and kissed me full on the mouth, prying my lips open with his tongue.

Without any comment he untied the rope from around my waist and pushed me ahead of him toward the village. Our route ran between the legs of the aqueduct; cold mountain water dripped onto our backs as we walked in its shade, and we could hear the rushing of the river encased in stone above our heads.

"Why do you cry?" the merchant asked. "You are a very lucky boy."

I return later than promised and wait at the door for the porter before entering the room. He winks as he hands me my package. I stand in the hall holding the door closed so that he cannot see the boy on the bed.

Adrian stirs, cuddling the pillow; my notes and papers lie spread across the bed. I sit beside him placing the gift between us, certain that he is not asleep, and gather my papers together. As sleepy as he can pretend to be, he curls about the package and begins to unwrap it. The tips of his fingers pick delicately at the tape. I have bought him a camera and many packets of film. I had intended to buy him a radio, for which I had already given him the money, knowing full well that he would not use the money as promised.

"Is it so dull you fell asleep?" I ask.

The boy holds up the camera.

"I've seen these before," he says, staring at the ceiling through the viewfinder, ignoring my question. "If you could be someone else, who would you be?" he asks.

"I don't think I'd want to be someone else at all."

"That's not what I was asking." He turns onto his side, resting the camera on my chest.

"Seriously? I don't know. I'm quite happy as I am right now. Who would you be?"

"I'd be," Adrian rolls on top of me, his legs straddling my thighs, "someone's love slave." He laughs rocking his hips. "Come on, take a picture," he begins to undress. "What's wrong?"

I shake my head and take hold of the camera. He jams himself against the headboard, his shorts caught at his ankles.

"Take pictures of me."

He stands on the bed shaking his dick at me. His skin is very pale, very light, almost made of light; fluorescent in this dark room. He still has some vestige of stocky, youthful puppy fat—a smooth unmuscled stomach, a thick waist, and full round, pale buttocks.

I place each picture on the carpet, and wait for them to develop. The boy kneels on the bed behind me.

"Look at that," he laughs.

In one photograph Adrian has his knees up tight to his shoulders; his fingers point toward the small brown walnut of his asshole. He is laughing as hard as can be imagined.

"Boy-pussy," he sniggers as he skips off the bed and into the bathroom, "costs you fifty."

"What about the story?" I say.

"If it's any good I'll let you fuck me for free," he bargains, calling from the bathroom. "But if it's lousy you'll have to pay double."

I sit up wondering if I can trust the valet to have my suit pressed. Adrian checks his mouth and searches the bathroom cabinet for a mouth rinse, which he brings with him to the bed.

I motion for him to come and sit with me.

"It's okay," I reassure him, "really. It's perfectly safe. You don't need that." I place the bottle of antiseptic on the floor. I feel stupid with my trousers at my knees, and the photographs about my feet. He straddles my hips for a second time and unbuttons my shirt. I cradle his head into my shoulder, cup my hands about his back and whisper into his ear.

The magistrate's villa stood at the head of the square. The sun had bleached and powdered the ocher walls white. The lower windows were shuttered. Before a solid wood door were mounted two cumbrous wrought iron gates, the tips of each iron spear fashioned as a lily flower. The doors themselves were of a heavy, dark wood, embossed lilies bound in coils around each of the panels, black varnish blistering on each of the petals. The marble staircase too had a fine trace of lilies etched into the stone steps, but many feet had worn the design away, except at the sides, where the grooves held rain or dew from the night before.

The merchant unlocked the gates and swung open the doors. Snapping his fingers he ushered me into the hallway.

I began to cough in the dry dusty air. Another cough, lighter than my own, echoed through the hall, though I could not determine from where as my eyes were unused to the darkness. A creature, a monkey, which I first mistook for a small dog, stepped delicately out of the shadows on all fours. A long, bushy tail, easily twice the animal's length, struck upright and curled tightly at its tip. It sat upon the marble and began scratching and tugging at a collar bound too tightly about its neck. I reached towards the monkey, convinced by the seeming distress in its wide, maudlin black eyes; but the wretch lashed at me, screeching like a cat and bearing its teeth. If it had not been for the length of the leash he would have savagely bitten me.

A tongue clicked in the darkness and the monkey resumed fidgeting with its collar, its black-tipped tail curled about the leash. The cord stretched back into the black socket of a doorway. Tall and lank, the magistrate walked unsteadily into the light. Leaning forward on his cane, he swaggered stiffly and extravagantly as if he would topple without it. His breath hissed softly between his teeth and his metal cane sang as it struck the marble flagstones. The monkey cowered as the magistrate approached, and chattered nervously at the shadows.

The merchant opened my shirt for a second time and pushed me towards the unsteady old man. The magistrate ran his finger across my chest from nipple to nipple. A small bubble of spittle slid across his lower lip as he gently teased them. He pressed his hand against my stomach as if it would leave an impression.

The monkey sat on the magistrate's feet and tugged at his

trousers. The old man stopped to pat its black pate, and the creature clambered up his arm and hung from his back, threatening to unbalance him. Understanding that the audience was over, the merchant opened the grill and offered his arm to the old man for support. The slender, suited magistrate teetered in the doorway, apparently dazed by the sunlight, and wiped the spittle from his lip. Then, taking the merchant's arm, he unsteadily walked out of the villa. In a moment the doors were locked, and the magistrate, monkey, and merchant were gone.

I ran through the vast, vacant halls exploring the dusty white rooms, with their patterned marble floors, faded frescoes, and vaulted ceilings. In several chambers the plaster had collapsed to the floor exposing the lath. Although the furnishings had long since been removed, a musty odour of decaying fabric lingered in the rooms. As I ran, a fine chalk dust raised in my wake. To my disappointment I found that I was quite alone.

In a chamber furthest from the entrance on the first floor, I discovered a mural of an angel, an impressive figure, twice, three times my size and blackened by soot. In one hand he brandished a white sword; in his other he held a scale, weighing the small naked souls of the penitent, their hands clasped in prayer. This was the room in which I chose to sleep, under the angel's doleful, protective eye.

That evening the old man brought me my food, bread soaked in sherry, and salted meat. Silently he watched me eat as the monkey chattered at his feet. When I had finished he picked up the bowl and oil lamp and departed, without uttering one word. Without light I searched through the apartment for bedding. Gathering black drapes and decrepit tapestries, I arranged a bed of sorts, but much of the fabric was so brittle that it would disintegrate upon the slightest touch, sending out flurries of dust.

Adrian rolls away from me on the bed as I stroke his ass.

"I'm not a charity," he says.

I slip my hand between his buttocks. The boy shakes his head.

"Too sore." He shifts forward. "You'll never get it in like that."

He suddenly smiles and slides slowly back and forward on my hand.

"Fuck, say fuck," he whispers bending to pick the camera up from the floor.

"Fuck," I say.

"You English kill me. Fuck," he says, "fuck," imitating my accent. "Which word do you prefer? Cock or dick?" he asks.

"It depends," I reply.

Adrian turns around on the bed, and focuses the camera at my crotch.

"On what? Size?"

"No. The situation perhaps."

The boy gets up and goes to the bathroom. After a moment I follow him.

Adrian straddles the sink washing his genitals. Water splashes onto the tiled floor.

"I should make you pay for this, too," he jokes.

"Can I ask you something?" I lean through the doorway, watching the boy. "Do you like sex?"

He stops washing and begins to laugh.

"That's a stupid question. What else am I here for?"

"No. I wanted to know if you liked it."

He stops laughing.

"Of course I do," he seems annoyed. "Doesn't everyone?"

"You're right—stupid question."

I return to the bedroom and lie down on the bed.

During the evening I would exercise, running through the apartments busying myself so that I would not fret over the magistrate's visits. At nightfall the magistrate would arrive with a lamp and a covered tin plate containing my food. He would then sit silently in his chair and watch me as I ate while his monkey restlessly climbed over him. After five days I became used to the procedure, and used to his scrutiny.

On the sixth night the magistrate arrived with a dress, which he threw upon the bed. Swaddled in the tapestries and worn velvet drapes I feigned sleep and ignored him. At the scrape of the tin plate on the floor, I pretended to awaken and stretched my arms fully over my head, allowing the drapes to fall from my shoulders. Drawing the bowl closer, I turned away from the magistrate and began to eat. As he watched, I slowly raised one leg, causing the drapes to open still wider, and the dress to fall upon the floor. Finally, having finished my meal I lay fully stretched out on my stomach, naked, the drapes free from my buttocks.

The old man turned the dress over with his cane.

Taking the dress, I rose from the bedding and stood naked before the magistrate. In the faint yellow light from his oil lamp we watched each other, but the old man did not stir. The monkey stretched on its leash, reached into the dish, and picked at the food.

The dress was fashioned from a deep red satin, and appeared to be stained. Although the skirt was wide, the bodice was too small to fit me or be fastened. It had many sharp stays or hooks which stuck through the material.

Wearing this odious and ill-fitting garment I leaned forward and kissed the magistrate's neck, seized by a rash desire to tease him. His skin was cold, and I could smell his rotten teeth. Money or keys jangled in his pocket as I pressed against him, brushing his linen shirt. Unblinking, unmoved, his clear gray eyes stared resolutely into mine.

"It's too small for me," I spoke, "and its stench appalls me."

The old man clucked his tongue at the monkey. Climbing up the chair, the creature settled on the armrest and tugged at the magistrate's sleeve, searching in his pockets for food. Producing a fig, the old man placed it between his lips, and the monkey delicately took the fruit with its teeth, its hands tenderly resting upon the old man's cheek and chin as if they were exchanging a kiss.

Feeling foolish, I undressed and returned to the makeshift mattress. A small droplet of blood beaded on my shoulder, where the dress had scratched me. The old man leaned forward to inspect, as if he could smell it. Turning my back, I quickly fell asleep, comforted by the thought that he was too old, too frail, to pose any threat to me, and that he could easily be overcome.

In the morning the dress was gone and I could not find my clothes.

* * *

Adrian bends towards the mirror, stretching out his tongue.

"What's wrong now?" I ask.

The boy steps back.

"Nothing," he replies.

"Then can I shave? What's all this hair in the sink?" I ask.

There are small blond hairs tufted in the drain.

"I shaved my armpit."

"What for?"

"Because," he replies.

He holds up his right arm and stares at his armpit in the mirror.

"You shaved only one armpit?" I pull the hairs from the drain. "Don't do this, please don't leave hairs in the sink. Did you use my last razor?"

The boy tuts under his breath and marches out of the bathroom. I hear him jump upon the bed. I find my razor in the trash.

"Is there anything you want today? Anything special I can bring you?" I ask.

There is no reply.

I peep around the bathroom door.

"Are you feeling alright?"

He is lying on the bed with his back to me, facing the windows. I repeat the question.

"Do you want me to bring you something from downstairs?"

"I'll need some more money today," he speaks to the window.

"Why, do you have plans?" I ask.

"Nothing special," he turns about smiling.

I walk over to the bed and sit at his feet.

"Are you alright?" I ask.

"Fine," he smiles, "just fine."

I squeeze his foot.

"How's about we go somewhere tonight?"

The boy shakes his head.

"Really, I'm fine," he insists.

For the next two nights there were no visits, and my food was left wrapped in sacking by the doors. Although I wanted to believe that I had successfully intimidated the old man, intuition warned me that this was not so; that he was indeed more formidable than I had guessed; and that I had been sorely misguided in kissing him. On the eighth night the magistrate returned without food, but was accompanied by the merchant. Neither man made any attempt to find me. Standing by the open door with a lamp at his feet, the magistrate supervised the merchant as he delivered heavy burlap sacks, tithes of wheat and barley, counting them as they were tidily stacked in rows in the hallway. Before leaving, he cautioned the merchant that he kept a wild dog in these rooms, and that he should not stray about the apartments on his own. The merchant laughed and asked if he might exercise the dog, and said that, should it need taming, the magistrate should keep him in mind.

The next night and the night after—every night for a fortnight followed the same routine. The old man would open the apartments for the merchant, count the sacks, and then leave. Only occasionally would he bring me my meal. Many nights I was forced to chew upon dried grain. As the tithes were delivered, the merchant would stack them along the walls, as high as the window ledge, building low corridors through which I could silently follow him. Once the night's work was completed the magistrate would return, inspect the rooms, and offer the merchant a drink. They would leave together, the younger man supporting the elder.

By the third night of the second week I realized that the merchant had contrived his own scheme to ruin the magistrate. As soon as the magistrate departed, the merchant would redouble his efforts and redirect his route. Taking the sacks two at a time from the walls he had constructed the previous night to one of the upper rooms, he would slit open the burlap and empty a quarter of its contents onto the floor, storing the grain, I assumed, for himself. The merchant worked skillfully and swiftly, stitching the bottom of the sacks so that they appeared full. Returning the sack once more to its place downstairs he would then urinate upon the tithes, for what reason I could not be certain.

On the last night, when all the tithes were stacked and stored, the old man again brought wine for the merchant. The

merchant drank alone and soon became rowdy. With consummate skill the magistrate encouraged the merchant's rau-
cousness and asked if he would care for some sport, telling him
that it was time they dealt with the dog and that he should
receive full payment for his labour. He spurred the merchant
on, plying him with more and more drink, riling him, until
the man spun drunkenly on his heels ready to rampage through
the apartments. With alarming agility the old man steadied the
merchant and produced the foul red dress which he had
brought to me several weeks before and my trousers which he
had stolen. Thrusting the garments to the merchant's face, he
had him breathe deeply their rank and treacherous odours.
Strangely sobered, the merchant raised his head, which the
magistrate patted and stroked as if he were petting his favourite
hound. Piece by piece, the magistrate threw the clothes into
the hallway and sent the merchant after them as if releasing a
dog upon its chase. The merchant howled as he ran through
the rooms, barking and screeching like a wild beast. I ran ahead
of him through a maze of sacks, frightened for my life, until
cornered in the last room, where there was no place further
for me to hide. I cowered in the corner, praying that I would
not be discovered.

The monkey scampered into the chamber and jumped upon
the sacks, seating itself just above my head. The creature non-
chalantly scratched its genitals and hissed at me.

The merchant teetered in the doorway, drunk and sweating.
The magistrate hurried into the room. Hectic and unsteady,
he settled himself in his chair and commanded that the man
undress. Happily the merchant stripped, throwing his clothes
across the chamber, stretching as he did, as if nakedness re-
newed him. Light from the magistrate's torch flit across the
younger man's skin, illuminating red welts and wens across his
body. His skin appeared as wart-ridden as a hog's hide. He
stood in the doorway slowly flexing his arms, his shoulders,
his legs, massaging his limbs as if bathing or shedding an invisible skin; discarding labour as if it were clothes.

There is an accident. A car straddles the sidewalk and road,
blocking the driveway between the hotel and the supermarket.

Two firemen tend carefully inside the car, leaning through the open side windows. Except for its broken windshield, the car appears undamaged. An ambulance arrives while firemen place cones around the vehicle. One fireman attempts to open the trunk, while another indicates that there are two people inside the car. White blankets are brought from the ambulance, two stretchers are brought to the car, but there is no haste. I watch the firemen force open the trunk. Someone shouts, and he returns with the bolt cutters to the fire truck.

I realise that the occupants of the car have died.

It is a futile response, but I wind down my window and ask if there is anything I can do. The fireman is wearing white rubber gloves. He holds out his hands and gently shakes his head. There is nothing he can do, there is nothing that can be done by anyone. I apologise and close the window. There is something expedient, old fashioned perhaps, about dying in a car.

Adrian sleeps with the television on, his reflection held in the window above the lake and the fire trucks, porcelain pale. The boy wakes as I prepare for bed. Plumping up his pillow, he watches and smiles as I undress.

"Tell me about the merchant," he asks. "What happens to you?"

I stand in front of the mirror and imagine the fireman, naked except for the tight white rubber gloves, finding me behind the sacks, his hands at my thighs, his fingers in my ass.

"When the merchant tossed aside his clothes, he threw up a curtain of dust, which caused me to sneeze."

I untuck the sheets at the end of the bed, and crawl beside the boy, climbing between his legs.

"He finds me. He finds me cowering behind the sacks, and takes me as the old man watches."

During the days I watched the merchant tend to the citrus groves that wrapped about the villa. The trees were cropped stumpy and round, planted in rows, each plot enclosed by tall cypress. As each tree produced fruit the merchant picked them bare, storing the fruit in boxes which did not carry the magistrate's insignia. Selecting the most fruitful trees, the merchant severed their roots, and poured lime into the irrigation channels.

The next time the magistrate visited was the night that the rains started. The days remained hot as before, but the nights became much colder.

The old man arrived leaning on his metal cane. The merchant followed with a brazier, dressed similarly to the old man—in a black suit and black shoes—but without shirt and socks. The monkey clung to the magistrate's back, and in the shadow cast by the lamp the magistrate appeared to have a tail.

"It is winter," the old man said. "We cannot have you sicken."

Inside the brazier was a small sack of meats and cheeses, which the merchant spread upon the floor. He began tearing the meat into small strips and cautiously fed them to me by hand as if I might bite him. After I had eaten what I could, the old man impatiently tapped the metal brazier with his cane, instructing that it should be lit.

"I give you what you can use of this boy," the magistrate spoke quietly, addressing himself to the merchant, "but what you take must be clearly marked; the rest is mine."

The merchant did not understand.

"It is simple," the magistrate explained, pointing at me with his cane. "I have given you this boy's ass, and you must mark it as your possession as clearly as you would mark a pig or a sheep or a horse."

He handed his cane to the merchant, who then thrust the cane deep into the kindling coals. Siezing me by my hair he forced me to the ground, pinning my shoulders to the floor with a knee across my throat. The more I struggled, the harder he knelt upon my neck.

The drapes shone red from the coals, and the angel's face flared, sanguine and distressed. Then with one hand the merchant drew my knees over my head, so that my ass stuck upward. With his other hand he haughtily slapped and pinched at my buttocks. I could hear the cane scrape against the tin. The merchant paused and held it over my face, and I could see that the tip was fashioned as a blade, one side inscribed with a lily motif. The flower blazed as scarlet as the coals.

Sharp, scolding pain seared my buttocks as the merchant branded me.

A sweet, pungent odour filled the room.

My cries sent the monkey charging in circles, screaming, leaping from sack to sack, ripping the burlap, scattering the grain wildly about the room.

Returning the cane to the fire, the merchant spat into his hands and massaged my ass.

"Well?" the old man leaned forward and sniffed at my ass, anxious not to be cheated of some sport. Still holding me to the floor the merchant released my legs and spun me about, pressing his lap into my face. Unbuttoning his trousers with one hand, he pinched his fingers into my jaw and forced my mouth open, obliging me to kiss where he placed my head. Pubic hair and calloused skin bristled against my lips as he ran his cock into my mouth. I could barely keep from retching at the stench.

The merchant drove slowly into my mouth, turning my head so that the magistrate could easily see without having to rise from his chair. The fat red cock head swelled, and I tasted salt. Withdrawing abruptly, the merchant pressed against my cheek and came upon my face.

Taking my head from his hips, the merchant pulled me up and kissed me, licking the jissom from my lips. Binding my legs fast about his waist, and my arms about his neck so that he could not withdraw, I whispered to him: "I have watched you spoil the magistrate's grain and poison his trees."

The merchant began to chuckle and twisted my ankles, releasing himself from my grip.

I arrive home to find Adrian pacing about the room, carving a path from the bathroom to the bed. When he sees me he rushes forward.

"Come here," he says. "Here."

Marshalling me over to the bathroom, he points into the toilet bowl.

"There's nothing in there, Adrian."

He impatiently slaps his side.

"I know that. I flushed it away."

There are a few tobacco grains in the bottom of the bowl, and the water is almost up to the lip.

"Did you spend all of that money on dope?"

The boy shrugs.

"And how come you threw it down the toilet?"

Slowly and with difficulty the story comes out. He had bought some hash from the porter. While he was lying, smoking, on the bed, the maid knocked on the door wanting to change the sheets. Adrian panicked, believing it to be the police. He dumped the whole bag into the toilet.

"How long ago was this, Adrian?"

He holds up his hands. His face is scarlet.

"What possessed you to do this?"

The boy stands tearfully in the centre of the room becoming more and more distraught. For some time, he tells me, he has had a lump under his left arm. He begins to sob. I make him stand still and pull off his shirt. It is the armpit that he had shaved. On the first attempt I cannot find it. Only when his arm is at its side can it be felt; a swelling about as large as a hazelnut.

"Is this what you're worried about? Everyone has those. Here let me feel."

There is no swelling under the right arm. I ask him how long it has been there. He isn't sure, a while, maybe several months. The lump moves slightly when pressed. He shows a little discomfort. He says that it aches, that it sometimes keeps him awake. He does not like to touch it as it worries him.

I ask him somewhat foolishly, "Why does it worry you?"

He hands me a magazine already open to an article. I read carefully, anxious not to upset him.

"I wish you had told me earlier. We could have saved you this worry," I throw the magazine onto the bed. "I don't think you can rely on this. I really don't. Everyone gets swollen glands; it's probably just sex."

He will not listen. "I have a temperature."

I argue that that would be the dope, and that now he is becoming both paranoid and unreasonable.

"I really don't think you have cause to worry. I think you're overly anxious. It's not as if you've exactly done anything to worry about. Have you? I think it's far more risky buying drugs from that porter."

Adrian wakes me at five o'clock, pulling the sheets over to his side. He tells me that he is cold. Within ten minutes he is hot again. I try to convince myself that this is not so strange. He asks for a doctor but stops my hand as I am dialing.

"They'd put me away if they caught me with you."

I try a "don't be ridiculous," but cannot make myself redial the number.

"You should try to sleep." I hand Adrian two tablets. "And we'll see how you are in the morning."

He shakes his head and hides his face against my arm.

"Perhaps it will just go away," he says.

I consider asking him why he hasn't told me about his arm earlier. I massage his shoulders as I talk.

Although I could often hear water rushing in the aqueduct, the apartments did not have running water, and I soon exhausted the places I could use for my toilet.

Within one week of the merchant urinating upon the magistrate's sacks, I could detect a faint whiff of alcohol. Each sack had sprouted into a soft pillow of green, thin yellow blades of wheat stuck through the burlap, tracing a line where the sun had fallen upon the sacks. But the vinegar smell of fermenting grain I tracked not to these tithes but to the grain that the merchant had stolen for himself.

The room was small and dark, having two square boarded windows, each no larger than a man's head, and a large marble fireplace. Water seeped down the wall from one of the windows, sprouting the corn on the floor. The floor of this chamber was laid thick with rotting corn and barley grain. Nature had outwitted the merchant.

So close and fetid was the atmosphere that I was obliged to open one of the windows. Stepping across the sodden corn and climbing onto a ledge I was able to pry back a board. There was no glass in the window, and within an arm's reach was the wall of the aqueduct. A small leak had sprung, leaping the gap between the aqueduct and the window. When I examined the wall of the aqueduct it seemed that the hole had been fashioned deliberately, scratched from the living stone.

As I picked between the stones, the mortar began to cake like putty under my fingernails. The deeper I dug, the damper the mortar became, until a small vein of cold water began to trickle along my arm and down the warm white stone. I worked until my fingers bled. I had enlarged the trickle to a small spout.

Exhausted, my hands sore, I sat down in the windowsill. Sunlight fell obliquely upon the wall of the aqueduct and reflected into the room. In the half light I could discern scratchings upon the window ledge. Although I could not comprehend the text, I was certain that there were names etched clumsily into the stone sill. More horrifying still were singular repeated scratches, marking days, weeks of imprisonment. There were perhaps twelve separate markings. I realised that I was not the first boy to be brought here, and not the first to realize that the aqueduct offered the only escape. In terror I fled from the room, frightened by thoughts of what had happened to those imprisoned before me.

Adrian flinches as I kiss his shoulder.

"How do you feel now?" I ask. "Is your arm troubling you?"

He nods.

"Would it help if I rubbed it?"

Adrian shakes his head. "I couldn't reach it," he says. "It's right in there"—lodged in the cleft between his arms and his shoulder.

"I wish I hadn't shaved," he complains. "It's really itchy now."

"Does it hurt anywhere else?"

Again the boy nods.

"Show me. Show me where."

He points to either side of his jaw, and both elbows and ankles.

I roll up my sleeves and run the boy a bath, steaming hot, and make him bathe. I stand over him as he lies sulking in the bath. Thankfully he is too tired to argue. His hands cover his genitals, and the water comes up to his chin.

"See this," I say, sticking my finger into the water. "See how my finger bends?"

He nods.

"My first boyfriend was equiped with a dick that bent just like that."

Adrian huffs. Sweat runs from his brow.

"Might be useful if you're really ugly, no one would have to see your face."

I gruffly sit the boy up and soap his arms and legs.

"Soap," he complains.

"What about it?"

"There's soap in my eye," he screws up his face and slaps his hand on the water.

"I didn't do it on purpose."

The boy raises himself from his bath, pulling on my tie.

"Thank you," I say. "Very nice. Very nice, indeed."

I spread the towel on the bed and have him lie on his stomach. He says that he is becoming cold again and that his eyes still sting. Taking some baby oil into my hands I begin to massage the boy's back. The bath has done little to relax him.

"Have you slept with many men?" I ask. Adrian stiffens. "It just might be that if I'm the first person, the first man, you've been involved with— It just might be that there's nothing wrong. You could just be unduly worried. That's all. I'm not really talking about sex. It's just that the first time you're involved with someone, someone of the same sex, in a relationship, that's essentially what we have here."

Adrian half turns, raising on his elbows. My hands rest on his buttocks, slippery with oil.

"Sometimes you ask the oddest questions," he observes.

"I had the hardest time, my first time. It could just be that. That's all I'm saying."

I was awakened by a whistle. Pressing my face against the small leaded panes I could see the merchant crouched in the vines beneath the aqueduct. A basket of lemons sat at his feet. Cautiously he waved me away from the window. As soon as I stepped back I was surprised by the monkey, which sprang upon the ledge. With great care the creature began to pick at the lead which held the glass in place, deftly prying away one of the small panes. The merchant cut the lemons into quarters and called the monkey back down to him. Piece by piece he handed the segments to the monkey. Again the creature scaled the wall and gingerly handed the segments to me, piece by piece. If ever I extended my hand too quickly toward him the monkey would fiercely screech and bare its teeth. I was in little doubt that he would bite me.

The fruit was ripe and sweet. Some of the segments had blood tracing the fat juicy cells, from where the merchant had cut himself. The citrus stang my lips and gums which had grown sore on the magistrate's meager diet of meat and bread.

"How much do you think you have seen?" the merchant questioned.

I withdrew from the window, pulled a tuft of sprouting corn from a sack, and tossed it through the window. The merchant caught the grain and with great care inspected what had landed into his hands. The man shook his head and looked back up at me. So anxious was his expression that I stepped back. When I returned to the window the merchant and monkey had gone.

I returned to my makeshift mattress, wondering what leverage I now had over the merchant. Disturbed by a noise from the hallway I quickly concealed the lemons and the rinds, afraid that this would be the old man.

The merchant warily approached the chamber and waited in the darkness of the hallway, holding out his hands.

"You have seen nothing," he said.

Walking slowly toward me, he again unbuttoned his trousers. This time he pulled out his cock so that it swaggered in front of him, lolling against the cloth as he walked.

I covered my mouth, certain that I would retch.

"To blackmail me serves you no purpose at all," he whispered, leaning over the bedding.

The merchant knelt and began to piss upon the sack. His hot, sweet-smelling urine ran between my legs. Taking a lemon from my hands he squeezed the juice upon his cock. Using his other hand he massaged himself, stretching his cock until it became full and firm. Taking another lemon he instructed that I should turn over, my stomach on the wet sack. Squeezing the juice onto the small of my back, he allowed it to trickle down between the cheeks of my buttocks, which he then spread open with his hands. Using his tongue he caught the lemon juice and wet my ass. With great care he teased his sticky fingers between my legs and twisted a finger into my asshole.

"It would be better for you if I were the magistrate," he whispered, kissing me on the mouth. Tearing the rind with his teeth, the merchant crushed the juice from several lemons. Wetting his hands, he thrust his finger deeper into my ass. He lay down on the sacks and had me bathe him, rubbing the sweet aromatic juices into the tough black hide of his shoulders and arms until we were both sticky and entwined. The hotter our bodies became, the sweeter and sharper became the aroma. Dark velvet drapes swung in the slow draft that filtered through the halls.

Adrian's breathing is now regular and deep. I have the urge to wake him so that I can continue with the story.

He will not come down to breakfast. Although his fever has passed, his mood will not lighten.

"I still feel sick," he says. "My shoulder still hurts and I think it's gone to my lungs."

I have room service bring his breakfast to the room. The porter asks if my son is sick.

As I unfold the tray on the bed, I ask Adrian if he needs more Polaroid film. I watch him pick at the plate, slowly turning over each item. Apparently the camera is broken, and anyhow, what would he take pictures of?

"I don't understand why you won't see a doctor."

He begins to pout. I remove the tray from the bed and sit next to him.

"I found a clinic and I've made an appointment."

The boy's eyes widen in anger.

"Alright. Alright. You don't have to go. Nobody's making you do anything you don't want to."

I slip my hand under the sheets.

"Tell me where it hurts."

He shrugs.

"All over?" I ask.

Adrian nods once.

"Is there anywhere I can kiss?" I jokingly pucker my lips.

For a moment the boy looks panic stricken.

"Maybe I'll get up this afternoon," he coughs. "Did you really get me an appointment?"

"No," I lie, "but I would have—if you had said yes."

No sooner had the merchant left than I heard the old man unbolting the front door. Wrapping myself in the drapes, I pretended that I had been sleeping. As drowsy as I could manage to be, I stretched and yawned, watching his approach. In each hand he carried a small silver bowl.

"I have brought you a gift." He smiled, placing the two bowls upon the drapes at my feet.

The bowls were of a fine filigree silver, containing small packages wrapped in linen. The old man nodded and I unwrapped the gifts. White eggs of sugared almonds, as large as knuckle bones, were contained inside. Lemon blossoms decorated and scented the packages.

"In your own time." The old man shook his head then and paused. The sweet scent of lemons still hung in the chamber, but far worse and far stronger, was the fetid stench of the rotting corn. His eyes narrowed and he cocked his head. With surprising briskness he walked through the apartments, pausing in the doorway of each room, as if testing the air. I listened to his cane tap along the marble floor as he searched and returned, it never occurring to him to look at the sacks beneath his very nose.

The magistrate stood in the doorway leaning upon his cane, dust settled behind him. The monkey pulled on its rope, lunging for the bedding where I had concealed the rinds. Impatiently the magistrate snapped back the leash, and the monkey sat on its hind legs, grubbing through the brindled fur on its belly. The magistrate tapped his cane upon the floor and pointed at the sugared almonds.

"In your own time," he repeated.

Adrian is not in the room when I return. Each time this happens it comes as a shock. I regret that I had teased him this morning. I prefer for him not to leave; without him the room is reduced to a foul orange carpet, with hideous beige furnishings, the place is hateful to me.

I check under the bed for his sports bag, which mercifully, is still there. This is the bag he arrived with. I have no intention to look inside but the zipper is undone, and by pulling the bag out from under the bed by its strap I can see inside. There is my pair of brown shoes. Enclosed in each shoe is a wad of money, perhaps twelve hundred dollars. I am surprised that I have such a thrifty banker on my hands, and realize that if the money is here then he will return.

It is still, however, a relief to me to hear his key in the door.

I managed to sleep, soothed by the rainfall, but awoke early, uncomfortable and itching. Tiny black ants covered my hands—after whatever remained of the fruit. I looked behind the sacks and found to my disgust a great number busy about the peels. I stamped fiercely upon them and traced their line across the room, crushing them with my hands.

The ants climbed the wall, following a fissure in the plaster, running a fine and crazy path across the cold and damp plaster, from the angel's feet to his face. Pressed into my palm I discovered a single wheat grain. The ants ran across the angel's lip and disappeared where the crack widened at the corner of his mouth, grappling with small morsels of lemon pith, paper thin flakes of plaster, and grains of wheat.

Intrigued, I explored each room, checking the floors and walls behind the burlap sacks. As I searched up the stairs and through the hallway the rancid odour of fermenting grain grew stronger, leading me back to the room where the merchant had stored his stolen tithes. The corn, indeed the entire floor, appeared as black as molasses and seemed to shift and seethe as indeterminate as water. The corn was carpeted by a thick mass of ants, a colony the size of which I had never seen. Many thousands of ants burrowed, tumbled, and laboured with grains swollen twice their size.

With such a mass of ants, I could not see my way to the window to continue digging at the stone. I crept along the wall to the fireplace. Sliding my hand across the cool marble lintel, my fingers chanced upon a soft cloth package. Lying on the fireplace, wrapped in a velvet pocket, was a slender ebony cross fixed with an ivory carving of the crucified Christ. Catching what little light there was, the gaunt white body shone like phosphorous.

"Help me," I prayed. "Save me as I cannot save myself."

Even as I wept, I heard footsteps behind me in the hall.

Adrian has spent the whole day in bed. I try to persuade him to dress, saying that when he is ready we will have dinner in the hotel, but he complains that he has no energy. Instead he sits at the table in his shorts drawing over an old comic. I can hear him scribbling while I shower. Pretty soon he begins to rip the pencil through the paper, furrowing into the wood.

"What did you mean when you said the government paid for this?" he asks.

"When?" I ask. "It was a joke. They're giving us some assistance to locate a new factory here. I have just spent four hours with three city officials in a swamp twenty miles from here. Niles? And they're promising me that they can have the land drained in four weeks. Look at my trousers." I hold up the soiled cuffs. "Sodden. Their new enterprise zone is nothing more than a godforsaken bog."

"I went to school near there."

"I told them it would be nice for a garden centre maybe. But this is the last of their sites, and I think they could just see it disappearing from them. But it doesn't have to be here. How would you feel about a trip?"

I look at the boy. He is staring down at his magazine.

"We can talk about it later," I say.

The boy slaps his forehead.

"Do you intend to join me, or do you intend to sulk?" I ask, standing beside the bed drying myself. Adrian sharpens his pencil.

"Well?"

In a flash of anger the boy hurls the pencil at me. I am so surprised that I do not even duck, and the pencil strikes me on the forehead. Rubbing the spot with my finger I see that I am bleeding.

"What did you do that for?" I point the finger at him with a very small smear across it.

"Stupid idiot. Why didn't you move?" he replies.

"I don't believe you just did that," I exclaim.

Adrian tuts, "Pathetic," and leaves the room.

"What's that you said?" I ask, doubly wounded.

"Nothing," he slams the bathroom door shut.

I check in the mirror; there is a tiny red puncture high on my forehead.

"You might have blinded me."

On the mantlepiece is a gift, a cassette recorder, which I had left that morning. The money has been taken but the gift remains wrapped. The wrapping tape peels up the side where it will not stick.

"All I want you to do is see a doctor. I'll come with you."

"What do you think they'll want to do? Hold my hand? Take my pulse?" he shouts from the bathroom. "They'll talk about partners. They'll ask about you."

"Hold on a minute," I knock on the bathroom door. "Did I miss something?"

"I have mouth ulcers, swollen glands, a fever, my lungs hurt."

"Adrian?"

He turns on the shower to drown my voice.

"They will make me take an AIDS test," he screams.

I clap my hand to my mouth, horrified that I would want to laugh.

"Adrian. I think you should at least allow a doctor to make that decision. Let me in. Nobody will make you do anything."

The boy is silent. The door will not budge. "I'm going to call the front desk unless you let me in," I say.

There is still no answer. I walk into the bedroom and stand over the telephone. "I'm at the phone right now. Think about it. I'm picking up the receiver." This is stupid, I tell myself. "I'm dialing the number." I have no option but to call the front desk. "It's ringing."

"Big fucking deal," he shouts.

The door shudders as he kicks it.

I hang up and sit on the edge of the bed wondering what to do.

"Adrian, where did you go yesterday?"

There is a click as the bathroom door is unlocked.

The boy sits naked on the wet floor. The tiles are slippery with steam. I sit beside him and offer him a towel. Water bleeds into my shirt as I cuddle him.

"Just lay off me." The boy shrugs me away.

"What's happening here? What's this all about?"

There are blue and red lines scribbled across his chest and forearms.

"What's this?" I ask.

"What?" he bluntly replies.

"These lines."

"It's a marker pen. I was bored, so I drew in my veins and arteries."

"What for?" I ask.

"I said I was bored," he shouts. "Bored, bored, bored, bored, bored."

He shuffles across the tiles, out of my reach.

"I don't understand what this is about." I try to make him speak. "Do you? And why have you saved all of the money I gave you?"

The boy turns briskly.

"What money?"

"It's in your sports bag, under the bed."

"What are you doing going through my bag?" he asks very quietly.

"I didn't do it on purpose. I just pulled it out." I stop excusing myself. "Under the bed is hardly a smart place to put something you want to keep private."

"Where else is there?" he retorts. "This place is so fucking small."

He slaps his hands onto the tiles, stands himself up, and leaves the bathroom. I remain seated on the bathroom floor.

"I only want to help you," I say.

"When I was first here—" He leans back into the bathroom. "—there was this guy I worked with. He was older than me, like maybe twenty, twenty-two. One of the porters would get us into this hotel, mostly just for old men. Once or twice we'd fuck and they'd watch—that way we'd get a room for the night. Mostly they just wanted to watch us jack off."

Spitting on his forearm he tries to rub away a red felt tip drawing of a flower.

"This was about three, four months ago. After I moved in here with you I barely ever saw him. He said I was being ripped off, that I was soft. Every time he came he'd steal or cause trouble. In the end the porter wouldn't allow him into the hotel. He got to be sick, real sick."

All the time he is talking he rubs at his forearm, trying to erase the flower.

"I kept all of your money, I'd been putting something aside for him 'cause I felt guilty. Like I'd abandoned him. Seeing as how he'd helped me out.

"I didn't want to turn up with nothing. I had to save. I kept thinking that whatever we could do with a hundred dollars we could do better with five hundred. And then I didn't know what to do about you. The longer I stayed here, the more difficult it became to leave."

"What was wrong with him?" I ask.

"What do you think?" he replies.

"Was he sure?"

"How sure can you be? At first he thought it was hepatitis, because he'd had that before." He pauses. "Maybe it was. I haven't seen him since. Maybe he was just blowing me off."

"But it worries you."

"What do you think," he shouts at the top of his voice, shaky, high-pitched, verging on tears. "What do you think?" he asks.

For a while I stared into the darkness. As quietly as I could, I slid down the wall and crawled on my belly along the floor and into the fireplace, acutely aware of every sound of my hands and knees scraping across the stone, and my uneven breaths.

The merchant stood in the doorway and called me to him.

"Quickly," he whispered. "If you leave now you will have the whole day, and he will never find you."

"What will happen to my family?" I asked.

"The grain has been sold," the merchant replied, "sooner than I expected. It is better that you are not here."

"How far can I expect to travel on my own?" I huddled, uncertain, in the mouth of the fireplace. The merchant did not reply.

"You aren't going to let me go, are you?" I asked.

As I waited for the merchant's reply there came sounds from the hallway. From behind him, I could hear the magistrate's cane clicking irregularly upon the flagstones. The merchant ran across the room and fell to his knees in front of the fireplace.

"Not one word," he whispered, forcing me inside the fireplace.

The cavity was barely large enough for both of us to stand with our heads inside the chimney funnel. The merchant pressed me to the stone wall, clutching my head to his chest.

We cowered together listening to the old man's familiar uneven footsteps as he walked toward the chamber. The merchant tried to scratch himself but was unable to raise his hand without his elbow striking the stone.

"Ants," he whispered.

The magistrate's footsteps became softer as he stepped upon the ants. A low guttural wail rose from the old man's throat and filled the room as he howled at his discovery of the spoiled grain.

Soundlessly the merchant unbuttoned his jacket and hitched up his vest, and pushed my hand inside. Running my hand across his skin in the darkness I could feel hundreds of ants swarming across his sweaty stomach. Small black mites agitated through the scabs and hairs on his chest, and try as I did to crush them, his irritation grew. He fidgeted so much that I was afraid that he would break into laughter and give us away.

I could smell the old man, his rotten breath and the stale scent of cigars were even stronger than the fetid stench of the rotten corn. So close were his sobs, that I guessed him to be standing beside the fireplace.

In agony the merchant rolled his head, chewing his knuckles so that he would not cry out. His abdomen flinched as the ants swarmed over his belly. Fearful that his restlessness would give us away, I kissed and twisted the man's nipples. But he only began to writhe more. I unbuttoned his trousers and grabbed his testicles. Ants swarmed over my hand and his hard cock.

As quietly as I could I raised my left leg and bound it about his buttocks, and had him crook his elbow under my knee to draw our hips closer. Holding his cock I carefully sank down and gingerly inserted him into my ass until I could feel his trouser buttons scratch against my leg. Fixing my hand about his sack I again twisted, making him swell inside me. I could afford only short brisk movements.

The magistrate's monkey sprang into the fireplace. It seemed certain that we would be discovered. But as soon as the creature settled on the hearth it began to scratch and pick and slap at its fur, tormented by the ants. The monkey leapt wildly out of the fireplace, crazed by the ants, and sheltered on the magistrate's shoulders.

Unaware of the monkey the merchant began to thrust, jamming my back against the sooty wall. He teased the bulb of his cock between the lips of my ass until he slipped out altogether. Pushing violently back in, he thrust up and spat jissom inside me. I bit hard on his hand and tasted blood. His body knotted hard and jolted. Slowly he exhaled, and although the ants continued to crawl over him, he no longer seemed to mind.

Unaware of the commotion, the old man whispered a benediction and slowly shuffled through the spoiled grain.

As the magistrate walked down the hall and out of the apartments the merchant began to chuckle. Finally, when he could no longer hear the click of the cane, the merchant burst into laughter. Concerned that the magistrate would return I placed a hand over his mouth, but he brusquely pushed me aside.

Together we rolled from behind the fireplace. Kneeling across my chest he slapped and brushed away the ants; as he buckled his trousers a knife fell to the floor.

The merchant picked up the knife and crossed himself. On the wrist of his right hand was a small tattoo, an outline of a lily flower.

"How many others like me have been here?" I asked.

The merchant shook his head as if there were too many to count.

"Then kill me."

The merchant raised the knife and pressed it against my neck, but he was unable to draw down the blade.

*　　*　　*

The porter shifts his feet and crosses his arms as I talk to him. I have a small roll of money in my hand.

"What do you want this boy for?" he asks, smiling at the money.

"I understand that he's been working here. In the hotel."

"You could ask at the reception. They would be able to help you with employees."

"You've never heard of this man? He's about twenty-two."

"I'd try reception." The porter nods.

"I wouldn't actually say that he was employed by the hotel," I insist. "I'd say that it was more like he was working for you."

"But I don't have any staff under me, sir," the porter says, smiling.

I shake my head and return the money to my pocket.

"I would try reception," he repeats.

With the telephone directory open on my lap, I call the hospitals, using the telephone in the hotel's lounge. The receptionist is insistent. "If you don't have a name, then there isn't much I can help you with," he repeats himself. "You will have to try the police department. Though frankly there isn't much for anyone to go on."

I have, it seems, been on the phone all morning. The more I pursue Adrian's friend, the more ridiculous it seems. It is beginning to dawn on me that there might easily be no friend.

If the story is a lie, then I am unable to fathom its purpose. Certainly the whole body of the story is not false.

The next morning as I was trying to clear a pathway through the ants and corn, I heard the iron grate and the doors being opened. Running to the stairwell I watched as twelve pigs were herded into the hall. I counted as each pig was thrown through the doorway. The pigs ran screeching about the rooms, raising dust, trampling over the drapes, and fighting fiercely with each other. As soon as they were all inside the gates were closed and the doors were bolted.

Adrian swims surrounded by blue as I watch him from the balcony. The chlorine is so strong that it makes my eyes sting. He lies on an inflatable raft, kicking his feet so that he spins slowly round. He knows that I am here but chooses not to acknowledge me.

I walk around the pool on the running track and remove my jacket—it is uncomfortably hot.

"Adrian Darling," I call across the pool. The boy tilts his head. "How is your shoulder?"

He answers "fine," and looks down into the water.

"Do you intend to do anything about it?"

He does not reply.

"Or do you think it will just go away?"

"Just shut up," he shouts, turning his raft about to face me. "You're always on at me. Leave me alone."

He suddenly stops. I hear a door beneath the running track open and close.

"What's that?" I ask.

"Somebody else wanting to swim," he replies in a calmer voice. "He's gone now."

He stares into the water as if thinking.

"I'll come with you. Whatever happens."

"Look. Just leave me alone, Mister Chocolate Salesman. I know all about doctors. My father's a fucking doctor. Just leave me alone."

I woke early to the squeals of pigs. Drunk on the fermenting grain, they had begun fighting. Unable to sleep I made my way upstairs. Water dampened the steps and I began to run, eager to check the hole that I had made in the aqueduct.

It was still dark and raining torrentially. On entering the chamber I could clearly hear water pattering into the room. The ants had gone, and the stench had subsided. What had been no more than a spout as wide as two fingers had enlarged itself to a runnel as round as my wrist. I pressed against the stone and found that it was loose. Pushing harder, I was able to rock the stone; each time it crept further forward pushed by the great weight of water in the aqueduct. I needed something to pry the stone out.

Remembering the cross, I climbed down and ran to the fire-place, sliding against the grain. As I unwrapped the crucifix a pig ran shrieking into the chamber, the magistrate's monkey riding on its back, gripping the swine's ears. The animal listed to one side, unable to run straight; it veered towards me, until it suddenly collapsed. The monkey leapt onto the grain. Kicking its heels the hog continued screeching, ripping at its belly with its hooves. Blood frothed from its mouth and I realised that it had been poisoned.

The stone dislodged from the aqueduct and hammered onto the floor. A funnel of water belched into the chamber swilling the blood from the pig's mouth.

I ran out of the room and slipped as I hurried down the stairs. The monkey scurried before me. As soon as I ran into the hallway, the merchant sprang in front of me, and punched me in the throat, knocking me to the floor.

At the end of the hall in my bedchamber sat the old man, in his black suit, both hands resting upon his cane. The red dress lay at his feet. The monkey leapt upon his lap and climbed onto his shoulder.

Beside the dress were the two bowls of candied almonds.

The merchant kicked me, coughing, across the floor towards the magistrate. Beside the magistrate's chair lay another pig, twitching, labouring for breath.

"Kill me," I begged the merchant. "Kill me now."

But the merchant continued kicking, shunting me across the floor. I gripped his feet and implored again that he should swiftly kill me.

"It wasn't me. I didn't spoil the tithes. I didn't touch the tithes." I appealed to the magistrate. The merchant punched me again in the throat and I could not talk. Picking me up from the floor, he violently swung me across the chamber to the magistrate's feet.

"Yesterday I brought you a gift," the old man said, pushing the bowls forward with his cane, his head shaking with irritation, "and I see that you have not eaten one of them." Bending down he carefully selected one, and popped it into his mouth.

I could not answer, and looked from the magistrate to the body of the pig. Water dripped from the ceiling, beating steadily upon its hairy hide.

"Permit me." The magistrate reached down and picked out another sweet, and rolled it in his palm. The merchant fastened one hand to my forehead and another to my chin and forced me to open my mouth. The old man placed the almond on my tongue.

Immediately it began to fizz and make a bitter froth. I tried to spit out the candy but the merchant clapped his hand over my mouth and would not release his grip. The old man rubbed his cane against my throat waiting for me to swallow. The sugar around the almond dissolved in a sharp, caustic phlegm, numbing my tongue. My chest burned for air. My eyes began to water.

I feigned a swoon and spat the almond into the magistrate's lap, but could not prevent myself from swallowing the phlegm. My tongue became numb, and I could not talk. My stomach burned, my eyes rolled, and my body sank without will against the merchant.

The merchant pushed me forward so that my head slumped upon the old man's lap. I heard the bowls of sugared almonds tumble across the floor, and watched the small white eggs spin across the flagstones at the magistrate's feet. Help me, I prayed, because I cannot help myself.

The merchant pulled the dress, red, stiff, and stinking of blood, over my head. So poorly had I been fed in the last few weeks that the bodice could easily be fastened. Sharp hooks stitched on the inside of the dress snagged at my skin.

The merchant hitched up the skirt, spread apart my legs, and opened his trousers. As he pressed into me, the skirt fastened tighter, its hooks digging deeper into my flesh. I began to bleed upon the magistrate's lap.

"Wait." The old man turned my head, and looked into my eyes. "Not yet."

The merchant thrust hard, forcing my breath out. A spasm caused me to retch up onto the old man's lap. The seizure left me shaking. My arms, splayed on either side of the old man's legs, began to shake involuntarily.

"Wait," the old man pushed the merchant back. Help me as I cannot help myself, I prayed.

The merchant's limbs shook with pleasure, and the magistrate took his sharp cane and pressed its blade to my neck, waiting for the merchant's signal to slit my throat.

The merchant thrust harder and faster. Soon he began to moan. The magistrate twisted the blade, ready to draw it down.

A formidable crack echoed through the apartments, and the wall behind the magistrate's head appeared to breathe out. Water streamed from the angel's mouth as a fissure rent the mural in half. The whole ceiling swelled and burst in a great torrent. A massive surge, a wall of water, tumbled into the chamber. Sacks swept from the upper floors battered through the wall, sweeping the merchant away.

The initial cascade forced all across the marble floor, filling the chamber with such a rush that it was impossible to stand or raise oneself without being forced down. My mouth filled with silt and grain as I slid across the floor. What appeared to be other human forms were pigs caught by the torrent and swept into the chamber.

I found myself swept across the slippery floor, into the hall, stomach and lungs full of grit and water. A second wave greater than the first burst through the wood doors, pushing the iron grill open, vomiting a thick black viscous mud into the hall. Furniture from the street, tables and chairs, rode the flood, spinning rapidly, seeming to struggle like the livestock.

The torrent turned as abruptly as it had begun. Water continued to pour from the aqueduct but the current had found its route, and swept past the villa's doors with a mighty roar, drawing with it the water which had destroyed the room. Water cascaded down the marble steps, pushing the sludge back into the street and closing the iron grill.

I was able to stand, retching into the water. My wrists and ribs ached, the dress gripped tightly about my chest, and I bled profusely. Light shone through the doorway. All about me lay crushed lemons swept from the orchards, and furniture shattered and broken against the walls. Above the brackish earthy smell of the mud was a more terrible odour, a base stench of animal, odours which our skin holds in. Chickens and pigs lay face down as if the flood had sprung from their mouths. The crucifix stuck upright above the water, protruding from the body of a pig.

The monkey had kept itself above the water riding and jumping to whatever flotsam came in its path. As the flood subsided, the creature leapt up the balustrade, its dun-colored, olive green fur matted to its skinny body.

The merchant sat clear of all the debris, eyes open, the water still about his calves, his hair matted to his forehead. The man bound one arm about his stomach, concealing a fearful gash, and picked with his other hand at the bark and citrus blossom which had stuck to his body.

The old man was trapped against the grill, held beneath the water by the dead body of a big black pig. Of his face all I could see was his open mouth; a ruby red pool streamed from his lips. His teeth had pierced and half severed his tongue. Sugared almonds fizzed in the water about his face. I rolled the pig aside. As he rose to the surface his eyes moved. I stood twice upon his chest to force out his breath, as he rose gasping to the surface a second time, I scooped up the sugared almonds and thrust them into his mouth, but the old man spat them out.

Plucking the crucifix from the pig's flank, I was able to break his clenched teeth and pry open his mouth, forcing the tablets one by one into his mouth.

Three villagers intent on pillaging ran up the steps. They stood uncertain beside the grill, watching me hammer at the old man's mouth with the crucifix. Forcing the gate open, they pulled the magistrate free, and held him high above the water. Red foam issued from the old man's mouth as he spat out the almonds, and his hands grasped at the doorway, flailing, attempting to draw himself down to the water.

Seeing the magistrate being taken from the villa, the monkey sprang from the balustrade and tore at the neck of one of the rescuers. Loosing his grip the man fell backward, dropping the magistrate so that his head cracked against the marble stones.

Blood spilled from the magistrate's open head, flowing into the grooves of the lily flowers carved into the stone steps. The monkey sat upon the magistrate's chest, plucking at his bruised mouth, bending forward as it had for food, its black nose brushing his lips as if kissing or drawing out the magistrate's breath.

Squatting in the water beside the merchant, I fished out the last of the sugared almonds from the mud and fed them to him. Beside him lay the magistrate's cane. Taking up the cane,

I pressed it to the merchant's neck, and ripped the blade across his throat. A black and bloody fountain burst from the merchant's neck, spattering the room, dropping and dissipating into the water.

I stand beside the pool, washing my hands in the water. The boy swears.

"What's the matter?" I ask.

He paddles the raft round to the side of the pool. Water catches in the small of his back as he kicks his legs.

"Look. I scuffed myself."

He shows me his elbow. There is a small red rash about the size of a penny where he has cut himself.

"How did you manage that? You'll wither like a prune if you stay in there much longer."

As he puts his arm back into the water a thin wisp of blood catches on the hairs of his arm.

"What are you staring at?" he asks.

"Why don't you come here and kiss me," I ask.

He slides off the craft and swims closer to the edge. As I reach over he suddenly smiles and slips backwards into the water, closing his eyes.

I pick up my coat and decide to wait for him in the lobby. I watch his body change, alternatively stretched and compressed by the water's refraction. Now he is a boy, now he is a man, once more he is a boy. Just for luck I touch the water.

TEN REASONS WHY MICHAEL AND GEOFF NEVER GOT IT ON

• RAYMOND LUCZAK •

1. THEIR PHYSIQUES DIFFERED FROM EACH OTHER'S.

Geoff was six-one with broad shoulders and a thick back; he didn't like to think too much about his growing pot belly. He recently had to go out and buy a whole week's worth of 38-inch underwear, and the other morning after a shower it struck him that through his blondness he was balding in very much the same pattern as his father's.

Michael was five-eleven with narrow shoulders. No matter what he ate, he just couldn't add another pound, and it had taken him a long time to feel comfortable enough to play volleyball at a nudist beach the previous summer. Some men had found the different colors of hair on his body fascinating: the blondness of his short bangs, the redness of his beard, the blackness of his chest hair, and the brownness of the hair on his arms and legs. Michael's red beard complements the shape of his slightly weary face very well. He dresses as if everything is an afterthought; no one at work minds, because he works in Creative at an advertising agency in the East Forties.

Michael is something of an oddity where he works, though. He wears a hearing aid in one ear and his speech is clumsy, sometimes incomprehensibly nasal. He figures that as long as hearing people already realize that he's slightly different because of this, he will refuse to hide his hearing aid in a mass of his strawberry blond hair. He keeps his hair cut around his ears.

They both desired a physically bigger, older man. Michael was 23; Geoff, 32. But when they first saw each other, each had thought the other was older. Later, when they were introduced, Michael was relieved to find that Geoff didn't mind the fact that Michael was nine years younger; after all, Michael was used to being taken for 30 because of his full beard.

When Michael first saw Geoff in the copy room on his floor, he had thought, He must be at least three years older than me. Geoff was clean-shaven, had slightly curly blond hair, and an eaglelike nose.

And when they first saw each other, their eyes locked.

2. THEIR AMBITIONS WERE TOO DIFFERENT.

Michael was a graphic arts student at Gallaudet University in Washington, D.C.; he was able to sell a few of his collages, and they were included in a group show here in New York. But he'd come to the point where he wanted very much to be in the same position as Lorraine Louie, who had her name printed on the back covers of Vintage Contemporary Books and Random House's *Quarterly*. He felt some of her stuff was beginning to look contrived, but her graphic style was instantly identifiable, which counted for something. That was the kind of reputation he longed for. Otherwise he was content where he was, working as a storyboard artist. He agreed with the aphorism his younger sister had once repeated to him when he became frustrated because he couldn't understand the deejay's voice on "America's Top 40": "Keep your hopes high, but keep your feet on the ground." He knew he wanted to continue making those collages: People kept saying that they'd make him famous. He wasn't sure he wanted fame. It was far more important to find a man who didn't treat his deafness as something cute but as just another part of him. And for the time being he was very content to live where he was, on the northwestern fringe of Park Slope in Brooklyn; the apartment was generously large for the rent.

Geoff had for years been a pipe dreamer, but lately he'd

decided to make money. That was his biggest reason for putting in so many hours in the first six months at the agency before bypassing three positions to become budgeting supervisor for six of the company's biggest accounts. He was fairly pleased with himself, considering he'd never actually completed his finance degree at Washington University in St. Louis. Maybe in two years' time he'd have enough for the first down payment on a nice co-op somewhere on the Upper West Side. He would've preferred to live on the Upper East Side, but he knew that neighborhood was completely unaffordable. If only he could meet a handsome rich man. . . .

3. NEITHER COULD AVOID MICHAEL'S HEARING LOSS.

Geoff does not remember seeing Michael's hearing aid at all until they happened to ride down the elevator together at the end of the day. Geoff had run to make the elevator as its doors were closing, and he stepped in right next to Michael. "Oh hello," he said. They'd never spoken.

It was then he saw the hearing aid up close, a flesh-colored comma perched on Michael's ear. The earmold caught a little of the fluorescent lighting from the elevator's ceiling, and Geoff wondered how much Michael could hear. He knew something about deaf people; his sister Ruth had told him some about her deaf students in White Plains, north of New York City. He didn't know any sign language, and he wasn't even sure if Michael knew it. Well, he'd find out soon enough.

Michael nodded and smiled slightly.

Geoff noticed how easily Michael blushed. Michael's freckles seemed awash in that peculiar pinkness; seeing this turned him on. While they didn't speak any, Geoff was suddenly very aroused by noticing the way Michael was trying not to look more closely at him. He thought, *I have to know this guy.*

When they got off the elevator, Michael nodded again while they moved through the revolving door out of the lobby. Michael wanted to follow Geoff, but he didn't know what to do, so he walked uptown, with furtive glances back at Geoff, who was walking the other way to his subway station.

A few days later, when they met again, homeward bound, alone on the elevator together, Michael surprised him by extending his hand. "I'm Michael Osbourne, and you are . . . ?"

After such a bold introduction, Geoff was relieved that he couldn't blush. "Geoff Linnesky."

"I'm really busy tonight but let me give you my number. I'm not so deaf that I can't use the telephone."

"Sure. Sure." Geoff watched Michael scribble his number. He was struck by the volume of Michael's voice, and the slightly pinched enunciation.

"Here. Now it's all up to you." Michael smiled.

Geoff took the number and thought, *He wants me to take care of everything. But if Michael made the first move, he was supposed to call, wasn't he?*

The third time they boarded the elevator together a few days later, Michael leaned over and said, "I didn't catch your name the last time. How do you spell it?" He had his pad out already.

Geoff wrote it down and smiled. "Are you busy tonight?"

They ended up walking through Central Park. It was May, and the evening was warm. They walked through Midtown, and in their conversations about their lives, Geoff noticed how difficult it was for Michael to lipread him. He had never heard "What? Pardon? I'm sorry, I didn't catch that," so many times in the space of a few hours. A comment from Ruth came back to him with some force: "You have very expressive eyes, it's too bad you have to mumble so much." Of course he'd always been interested in sign language ever since he learned how to fingerspell as part of his Boy Scout training—why couldn't he remember the letters now that he needed to? He felt somewhat frightened because he could understand Michael's speech well enough to know what he was talking about, and that created a feeling of inadequacy: *I can understand him but he can't understand me.*

So Geoff asked Michael to show him various signs, and among these was "fuck." When Geoff repeated back to Michael, he felt giddy when he saw how Michael blushed.

As they reached Columbus Avenue, Michael said he had two tickets for that evening's spring production given by the National Theater for the Deaf. Geoff agreed to go, once Michael told him it would be voice-interpreted. Michael also said he knew quite a few of the people who would be there, and he assured Geoff that he could show Geoff a few conversational signs—besides "fuck" and "asshole." Michael told him that if he showed that he was willing to try to use sign language, he'd do just fine. Geoff nodded, not wanting to wonder too closely: What if he didn't know how to read a sign? Or what if he fumbled with his hands the way he mumbled? Or . . . ?

Before the play began, Michael tugged Geoff over to a small group of friends. He introduced Geoff to them, and they nodded and smiled, but then they all had curious, waiting looks on their faces, as if they had expected something more from Geoff.

Geoff felt suddenly intimidated. What was the sign for "Sorry"? He didn't know, or he had forgotten, or both, and he wished he were somewhere else. He wanted just to stand around and talk and laugh the way he usually did in the lobby before a show began. He felt even more lost when he watched deaf people hug their friends and sign so quickly, and even though he tried to watch them closely, he just couldn't understand them. What were the signs Michael had taught him? He felt like he was treading around the lobby with useless hands. He just nodded, "How do you do?"

During the play, though, Geoff felt deeply aroused by the way Michael pressed his fingers warmly under Geoff's elbow; he was afraid to look at Michael when he did that. Finally, he did look, and he saw that Michael's unblinking eyes were shining brightly from the lights from the stage. He had never felt such warmth shiver up his spine, and he grinned. He wished he could learn the sign for that shimmer in Michael's eyes; there had to be a way. He'd seen enough of Michael's signs to believe that hands could most certainly convey such specifics.

Geoff found the play itself touching—not so much the play, which was a rendering of a Restoration farce, but how clear and comprehensible the deaf performers were on stage. He heard the voices, but his eyes were riveted on the deaf actors. There was a logic, a beauty to what they were doing. He found himself wondering why he had been so intimidated by the notion of interacting with deaf people. They laughed at themselves, but he still felt a little embarrassed when he laughed too. He could tell that his laugh was among the few that sounded "normal" among the dozens that were raw and strange and howling—but primal in the pleasure they took from the visual jokes. They weren't afraid of their bodies, either. Maybe that was what seemed to make Michael so different, Geoff thought.

At the reception afterwards, Michael took Geoff around again and introduced him to his friends. Geoff just nodded, mumbling, "How do you do?" He had forgotten how to sign, "Nice to meet you."

When they left the theater, Michael said, "You could've at least *tried* to sign something. I showed you how to greet. . . . Deaf people do really appreciate it if you just *try*."

"I'm sorry."

Michael said nothing for a while as they walked toward the Times Square subway stop. "I wanted them to like you as much as I do. I just feel like shit for going to all that trouble for nothing."

Geoff looked down. "I'm sorry."

"Please."

"What?"

"Don't look away from me when you talk to me. Otherwise, how can I read your lips?"

"I'm sorry, okay?" In that moment Geoff forgot how warm he'd felt while he watched Michael's eyes shining so brightly during the play, drinking in the performers; he forgot about asking Michael to come to his apartment that night. He said instead, as they parted to their own trains home, "I'll see you tomorrow."

While Michael took the long ride to Brooklyn, he continued to feel like shit. He knew it would've been better to attend the play alone and not have to worry about enunciating clearly for Geoff. He could have just let his hands do everything. *Fuck.* He should've waited till he knew Geoff better.

He took out his hearing aid and fingered it a little inside his denim jacket pocket, hoping that he would run into Geoff tomorrow.

They would have to talk about this.

4. THEY WERE BOTH LONERS.

Geoff had never gotten along with his parents. He never went back to synagogue after his bar mitzvah. In the seventies, he grew his hair into a weird afro, sought sex in bathhouses, and fell in love with pot. He left St. Louis for New York only two months before he would have received a B.S. in Finance. At the time, he thought, *Why not? Fuck everybody*. He could graduate somewhere else.

Through the years, he found he enjoyed being alone, yet he was beginning to get tired of drifting around. In New York, he gradually became the consummate sexual drifter: He knew which porn movie theaters had the best dark places, which doors in which peep booths could lock or not, which hours attracted greater numbers in which places. He never actually thought much about these things; they had simply become part of his routine. He was too much the hunter to worry about the annoying flashlight checks of the attendants. He had thought, when he first started frequenting the same kinds of places in St. Louis, that he might eventually find love. He could at least expect to chat a while with regulars, but even that made him feel uncomfortable. He didn't see himself as a regular patron of these places; yet he was. Although he couldn't admit it, he was absolutely terrified of the fact that he'd evolved into leading a double life: by day, an openly gay man with a good-paying job, and by night, a guy who was willing to grope just about anybody in the dark. Still, the allure of these encounters, the efficient pleasure they provided, and the ongoing possibility of connecting—he'd exchanged phone numbers with over fourteen eligible guys—made returning to these sexual emporiums seem sensible enough.

Michael had grown up reading. Books were a land where he never had to lipread; he could eavesdrop on everything. He grew up in a family of seven children, yet he felt alone; he was used to people turning their faces toward him, whenever they spoke to him, but from an early age he began to feel set apart. If everyone turned their faces toward each other whenever they talked, then he wouldn't feel so different.

As for sex, he couldn't talk about it. It wasn't in his nature to brag, or to wish that a man he'd met would call again; he had been let down far too many times. He eventually decided that some men wanted to sleep with him only because they found the idea of tricking with a deaf man exciting in some way, but none of them seemed to care for anything more. Michael quickly got enough of drifting around.

Michael wasn't like some of his deaf friends who were eager and willing to accept whatever hearing people said at—so to speak—face value, and this actually became a kind of burden for Michael himself. Why weren't there more intelligent deaf men out there? And why couldn't an intelligent hearing man be willing to learn sign language? He often shuddered at the prospect of misunderstandings during an argument, and because of this, he decided that his next lover would have to learn it. If not, then he'd have to leave. He was used to being alone anyway.

5. EACH WAS CONCERNED HOW THE OTHER WOULD APPEAR TO HIS FRIENDS.

By the time Geoff had lived in New York for nearly a decade, he had accumulated a small group of friends either from having slept with them, or from finding they had similar interests. Most of them were concerned with making money and living well, while Geoff had lived in his cramped apartment on Ludlow Street for over eight years.

He thought often about the feeling he had whenever he entered their apartments: how beautiful, how white, and how spacious their places were. He remembered waking up the morning after meeting one of them, and thinking, *If I could be his boyfriend, then everything would be just perfect.* He concentrated on making a go of it, but he found each man unwilling to be more serious. But how could anyone with money take him seriously once he told them that he lived on the Lower East Side?

Whenever he received invitations to weddings and house-warming parties, he felt envious, but he was careful not to talk about it. "Lucky you." People always laughed. "You're still single, you're still eligible, you can sleep with anyone you want."

Not only that, he felt he wanted somehow to become closer again to his sister Ruth. When he'd moved to New York, she let him stay with her, and she'd showed him around the city. Walking the streets of Manhattan, they'd become very close, talking always about what they hoped their future boyfriends would be like. The similarities of their hopes were often a revelation.

But when Ruth met John, everything changed. She married him, and now he'd become some kind of an executive for a large food company in White Plains. She got a teaching job at the local residential school for the deaf, and the school in White Plains was so much nicer than the one in New York. John told both of them that he knew all about Geoff's "lifestyle," and he kept himself at a distance, much to Ruth's chagrin. Geoff didn't much care; as far as he was concerned, John was a complete asshole.

Meanwhile, Ruth began trying to convince Geoff to stop working at his low-paying accounting firm job downtown and to start looking for a higher-paying job. "You have to dress well to attract the kind of man you want, so how else will you be able to do it? Steal?"

In truth, it was rather obvious from his clothes that Michael didn't appear to care about making a whole lot of money.

Michael wanted just enough to live on comfortably; when he met Geoff, he began to fret: Should he dress up like him, or should he dress the way he always had?

After much thought, Geoff decided not to tell Ruth about Michael, even though she might be tickled by the idea of him falling for a deaf man. She was fluent in sign language; he had thought about asking her for some pointers on how to communicate better with Michael, but decided against it. It would be a waste of time: Michael could never fit in with Geoff's friends anyway, or even with Ruth and John. No, it was better that Ruth didn't know about Michael.

And Michael was sure his deaf friends would surely turn stony toward him whenever Geoff was around; Geoff was so hard to lipread, and he was so unsure of Geoff's ability to sign with them. Maybe they still resented the fact that he could communicate with almost any hearing person he liked. They couldn't do that so easily. Still, they were his friends because they shared the language. Unlike anyone else, they understood how separated from the rest of the world life could feel because one couldn't hear the radio, or because one had to wait to watch a TV news report that was close-captioned. Michael knew from experiences growing up that something that's funny—in a group conversation—is killed when it's repeated so soon after its first occurrence. The joke is no longer spontaneous; it sounds contrived. So Michael had always felt ambivalent about having a joke repeated. Having to endure such second-hand humor all the time without asking was bad enough.

Michael wished more than anything else that Geoff would take a sign language class at the Chelsea School of American Sign Language, where he taught two nights a week; he had even teased Geoff about being his teacher there. If Geoff didn't try to learn sign language, then all his friends would whisper among themselves, Why did Michael pick *him*, when it seemed so obvious that Geoff just wanted to use him, the way a lot of hearing guys always did?

But why couldn't they be patient with Geoff?

6. MICHAEL DREW A CARICATURE OF GEOFF.

Michael rarely did caricatures of anyone he knew, but one afternoon when he stepped out of the 3rd Street exit of the West 4th Street subway station he saw the portrait artists and cartoonists lining up on Sixth Avenue. This gave him an idea.

At home, after trying many approaches, he finally settled on patterning Geoff after James Bond in his trademark tuxedo, substituting Geoff's head for Sean Connery's. As he sketched carefully in charcoal and added dramatic touches with India ink, he found himself unable to stop smiling.

One morning as they happened to step aboard the same elevator, Michael said, "Can I show you something in my office?"

"Sure, sure." Geoff was curious to see how Michael might decorate his office. It was like anyone else's, festooned with posters of Prince and wiggly Keith Haring drawings; Geoff noticed a light-flasher switchbox near his telephone.

Michael took out the drawing. "It's for you."

Geoff coughed. *The craft was amazing, but really, this was too much.* "Well, I don't know what to say," he said. "I—I like it, though."

As Michael gauged Geoff's reaction, he immediately wondered why he'd even bothered. He nodded instead, and said, "I'm glad you like it."

Later that day, when Geoff took the Second Avenue bus downtown to the Lower East Side, he thought, *Michael is a romantic.* He remembered the men he had dated and how they had set up their apartments in candlelight with a rose in a slender vase on the table between them—and how extremely uncomfortable he'd felt. He didn't like the idea of going through all that trouble to make everything so romantic. Geoff thought, *Last thing I need is another romantic in my life.*

7. THEIR DEFINITIONS OF THE IDEAL LOVER WERE DIFFERENT.

Geoff was most attracted to men who were tall, rather clean-shaven but with a healthy spurt of dark hair out of the collar just below the neck, and slightly older. The ideal lover would be muscular, monied, and masculine in his interests; he would be interested in the woods and not care so much for shopping at Bloomie's. He would be well read in many areas, and would be able to conduct intelligent conversations about anything. He would also have a sarcastic sense of humor. He wouldn't feel the need to tickle Geoff, because that always made him feel more tense afterward. He would want to live in a very nice co-op on the Upper East Side, and have a great group of friends who were always a blast whenever they got together. They would smoke joints now and then, and giggle away their highs together. His ideal lover would be well versed in classical music, Mozart and Verdi most of all. He would be a great fan of experimental films, and he would beg to see another Alma-dovar movie if one was being shown in New York. They would play Trivial Pursuit occasionally and make the most passionate love. His ideal lover would have a big dick, and a very hairy and very round ass, and nipples that got hard whenever Geoff's fingers touched them through his Ralph Lauren shirt. His ideal lover would have style and an elegantly casual way of looking at things. He would never grow into a tacky old queen with friends who never quite made it to the altar; he'd stay very virile while they grew old together.

And Michael was most attracted to a man who was tall, had a nice beard, and was slightly older. His ideal lover would be hearing and have a natural ability to learn sign language easily and quickly; he would be very affectionate with Michael in public and in private; he would enjoy their strolls through art museums together. He would enjoy cooking gourmet meals, he would prefer to rent close-captioned videotapes than attend nonsubtitled movies at the theater, he would buy a TDD—a Telecommunication Device for the Deaf which would transmit through the phone whatever the person on the other end typed on the screen—so he could talk with Michael anytime without having to rely on the TDD/voice relay service; no matter that he would also have a crystal-clear voice easily understood over the phone. He would never mumble. He'd be very expressive in his humor. He'd tickle Michael under his feet because that was one of Michael's favorite turn-ons. And his ideal lover would love books. He would enjoy going to sign-interpreted theater performances and deaf theater productions. And everyone who met him would accept him as one of them. Not only that, he would be propositioned often, and he would shrug them off in ASL with, "Me-sorry but me-taken. Ask Michael first." And of course, no one would dare ask Michael for permission. They'd live together in the Village, and their neighbors would be couples who wanted to be couples and who wanted to learn sign language too, and they would play pinochle and have elaborate dinner parties at each other's place. . . .

8. BOTH HAD LIVED WITH A LOVER A FEW YEARS BEFORE.

Michael had lived with a deaf lover for over two years, long before he'd moved to New York; in fact, his sudden move to New York was his attempt to lessen his ex-lover Tom's fierce sense of unrequitedness.

Geoff had lived for four years with Nick, who was six years older, and it had taken him two years since the breakup to concede that it had been a very bad relationship, that Geoff had been cheated on so often, and that he'd hoped for too much too soon. But he sometimes thought about Nick, only because he hadn't yet found anyone who really wanted to live as a couple, to build a home.

So, while Michael and Geoff were both willing to try again— this time with someone new and different—each arrived in the other's life with a separate set of expectations, and each felt like—though they weren't—damaged goods.

9. MICHAEL WAS TOO DIRECT FOR GEOFF'S COMFORT.

During one of their lunch breaks at a public fountain on East 50th Street, which turned out to be their last together, Michael asked, "Did you have a chance to look at the schedule of sign language classes? You know, the one the Chelsea School sent you?"

"I just don't have the time."

"Well, if you need to borrow some money to go, I'd be happy to help you out. I'm just tired of guessing what's on your lips." His eyes didn't seem to Geoff to shine as brightly as they had before. "I can arrange a discount for you, if that's a problem."

"I'm sorry." Geoff wondered again why Michael had to make him feel so inadequate. What about Geoff's *own* needs, god-dammit? Couldn't he just talk about anything and not worry about being misunderstood or having to repeat some things twice? Why couldn't they just be telepathic, the way all true lovers were supposed to be? "You know how busy I am," Geoff said at last.

Michael said, "Well, I believe that if something is important enough, I make the time for it. I'm busy too, but if you're willing to make the time for us, I'm willing too."

Geoff said nothing for a moment. Finally he said, "You're too romantic."

"What was that?"

"I said, *You're too romantic*."

"I don't understand what you mean by that."

"It's like—you want flowers, poems, and all that, and I'm just not that type of guy—"

"You have an ideal lover in mind, right?"

"Well, who doesn't?"

"Lots of people don't. But people who *do*, I call them romantics. And they seldom admit it." Michael stood up, his sandwich half-eaten. "You're a romantic, Geoff. Fuck you if you think I'm too romantic for you. Ideals change. We could have been wonderful."

And Michael left the sound of the fountain thundering in Geoff's ears.

10. GEOFF DID NOT KNOW HOW TO APPROACH MICHAEL.

After that, Geoff stayed more and more in his office, knowing how Michael liked being outside for lunch. He kept an occasional eye on the pedestrian traffic below his office window; it was the only time he could observe Michael without him knowing it. He went instead to the company cafeteria for lunch, chatting almost listlessly with his co-workers and trying not to remember.

One morning Geoff was standing at a urinal in the men's room when Michael came in. Michael looked away as he stepped into a stall. Geoff shook off his dick and zipped up. But he took his time, washing his hands with soap and glancing back under the stall door where the jeans were crumpled atop Michael's black Reeboks. He wondered what kind of underwear Michael wore, and then it occurred to him that Michael must be waiting for him to leave.

Then there were those elevators in the morning. Michael stood at a distance while they waited in the lobby, smiling hellos to everyone except Geoff. Meanwhile, Geoff would pull his *Times* over his face until they arrived at their floors. Such scenes repeated themselves in Geoff's mind all day: Why couldn't Michael live and let live?

He wants to be able to say, "I'm sorry," but he doesn't know the signs.

Geoff starts to see other men, but it's not the same. The *men* are the same as before, but something about Michael will not let go. He looks at the small handbook of signs and realizes the only sign he remembers is for "fuck."

He stares after Michael now and then as he walks down the corridors of their office building, and feels his heart opening a little again. *No.* He must go on looking. And no, he is *not* a romantic, goddammit.

In time, Geoff does leave for a better job, this time on Madison Avenue. He has mostly forgotten about Michael, until one day he notices a messenger in Spandex shorts pulling out a package of storyboards for the receptionist. He recognizes that it is unmistakably Michael's artwork; he closes his office door quickly.

Michael also notices Geoff's absence and goes on to date other men occasionally. But it's not the same. When Michael falls asleep beside them, he imagines himself curling a little closer to Geoff's chest, trying to hear the sound of his own heart beating.

THE GREEK HEAD

• PETER WELTNER •

OUR WORLD, MINE and Charlie's, resembled theirs, Don's and Roger's, only superficially. It was curious that Don and I both managed record stores, though his was twice as large as mine and three times more successful, and that Roger and Charlie were both vice-principals at middle schools here in the city; that Roger and I both came from Providence and that Charlie and Donald grew up, if thirty years apart, nonetheless within blocks of one another in San Mateo; that Don and Roger had met in 1946 in a bar located in the same block as the bar in which Charlie and I met twenty-nine years later; and that the first several letters of our pair of last names were the same, Don Ross and Roger White, Charlie Roberts and Sam Whitten. But it was only curious, nothing more. People are constantly taking accidental facts and arranging them into some kind of order, as if to show, in this instance, that the two of us were destined to become friends with the two of them. But that's not how it happened, of course. We saw their "For Rent" sign before someone else, that's all. And, if the truth were told, we didn't really get along all that well, not well enough to be described as truly successful friends.

When an artery in Donald's brain, having apparently already ballooned, finally exploded, I was at lunch with a guy named Rick whose ad I'd answered—eyes wide open and skeptical, not expecting much. Of course, it turned out he was the one to be disappointed since he had apparently believed, when I'd told him on the phone that I was currently uninvolved, that I'd meant "really." Though we'd agreed nothing would come of it, the meal still lasted too long because I had been trying to justify myself to him and to myself at the same time, attempting to explain that all I had meant to say was that I was unhappy. Nor was I home later when Roger first pounded on our door at a time when I'd told him I'd be sure to be back from work in case he heard anything from the hospital. He had heard something. Donald was dead.

I knew that there was no need for me to feel guilty. It was just a mistake, something bad that happened while I was looking for a way out of my life and not paying attention to much else. Still, if you were to ask me how my life was going these days, I'd answer, as Don used to when he was down in the dumps, "In low water." I knew one of us, either Charlie or me, should have made the break and gotten it over with long ago. But neither of us did, perhaps because it's so hard nowadays to be certain whether one is behaving rationally or from fear. Charlie figured I was safe, I figured he was safe, so it was OK. We were all right together. Or that's what we pretended: safe, safe, discontent, and safe.

That's just another way that Roger and Don weren't like us, only seeming the same. They argued all the time too. But the difference is that they were never afraid. They had never been afraid of anything, not of each other, not of splitting apart, not of the world's opinion of them, certainly not of dying. They understood as well as anyone that nothing was forever. But they endured. They stuck it out anyway. They had become famous for lasting. Thirty-nine years they had been together, thirty-nine years and counting, Roger had said when Charlie and I had helped them celebrate their anniversary right before last Christmas.

It was a familiar number by then, they'd repeated it so often, but all of a sudden it seemed a miracle to me. Their entire lives were somehow like the one brief moment when Charlie and I had just become lovers and we'd flown to the Cape to rejoice in our success. All week long the weather was beautiful, mild. We rode rented bikes, swam, walked the beaches, strolled the strip, danced at the Sea Drift, drank too much, ate too

much, got too much sun, made love, were happy, the night
sky so clear as we lay back on the sand it seemed as if the
souls of all our just spent seeds' unborn children were blinking
to us from the stars. It didn't last. The first fight after our
return to San Francisco almost destroyed everything. Like pil-
grims in search of consolation, we took another trip, this one
to Seattle. It worked. When we got back, we found the apartment, its garden for our use too.

The days after Don's death as Roger waited anxiously for
Don's sister Susan to arrive, we could hear him pacing overhead, especially at night. It kept even Charlie awake, who if
tired enough could easily fall asleep while having sex. In earlier
years, we might have known what to do about Roger, might
have known better how to behave and what to say so that we
might have believed some of it ourselves. But we had given up
speaking about such things or trying to affect the course of
grief, Charlie months before me. Don's was the third death of
a friend in a year that was barely a month old. The other two
had been twenty years or more younger, and their dying had
been much more painful, taken far longer, and been terrible to
witness. Why waste more useless words on Don's death? It
had been easier, much easier, than most. He was almost old.
He'd been, he said, a happy man. Wasn't that enough? Let
Roger remember all of that and quit stomping down on the
floor, on our ceiling, as if it could do any good.

A big and awkward man, Roger seemed to be foraging for
food, the refrigerator door opening and slamming shut over and
over. Or was it only ice he was after? It annoyed us and was
meant to annoy us. I was sure of it. We could hear the anger
in it, expressed as well in the clogs he had apparently exchanged for his usual soft slippers, an anger directed against
us and our silence, I figured, at our failure to have offered him
any comfort, sham though it might be. It was funny in a way,
like the bratty kid spoiling it for all the others because he hadn't
been invited to the party. For the first time, Roger had to
envy us for something more substantial than our relative youth.
Unhappy as we were, we still had each other, if we wanted,
for a while longer. There was still a party of sorts downstairs,
even if it was breaking up. And, momentarily at least, he hated
us for having it. I knew he did.

Because of him, we were eating breakfast much earlier than usual. "I didn't know they bothered to carve clogs in a size fifteen," I remarked. "Those things must weigh ten pounds each." It sounded like dumb bells falling in a gym or like furniture dropping.

Charlie said nothing. He was quietly furious. He had just found the new ad I had cut out and boldly circled, and he was refusing to acknowledge it. It didn't puzzle me why I had left it out on the top of the bureau like that, exposed so blatantly under the lamp's light in an otherwise black room as if deliberately to call his attention to it, the way lately he had been calling my attention to the fact that he had masturbated while I was gone by leaving a porno mag or two lying on the night stand top rather than hiding them back in the drawer where he knew I knew he kept them. The previous night I'd been searching for my one pair of black socks in the back of my bureau drawer, thinking I'd need them for the funeral or whatever. But I didn't put everything back in. That was why I was pretending to look for those socks. I was preparing to pay Charlie back for the golden boys he had been fucking in his imagination yesterday afternoon—if it was only in his imagination, since Duane had entered the picture. So it went. We were each trying to let the other know he wasn't necessary anymore. We had been trying to tell each other that for a long time. Only in the past we had bothered to be subtler.

Charlie chomped down hard on his toasted bagel and with one hand opened the interior shutters behind the kitchen table. The sky was already a radiantly pure blue, the surprising storm which had sailed through last night having netted up all the junk that usually floats in the air and left in its wake only a few wisps of clouds.

I sipped my coffee. Why does it never taste as good as it smells? That had been Donald's annoying question nearly every morning when we four were in Baja together on a week's vacation four years ago last winter.

"Which of these shells do you like best, Charlie?" I prodded. "I think this one is probably my favorite." I shoved it over towards him from the pile in the middle of the table that Roger had arranged as a centerpiece, though it had early become unglued. "What do you think?"

He picked the shell up, examined its shape, so much like a dragonfly's wing and nearly as transparent, and tested its firm, sharp edge, like a knife's. His duty done, he tossed it back to join the others, no two alike, Roger had boasted. "It's OK. It's pretty."

"Right," I said and stared back out the window. It had been a dumb question on a lousy topic, the centerpiece itself something we kept on display only to please Roger. I'd hated the foul, variously infested town on the southeastern coast where Don had directed us all because it was supposed to be such a great spot for diving. Charlie, of course, liked it. Ever since, each time I had mentioned anything about it, Charlie scowled at me exactly in the same way, as if he owned this one special mask whose sole purpose was to remind me that my bad time there was no one's fault but my own. But that was like Charlie. The bad times anywhere with anyone were always another person's fault, and he had designed lots of different scary masks to let them know it. Yet the truth is that Charlie is much better company than I am. Nearly everyone says so. I've told him so many times myself.

I glanced up at the ceiling. "Roger seems to have settled down."

"So it seems. Maybe he's gone to bed." Charlie checked his watch. "Finally." He folded our newspaper and laid it on the table next to my elbow. "Talk to him today, will you? Find out what's going on with him. What did that note say? That Don's sister was to be here at least by tomorrow, didn't it? She's next of kin, for God's sake. Roger's got to have his wits about him, even in this enlightened era. Try to calm him down some."

"Why don't you?"

"Because I'm going to work." He took a last swallow of his yogurt drink and stood up.

"So am I."

"Yeah. But not for four more hours."

"So what? I don't get it. What's the big difference?"

"You don't have to get it. Just do it."

"Why are you avoiding him, Charlie?"

"Why are you?"

"I'm not."

"Like shit you aren't," Charlie said. "You're avoiding Roger every bit as much as I am. And we both know why."

"We do?"

"Oh, cut the crap, Sam. You don't want him to know we're really breaking up this time. I don't either. Not now, not yet. It's that simple."

"Are we?"

"What?"

"Are we really breaking up this time?"

"Of course. Don't be an ass. We've been doing it for months and months. I suppose it's just taken me this long to find the guts to say so. Now all you have to do is to find the guts to admit it." He walked around the table to position himself behind me and bent to kiss the back of my neck. I shivered. "No scenes now. We promised, remember? I've got to go. I've got a lazy teacher to bawl out."

"It's still early," I protested.

"I know," he said and left the room.

I sat in my chair motionless, nearly rigid. Outside our window, the city looked dazed too, as if it had yet to recover its breath from the blow of last night's storm's wild punch. Twenty or thirty minutes at least must have passed in silence as the sun strolled over a golden flank of Telegraph Hill. Never had a place seemed more beautiful to me than San Francisco at that moment, until Roger resumed his pacing, the thud, thud, thud, pause, thud, thud, thud, pause, and turn as regular and as infuriating as a madman's dance.

So I didn't go up to Roger's. I couldn't yet, I just couldn't do it. I was too angry at everything and at everyone, at Donald for dying and messing things up this badly, at Roger for grieving and carrying on, and most of all at Charlie for having walked out on me before I'd summoned the courage to leave him first. I was furious at all of them for their not having asked me whether this was the way I wanted it or not. And something, maybe it was my heart, was jumping up and down inside of me like Rumpelstilskin in a rage at having been found out.

To pass the hours before work, I watched two "I Love Lucy" reruns, early ones full of the kind of slapstick and mugging that Charlie hated, and then I took a long intense shower,

soaping my whole body repeatedly to feel the pleasure of washing myself clean over and over again—in the process, however,
apparently stripping my pores of all their oil because after I'd
dried myself off my skin was like an old man's, like Roger's,
old parchment from which all the legible writing had long ago
faded.

I stood in front of the mirror, disgusted by my own body,
then opened the medicine cabinet door and drenched myself
with Charlie's precious baby oil, watching it soak in and bring
me back to life like the rush of tide over the body of a beached
and dying starfish. It worked. The evidence was that I wasn't
so bad off after all. I'd panicked needlessly. There was some
semblance of youth left in me, not much perhaps, but enough
for a while. Basking in the sunlight piercing through the bathroom window, I almost glowed, the oil covering my body like
an unguent that might protect it from the world and time.
Before I could dress, however, I had to wipe most of it off
with a towel to keep it from seeping into my clothes. So much,
I thought, for magic.

I left Roger a note taped to his mailbox, assuring him I'd
drop by that night, after I got home. I walked to work. There
was still time, lots of time, and the day was too near perfection
to lose altogether, the winter's light pure, the views unimpeded
for miles, all colors everywhere reduced to either bright blue
or stark white, like the earth in pictures taken from the moon.
Chinese New Year was to be early this year, apparently. Firecrackers were exploding somewhere up Jones Street and down
Greenwich too. As I turned to walk up the steps, a cherry
bomb exploded behind me.

Don always dreaded these weeks because the noise reminded
him of the sounds of battle and especially of the time when he
was wounded on Kwajalein. That was practically all he ever
mentioned about it, just a little grumbling during the two
weeks or so every year when firecrackers burst all around us.
The festivities didn't bother Roger though, Don said, because
Roger had held a desk job in Honolulu throughout the duration. Don's eyes gleamed as Roger blushed.

As I paused on top of Russian Hill for a couple of minutes,
standing in one corner of the park on what Don liked to call
"our" hill—meaning his and Roger's, mine and Charlie's—and

gazing northward over the bay towards Marin, I remembered his saying how the sky here on such brilliant, weightless days was like the Greek sky he and Roger had seen so often, a strange, oddly suspenseful sky as if some god were just about to step out from it. Constantly in Greece, he said, it came as a shock to discover that eyes so dazzled could see so clearly. He had winked at me, a bright glint in his imp's eyes, touched me briefly but firmly where he knew I wouldn't forget his fingers had been, the running shorts and jock that separated my flesh from his flesh somehow immaterial for the moment, and he walked away, never again to make that sort of advance. Charlie and I had been living downstairs for only six months. I still don't know what sort of claim Donald was staking that morning, if any. But recollecting it, I cried a little for the first time about his being dead, until finally I pulled myself together and hauled ass the rest of the way to the store.

Only later that night, after I'd closed the shop and turned off all the lights except for the one over the counter and gone in the back to use the john, while I was sitting there in the dark without accomplishing very much, did I think of Don again with that sort of clarity, as if he were standing in the flesh by the door, grinning that half-salacious, half-beatific smile of his, like that time he caught me coming out of the shower. I had stomped back into the bathroom and grabbed a huge towel to wrap around my middle.

"Don't you ever knock? What the hell are you doing barging in here like this, Don?" My hands were shaking, I was so mad.

"You're angry," he said calmly and started to whistle "Danny Boy," which he called "Sammy Boy" to irk me.

"Stop it, Don."

He quit, leaned back against the jamb, and crossed his legs at the ankle, looking quite pleased with himself. "Care to join us for dinner tonight?"

"It's late, Don."

"But you haven't eaten?"

"No."

Without moving any part of his body, not even his eyes, he surveyed the room. "And Charlie's not here," he observed.

"He's at some gay political meeting. Get out of here and let me dress, will you?"

"What are you ashamed of, Sammy?"

"Don!"

"Charlie's never minded. But then he has a better sense of fair play. It's only a peek I want, after all." I let the towel fall. "Very nice. Sam, Sam," he clucked. "You think the whole world's out to make you, don't you? That's why you're always so on edge, doll, like some sweet young thing out on the streets alone late at night checking over her shoulder to make sure no one's there. But you'd like someone to be there, wouldn't you? Wouldn't you, Sammy?"

I dressed quickly. "Maybe Charlie and I should move out."

"I thought we were going to be friends, we four."

"I'd hoped so too, Don."

As he two-fingered a cigarette out of his shirt pocket and lit it, I wanted to beg him to stop, but it was absurd to try. Don would smoke even after he was dead. We all knew that, though he did manage to refrain sometimes, like when we were all driving somewhere together. "Listen to me, lad," he said and drew in a lungful of smoke. "You imagine I'm on the make, don't you? Well, maybe I am in a way. But Roger and I are happy. We've been happy together all these years. And do you know why? Do you know why he's really all I want, old fart that I am?"

"I wish I did," I said honestly enough. "I wish I did know, Don."

"It's because neither of us ever expected more from life than what it gave us, including each other. I mean, Roger was pretty spectacular when I first met him. But so were lots of other men, if you get my drift. We just never wasted any time hoping or waiting for something more or better. We made it work, doll. Do you understand me? Is my message clear? We made it go."

"You're not telling me very much, Don."

"You kids," he said, snickering, gazing down absent-eyed at the ember of his cigarette. "You young pups. You know what? I wouldn't see the world as you kids see it for all the hunks in this town. It wouldn't be worth it. It just makes you all so angry, thinking you can have everything and everyone, because you can't. You never could. It's such an elementary truth.

Roger and I, we made do," he stressed once more. "Who believes that's enough anymore?"

"I don't know. Don?"

"What?" He grinned at me, his smile as pure and as enigmatic as any virgin's.

"Please don't do this again."

"Do what?"

"Surprise me."

He chucked my chin. "Dinner's at nine," he called behind
him as he strolled out the door, turning back briefly only to
disentangle his favorite fraying red cardigan sweater from the
latch where it had caught.

It was after ten and I was still thinking about Don by the
time I wearily walked in the door of our apartment and
switched on the light. Charlie had left a note in an envelope
out on the mantle, but I didn't want to read it. Instead, I made
straight for the kitchen, grabbed a bottle of scotch from the
cabinet over the sink, and carried it upstairs.

When Roger opened the door, his appearance shocked me.
Why was I so disappointed? What had I imagined, or hoped,
I'd find? He looked great, clean shaven, casually dressed but
dapper as always, his dark eyes bright and quick as a curious
child's, no heavy clogs on his feet after all but only his usual
well-shined loafers.

"I could use a drink," I said, offering him the bottle. It was
less than half full, but it didn't matter. Roger wasn't much of
a drinker either.

He accepted it. "A hard day, Sam?"

"You could say that. I kept thinking about Don."

Roger smiled down at me sympathetically. If he and Don
had ever played good cop/bad cop, Roger would have been the
good cop, the pal, the buddy, the one with the smile you could
trust until you confessed. I followed him into the kitchen where
he filled the glasses with ice cracked from the tray and poured
in enough scotch on top of it to leave room for only an inch
or so of water. He tasted it, grimaced, and pointed back out
to the living room where, glass in hand, I pursued him to
the window which overlooked the deck and garden with their

splendid views of the bay. "What a clear night!" Roger exclaimed.

"Yes," I agreed. "It's swell. Roger?"

"Sam."

"I'm sorry."

"I know you are, Sam." He laid a kindly hand, wide and warm, on my shoulder. "I know you are. Don was cremated today, incidentally. Around noon, I think. We'll sail him out onto the bay in a few days, perhaps Sunday, and sneak him into it, just as he wanted, you and me and Charlie. His family." He withdrew his hand.

I didn't know what to do or to say so I said only, "That'll be fine, Roger."

"Good. Good."

"Roger?"

"Yes?"

"I haven't meant to be avoiding you." When I jerked around to look, he was no longer even pretending to smile, his face creased with a frown like that teachers use to express disappointment at your failure. "I mean I haven't known what to say. I still don't know what to say."

"Yes," he nodded too eagerly. "It is difficult, isn't it?" He took a sip of his drink. "Come over here," he directed me, indicating the love seat opposite the one he had just flopped into.

A small, restless fire burned in the fireplace to my right. Between us stood a glass-top coffee table covered with the usual art and travel magazines scattered about. But the Greek head sat as always exactly in the center, handsome and proud and serene. I bent over to touch its eyes, as if to keep them from staring up at me.

"You know I wasn't with him when Don stole that," Roger said.

"I know," I said. "You were . . . ," but I stopped myself.

He placed his sweating glass carefully on top of an old *Holiday* and folded his arms across his broad chest like someone with a chill. "Only that strange, wonderful woman who had attached herself to us in Perugia. By the time we reached Rome, Cecille was simply a part of us and our vacation. To this day, I don't understand how it happened. She had broken her leg climbing up to some forbidden monastery high in the Tyrol and was on crutches when we met her in that little café. How she had managed to see so much on crutches without our help I never figured out either. Without a word from either of us, she understood the score right off and never once tried to interfere. In fact, if anyone became jealous, it was us of her. How that woman enjoyed Italy!

"Then, when I got so sick in Rome, Don and Cecille went everywhere together and immediately afterwards told me all about it so I might feel I'd done it all too, been everywhere, seen everything with them. Nine years later, when Don and I returned to Rome, it was so strange because I did have this powerful sensation I actually had done everything they'd told me about. It was Don who was all the time having to straighten me out. 'No, no,' he'd say, 'Cecille and I told you about this place. You weren't here. You were flat on your back in that miserable pensione, poor guy.'

"He was right, of course. And yet it all really was that vivid. The whole city. Cecille and Don had described everything so perfectly it was like life. It was like having lived the words in a book." Roger took another sip from his drink and settled back deeper into the couch's plush cushions, staring into the flickering fire. The apartment was too warm. Don's and Roger's rooms, wherever they were, were always too warm. Yet they were both big, husky men. "I miss him, Sam."

"So do I. So does Charlie," I added as an afterthought. "Already very much."

"Maybe that first trip was our best," he mused. "We felt so lucky to be alive after the war, especially Donald. It had been terrible, but for us in a way it had been lucky too, since it had brought us to new worlds and eventually here to San Francisco. I'd just finished at State under the G.I. Bill. Don had made some money at that original store he'd opened downtown. We were in love. I mean that. We were really in love. We neither of us had ever been to Europe before. It was wonderful."

I couldn't look at him. "First trips can be like that," I suggested. "The best. Or the worst. So much is being tested."

"Tested? Perhaps." His eyes seemed fixed on the fire. I could only hope that he, unlike me, wasn't picturing Don's naked body on a pallet sliding into a burning chamber. He had started to cry, very quietly.

"Roger?"

"I'll be all right. In a minute. In a minute. It's just that we hadn't expected it. We thought there would be more time." He attempted a smile. "But I suppose that's only human, always hoping for more time than fate is willing to give you."

I reached over, picked the Greek head up off its stand, and fondled it in my lap. "It's very beautiful, one of the most beautiful, sexy heads I've ever seen. It must weigh twenty pounds, Roger."

"Surely not so much. It's funny, though. We've never weighed it. Think of all the countless things we must have weighed in a lifetime, but we never weighed the head. We shipped it home surrounded by many, many cans of olives that concealed what was placed in sawdust in the center of the box. To fool customs. And it worked. So I only know what it weighed with the olives, not by itself. Don and I were eating those olives for years afterwards," he said, laughing, "serving them to guests too, especially in martinis. We saved one can, for good luck. It's still in the cupboard, the last I looked.

"The Italians were digging up heads and other bits and pieces of classical statues, Greek and Roman, all over the place in those days. It was the war. It had disturbed so much earth that practically every backyard or field yielded one antique body part or another. They simply didn't know what to do with them all. Too many living people had lost parts of their own bodies, or their loved ones, for them to care much about bits and pieces of broken statuary. There are times in history, and this was one of them, when art doesn't mean a thing. Not a thing. So some museums were actually littered with fragments of classical sculpture lying around in basements, in courtyards, in gardens, scattered all over floors. Nobody had the time or the money to do anything with it except pile it all together somewhere.

"I'm exaggerating, of course. Still, it was quite easy, Don said, for him and Cecille to steal this one. She was on her crutches, of course, and had to carry a big bag, more like a sack, draped over her shoulders to hold her belongings, like her wallet and all those mysterious woman's things that in those days seemed so indispensable. Don simply waited until the coast was clear, decided upon that head there, lifted it off the cluttered table where it lay with other black marble pieces, and dropped it in Cecille's bag. Then they walked calmly out—or rather he walked calmly out and she somewhat nervously, she reported, hobbled out behind him. Isn't that amazing? You see, Cecille didn't want Don implicated if she were caught. She was convinced, she said, that she could easily charm her way out of any Italian jail. I imagine she could have.

"It was to be a present to me, for having missed so much. It's funny. I don't recall feeling I'd missed anything at all. And yet if I hadn't been sick, maybe Don wouldn't have gotten the nerve to pull off the heist. Cecille, well, for her it was a game mostly, something to do so that she could prove that she could do it. But Don wanted to accomplish something spectacular for me. For us, I mean. No matter what else might happen to us in our life together, we'd have this special thing no one else like us would own. A real Greek head, early fourth century B.C., Cecille said. Ours, Don's and mine. A work of art for her two Greeks, Cecille said. She loved that phrase. Her two Greeks. Because it was her gift too, after all, the beautiful thing that remains after everything else has died, she said."

I carefully placed the head back on its stand, the one Don had built for it thirty-five years ago, picked up my drink off the floor, and drained it. "Are you going to be all right? Would you like me to sleep up here tonight? Roger?"

He wiped his eyes. "I must have bored you with that old story."

"Not at all," I protested, though in fact the story had bored me. I couldn't concentrate on it and kept shifting to Charlie, as if he were naked and aroused downstairs in bed. "What did you say, Roger?"

He shook his head. "I said, 'Don't be silly.' I'm fine. Do me a favor tomorrow instead though, will you?"

"Certainly."

"Help me entertain Don's sister. She'll be here around five or so. Come for dinner, why don't you, you and Charlie. Let your assistant handle the store tomorrow night. I'll need to talk to her alone first. But I'd like to spend as little unprotected time with her as possible. She's always blamed me for Donald's problem, as she calls it."

"Blamed you?"

"For making him abnormal or something equally nonsensical. I don't pretend to understand such people. Wouldn't it be marvelous if we actually did have such power? She'll have a fit about the cremation, of course."

"She didn't know?"

"There's a family burial plot outside of San Mateo, someplace up in the hills. They all expect Don to lie in it. He said no way. But they didn't believe him. It's strange what some families won't believe, isn't it? I have Don's will to back me up. I've already had to refer to it a couple of times, though I confess I haven't been able to bring myself to read it yet. Don told me the essence of what was in it. That was enough for me."

"You ought to read it," I recommended.

"Yes. Eventually."

"I should go, Roger."

"Thank you, Sam." He stood up and pecked my cheek.

"For what?"

"For conquering your fear at last and coming up. You see, I'm really all right, aren't I? There's no need to be afraid."

"I wasn't afraid."

"And Charlie? He's not afraid either?"

"He'll be up to see you tomorrow, Roger."

"Good." The toe of his shoe poked at the rug. "I guess I'm the odd man out, now, aren't I? Our traveling days together are done."

"I don't see why," I said, though I knew exactly what he meant. "Don wouldn't want your life to stop anymore than you would want his to if you had died first," I counseled.

"But I didn't," he said bitterly. "I didn't die first. Good night, Sam." He opened the door for me. "Oh, by the way. What was Charlie doing at home much of the midafternoon? Is he sick?"

"I don't know," I said and almost stumbled out.

I lay still dressed on my bed, unable to sleep and impatient with all the night sounds of the city that seemed determined to keep me awake, and I could hear Roger pacing again, more quietly this time, the circle he was making growing steadily smaller as if he were spiraling towards some still center where he and I both might find some rest. The first time I woke up, the light I'd unknowingly left on in the hall, dim as it was, nonetheless nearly blinded me when I opened my startled eyes. After I'd jumped out of bed and switched it off, however, the moon's light bathing the living room was as soothing, as refreshing as the morning sun on those late summer backpacking treks Charlie and I used to enjoy in the Sierra when we'd hiked high enough to be alone, leaving Roger and Don a couple of thousand feet below, since the rare air wasn't good for Don's heart and Roger was afraid of heights. So it goes. So it went. Later, I would fall behind too, as afraid as Roger, while Charlie and Don, to all our surprise feeling stronger again as he got older, climbed far above.

My stomach growled, my head ached from hunger, my toes itched. Propped there on the mantel, Charlie's note seemed not so much to glow in the moon's rays as to be illuminated from within, like a child's night light. For a moment, long enough for me to reach for it, it consoled me and made me feel safe. But then I read it.

> Roses are red,
> Violets are blue,
> I'll be back for the heavy stuff
> When the rent is due.

In the bathroom, I flushed the bits of torn paper down the toilet and tried not to look at myself in the mirror. It was dark enough that I almost succeeded. I didn't look in Charlie's empty drawers or closet either.

Half stripped of what belonged in it by Charlie, the bedroom began to smell slightly of disinfectant, like a hospital corridor. For a well man, however worried, I had been in too many sick rooms lately. You can't suppress the smell of death. Clean the walls and floors, the glass, the tiles, the chrome, the sheets and other bedclothes. Take out the bodies. Death still sticks to things. It can't be hidden, any more than old people can conceal the smell of their dying flesh with fragrances or young bodybuilders can hide it beneath their sweat. The skin always stinks of it, lurking just beneath the surface the way the rain-drenched earth, full of rot, lingers just under the sweet, musty odor of any rose or the taste of a ripe peach. It was there, too, in the absence Charlie had left behind.

For the first time in nearly three days, I heard Roger walk the long way down the hall to their bedroom, tucked back in that part of the house which cut into the hill, for their flat expanded considerably beyond ours. He moved slowly, almost staggering across the floor as if something heavier than the weight of sleep drew him on. A door shut. Then the whole house grew quiet, as if it, like me, had been waiting for Roger to find his way back to bed and rest.

Though the night was chilly, I undressed and walked out onto the deck naked, as Charlie and I would sometimes do to make love on a couple of air mattresses, pretending we were back in the high country. The moon had just slipped out of sight. Directly overhead, an airplane flew, its red warning lights flashing, and banked towards Japan. Early last September, Don and Roger had tried to talk us into going there with them the next summer. Don said he thought he'd almost forgotten enough about the war to enjoy a visit. Roger maintained all he cared about was seeing a real rock garden, not an imported one, since theirs was obviously missing something, but that if he had his way they'd be going to the Dordogne. Charlie jumped at the proposal. I was less certain. I had been promising myself someplace alone with Charlie, though I didn't know why or where.

Now there would be no trips. I hunkered down and gripped the deck's railing with both hands to keep from toppling over, a sudden gust of emotion blowing through me without doing much damage. I wanted to feel sad, I really did. I wanted badly to feel sad about something real, at least about Don's death or Charlie's leaving, if not about all those other deaths and departures that were taking place around me, as if daily. I needed to grieve, but I couldn't. Real sadness, I thought, had to be like fierce desire, a thing of the moment, doomed not to last, but nonetheless profound and enduring in its effects. I believed that once Charlie and I had experienced such passion. It hadn't lasted much longer than the first six months, if that long, and yet I thought we could live off it for the rest of our lives. Apparently I had been wrong. We had both been mistaken. But, if I couldn't love him anymore, I wanted at least to feel the sorrow that was supposed to follow his going. Then I could grieve for Don too, clinging to the memory of each of them as to a lost hope.

I slept poorly, went to work early, left the store early, having put my best clerk in charge for a few days. While waiting downstairs for Susan to arrive, I pictured her as a tall, gaunt woman dressed in severe black, a handsome woman, handsomer than her brother, her hair the same iron gray as his, her eyes dewy, her lips atremble, her fingers still nimble enough, however, to turn the pages of a will with care. As usual, my fantasy was wrong. When, having heard a car turn into the driveway and park, I peeked around our living room curtain, I saw a short, dumpy, henna-rinsed, slightly comical-looking old bag dressed in a white frocklike dress dotted with cute little blue birds. She was so pudgy that she had to use both hands to haul herself up the stairs. Once on the stoop, she stood there panting, the loose skin on her neck quivering like a biddie's wattle, and she repeatedly poked at the buzzer with an uncertain finger. She was still breathing too hard to speak when Roger opened the door for her.

Less than an hour later, Roger stamped down on his floor three times, paused, then pounded down three times more, the usual signal that he and Don were ready for me and Charlie to come up and join their festivities, whatever they were—drinks and dinner, a sample of a just discovered Burgundy, fresh brochures from their travel agent or a consulate, more recently a new movie on their VCR. They wanted us to share in nearly everything they bought and participate in almost everything they planned because, Don enjoyed saying, they were that rare phenomenon, a one-couple couple and thus truly monogamous.

Neither Charlie nor I ever got around to telling either of them how uneasy that attitude made us. Instead, we simply went along with it, coasting, since we liked them and since they, unlike ourselves, were always so full of plans. Yet Roger's coded stomping on the floor had early on irked us both, perhaps because it sounded too much like an official summons, and Charlie and I resented all such commands, all orders, anyone's telling us what to do. Someone's telling somebody, the wrong somebody, what to do was the origin of all the world's revolutions, Charlie remarked one afternoon, glancing up at our throbbing ceiling. I was positive that it was the origin of most of the trouble between Charlie and me. Or maybe Charlie and I just didn't have the patience for the long haul.

Roger clomped down again, this time, however, only twice and with so little force to it, so weakly, that the message it sounded seemed more like a plea than a command. When a few seconds later he met me at his door, he boldly shoved me back down a couple of steps and dramatically shut the door behind him, his pale face as sad as a mime's. He was panting. "Sam, oh Sam," he said. "You wouldn't believe what I've been going through with her." He gestured behind him.

"Try me."

"She's a—a—a Baptist," he finally managed to say. "Can you believe it, in this day and age? I mean, she believes in it all."

"That spells trouble, Roger," I warned.

"She's already informed me three times that she intends to leave all her money to the church and has recommended at least as often that I do the same, for the good of my soul. Why do I have this feeling that she thinks the sooner I go to perdition the better it will be for everyone? What a gabby woman." Roger wiped his brow with his handkerchief, his eyes blinking too rapidly. "You know what I think? I think that old bat is going to contest the will. I think she believes it's her Christian duty. Christian duty," he spat. "Can you imagine?"

I didn't try to hide my surprise. "She's read it?"

"She's reading it," Roger sighed. "She insisted."

"And what about you? Have you? Have you read it yet, Roger?"

He shook his head nervously. A lock of hair, dirty white like raw cotton, fell over one eye. He pushed it back. A truly handsome man, it occurred to me once more. "I've wanted to, Sam," he said. "Truly I have. It's only . . ."

I tugged coaxingly at the sleeve of his blue dress shirt. "Only what, Roger?"

"I'm not sure. It sounds so silly to say it out loud. I've been afraid, I guess."

I took his hand gently in mine. "Afraid?"

"Of surprises. I didn't want to discover any surprises. Isn't that strange? After all these years, after forty some years of Don's and my having been together one way or another, in good times and bad, I'm still not completely sure of what it is that we were together. And wills are such absolute things. You understand. There's no going back and changing them, is there?" He glanced over my shoulder. "Isn't Charlie coming too? I had been hoping he'd be here as well. I need all the support I can get."

Though I had been expecting it, the question nonetheless startled me. I pulled my hand back and, awkwardly shifting my body away from his, began to fall backwards, grabbing for the railing. Roger caught me by the collar of my shirt and held tight until I regained my balance. "Well," he said. "I suppose that answers that question."

"Does it?"

"Yesterday, wasn't it? Yes, it must have been only yesterday. He was carrying too much out for just a trip. But I suppose I pretended not to notice. Give him a day or two more," Roger advised. "Then, if you don't hear, call him. That's what I always did with Don, the few times he left me. That's what he did with me, the one time I left him. You know where he is?"

"Not really. But I can guess. He's at Duane's, I'd bet anything. Or at some other blond's with muscles you could see rippling through his clothes."

"Maybe. But maybe not. Give him a day or two more. You boys will be fine. A day or two more is all," Roger repeated, gazing down the stairs wistfully, as if he were wishing he were waiting for someone to come back in a day or two more. "That was all that Don ever needed when he got restless. Well." He took a deep breath. "Ready for Susan?"

"No," I said, grinding my index finger into his stomach. He sucked it up tight.

She sat at the dining room table, her overfed purse resting next to her right elbow, her broad, bulging bottom spreading out over several pillows that lifted her up closer to the document she was reading as she whistled through her teeth, her lips moving to no word's shape, her chubby little fat girl's legs dangling, shoes kicked off, nearly a foot above the carpet. She licked the point of the pencil and laid it down, smiling as if her best friend had just entered the room. "Why, who's that? How nice, Rog. You didn't mention anything about company coming."

"I'm not company. I'm Sam Whitten," I said, holding out a hand to her. "I live downstairs."

"Why, that's nice, I suppose," she said, ignoring my offered handshake and returning to the will to examine it further. "Let's see. Donald mentioned someone who lived downstairs to me once. From San Mateo too, he said, over on Thirteenth Street, just two blocks away from where we was born, him and I and our little sis. But it wasn't you. It was Charlie Roberts. Charles Simpson Roberts, it says here. Oh, Donald was full of high praise for this Mr. Roberts. But I guess he must have moved out," she said to me, smiling for all the world as if I were her darling grandchild, "because you live there now. That's what Roger just told me was the case, wasn't it? Wasn't it, Roger? This man lives there now."

"Yes, ma'am," I said, pleasantly enough, I thought. "Charlie Roberts moved out."

"Isn't that just the way of the world?" she said, smiling brightly, as if this were the sunniest thought she had had all day. "Here today, gone tomorrow, what starts in joy, ends in sorrow. You've got to put your trust in the Lord, Sam Whitten. My poor brother Donald didn't, don't you see, and so everything in this foolish document"—here she gave it a shake in the air—"everything in it is Roger this or Roger that except for this Mr. Roberts once and not one mention of Jesus in it at all. Not one. And He's our only salvation. Well. . . ."

" 'Well' what, Susan?" Roger inquired, his voice quivering, though whether more from nerves or anger, I couldn't be sure.

"Well, some things will have to be changed, I reckon." She had begun to hum the big tune from the "Blue Danube."

"Could I fix you a drink?" Roger asked me.

"Nothing alcoholic for me," Susan sang.

"Orange juice?" Roger offered her.

"Fine, fine," Susan smacked. "A glass of cold orange juice would hit the spot."

"A jigger or two of vodka in mine, Roger," I said.

"At least," Roger agreed. Susan wrinkled her pug nose at us.

"How do you spell 'genealogy'?" she quizzed me the second after Roger had left the room.

"What?"

"How do you spell 'genealogy'?"

"G. E. N. E. A. . . ."

"Oh, heck," she said. "Most people spell it with an *O*. Let me ask Roger again. Roger?"

"Yes?" he called back.

"Susan wants you to spell 'genealogy' for her," I said.

"I just did fifteen minutes ago," he said, exasperated.

"Just do it, Rog," I recommended.

"G. E. N. E. O. . . ."

"You see," she said, winking at me.

"I guess I'm not 'most people' then, Susan."

"Well, neither am I. I'm a genealogist," she boasted, pronouncing the *A* with great care. "I have traced my family's history back seven generations."

"Good for you," I said.

"All the way back to Scotland," she said.

Roger marched into the room, drinks on a tray, and sat Susan's down on a coaster next to her purse. She sniffed it to confirm that hers was the one without the alcohol. "We got rights to Texas oil property," she bragged, "if I can ever get my no-good, no-account grandson Dickie interested in it. Little Bernard, my son by my first marriage, he couldn't care less either. One day I'll be sitting pretty and they'll all be coming begging, you wait and see, though I've already been blessed beyond my hopes and dreams, amen." She began to flip back and forth through the will again until she'd found the section she wanted and reread it, humming all the while some tune that sounded remotely like "Stranger in Paradise." "You answer me this, Rog?"

"I'll try, Susan," he said from his seat way across the room near the fireplace. I was standing to his right, straddling the living room and the deck, leaning against the edge of the open glass door, watching her warily.

"What's a Greek head?" she asked, her eyes glued to the

words which her fingers repeatedly underlined. "Don't it sound gory?"

I scurried over to the coffee table, put down my glass, and lifted it up to show her, stand and all. "This," I said almost proudly, holding it aloft for a few seconds and then carefully setting it back down again.

"Well, it's his," she said, without having bothered to pay it much attention.

Roger blinked once. Otherwise he didn't flinch, he didn't blanch, he didn't falter in any way. He simply quit breathing. "What?" I said.

"It's his," she said and checked the will again. "That Charles Simpson Roberts. The one from San Mateo I was recollecting Don having mentioned before. Oh, the few times we talked and yet Don always had high words for him, all right," she clicked. "I remember now Don's singing his praises, going on about how lucky he was to have such a fine neighbor. What is it, anyhow? Some kind of old art? It looks broken."

"You're kidding, right?" I said to her. "You can't be serious. I mean, you have to know how valuable this is, don't you?"

"Valuable?" She smiled at me scornfully. "Son, only your soul is valuable. Well," she sighed, as if closing up shop, "I reckon I've seen all of what I came to see. It saddens me to think on it, but I guess poor Donald is burning in hell today. He led a wicked life, and who can question the justice of the Lord? It's my duty now to make sure he gets a decent Christian burial in any case, owing to how he might have repented in the end without our knowing it. My poor brother needs at least that kindness, Roger."

"There's not going to be a burial, Susan," Roger said flatly, moving only his lips and jaw, the rest of him motionless, rigid, purple with anger.

"Course there is."

"No, there's not. I had him cremated. Yesterday. In accordance with that will of his you supposedly have just read."

"There's not a word in it," she said. "Not a word about any cremation."

"There must be."

"Not a word. Read it yourself," Susan challenged him.

"Oh, God. Please," Roger exclaimed and covered his face.

Susan blandly hummed to herself the melody of the "Emperor Waltz," her compact out as she layered more powder on her already overpowdered face.

"We're going to scatter his ashes in the bay, Susan," I informed her, for the nasty fun of it. "Roger and I. In a few days. We're going to take Don's ashes out in a small box and dump them into the currents of the bay. You should come along."

"Please, Sam," Roger muttered, his head still in his hands.

She slid down onto the floor and effortlully bent to pick up her shoes which she carted over to the love seat with her to put on. The Greek head caught her eye. "Heathen work. Devil work. We've been warned," she said, dismissing it at a glance. "Mind my words, the Lord chastizes. I don't know why Donald wanted such a thing in his house. Do you know, Roger? It's all so puzzling."

"No," Roger said, shaking his head in a kind of amazement. "No, I don't know." He sat upright again. "You're not staying for dinner, Susan?"

"I think I've changed my mind, Rog." Her shoes back on, she heaved herself up and straightened out her dress, picking at one of the blue birds on its design as if it were a spot she were trying to remove by peeling it off. "You took my brother," she said to no one in particular, certainly not directly to Roger, neither anger nor hatred nor emotion of any other kind in her singsong voice. "And now I can't lay him to rest in that hill where Mom and Daddy and my Frank and our little sister and all the others lie so peaceful. So I guess I'll just drive on back down to Foster City." She checked her tiny gold watch. "It's getting late for a tired old woman like me. You're going to be old too, even you," she warned me. "It's time for you to be making your case before Jesus."

"Oh, do shut up, Susan," Roger snapped, leaping to his feet.

She chose not to hear him. "You play the piano?" she asked me. She'd wandered back to the dining table to retrieve her purse and seemingly had just noticed the baby grand that stood far to the other side of it.

"No," I said, bewildered. "Why?"

"It would be so sweet to hear a little piano music now," she said. "Donald always did play the piano so sweet, don't you agree, Roger? He could have had a major concert career if he had wanted one. A major concert career. But what did he do instead but waste his God-given talent selling records of other people playing trash. Frittered his life away is what he did. It don't make any sense. I never did hear another human being who could play so sweet."

"You loved Don a lot, didn't you, Susan?" Roger offered.

She was swaying back and forth to some imagined music in her mind. "He was my baby brother. I blame that war. It took him from us and unsettled him and changed his way of thinking. He had been such a right-thinking boy. And then he was called away to fight and came back to . . ."—she looked around the room, her eyes bleary—"to some other place, and none of us ever saw him again, not really. He would have been better off dead, Daddy said, killed on one of those islands. We all said so. Something bad happened to him that made us wish it. Something did." She'd found her keys. Roger opened the door for her. "Help me down, Roger," she directed, slipping her free arm into his. "These stairs frighten me." Her wandering eyes settled on me for a moment. "What you'd want with that ugly old head is more than I can understand," she said, clutching the railing with her other hand, her purse swinging from the crook in her arm and bumping against her bosom. They had maneuvered almost halfway down. "Why did Don give it to him anyway?"

"He didn't," Roger said.

"My brother was a strange man," Susan said.

"Yes," Roger agreed. But Susan wasn't listening. She had started to hum "Autumn Leaves," her voice pitchless and warbling, weaving back and forth over the tune like a drunk trying to walk a straight line.

"Well, at least that's over," I said to Roger to console him when, a few minutes later, he joined me out on the deck. The sky was bands of lavender, silver, lace. Then suddenly it was almost night.

"Poor Susan." Roger collapsed into a lawn chair and closed his eyes, his head sinking into his pillow.

"You feel sorry for that dotty old bitch?"

"No." He held his head between his hands as if it were throbbing beyond any relief. "Fix us both another drink, will you, Sam? A real one this time. Something brown, not too translucent, with a kick to it."

When I handed him his, he sat upright to accept it, pulling the back of the lounge up too.

"So," I said.

"Yes."

"How are you feeling?"

"Peculiar."

"Is that all? Aren't you furious?"

"I don't know," Roger said, stretching out. "I was just thinking about that time on the Hoh River trail when you and I didn't want to cross that ledge and stayed down at Elk Lake, and Charlie and Don hiked the rest of the way up to Glacier Meadows by themselves. Remember? How long were they gone? Two days? Three days? I wondered at the time why you were so unpleasant about it. It was hardly the first time they had taken off on their own. But it had never bothered me until I saw how much it was bothering you. So when we got back to the city I asked Don about it."

"And?"

"He said he loved both of you. He loved me first. And then next he loved you, meaning you and Charlie together."

"And?"

"That's all," he said easily.

"That's *all*?"

"It was enough, Sam. I didn't press him any further. Why should I? I was satisfied by what he said. It would have demonstrated a lack of trust to ask any more. You have to have faith, you see. Otherwise, it's no good."

"I see." I squinted out towards Alcatraz where the light had begun to revolve in the gradually thickening dark. I didn't see. "You're kidding yourself, Roger."

"Am I?"

"Admit it. He left the head to Charlie, Roger. He left the head to Charlie."

"Yes." He set his drained glass down on the floor. "As Susan would say, it's puzzling."

"Not to me."

"No, I suppose it isn't to you." He struggled out of the lounge chair, joined me where the deck's stairs led down into the garden, wrapped an arm around my waist, and would not let me pull away. "You know, Sam," he whispered, "Don and I always worried about you and Charlie. You were both very good companions to us, of course. We always enjoyed your company immensely. Our last ten years would have been greatly diminished without it. Yet we found you two to be very strange because, although you were both lovely boys, neither of you seemed to be able to feel anything permanent about the world. I don't know how to explain it, but try to understand that even if Don and Charlie did have some kind of fling together, which I doubt, it can't matter now, don't you see? I mustn't let it. I mustn't have wasted my life."

"Don't let him have it, Roger," I whispered back.

His fingers loosened from my belt. "It was mine. It was my gift."

"That's right," I prodded.

"Why would he have to give it away?"

"That's the question, all right."

"To Charlie?" He gazed at me through the shadows, utterly bewildered and dismal.

"To Charlie," I underlined.

"It isn't true," he said quietly.

"You were the one who didn't want to read the will. Why not? Did you know?"

"It isn't true."

"Get rid of it."

"Nothing happened."

"Get rid of it. Get rid of the head. Don't let the bastard have it."

"Nothing happened, I said."

"Sure. Get rid of it. Sink it in the bay with Don."

"Don't turn your anger on me, Sam."

"That's why Charlie moved out three days after Don died. That's why. Why should he stay any longer? His lover was gone."

"Don't, Sam. It's nonsense. Preposterous nonsense."

"Nothing happened," I mocked.

"It didn't. I know it didn't. Don wouldn't. Neither would Charlie."

"I know all about worst fears, kiddo. They always come

true. Sacrifice forty years to him and his need to be flattered. See if I care. I only sacrificed ten. What idiots we all are."

"Get out, Sam." Roger had retreated to the glass door and had already pulled it halfway closed. "Now."

I stepped onto the first stair down. "Sure. That's right. Blame it on me. Kill the messenger."

"I mean it, Sam."

"Do you want to give it to him or should I? Some lawyer's going to have to check it all out, you know. Tell him it's gone. Tell him it disappeared. That's the thing to say. Don't let Charlie have it, Roger. It's yours. Get rid of it. Sink it."

"Now, Sam."

"Drown it. What the heck? You couldn't stand to look at it again, could you?"

He slowly shook his head. "No," he said and slid the door all the way closed, backing into the room so that he wouldn't have to notice the Greek head in the place of honor where it had sat for decades.

I lay on our bed, on the guest bed, on the couch in the living room, clutching the dark. Nothing worked. I got up, turned on a lamp, rearranged books from one shelf to another, separating mine from Charlie's. One of them, a hardback Durrell, was Don's. I set it aside, then placed it on the stack with the others that I knew weren't ever mine. Some kind of pain grabbed the back of my neck and yanked on it, like a not quite legal wrestling hold just before a fall. I jerked on the lamp's chain to turn it off, nearly stumbling over a pile of paperbacks in the process, and fell against the wall, the cool of its plaster like smooth marble against my face.

In the hall, a sliver of light shone around the perimeter of the closet door. Charlie must have left it on yesterday. He was always leaving lights on somewhere. But why hadn't I noticed it earlier? Maybe he had been back today, too, while I was up at Roger's, though that was highly unlikely. Why would he have come back here? It didn't matter. Whenever, he had knocked over one of the boxes of letters and postcards we saved there. Or had they spilled out as he searched for one particular card or letter? That couldn't matter either. I might have done it myself, after all, and forgotten.

I picked a handful up. "Our winter was less productive than I had hoped it would be. We have been seduced by the lawn furniture. James studies his law books. The weather is blissful here. And yours?" Another: "Yesterday Delos. Tomorrow Rhodes. Then on to Turkey. Don is exhausted but looks forward to seeing his first camel caravan. So do I. Miss you two. All best." Or another: "The one hurtling off the cliff like Greg L. is mine. The one waiting his turn in the white bikini is Al's. Hi! This island's just what the doctor ordered, guys. It's like no one alive has ever been sick. Al says he could live forever. But what the hey, huh? We've had our fun." One more: "You two have got to be the best tour guides in that crazy town. Thanks for the sack space. That couch is better than my bed back home. Really! Don't apologize about the guest bed's being occupied. Actually, I got in it once. That Tom is wild. Did he tell you? It gets lonely here in Kansas. I wish I could have stayed out there for good. But I guess I'm needed where I am. Needed? Lord! Love ya."

I didn't leave right away. I flipped through several more cards, the pictures on each one like photographs taken by the same uncurious tourist's camera, always aiming for the obvious, for the cliché, so that you'd think the world was everywhere equally dull until you flipped the card over and read the message, only to find out that instead it was merely hopeless and sad. I tossed them all back into the box. Whatever I was going to do, I knew I couldn't stay all night confined by these walls. I was too angry, at Don and Charlie, of course, but at Roger and myself as well, furious at all of us for not being better at life than we were.

I clicked on a light in the bedroom and retrieved from the back of my dresser's top drawer the fragment of the page from the personals I had torn out about a month ago on which I'd jotted down Rick's number when he called after receiving my letter. Rick was surprised to hear from me, of course, and cool to the idea at first. But, when I told him that Charlie and I had really split up this time, he agreed to meet me an hour and a half later at a bar we both knew in the Haight just a few blocks from my store. And the thought of seeing him again actually revived my spirits for a while.

I neither changed nor showered as I usually would have. I

didn't have to. Since Charlie was gone, there was nothing I needed to shed. Though I hopped on a bus for the middle part of the trip through a risky part of town I didn't feel much like braving in the night, it still took me over an hour to get there. Rick was already in the bar when I arrived, just as I hoped he would be. He didn't seem to recognize me at first, but that was all right because it wasn't recognition I was after. First he said how pissed he'd been about my having lied to him during our first conversation on the phone. But when I explained to him about my life now, not having to lie at all this time, he said he guessed he understood. Then he smiled like a man who knew he had just been lied to again, even if only a little, and who plainly had decided he wouldn't mind. He was used to it. We were all used to it. No big deal.

In the morning, I wandered home slowly and stopped at a travel agent or two to check out their new brochures. There was a special on Catalonia that looked inviting and another to Tibet which, though still very expensive, promised the ultimate in exoticism and a third to the Marianas that Don would have avoided at all costs and a fourth to Great English Gardens and a fifth for a cruise to Alaska and a sixth for another through the Panama Canal. All specials. Every place was special, every place on sale. I gathered them all up and carried them home, studying each off-and-on along the way, wondering what it was that Don and Roger had hoped to find by traveling. If Don knew, he never told us. I would have to ask Roger one of these days, before it was too late. Whatever it was, however, they plainly hadn't discovered it any more than Charlie and I had, because in a way they were even more restless than we were. If Charlie and I needed an occasional strange body, Roger and Don had demanded whole strange new worlds, none of which was ever quite strange enough to hold them there. So maybe it wasn't so surprising that in the end Don had settled for an ordinary faithlessness after all, just like the rest of us.

Back at the house, I knocked on Roger's door to see how he was doing, but he either wasn't home or, mad at me, didn't answer. Sitting on the stoop off the street, I watched the mail-man slowly work his way up it, a buckle on the strap of his bag catching the sun and reflecting it brilliantly, like a shiny new silver dollar back when we were kids. Maybe there would be a letter from Charlie. I knew there wouldn't be a letter from him. Yet maybe there would be.

I perched myself eagerly on a higher step for a better view since Charlie had said recently that our new mailman was by far the best looking in the city. When I asked him how he knew, he didn't answer. "There couldn't be much competition," I said. He said, "Maybe not, but check him out anyway." OK, for Charlie's sake, I'd check him out. But the letter carrier passed me by, not even delivering any junk mail and carefully avoiding my eyes, as someone accidentally encountering a funeral party will avoid the eyes of the mourners, eager to get on with his business and not wanting to be implicated in their grief, however slightly. As usual, Charlie had been right. He was a babe, his calves and thighs bulging like plates of armor beneath those floppy dull gray trousers they make them wear.

But, because he hadn't opened the gate, come up the walk, mounted the steps, my life would go on just the same, unchanged. So why did each tick of my old wind-up wristwatch seem dimmer, until at last there were no sounds left at all? No firecrackers bursting, no children's voices from the school playground across the street, no backfires from the truck struggling up Jones Street and spitting out black fumes from its tailpipe, no hammering noises from the workmen repairing the roof on the stark Victorian near the corner, though I could see their arms continue to drive in nails, row after row. Although the chill wind off the bay quietly prickled my skin, it did so without once whistling through the gutters. Not hearing anything, not a thing, I sat there, arms wrapped around my knees, and stared happily into the silence, watching it grow steadily brighter as the sky does in mountain valleys long before you see the sun. One of the neighbor's scruffier cats scaled the front railing, slunk along the coping of the wall, pounced, and landed in my lap. I could feel it purr, I could see it meow when I yanked its stubby tail, but that was all.

It wasn't that I had gone deaf. Not for a second was I afraid that I had lost my hearing. I simply had made a choice and without knowing it had chosen silence. As if by magic, I had been able to still the world, especially the raucous world of my

own body, and keep it hushed for a while. I stood up, unbuck-
led my unwanted watch from my wrist, and read it, astonished
at the time. Back inside the apartment, I dropped it into the
hall wastebasket, grabbed a chair from the kitchen table, set
the chair on the deck, sat down, and wondering if blindness
might be equally liberating, stared briefly up at the heavens,
the whole sky in flames, all of it, save the huge white disc at
its core, burning with the clear, clean blue translucence of a
Bunsen burner. In the back of my eyes, orange and red dots
began to swirl and collide, battering one another, but I refused
to blink.

"Don't," I could hear Don advise me as if he were actually
there. I didn't have to see him to know it was he. I could smell
him and his cigarettes and almost feel his knobby fingers grip
my shoulder.

"All right," I consented, though I lowered my eyelids
slowly, as if I were gradually letting down shades in a too
sunny room. The bitter, acrid odor of those French cigarettes
he liked so much, the ones with the strong Turkish blend (of
Turkish men's sweaty pits, Roger used to joke, holding his
nose) left an aftertaste in my mouth. Then all the city's shrill
noises swelled up once more into my ears. It was rush hour
already. How had it gotten so late? Hours must have passed.
I breathed in deeply, but the air had changed again. Now it
mixed dry earth, fetid water, and redwood and cedar chips
with a hint of gardenia sweetness and the sour odor of too
many neighborhood cats. Another cat, different from the one
earlier, bounded into my lap, digging two of its claws into one
knee. With a wicked swipe of my arm, I knocked it off. When
it hit the brick wall, it squalled like a baby.

"Meditating?" I heard Charlie ask. "Is that what you do
when I walk out on you? Sit around and meditate? That and
attack cats?" He was standing just inside the sliding doors
which I had left open, sweating hard, back pressed flush against
the kitchen wall, the sleeve of his sport shirt ripped at the
shoulder exposing a bad bruise.

"Something like that," I said. "Who's been beating up on
you, Charlie? Duane?"

"This?" He examined the spot. "I tore it on that new hook
in the closet, the one with the sharp point you've been com-

plaining about. Which of course made me lose my footing. Which made me collapse into the corner of that wardrobe of yours. So I fell. Backwards. You mean you didn't hear? You really haven't heard all the racket I've been making? I've been so noisy, chum, I might as well have been building this house all over again."

"You're moving back in then, Charlie?"

"Sure. I figured the point's been made. What the hell, huh?"

"That's nice. What point?"

He flipped something off one finger with his thumb. "The same one as always. You know. The one that says we'd better stick together because anyone else we'd choose would be that much worse. Incidentally, you certainly have been acting strangely for the last couple of hours or so. I figured it was some sort of quiet fit you were throwing for my benefit that we'd have to talk about later."

"Uh-huh. Maybe I don't want you back, Charlie."

"Of course you do, booby," he said, gnawing on a fingernail. "Nobody else would put up with you."

Roger peered over the upstairs railing. "Is that Charlie I hear?" Charlie stepped out onto our deck to offer him a little salute and a click of his heels. "Welcome home, lad. I thought I heard you hard at work down here. I just got back myself," Roger offered as he joined us, "from an important trip. A most important trip. It feels wonderful to be so free of it, I must say, much to my surprise."

"Oh? Where to, Rog?" Charlie said. A swallow landed on the head of the statue of Eros which stood as if to pee in the middle of the birdbath in the middle of the almost dry pond, and immediately flew off again so that another swallow could pause briefly after it on the same spot which, once the second had departed, was followed by a third. While I waited for the fourth, Roger positioned a white wrought iron lawn chair at almost exactly ninety degrees to my left, much closer to Charlie.

"So, welcome home," Roger said to him again. Crossing one leg over another, he fixed the crease in his trousers.

"Thanks," Charlie said, blushing. "I'm sorry, Roger. Please forgive me. It was a lousy time for me to have run out on you. I guess I just got scared there for a couple of days. Certain

. . . problems between me and Sam came to a boil. I had to go away and think."

"I understand," Roger said. "I really do quite understand." There was a sharp, slightly rusty edge to his voice, though. He two-fingered a cigarette from his shirt pocket and lit it. It was one of Don's cigarettes and he lit it with Don's lighter. "Yes, you needn't tell me. I know," he said, acknowledging our stares, "it's an odd time in my life to start so disgraceful a habit. But it comforts me. I thought of it last night, Sam, after our discussion and it comforted me some. There are so many little things that I didn't like about Don which now, of course, I find myself missing. Remember that, you two. Sometimes what you disliked, even hated, is no easier to lose than what you've admired or loved. It makes it no easier to sleep recalling one more than the other."

Charlie reached to pick a pebble from the ground and pitched it into the pond where it hovered, suspended in green scum for several seconds before it sank. "We must clean that soon," Roger suggested, "and buy some new goldfish. It would be nice for the spring."

A brown rat poked its head out of the end of a broken piece of drainpipe and dashed down the retaining wall behind me heading straight for the neighbor's. Below, one cat after another arched its back and hissed. Roger surveyed his garden, which had grown almost entirely shadowed by the hill. "We should water tomorrow when it's light enough. We've been neglecting it."

"I will," Charlie promised.

"But early," Roger emphasized, "before the sun is too high."

"Yes," Charlie said. "I know how you like it done, Roger."

Extinguishing one cigarette, Roger lit another. "I don't inhale. I'm afraid to inhale."

"That's good," Charlie said.

"Don always inhaled. Deeply. He did everything deeply. 'Don Profondo,' I called him. Did you know that?"

"Yes. I think so," Charlie said.

"That was Don. If you're going to fight, really fight. If you're going to love, really love. If you're going to smoke, really smoke. So he smoked like a fiend."

"Say. Isn't that one of Don's sweaters you're wearing?"

Charlie observed. "I've never known you to wear bright red before, Roger. It looks good on you, really good. You should keep it up. Very sexy."

"Do you think so?" Roger said. "I suppose I have always been too conservative. Don always complained that I was too conservative, that I should take more chances, more risks. And I thought maybe I should put his things to some use. Just a few things, of course. I'll give a lot away. I'm making a list. But I've always liked this old sweater. It's Italian."

"It looks Italian," Charlie said, admiring it some more. "It has that flair."

"But I won't give everything away," Roger insisted.

"No, not everything," Charlie said. "Why should you?"

I shivered. In the shade, the air had become cool and damp. Overhead, several flocks of swallows were flitting this way and that seemingly without direction or purpose, like radarless bats, beating their wings all the more furiously, I surmised, because there was no sense to it.

"Not the Greek head, for instance," Roger said, that dangerous cutting edge returning to his voice. "Not that. I've taken care of that." He took a puff, long, leisurely, and pointed, and would glance neither to his left nor to his right. We were both being told something. Charlie started to speak, hesitated, and looked away uneasily.

"Look behind you," Roger said to Charlie where he sat hunkered on the bricks. "How beautiful even the shabbiest of our westward facades become at sunset. They seem to be clutching at these last rays of light like some miser his gold, just as it's to be taken from him. It's why we go to museums, Don used to say. To get some of that lost gold back, the lost gold of the sun. Don was a wonderful traveler. Well, you know that. You can appreciate that, how well he saw everything. He was the most impartially curious man I've ever known."

"Yes," Charlie acknowledged.

" 'Don Impavido,' Cecille would call him. I've missed her so much these last few days, regretting all the more the rupture that both Don and I felt was nearly unhealable between her and us after she married her second husband, a piously conventional man who couldn't help expressing his disapproval of us in numerous petty ways. 'Don Intrepido' was another of Cecille's names for Donald. I especially liked that. Don Intrepido."

"What about 'Don Giovanni'?" I scoffed.

"What is your problem exactly?" Charlie said to me.

"Hardly," Roger said. "No. Don was no Don Juan. To me he was pure pleasure, a fine lover, but he was no Don Juan and he knew it." The night had blackened the lines on his face and deepened them so that it appeared that Roger was wearing a mask which, as he smiled, turned comic, a satyr's mask strangely befitting him.

Charlie had taken a cushion from a deck chair and was leaning back upon it where he had propped it against the pond's brick wall, an unopened six-pack next to him. When had he brought the beer out to the garden? What was happening to my ability to observe things? Did all men become handsomer, like Charlie, in the dark of night and shadows? If so, did that explain why Don liked black marble best? Something deep inside of me had finally started to hurt. "Charlie," I called to him. He grinned and pitched a can over to me, carrying another to Roger. I opened mine gingerly, spilling none.

"Rog?" he prompted. "You said you took care of the Greek head. What did you mean, 'took care of it'? Because Don wanted me to . . ."

"Please," Roger interrupted him, holding his hand up as if to warn him to stop. "Let me finish what I have to say first." With the toe of his shoe, he squashed his cigarette into the ground like a hated snail. "You see, Charlie, I just got around to reading Don's will last night. Sam already knows all about it in a way. I'd been putting it off and putting it off because the prospect of reading it frightened me. You'll know what I mean some day if you're the one that's left. But once his ineffable sister Susan had perused it, I felt compelled to do so myself at once. And of course she was completely wrong about the cremation. There it was, all spelled out quite clearly, just as Don had told me," Roger said to me without taking his primary attention from Charlie. "That woman is either dinghier than I thought or crazed by religion. But about the Greek head, which she had no personal interest in, she was nonetheless exact. And

I don't understand it. I simply can't understand it, Charlie. Can you? You do know what I'm talking about, don't you? You must."

Charlie flipped his empty can into the open trash barrel hidden under the upstairs deck. "About the head? I know that Don left it to me to take care of, if that's what you mean. Is there something else I'm supposed to understand, Roger? Because, if there is, I don't . . ."

"I'll be plainer then. The question is this. Did you or did you not have an affair with Don, as Sam so cruelly insinuated last night? Or is 'insinuate' too benign a word for what you did, Sam? Explain it to me. Why did he leave it to you, Charlie? It was the possession of ours we both loved most, our symbol and his most precious gift to me. Yet he left it to you. Why? I have to ask. I have to ask, Charlie," he pleaded.

"Of course you have to. It's my fault. It's all my fault, Roger," Charlie apologized quietly. "I should have come to you first. Days ago. Right away. You see, Don didn't trust you."

"Didn't trust me? Of course he trusted me. I never gave him the slightest reason not to . . ."

"I don't mean it in that way, Rog," Charlie said.

"Then how?"

"Yes, how?" I interjected.

"Oh, do be quiet, Sam," Roger said. "You've done enough harm. Please, Charlie. How?" Roger repeated.

"He didn't trust you to give it back," Charlie said, casually popping the top on another can and setting it aside to dry his hands off on the front of his shirt. "He told me what he was going to do a couple of years ago, that time he and I went on up to Glacier Meadow and left you guys behind at that lake. He swore me to secrecy, of course, because he knew how you'd resist the idea. Don't you see, Roger? For three and a half decades, Don had apparently felt guilty for stealing that thing, for having taken it from its own soil and secluded it here in this house so far away from where it belonged among all those other beautiful things the Greeks had made in Italy. He didn't want you to know, Rog, but he longed to send it back. That was to be my job only because he said you loved it too much. You understand? You loved it too much. So did he, almost as much as you did. That's why he knew he'd never get enough nerve to do it himself. And he wouldn't ask Sam over there because he figured Sam would probably just go ahead and hold on to it, pissed that anyone should have to give anything up. Don said he knew I'd do it if he asked me since he believed I didn't cling to things. I don't think he meant that as a compliment, Roger. It was just something he'd observed, like he knew you'd never read his will until you absolutely had to.

"I have the address and all the instructions written down in my desk at the office at school. I thought I'd lost them, but I found them last evening when I snuck in here while you two were upstairs talking.

"Please don't worry, Roger. It's yours to keep until, well, you know . . . I mean, all this I'm telling you now isn't written out in the will, because Don only wanted to make sure it got done some day, that's all. And he thought that meant I'd have to be made the head's legal owner. He knew I'd explain everything to you. It was only that my timing was off. I mean, I should have been here to tell you. Don said he would rest easier knowing that it would find its way home eventually. I promised him I'd see to it. That's all. So," Charlie said, slapping his hands together. "That's the story, Rog. Believe it."

Roger stood up, his back cracking, and walked cautiously towards the stairs like an old man, the gentle breeze after sunset blowing his hair about so that it glittered like sea grass in the moonlight. He reached for the handrail and grabbed it firmly. "I do believe you, Charlie," he said softly. "I believe you, and I believe Don. It's so strange. This afternoon, I was so maddened by jealousy, I packed it up in a crate all by myself and drove it to the parcel service, and shipped it back to that museum in Italy. I didn't want you to have it, you see. Better them than you. So I don't blame Sam, despite all his unfortunate insinuations. Not really, no more than Othello could blame Iago. The doubt was in me, the anger was in him, the two matched almost perfectly. That's all.

"Don would be laughing now, that great belly-walloping laugh of his I always found so sexy. He would be enjoying it, the irony of it, I'm sure. It happens only rarely, but sometimes worst things can come to good in the end. It's our one hope. Goodnight, gentlemen," he said, waving at us both. "I'm very tired all of a sudden. We'll talk more tomorrow?"

"Roger!" I stopped him. "I'm so sorry. I . . ."

"Yes," he accepted. "Goodnight. Oh, only one thing more," he said without turning around again. "Did it ever strike you as odd, Charlie, that Don thought the head was his to give back? Well, never mind. Goodnight once more."

Charlie and I stood opposite one another, waiting, as we had so often waited, for the glass doors above to slide closed. "I'm sorry for so much," I said to him.

"Yes. I know," Charlie said. "So am I." He pointed upstairs. "Our voices carry. We should go inside. Come on inside now, Sam. Come help me finish my unpacking."

The following Sunday, the three of us poured Don's remains into the bay, each taking his turn holding the ciborium-shaped vase as, once the rented boat was safely stabilized, we scattered the ashes and bits of bone into water and wind. The night before we went out, the weather had soured and it stayed bad all morning, the clouds immediately overhead dirty gray and feathery as a pigeon's wings, the bay's water surging up over the gunwale cold and bitter, the boat rising and falling over and under surprisingly high swells. But none of us was sick. We were too sad to be sick for so little reason.

As we coasted back into the marina, though, the sky cleared and the sun shone brightly once more. All the while we had been on the water, Roger had retained his composure, but, the minute both his feet touched land again, he collapsed into Charlie's arms, sobbing. After we'd driven him home, we brought him a brandy in a warmed snifter on a silver tray and talked to him about his plans for a trip to the Dordogne next summer. We offered to go along. He listened politely to our enthusiasm and smiled and said, No, no, no. It wouldn't do. It was time for him to be alone now. He thought he'd sell the house and move to an apartment somewhere out in the Richmond, a smaller place, easier to keep up and closer to his school. He wondered if we'd like to buy the house. But Charlie and I couldn't afford it, we said, and our future together—this came out almost in unison—was simply too much in doubt. Roger smiled, his kind way of acknowledging that he knew better than we how doubtful or sure it was.

Charlie and I helped put him to bed and spent the rest of

the afternoon and evening in his apartment looking through photograph albums we'd never seen before that Roger had been reviewing the previous night.

"Let me see that first book again," Charlie said to me. I passed it to him. "You know," he said studying several early photos, "Don was right. Roger really did look like that Greek head when he was young. What a beauty. And so serene."

"I wonder if he really gave it back," I said, "or whether he only hid it someplace where he can look at it whenever he wants to."

"You're joking, right? Of course he did. Of course he sent it back. Roger doesn't lie."

"I wouldn't have," I said. "Don was right about that."

"Me neither," Charlie laughed. "Or maybe I would have. I don't know. I did promise him."

Back in the bedroom, Roger cried out Don's name once, then again. Charlie rushed in to check on him. When he returned to the living room, he was crying a little, his cheeks flushed and damp. "He's still asleep," he said, "all squeezed over on one side of the bed as if Don were still lying next to him. It's good that he's going back to work tomorrow."

"Yes," I said. "Very good. Pass me that album with the green binding, would you, Charlie? Look," I showed him. "We're not in this one either. And this was Baja."

"Let me see," Charlie said, taking the book from me, flipping through the pages himself, as surprised as I had been.

As we moved from album to album again, what unfolded before us with increasing clarity was the joy of Don's and Roger's life together, each trip, each special event, each important occasion carefully documented by the camera, as if to suggest that some day its meaning, not apparent at the time perhaps, would be discovered by people like Charlie and me. And yet Charlie and I seldom showed up in the pictures of the last ten years. We found ourselves in some of them, of course, and it was obvious that Charlie or I had taken many. But we agreed that we thought there should have been more, that we remembered having posed for many more, and wondered in whispers what had happened to them.

THE VALENTINE

• GREG JOHNSON •

WHEN CLIFFORD BANNON returns to his tenth-grade class on the second of January, after being absent for the entire fall term, there's a firestorm of gossip and rumor and speculation among his classmates—the talk is far more intense than the mock-sorrowful, mock-pitying discussions they'd enjoyed last fall, both the boring ones directed by the nuns in class (who said they must *pray* for Clifford, must try to imagine the hellish *ordeal* he had suffered) and the less formal, possibly less hypocritical buzz of conversation in the cafeteria, the hallways, the parking lot, where Clifford Bannon's name had been on everyone's lips throughout September and most of October. (Although, by the first of November, the talk had died down and the subject was discarded, like a piece of Juicy Fruit that had finally lost its flavor.) On Clifford's first day there are cheery hellos sent in his direction, there are plenty of offers to help Clifford "catch up" with his school work, there are a few brave attempts to get him involved in the CYO, or the basketball team, or the planning committee for the Spring Formal to be held in early May—but Clifford, to no one's surprise, greets all offers with a curt shake of his head, a barely audible *Thanks, but I'll pass*; and he gives that enigmatic half-smile of his, mouth turned down on one side, which none of his classmates quite knows how to interpret.

"He's the same old Clifford, if you ask me," Trudy Cravens whispers in the cafeteria one day in late January, her lips puckered in disdain. "He's still got his nose in the air, still won't date any of the Pius girls—"

"Trust me, Clifford is *weird*," says Mary Frances Dennehy, around a mouthful of ham and cheese. "I mean, anybody who likes Janice Rungren has *got* to be weird."

"C'mon, you guys," one of the junior boys says from the far end of the table, "give poor Clifford a break! That stuff is ancient history. Kathy McCord says he wouldn't touch Rungren with a ten-foot pole. Anyhow, Rungren's been dating some guy from public school."

"God, that's so *gross*!" another girl screams in delight. "I mean, *public* school, that's the most grotesque thing I've ever—"

"Yeah, well it fits. In Janice Rungren's case."

"But listen, you guys," Jennifer Jenks says in a heightened voice, making sure everybody can hear, "you know he's got to be hurting—I mean, can you even imagine your mother killing herself, and then you just walked into the kitchen one day and found her? Like *that*?"

"You've got a point, Jenny, but you heard what Kathy and Fritzie McCord said, last fall—said he just sits around their house and draws his pictures, which he won't let anybody see, and acts as if nothing ever happened. He never cries, never talks about it, just acts like he's been living with the McCords all along. And did you hear about last summer?—Mrs. McCord had to *make* him go to the funeral!"

"See, didn't I tell you he was weird?" Mary Frances says. "Just imagine!"

"Where is Kathy, anyway? I have trouble believing *that*."

"I know Kathy better than you guys," Jennifer says hotly, "and she never told *me*—"

"Oh, and get this—guess who Clifford had made friends with, now that he and Janice aren't speaking? Jimmy Tate!"

"The caretaker? *That* moron?"

"You've got to be kidding!"

"He's worse than a moron," says one of the tenth-grade boys, his voice fallen to an ugly whisper, "I heard he's a fucking *queer*. One day when Gallagher and me—"

"Hey yeah, that's *right*—Witherspoon told me Clifford goes down to the basement and visits Jimmy all the time, during lunch, during study hall—"

"There, I told you he was weird. I rest my case."

"C'mon, Mary Frances," says Jennifer Jenks. "I think he's sort of sweet, and he's got to be upset. I mean, wouldn't it blow *your* mind, if you came home one day—"

"Well, I guess you should know," Trudy says slyly, "since I heard that you and Clifford went out together—it was around November, wasn't it? And you thought nobody knew?"

"What?" Jennifer cries. "How did you—"

"Shush, you guys! Here he comes."

The whispering starts and stops, and starts again, and whenever Clifford turns down a corridor or enters a classroom his classmates in their tightly clustered groups break apart, grinning awkwardly, chagrined, and occasionally he troubles to wonder if they think they're fooling anyone; or if they think he really cares. All through January and part of February—until February 14, to be exact, when Clifford Bannon's career as a parochial school student meets its abrupt and ironic end—Clifford slips back into the persona that has served him so well during his years at this school. *Well-behaved, though a bit reserved*, Sister Mary Veronica had written on his final evaluation last spring, at the end of ninth grade. *Keeps his own counsel, and might do well to interact more with his fellow students*. . . . He remembers standing quietly in the kitchen on that May morning (two weeks before Senator Kennedy's assassination and the start of that final abrupt downward spiral in his mother's condition) while she read and reread the report, frowning. It was certainly far different from the one he'd gotten the previous fall, after Clifford's chapel detention and the infamous term paper and the two-week suspension just before Christmas; in fact, Clifford had thought, Sister might have been describing someone else entirely.

"If you misbehave, they complain," his mother had muttered under her breath, "and then when you *behave*, they still complain." Signing the note, she'd lifted her dark deep-set eyes to Clifford and, as if on cue, they'd begun laughing at the same moment. They both laughed so recklessly that their eyes filled with tears, and finally his mother had bent over double, trying to catch her breath. A few minutes later, Clifford had gone out to the school bus with a lightened heart; but, as it turned out, this was the last time he could remember that his mother had laughed.

By now, in January of 1969, at sixteen years of age, a tenth-grader at Pius XII Junior and Senior High School, he has lived for over five months in the hectic noisy household of Rita McCord and her genial husband, Larry, and already he feels like one of the family. Oddly, there hadn't been the "period of adjustment" everyone had warned him about, even though he had to share a room with Fritz McCord, a freckle-faced athletic boy a year older than Clifford, whom he'd never known very well. To please Rita, he did get involved in the household activities, sharing chores with the other children, observing curfew rules (set according to each child's age: Fritz and Clifford were expected home by 10 P.M. on weeknights, 11:30 on weekends) and television rules (one hour per evening) and rules concerning promptness at mealtimes and personal hygiene and the many details of Catholic religious observance. Because Father Culhane and Sister Mary Veronica and Clifford's father had all agreed that sitting out the fall semester might be the best thing for Clifford, he'd had plenty of time to get to know all the McCords, who had done everything possible to make him feel at home. Clifford felt both flattered and embarrassed by the attention they paid him. Fritz had tried to interest Clifford in coming to the basketball games and the CYO socials, and at such times Clifford would look up from his book or his sketchpad and smile, saying *Okay, sure*—though at the last minute he usually found some excuse to avoid going, knowing he would be bored, knowing there would be a certain amount of whispering and staring. His name was still Clifford Bannon, after all, not Clifford McCord; it was important to keep reminding himself of that.

One evening, when Larry handed Clifford a button, worn by all the McCord kids to school, that read "Stay Tough in Vietnam!," he had hesitated, confused; he remembered how hungrily his mother had watched RFK's speeches the year before his death, her eyes welling with tears as Kennedy parted company with Johnson on the bombing of North Vietnam and the escalation of the war in general. As she listened to Kennedy summoning up the uncomprehending terror of the Vietnamese peasants, the tragic spectacle of innocent mothers and their children, all hope gone, trapped in that scorched and ravaged landscape, his mother had stroked Clifford's forearm idly, weeping: "See, honey, there's someone who understands, isn't there? He *does* understand, doesn't he?" He'd felt a brilliant hectic energy in his mother's touch, like an electric charge. Yet Clifford, very uncomfortable, had sensed that she was responding to something other than the man's words, and had quietly drawn his arm away.

Though he'd hesitated, he finally did accept the pin from Larry McCord, and sometimes wore it around the house to please his new father. It was clear that Larry, an ardent Kennedy supporter back in '60, had developed serious reservations about Robert Kennedy in the months preceding *his* assassination, though in Clifford's presence he avoided this topic, perhaps unaware that Clifford listened so intently not because he cared about Larry's conservative politics or Vietnam or the drug culture or birth control—Clifford had no opinion about any of these things—but because Larry's innocent adult *certainty* so impressed and pleased him: the certainty that there were right and wrong ways to live, that there existed certain moral absolutes that need only be recognized and followed.

It pleased Clifford also that neither Larry nor Rita had attempted to coddle him in the matter of his mother's suicide— Rita, as always, moved forward through life with her nononsense relentless good cheer, and though Larry, soon after Clifford moved in, had offered a "sympathetic ear" anytime Clifford needed one, he'd never again alluded to Mrs. Bannon's death. Nor did they allude to Mr. Bannon, though for weeks after the funeral last August he'd gotten calls from his father, whose whining faraway voice spoke of Clifford coming to Atlanta to live, "anytime he wanted"—of course he wouldn't fight Clifford's decision to stay with the McCords, he knew how close Irene and Rita had been, but still if Clifford ever had the desire. . . . Clifford had stood in the hallway next to the McCords' noisy dining room, where kids were always eating or playing cards or talking in high cheerful voices, and he'd turned to the wall and answered his father in a quick low murmur, *Uh-huh, yeah, I guess so—no, I guess not—yeah, I'm sure, but thanks anyway. No, Dad—but thanks.* He'd been patient, not wanting to hurt his father; and to his relief the calls had tapered off gradually, painlessly.

He hadn't been so lucky with Janice Rungren, who called almost every night in the weeks after the funeral, who wanted to know how Clifford was *feeling*, if there was anything she could *do*—and though Clifford tried the same monosyllables on her, the same practiced indifference, she eventually became angry and shrill, demanding to know *when* she would see him, *why* couldn't they get together, there were two weeks of summer left and why should they waste this precious time, wasn't this an opportunity to get closer, and shouldn't they—

No, he'd said sharply, and he allowed himself a shiver of revulsion over the way she'd clung to him all these years, always coming back, always wanting something he couldn't give. She was so immature, really. At school she'd started getting in trouble again—the blond and pretty and privileged but still rather demonic Janice Rungren, the scourge of the nuns at Bosco and now at Pius too, a bundle of passionate misdirected energy who had, since they met in third grade, focused so much of that energy on Clifford Bannon—and he couldn't count the times she'd gotten *him* in trouble. So he'd said *No* quite loudly, rudely, hoping to settle this once and for all. Expecting to hear her shrill voice coming back through the line, making accusations, telling Clifford what his "problem" was, he'd been surprised when, after a long silence, she said softly, even meekly, "Clifford? Clifford, are you still there?"

"What?" he'd cried. "Where else would I be?"

"Clifford?"—again with that peculiar meekness, which grated on his nerves because it was so unlike her—"Clifford, what's happened to you, anyway? What's happened to *us*?"

"*Us*?" he said, exasperated. "*Us*? What the hell do you mean, Janice, what are you—"

"Everybody's been saying it for years, haven't they?" Janice said. "Haven't they said that we liked each other, didn't everybody just assume—"

"We're friends, Janice, we've always been just *friends*. Don't try to—"

"But what did you expect, Clifford Bannon"—she was raw-voiced, furious—"when you spent all your time at school with me, year after year, and never had another girlfriend, and never contradicted anybody who said we *were* boyfriend and girlfriend—what did you expect me to think? Or the other kids?"

She paused, swallowing hard; she took a deep breath.

"What were *you* thinking, Clifford, during all that time . . . ?"

"Who cares what anyone thinks!" Clifford shouted, but his own words were hollow, in a flash he saw how things had appeared to *her*. She'd been indulging her "romantic" day-dreams right before his eyes and he hadn't cared, hadn't really paid attention, he'd simply hung around with Janice because he liked her and because she was always *there*—energetic, laughing, pulling him along. He'd been so involved in his own passing infatuations that he'd never imagined himself as the object of anyone else's. About the same time he met Janice he'd been in love with that neighborhood boy, big blond good-hearted Ted Vernon, with whom he'd enjoyed some "horse-play" (Ted's embarrassed word, the next morning) in Ted's boy scout tent one summer night in the Vernons' backyard; and after Ted came the series of older boys at school, the football and basketball stars who scarcely knew that Clifford existed. They didn't matter as individuals, of course, but only as they perpetuated the romantic haze in which Clifford had lived until last year and which excluded not only Janice Run-gren but nearly everyone else. It was true that several times during their friendship Janice had cornered him, giggling, star-tling him with her aggressiveness and daring—that morning in fifth grade when she'd dragged him off into the woods beside the playground at St. John Bosco Elementary, saying it was time they "played doctor," saying it was for his own good and he'd need to be a brave little boy, and that day two years ago when she'd entered the small chapel anteroom where Clifford was spending his "chapel detention," quietly studying by him-self, and she'd shut the door behind her, smiling, her eyes a mischievous damp blue as she approached him, and he'd known what he was in for—yes these things had happened and he hadn't resisted, he supposed he'd even cooperated since after all her will to do them was so much stronger than his will *not* to do them. Hadn't she known that they were only playing around, "experimenting," did Janice really think he felt romantically drawn to her?—or to any girl, for that matter? So there had been no solution, he thought, and during that last phone conversation he'd listened woodenly, summoning all his patience, as Janice rattled on shamelessly about the "romance" they could have had, and how she'd never thought of anyone else as her boyfriend—and how much the other boys at Pius disgusted her with their stupid remarks, their dirty words and gestures—and how she didn't know what to *do* at this point, since she felt sure that Clifford wasn't leveling with her, that he was still upset over what happened to his mother and if only he would *talk* about it, if only they could get together and talk things out the way other couples did—

"No," Clifford said again, not sharply but wearily, absolutely needing this to end. His palms were sweating; he didn't think he could bear Janice's rambling self-pitying voice for another moment.

"Clifford," Janice cried, "will you please listen? Don't you know that I *love*—"

And so Clifford had no choice: Very gently, he replaced the receiver.

Though he felt guilty for a few days, he understood how pointless the guilt was, and soon enough began living through his days at the McCords' with a new lightness, a sense of freedom. Past was past, he thought. In a polite and reasonable tone he'd said to Rita McCord that if Janice called for him again he'd rather not take the call, and Rita had said of course, of course; but Janice had not called back.

So for Clifford the fall passed in a blur as he comported himself easily with the McCord household and its routines, not thinking of the future and seldom about the recent past. Sometimes, late at night, he would let the familiar procession of images rise to his mind's eye—the discovery of his mother that humid morning of August eleventh when he came into the kitchen for breakfast, staring at her body curled pitifully on the floor next to the wrought-iron telephone stand, a thin greenish vomit oozing out the side of her mouth; the arrival of the ambulance, the police, and finally Rita, who pawed the tears roughly off her cheek and literally pushed Clifford out the front door and into the back of her station wagon; the funeral a few days later, toward which she'd also pushed him, and after which he had to endure an awkward and pointless conversation with his father and Father Culhane, both of whom looked guilty and aggrieved, both of whom tried to explain what had happened, the two men stepping on each other's lines and apologizing to each other and casting the same timorous assessing glances into Clifford's expressionless eyes. Father Culhane had assured Clifford that his mother must have deeply regretted her act after it was too late to forestall its results, probably she *had* been struggling toward the phone when she died and this did suggest remorse, and the likelihood of God's forgiveness. Mr. Bannon's milder, more tentative voice had woven in and out of the priest's in Clifford's hearing, saying how Rita had told him about Irene's reaction to the assassination in June, that she'd even called periodically and suggested hospitalization because Irene had begun claiming that everything was over now, the world had no chance, there wasn't any hope—that kind of talk—and his father admitted that he hadn't wanted to hear all this and had put Rita off.

"I'm sorry," he told Clifford, "I'm very, very sorry—of course you can come live with Miriam and me anytime you want, or if you'd prefer—"

He'd broken off, bewildered, just as Father Culhane had done when he'd recited his words about God's forgiveness and then had seemed, abruptly, to run out of things to say.

Then his father tried again, his voice cracking: "Your mother had this sorrow inside her, Cliff, this deep *sadness* that would well up suddenly, without warning—and I guess it overwhelmed her this time, I guess she couldn't—"

Tears blocked his voice and Father Culhane had touched Mr. Bannon's hand, had given him a reproving glance, and then signaled Rita who stood waiting at a discreet distance, by the olive- and white-striped funeral canopy, to come and take Clifford away; which she did, herding him back to the station wagon with her other children, who stayed respectfully quiet all the way home; and Clifford had felt both embarrassed and nearly faint with relief.

It's over, he thought.

Over, he thought repeatedly in the following days and weeks and months, thinking back and remembering only to wonder at his father's and the priest's bewilderment; for if Clifford understood perfectly why his mother had died, why couldn't they? Why couldn't they see the world with the same heartless clarity his mother had finally achieved, why did they want to romanticize what was probably an ordinary and even sensible death, why didn't they just get on with their lives and squeeze out whatever pleasure they could and quit wringing their hands over the "mystery" of Irene Bannon's exit from the world . . . ? There was no mystery, Clifford thought, and the issue of having hospitalized her, of having "saved" her, was probably irrelevant; just as the issue of God's forgiveness, Clifford thought scornfully, was irrelevant.

Though school didn't seem to matter, either, he did his homework with faithful thoroughness like all the McCord children, and no longer indulged in blatant daydreams during classes or felt the need to ridicule the religious instruction still given out patiently, year after year. (Theology class was now taught by the smiling pasty-faced Sister Mary Sylvester, a young and supposedly "brilliant" newcomer who had all she could handle, Clifford noted, in the stepped-up antics of Janice Rungren.) And it was likely, he would later think, that he'd have finished his remaining three years at Pius with all A's (at the time of his expulsion, he had near-perfect averages in all his classes) and perhaps even as senior class valedictorian, if he hadn't happened one day in mid-January to enter the first-floor boy's bathroom at about 8:25 A.M., only minutes before homeroom period began.

He'd assumed the bathroom would be deserted, but he saw something—a shift of the light, a shadowy movement—as he hurried toward the urinals. Then unzipping himself he saw Jimmy Tate, the school caretaker, emerging slowly from the tiny supply closet over by the sinks.

"Oh, hey," Clifford said, as the man stood there for a moment, staring. "How's it going, Jimmy?"

He'd never really spoken with Jimmy before but evidently the man had worked here for several years, and evidently the kids considered him "slow"; he'd seen Phil Witherspoon mimicking Jimmy's slack-mouthed expression, his rounded shoulders and shuffling gait. Clifford hadn't paid him much attention, had never heard him say anything, but he'd noticed the way Jimmy would stare as kids passed by him in the hall, his lips parted vaguely, his pale blue eyes looking glassy and stunned.

Now Clifford felt a chill pass through his chest and abdomen and groin, a twitching anxious excitement that seemed only heightened in this rather dismal, poorly ventilated bathroom with its blended odors of urine and disinfectant, and that heavy damp pervasive smell of the cheap brown paper towels littering the sinks and the floor; in his discomfort Clifford edged closer to the urinal, his shoes scraping along the gritty wet tiles. Trying to sound casual, he spoke to Jimmy Tate over his shoulder.

"How's it going, what's new?" Clifford repeated. He felt embarrassed to be using the bathroom while talking to some-one, but now Jimmy was giving him that look, too, that baleful blue-eyed stare; when Clifford laughed, uneasily, the man licked his upper lip and smiled back, though his eyes still held their look of unabashed longing.

Keeping his gaze fixed on Clifford, he leaned his mop against the wall.

Clifford turned his head, ignoring him, looking down as if zipping himself, preparing to leave; but he waited a moment as Jimmy stepped up to the urinal next to him, undid his own zipper, then cleared his throat and said in a shy, deep voice: "Not much, I reckon. How about you?"

There were no partitions between the urinals and Clifford could feel the man's body heat, and imagined he could feel him glancing over, from the sides of his eyes. Blond and big-boned, Jimmy was over six feet tall, several inches taller than Clifford, and of course he could see that Clifford hadn't yet zipped his jeans. For a moment Clifford's heart pounded, but he took a breath and looked over as Jimmy stepped back and turned toward him, showing himself to Clifford, and in almost the same movement Clifford turned toward Jimmy, and as the man reached out to touch him the 8:30 bell rang, startling them both.

Clifford laughed, his hand trembling as he quickly zipped his pants, then flushed the urinal; Jimmy Tate didn't laugh.

Unwillingly Clifford thought about Jimmy all the rest of that day, and the day after that; he kept glancing over his shoulder in the cafeteria, or in study hall, expecting to see the man with his mouth ajar, his eyes vacant but eerily still, in some fixity of longing. All around Clifford his classmates were talking eagerly about Valentine's Day, asking one another if they were sending handmade or printed cards, and did they plan to send cards to everyone, or just to that "special person"?—and though no one dared to ask Clifford any such questions he felt as much angry resentment as if they had, he shouted into the shadowy threatening corners of his mind *No, Janice and I are not an "item," no, goddamn it, I'm not dating her nor will I ever date her, nor will I . . .* And out of those same mental shadows that were already threatening the clarity he'd achieved these past few months— which Clifford likened to a harsh fluorescent light that showed everything for what it was, reducing the world to a single unlovely substance that didn't bear much scrutiny—out of these shadowy dim corners stepped that slack-jawed caretaker, Jimmy Tate, who simply stared as if waiting patiently for Clifford to acknowledge him; as if he knew something Clifford didn't know but would wait as long as necessary—with more than patience, even perhaps with something like affection—for Clifford to recognize it too.

Several days later when Clifford went to his locker during lunch period, he saw Jimmy at the far end of the hall, dressed in his khakis as usual, holding a broom. He stared at Clifford, his lips slightly parted. When he nodded toward the basement stairs and disappeared, Clifford hesitated only for a moment; in subsequent days he never hesitated. Sometimes he and Jimmy talked for a while—friendly comments and questions on Clifford's part (in that new polite voice he'd developed since living with the McCords), awkward half-mumbled replies from Jimmy Tate. Over a period of several weeks Clifford learned a few facts about Jimmy: that he was from Abilene, that he'd fought with his father a lot and had drifted east, working odd jobs, getting fired a lot ("I wasn't no good at school," Jimmy told him), sometimes getting help from the Salvation Army or the local rectory. His mother had been Catholic—as a boy he'd gone to Mass and First Holy Communion—and he hadn't been surprised when Father Culhane had offered him a job and found him a rooming house right around the corner, even though he'd only asked for an evening meal. That was the luckiest day of his life, Jimmy told him. He liked working around Catholic kids, and around the priests and nuns; he liked his job, he was lucky to have this job. . . . When he touched Clifford his big calloused hands were almost reverent; he seemed nervous and abashed when he fumbled with the zipper on Clifford's jeans and looked more solemn than hungry as he slowly lowered the jeans and then Clifford's Jockey shorts and approached him with lips parted and tongue extended, like a communicant. He would suck Clifford slowly and thoroughly, a blurry deep sound coming from the back of his throat like murmuring underwater, but whenever Clifford's fingers brushed the smooth front of Jimmy's khakis the man would back away, dropping his eyes.

"No?" Clifford said. "How come?"

Jimmy wouldn't respond, and so Clifford quit trying; he was pleased enough, he thought, with things as they were. He'd begun to find Jimmy's company strangely soothing, as the man seemed to have no capacity for judging him, or perhaps simply no wish to judge him, and he asked for nothing beyond what Clifford wished to give. . . .

And so, on that February afternoon, just after Janice Rungren thrusts an envelope into his hand during library study hall (and just as Sister Mary Jerome turns her back, bending over an encyclopedia with Barbara Balfour), his sudden impulse feels inevitable: He gathers his books quickly, quietly, and sneaks out of the library. He goes immediately to the basement door, raps twice, hurries downstairs, and takes his usual place against the wall, next to a closet doorway where they could hide if anyone came along. On this particular day, he and Jimmy don't exchange a word, Jimmy coming forward at once and getting to his knees, Clifford not even glancing down as he takes the envelope and rips it open quickly, impatiently. Above the Valentine message, *Will you be mine?*, Janice has written his name, "Mr. Clifford Bannon, Esq.," dotting the *i* with an oversized heart, and in a tiny, ornately "feminine" hand she has written "I love you," and beneath that she has scrawled in big block letters, "WHY THE HELL NOT? (Ha ha)."

She didn't sign the card.

Clifford stuffs the Valentine inside its envelope and drops it in a huge waste barrel next to him, and at the same moment he hears a noise from the top of the stairs. He looks down at

Jimmy Tate's blond head, bobbing rhythmically; he knows that Jimmy's grateful guttural murmur keeps him from hearing, but after his first impulse of alarm Clifford decides to do nothing and at once he's flooded with calm. There are a few moments of exquisite pleasure when he is able to focus only on what Jimmy is doing, the fact that it won't last only increases his pleasure, and when Sister Mary Jerome reaches the bottom of the stairs and peers into the dim light of the basement—not yet with her pale fish-faced look of horror because she hasn't quite focused, her vision hasn't yet quite adjusted to what she's about to see—even at this moment Clifford is able to think, Whatever happens, happens, and why the hell doesn't Janice Rungren understand?

NEW YEAR

• JACK SLATER •

FOR CHARLES KUSCHINSKI

January 7

The hills, the mountains, the lake, the islands—everything this late Wednesday afternoon was bathed in a mercurial orange light as I walked home from Pátzcuaro centro, thinking of Ohio and Dad. Thinking of remaining here in Mexico forever, in the presence of this orange brilliance, yet missing—well, not Dad so much as home. Missing some home somewhere. I was feeling good and, ironically, humming that old song, "Why, oh why, oh why-oh, why did I ever leave Ohio?" and thinking that Ohio for me was not home. Not even a home. It was my father. Ohio was Dad, the place where he was, would always be. Ohio was his long body, his thick hands, his big laughter, his athleticism, the 50-cent pieces he used to give me for spending money, the Lincoln Recreation Center he used to direct, the slices of pie I could order on his tab at Babe's. Ohio was the Dad I was always missing, the home I was always wanting. I have a thousand memories of him and therefore a thousand memories of Ohio. But those moments, those memories have never been enough, because I've never really had enough of Dad, never had my fill of him. Never been satiated by him.

Sipping hot cider from a large mug, Howard Shaler wrote that journal entry in a large, black loose-leaf notebook as he sat before the blazing fireplace in his two-room adobe house situated in the hills overlooking Pátzcuaro. Later, long after he climbed into bed, he lay awake in the dark, hands clasped behind his head, still thinking of his father—summoning once again that masculinity he had often envied, recalling once more that indefatigable Christmas Day personality and the inexhaustible self-confidence, the eyes glittering with interest during any conversation, or, with the head thrown back, the laughter— always the big laughter—that could embrace you like a warm shower.

Yet the laughter, Howard realized, was always a promise, never really a fulfillment. It didn't occur to him until he became an adult that he and his daddy rarely went anyplace or did much of anything together. Sidney Shaler, the football and basketball coach, the swimming instructor, and the boxer— Sidney Shaler, the superb athlete, seldom got around to leading his only son into any crowded stadium or onto the mobbed bleachers framing any court to see any game; never showed his son how to hoop a basketball or make a tackle or slide into first base; never taught him how to swim, never how to run the hundred-yard dash. Why? Howard never knew, and by the time he began to wonder why he was of an age to shrug it off the armor he had constructed so well.

From his bed Howard watched the last glowing embers in the fireplace fade in the darkness, until he himself faded into sleep, remembering, remembering wisps and scraps and odd patches, a chaos of memories swirling inside him like a silent storm: his mother, who had died of cancer when he was a child, and his first lover and first friend, Wade; and Jessie, Jessie so fat and black and shy and always lonely, and so easily caricatured yet . . . well, he wondered if he had ever loved anyone as much as he loved her, his stepmother; and his aunts—even they swooped into view—those two dead aunts whom he had never known, his father's teenage sisters who drowned in some Kentucky river, drowned again and again in Howard's memory, because his father never tired of telling it. "My mom went a little off after that," Sidney Shaler used to say of that year when he was ten. "She never got back right. She used to go to the river to call my sisters, call them, until the women came and took her home. She did that for—oh, I don't know—about eleven, twelve months after the drownings, and the women would always come and take her home. Then she stopped. Gradually she just stopped. But she never got back really right. She was always a little off. Not crazy, but the life had gone out of her."

". . . the life had gone out of her"—for some reason, it was always those words that stayed with Howard whenever he thought of his father's mother. Even as a kid he had been fascinated by the thought that grief could actually take the life out of you. Now, sinking toward sleep, he wondered how the ghost of his grandmother's sorrow expressed itself in him. What face had she bequeathed him? What soul? What was her contribution to the thousand parts of himself? Then, as he thought those things, the phantoms and their voices vanished, and he slept.

The next morning, in the midst of preparing his usual breakfast of cereal and orange juice, Howard was interrupted by a knock at his front door. It was a delivery man: young, slender, bronze-skinned, black wavy hair, moustache—Howard's veiled glance encompassed him in less than a second. On the road, in front of the house, the young man's small pickup awaited him, motor still running. "*Buenos días*," he said, startled briefly both by Howard's six-foot-five frame and his black skin. "*Telegrama para Howard Shaler.*"

"*Gracias*," Howard replied, signing a paper the man had thrust in front of him. He too was startled. During the year and a half he had lived in Mexico, he had never received a telegram. Indeed, he had rarely received a letter. Only his father, who never wrote, and Jessie, as well as a friend or two, knew where he lived. Which was his choice. He had wanted to wall himself away from the world he had once known. Yet now some part of that world was reaching for him—with telegraphic urgency. But he didn't want to hear anybody's news, good or bad.

He found some change in his pocket to tip the young man. "*Gracias*," he repeated and, closing the door behind him, again encompassed the slender body, the bronze skin, the black wavy hair, the moustache. Listening to the pickup drive away, he returned to the kitchen and propped the telegram against the sugar bowl as he sat down at the table. It remained there, screaming at him silently as he began eating his cereal. He didn't open the envelope until after he had finished breakfast.

Then:

YOUR FATHER PASSED AWAY PHONE ME PLEASE JESSIE.

Howard read the message again, and once again, before carefully folding the paper and returning it to its envelope. At
length, he gathered the three or four dirty dishes from the
kitchen table, took them to the sink, and washed them repeatedly. And dried them repeatedly. After sweeping the kitchen
floor, after making his bed in the other room, he put on his
dark blue windbreaker and went outside in the stillness of the
cold morning to take a walk in the woods behind the house.
He often took short walks in these woods, brief forays into
what he liked to view as "my wilderness," before returning to
the house again to tackle the book he had been writing since
he arrived in Mexico. Today he remained longer than usual in
his wilderness. Sitting down on a familiar stump, he looked
up, beyond the towering pines, to the whiteness of the sky,
his mind shouting disbelief. He wanted to weep, but he did
not, could not. He continued to look up, entering the sky as
he did so, flying up—up beyond the gathering clouds, beyond
the morning moon, flying as he had often done when he was
a child, past the invisible stars into blue boundless space. . . .

Later that morning, he walked into town to the tiny telephone office near the Plaza Grande to make the long-distance
call to his stepmother.

"Thank God," Jessie said when she heard his voice. "I just
didn't know if the telegram would reach you."

Hearing that little-girl, Ella Fitzgerald voice again, he suddenly felt protective of her. He saw her once more: short, old,
fat as the letter O. And vulnerable—yes, she would always be
that, he thought. Did he love her because he pitied her? If so,
was that love? Did he love her because he saw parts of himself
in her? Was *that* love? He wanted to wrap his arms around
her, this woman who had just lost her husband.

"When did it happen?" he asked. In the telephone booth,
claustrophobia began to close itself around him like a casket.

"Yesterday afternoon."

Yesterday when I was thinking of him, wanting him.

"Yesterday afternoon," Jessie repeated. "About four-thirty."

*Maybe he was thinking of me, wanting me. Maybe he had actually
come to me.*

"It happened so quick," Jessie went on. "I was sitting at the living room window, watching him shovel snow from the sidewalk in front of the house. I was darning socks and putting new buttons on some blouses, and I happened to look up to see Sidney stagger and drop his shovel. And collapse in the snow. I got up. I didn't know what had happened. I got up and ran out of the house to him. He was nearly unconscious. Nearly gone, already. I kept saying, 'What's wrong, Sidney? What's happened?' I tried to drag him inside, but he was just too heavy, too big. I screamed for help. Mr. Collins from next door heard me, and he came. And we got him into the house, and I called the ambulance. And they came and took him to the hospital, but it was too late. They worked over him for forty-five minutes. But it was just too late. It was his heart. A heart attack." She began crying. "At least, he went quick," she murmured. "He didn't linger. Didn't suffer."

Why, oh why, oh why-oh, why did I ever leave Ohio? The song suddenly returned to him again, insanely, mockingly. "Well," he said at last, "I'm sorry this has happened. I'm so sorry." He didn't know what else to say. A faint sense of guilt washed over him. "I'll be home sometime tomorrow," he added, nearly whispering. "I'll be leaving here this evening."

Until he had uttered it, he hadn't realized that he was going home. But of course what else could he do? He had no other choice. Sons, he told himself as he left the telephone office, go home for the funerals of their fathers.

He went directly to the bank to withdraw enough money for the next week or two. Afterwards, he walked to a nearby *casa de cambio* to change his pesos into dollars. Later that afternoon, with a small suitcase in hand, he caught the bus that would take him east to Mexico City: the first leg of his journey. As he sped away from Pátzcuaro—already missing it, already longing for it—the sun seemed to be burning itself out, sending forth in its descent great veils of smoke. The hills, the mountains, the lake, the islands—all were screened by these veils, this dense orange mist that heightened the town's beauty even as it obscured it.

Watching it all vanish behind him, he panicked for an instant, imagining that it was departing from his life forever, imagining that he would never see Pátzcuaro or Mexico again.

He nearly flinched. For if he really believed that, he carefully explained to himself, he would have to get off this bus this instant. To abandon Mexico would be to abandon his future. It would be to leave behind the happiest year and a half of his life, the most fulfilling, because for the first time he was doing what *he* wanted, what he personally needed. Some of his Mexican acquaintances in Pátzcuaro wondered why he, a black man, had remained among them for so long. "The town's so small," they would tell him. *"También es muy indígena."* Or: "Don't you miss the United States? Living here must be different for you." Others of course understood why he had come and why he stayed. *"Es tranquilo, no?"* they would say. *"Sí, es muy tranquilo,"* he would agree, and add in Spanish, "Believe me, I want the quiet life. You can't know how much I want it." To find this quiet life—and to escape the futility of Los Angeles—he had scrupulously saved half of each paycheck for two years. Then, after he had accumulated enough money, he quit his job as a magazine copy editor, sold his car, sublet his apartment, and flew to Mexico to give himself another chance among the thousand chances he had blown. As it turned out, it was the best move he had ever made, because here, in this solitude, the old life and its compulsions began to fall away from him. Here, he was beginning to reconstruct something inside himself, rebuild—as well as excavate. . . . No, he could not leave Pátzcuaro—not yet. To leave would be to abandon hope.

> *My body is a torn mattress,*
> *Disheveled throbbing place . . .*

When his plane landed the following morning at Dayton International, he was remembering that Bob Kaufman poem:

> *My body is a torn mattress,*
> *Disheveled throbbing place*
> *For the comings and goings*
> *Of loveless transients . . .*

He was remembering Los Angeles and all the drifters there who had tramped through his body, one after the other across the years. All the baths in which he had searched and all the bars he had scoured. All the parks and the porno theaters. And all the men who could never love. Why had he continued to believe that love was anywhere at all to be found?

As he walked out of the plane and through the beige accordion tunnel that led into the terminal, he wondered if he and his body were now paying the price for accommodating all those transients.

"Howard."

Because now the diarrhea that had tortured him off and on since Houston began once again to press like a knife against his lower gut. Was it anxiety? Or was it something else, something more serious? He didn't even want to think about it.

"Howard?"

Startled, he turned and saw his old friend Wade Elliot moving alongside him.

"Wade!" He stopped, let his bag drop to the floor, and embraced the man he had known since they were teenagers. "What are you doing here? No, wait," he went on, "Jessie sent you, right?"

"Right." Grinning, Wade was delighted to see his oldest friend again. "After you phoned her from Houston, she called me. Gave me your flight number and all."

"I was gonna take a bus into town, then grab a cab. Hey," Howard said, all in the same breath, "you're really looking good." He wrapped his right arm around Wade's shoulders. "Not a line anywhere on that face." Wade was a slender, light brown–skinned man of medium height. A lively intelligence, as always, dominated his features, but now Howard noticed something childlike and forthright fusing with the intelligence, giving his friend's face a kind of youthful wisdom. It was the youth that Howard chose to recognize: "I can see the years have passed you right by," he observed.

"I wish I could say the same about you," Wade said with a sly grin.

"Bastard!" Howard responded, laughing the big laugh, his father's laugh. "At least I *look* my age." Then, referring to the years of their youth: "Are we still competing or are we still competing?"

"Not I, not I." Wade held up his hands in mock horror.

"Look, before we go any farther," Howard suddenly said,

stopping in front of the men's room, "I've got to go in here. I have a touch of diarrhea."

"Okay, I'll wait here. Leave your bag. I'll watch it."

Howard disappeared into the men's room for fifteen minutes, maybe twenty—he wasn't certain. When he re-emerged, he felt a bit weaker, and thirsty, but he was all smiles.

"Are you okay?"

"Yeah, I'm fine. Of course." Howard went on flashing his reassuring smile. "Let's go."

Outside, under Ohio's gray January sky, a blast of cold wind mixed with snow flurries rushed up to greet them with such force that Howard nearly lost his balance. "Wow! Somebody's glad I'm home." At that instant, he experienced what he had been hoping he would feel, the excitement of arrival—the sense of having flown into another realm, another kingdom.

"Well, *this* somebody is glad you're home," Wade declared, as he manuevered his car out of the parking lot and into the slow stream of airport traffic. "I've missed you. I haven't talked with you in so long. And you never write. I write occasionally, but you never write." Wade stopped the car at a red light. "And, listen, hey, I'm sorry about your dad. I'm sorry you had to come home to . . . to his death, but I'm really glad you're home. It's great seeing you again."

Howard didn't say anything immediately. Wade's candor was making him feel a little shrunken, a little guilty. He cuffed Wade's right cheek with a gentle fist. "You always did give me your feelings," he said, touched by his friend's great warmth and his openness. "Okay, since I'm gonna be home for a week or so, let's try to be with each other as much as possible."

Wade laughed. "Fine. But you know I intended to do that anyway."

They had been friends for twenty-one years. Which was, Howard told himself, no great length of time, really. Still, the awareness of those years awed him, since nothing else in his life had ever lasted twenty-one years. His marriage had stumbled along for two years. His various contacts with men— "affairettes," as he liked to call them—had never survived beyond a few weeks or a few months. His career as a copy editor, like his flickering interest in L.A. itself, had endured twelve years, the last five of which had seen him sleepwalk through most of his duties at work. And his new life in Mexico had lasted, so far, some eighteen months. "It's sort of . . . unusual to have known each other for so long," Howard remarked.

Busy with the traffic, Wade nodded as he managed a left turn onto the highway that would take them into Dayton.

"By comparison . . . ," Howard went on, as if to himself; but he didn't finish the sentence. "Have you kept up with anyone else from the old days?" he suddenly asked.

"Not really," Wade replied. "And I've stayed here. Unlike you." He accelerated to overtake a car on his right. "Oh, I see a lot of people. At least, I'm always waving to somebody. But I can't say I keep up with anybody. Of course, I was never exactly an overwhelming favorite, as you know. And when you and I went around together, I was always—well, suspect."

"And so you should have been," Howard recalled, smiling.

Wade beamed that sly, roguish grin: his trademark. " 'He was always'—as my mother used to say of me—'a little different.' "

Suddenly they looked at each other, remembering. *"Vive la différence!"* they whopped in unison, and laughed with some fondness at the memory of their high-school years—or rather, at the recollection of that high-school moment—when Howard had kissed Wade, who had been gloomy or morose about something; had kissed him in Wade's bedroom as they lay on the green shag rug. He was trying to comfort him, to shield him from—what? From whom? The demons of their adolescence? The vicissitudes of being black and poor and, even then, angry and almost fatally ambitious? "Well," Howard had said, referring to the kiss, "it seems kind of natural, huh?" Wade didn't reply immediately, didn't say anything for a long while, until finally, with his eyes averted, a "yeah" eked itself out of him, like a grunt. And Howard kissed him again, tentatively; and Wade held him tentatively, then drew himself against him with more assurance, more certainty as he returned the kiss. Because if being together in this way meant—well, of course, they weren't too sure what it meant. They did know they liked being with each other more than they liked being with just anybody else on earth, including girls. "So, hey," Wade told himself aloud (and Howard agreed and said it too) with that smart-ass bravado of seventeen-year-olds, "yeah, yeah, *vive la différence!*" It was a phrase they had just learned in Miss Whitaker's French I class, and Miss Whitaker, who had just seen an old MGM movie, had been quoting Maurice Chevalier.

"So," Howard now asked after their laughter faded, "how's your love life?"

Wade tapped his right temple with his forefinger. "It's right here," he replied, "consigned mostly to my fantasies. And yours?"

"The same, I guess." Watching the world glide past his window, he turned to look at Wade. "I don't know," he said, with the merest shade of defiance, "I don't think I want a love life."

Wade chuckled. "Bullshit!"

"No, really."

"Bullshit!"

"Besides, there's AIDS."

"Yeah, there's AIDS, which exists simply as one other excuse to avoid love."

"And death." Howard laughed nervously.

Wade shrugged. "Nobody can avoid death," he said, as Dayton's modest skyline came into view, "but it is possible for all of us to avoid life."

By the time they arrived at Jessie's home on Reisinger Avenue, Howard could feel the edge of the knife slicing into his gut again. He ignored it as he greeted his stepmother at her front door and ignored it again as he took her generous bulk into his arms and held her closely, briefly, before she said, "Pretty cold, huh? Colder than Mexico, I bet?" Eventually, as he and Wade stamped the snow off their shoes, he could ignore it no longer. After Jessie ushered them into the house, helping them off with their jackets, Howard put his bag inside the door, pleading, "Excuse me for a second," and ran upstairs through the hallway, past the door to his old bedroom, past his father's bedroom (the bedroom that now belonged only to Jessie), to the bathroom. He tore at his belt buckle, shoved his pants down past his knees, and nearly staining his underwear, sank onto the toilet seat. His body convulsed twice as it attempted to eliminate the curse that was gripping it. He thought of his father, even as he told himself, So this is how it begins: shit running out of me like oozy discharges from a gutter—his father, the great straight Sidney Shaler, who would have been so ashamed of him, him a river full of contaminated blood and poisoned semen.

He remained there on the toilet seat for a long while, elbows on his knees, head bowed. He remained longer than he suspected, because he soon heard Wade knocking at the door.

"Howard?"

"Yes?"

"You okay?"

"Yes, yes, I'm fine," he replied wearily, and hauled himself up, his thoughts shifting abruptly as he saw his father's shaving mug and razor on the bathroom counter, waiting, apparently still waiting for his return. Picking up the razor, Howard turned it over in his hand, examining it as though it might contain a message or a clue. As he returned the razor to its place, he looked up to see his reflection in the mirror, the mirror that had held his father's image only two days earlier. Only two days ago, he told himself, Sidney Shaler had stood here in front of this washbasin, alive. The thought astonished him. He imagined his father looking into his own eyes, shaving, trimming that anchovy of a moustache, toweling his face, brushing his teeth, never suspecting that his passage on this earth was about to end. Did he have time to say goodbye to anyone? Did he give anyone a message? He wanted to reach into the mirror to reclaim the man he had hardly known. *Who were you? And who are you now in me?*

Walking out of the bathroom, he saw Wade descending the stairs at the other end of the hall. "Are you taking anything for that," his friend called out softly, "or are you just toughing it out?"

"No, I have medicine," Howard replied. But he amended himself immediately. "Yes, I'm toughing it, because I'm tough, you dig?" Hunching his shoulders, he assumed a boxing stance. "Besides, I've only had it a few hours."

"Maybe you've got *turista* in reverse."

They were now walking down the steps, Howard behind Wade.

"Yeah, I'm allergic to home."

At the bottom of the stairs, Howard, who had been too preoccupied to notice, now became aware of an odor permeating the house: chicken and shrimp, oregano and okra and garlic. He and Wade found Jessie standing at the kitchen stove, keeping watch over a huge pot of gumbo. "It's nearly ready," she said. "I hope you boys are hungry."

Sitting down at the kitchen table, Howard looked at her with curiosity. "How you doing?" he asked. Their eyes met, and from behind her sorrow she smiled at him a little tiredly, nodding her reply, before returning her gaze once again to the brew she was stirring. Howard continued to look at her, this woman who had been a part of his life since he was in high school.

She was his father's third wife: a squat woman, with a round, puffy face and pendulous breasts, a woman who restrained her spreading girth, tamed it, with punishing corsets, constricting bras, and black dresses. A woman in perpetual mourning.

"Did you say you were hungry?" Jessie asked as she brought a platter of white rice and two steaming bowls of gumbo to the table.

Wade, who hadn't eaten breakfast, said he could eat a horse.

"I want some water, first," Howard announced, nauseated by the very thought of food. "About a gallon, maybe." Getting up, he moved to the tap at the sink, his mouth feeling as dry as Mexico in March. Remembering that diarrhea often led to dehydration, he drank two glasses of water and returned to the table with a third. "Now," he added, feigning enthusiasm for the food he knew Jessie had prepared especially for him, "let's eat."

"Come on, Miss Jessie," Wade urged.

"You boys go ahead," she answered, inspecting a pan of rolls in the oven. "I'll be right there."

As she peered into the oven, Howard watched the ghost of another Jessie, still luminous and alive, still enduring inside memory, calling him from the back door of this same kitchen.

"Howard?" she had shouted.

How old had he been? Fourteen, he supposed. He was in the ninth grade—that he knew for certain, because he had just entered high school when his father had divorced and remarried again, this time to this woman who always wore black.

"Howard?" she shouted again.

"I'm here," he spoke up from the garage where he was fixing the flat tire on his bicycle.

"Come here," Jessie shouted. "I've got something for you."

Howard left the garage and went to the back porch.

"A surprise for you," she announced, smiling, and turned as he followed her into the house.

The kitchen smelled of baking—that's the first thing that greeted him. Baking and brown sugar and sweet spices. Stepping farther into the room, he saw two pans of cinnamon rolls cooling on the kitchen counter. Jessie, standing in front of the sink, had fixed her gaze on the table. He followed her eyes to a pie placed there, like a bowl of flowers, in the center of the table. Remembering her promise a few days earlier to make him a cherry pie ("Just for you," she had said), he looked at her again, a question mark on his face. She answered the question with a nod, still smiling. Even so, he didn't believe her. "For me?" he asked himself silently. And asked himself again but dared not ask her, fearing he might have misunderstood. "Gee, thank you," he said at last, guardedly. And when she didn't withdraw her gift or say, "No, no, no, I didn't mean . . . ," he spoke up again, more certainly, "Gee, thanks a lot."

Over lunch, Jessie told Howard and Wade that she had arranged for the viewing of her husband's body, the "laying out," to take place the following evening, Saturday, at Barrington's Funeral Home. "A while ago Sidney told me he didn't want a funeral, just a laying out with a closed casket," Jessie explained in that diminutive Ella voice. "He said he didn't even want a memorial service. A laying out—that would be enough, he said. So I'm doing what he wanted," she added a little defensively.

"Of course," Howard responded, conscious once again of his stepmother's need to apologize. He had nearly forgotten that sense of uncertainty which nearly always enveloped her. Lifting a spoonful of Jessie's brew to his lips, he reflected, as he had so often in the past, that he could actually detect some music emanating from her, some sense of herself as blameworthy, forever blameworthy—wrong, wronged—*Miss Five by Five*,

Don't Give Me No Fat Woman, Ugly Woman Blues, something swirling about her malevolently, like a storm of black butterflies.

"When is the laying out?" Wade asked.

"About seven," Jessie replied. "Tomorrow." She had scheduled her husband's cremation for Monday. "Sidney wanted to be burned. He told me that a couple of times, so I told the funeral home about it, and they called out to where it's done— somewhere out there on Old Dayton Road, and they phoned me back to say, yes, it could be done Monday morning."

"The cremation?" Howard asked.

Jessie nodded.

"I'd like to see him before . . . before they do it," said Howard. "You know, by myself."

"That's what I told them at the funeral home. Your dad's there now, and I said you'd be calling them sometime today, after you got in. Their number's on the phone table in the hall."

"Is there anything you want me to do?" Howard asked. "Anything you want me to get?"

Jessie thought a moment. "Flowers," she said at last. "We should get some flowers for the laying out. Also, maybe we could put a notice in the paper. You'd know how to write it up, what to say." She paused, still thinking. "I don't know what else." Her voice trailed off. At length, more strongly but still with that little-girl timbre: "After all this is over, you might want to take some of your dad's clothes. They'll fit you. He's also got a couple of rings you should have, and a pocket watch. And his wristwatch."

Acknowledging her words, Howard nodded. Offerings from the dead, he thought. If you can't offer anything of your life, give of your death. Despite his cynicism, he was vividly aware that a part of him was afraid to possess anything of his father's, while another part was greedy enough to want to possess all.

They finished their meal in silence. Declining the coffee Jessie urged on him, Howard excused himself, got up from the table, and went into the hall to phone the funeral home. The first person he reached, a woman, told him he could view his father's body that afternoon at whatever hour he wished.

Returning to the kitchen, he announced, "I'm going over to Barrington's."

"Do you want my car?" Wade asked.

"No, I can walk. It's not that far. Besides," he added, looking at Jessie, "I guess I could use Dad's car, huh?"

"The keys should be on that nail by the back door," Jessie said.

Howard hesitated, trying to decide. What if the diarrhea should flare up again? With a car he could come home more easily or get somewhere else. "No," he declared, settling it, because he didn't intend to give in to illness, "I'll walk. I want to see some of the old stompin' grounds. I'm home, right?"

As he closed the front door behind him, he told himself again, I'm home, right? and kept repeating that sentence, that interrogation, off and on, like a litany, as he quickly moved past the sidewalk on which his father had collapsed and walked through the gray midafternoon toward Third Street. It was cold. Colder than when he had arrived at the airport. And it was still snowing. As he watched the white flakes falling from the gray invisibility above him, he thought of Mexico, his Mexico of the diaphanous orange mists, the green mountains, and the dead volcanoes, all as available to him now as the fragments of a dream. *I'm home, right?* And he moved onto Third Street, and immediately confronted the fast-food joints and the rib houses, the gas stations and the bars. The street was wider and busier than he remembered, and he watched it for a while, recalling the vanished Howard, that skinny black kid, all legs and arms and spectacles, who had stood at this street corner a thousand times on his way to school or to Wade's house or to the grocery for a loaf of bread ("And don't forget the pork chops, about six of them," he heard Jessie calling him from across the years).

Suddenly, another memory, all in a piece, shimmered in front of him, as he waited for the light to change.

"Where is Dad?" he remembered asking Jessie. It was the summer between his junior and senior year in high school.

"I don't know," Jessie replied, a tight expression on her face. "He said he'd be in Troy for the night."

That was the summer Howard became aware that his father had simply stopped coming home. At first, Sidney Shaler didn't manage to make it for dinner three or four days in succession. Then, on weekends, he was often gone, "to Troy," or "to Springfield," or "to Columbus," he'd tell Jessie as he walked out the door, "to talk to some people about a basketball game we want to set up." Soon his weekends away lengthened past Mondays and Tuesdays and, once, to a forlorn Wednesday night when, after he returned, the house literally vibrated with Jessie's screams and his shouts, screams that disintegrated into sobs, shouts that slid into defensive plaints: "You're wrong, sugar. Dead wrong. I don't care who's seen me. I don't care what your so-called friends say. I don't cat around. Are you listening, sugar? I do not cat around. Don't have to. And I don't like you talkin' like that with my son in this house of yours." After that July night, Sidney Shaler didn't come home for three weeks. It was about this time when Howard began to absorb Jessie's bafflement and her sullen loneliness; watched her sitting at the dining room table jockeying unpaid bills or wrangling via the phone with the corner grocer for credit. As he observed her preparing the most basic, the most meager of meals (she who loved to cook on a grand scale), he began to like his father less, worship him less. Sitting night after night at that silent, cheerless dinner table, Howard learned then that he could actually intercept his stepmother's thoughts or at least detect that dark music emanating from her: ugly, wrong, wronged. Embarrassed that his father was simply walking out of her life, he the stepson began to believe he had no right to be in Jessie's presence, creating more bills for her, while his father, who paid no bills, took up with some other woman. He believed he had no right to be eating Jessie's food, sleeping in Jessie's home, breathing Jessie's air—reminding Jessie by his very existence of her marital plight. So, one day, in the middle of the third week of his father's absence, he said goodbye to her, telling her he would return at the beginning of the new school term, and not knowing where else to go, boarded a Greyhound bus to Philadelphia to visit his mother's folks, his grandparents, who lived in nearby Darby. In effect, he was running away, away from Jessie and her bottomless misery, away from himself, and from a father he could never love again quite so completely. . . .

Then the light changed, the apparition vanished, and he crossed at the intersection, turned east, and continued along Third, passing trim red-brick apartment buildings and churches struggling for dignity, modest frame houses and homes in various stages of deterioration, until he turned right onto Summit and saw Barrington's across the street.

It was a largish, one-story, tan-brick building perched near the corner in a tree-lined residential neighborhood. Howard knew the building well. Throughout his years at Dunbar High, he had passed Barrington's twice daily to and from school. Occasionally, he had noticed the black limousines waiting out front, as well as the row of double-parked cars which meant that a funeral was in progress; but mostly he had passed Barrington's as indifferently as one might pass a streetlamp or a telephone pole. Now, as he stood under the white portico and rang the doorbell, the building seemed to throb with his uneasiness, his anticipation, his fear. The door opened.

It was a young woman—tall, dark brown–skinned, black hair caressing her shoulders—who ushered him into the reception area. She was wearing a gray suit and a white blouse. "Come in, please."

"I'm Howard Shaler."

"Yes, we've been expecting you," she said, smiling. She didn't introduce herself. Whether she was a secretary or a bookkeeper or the funeral director herself, Howard never knew, and he never asked. Like Charon ferrying across the marshes of the dead, she led him past the chapel into the interior of the building, through an all-white hallway, and past two closed doors, to a corner where the hall made a sharp left. Here, at a third door she inserted a key in the lock, turned the knob, and moved in front of him into the darkness. When she switched on the fluorescent ceiling light, Howard looked around him at an all-white windowless room. Directly in front of him, on a long stainless steel table, he saw the head of his father peeking through the unzipped slit of a large black body bag. "You can stay as long as you like," the young woman said, nearly whispering. Then moving past him, she closed the door behind him.

Conscious of the sudden silence around him, Howard stood near the door for a long moment, accustoming himself to this new world he had entered. He thought of Wade and longed suddenly to feel his friend's arms enfold him. He thought of

Jessie running out into the snow to help this man, to stay his journey, to stop his flight. . . .

With an audible sigh, he walked toward the black object in front of him and stood over it, his mind full of the echoes of a hundred memories. A little afraid, he touched the man's forehead, his cheek, his throat. The dark skin was cool and somewhat stiffened, like old leather. His head was turned slightly toward Howard. His mouth was partially opened. Slowly, very slowly, Howard unzipped the bag to the man's waist, as though he were trying to make him as comfortable as possible. Sidney Shaler was wearing what appeared to be a hospital gown: white, cotton, shapeless. Howard studied it without seeing it. Then he sat down next to him on one of the two barlike aluminum stools in the room, and waited.

Well . . .

He touched the face with his fist, the knuckles of his right hand.

Well, I don't know what to talk about, really.

He touched the face again: a caress.

I'm sorry you had to go like that, in the snow, in the cold, surprised . . . surprised and probably not knowing what was happening to you.

He stopped. He had wanted to say so many things, but now that he was here the words floated within him, disconnected, or came out as though he were pasting them, one by one, onto the wind.

I'm sorry . . . I'm sorry I couldn't have been there to help you, although I'm glad you came to me in your going. Came to say goodbye and to remind me that Ohio was you and you were the home I was always wanting. I'm glad you spoke to me that day. Maybe your speaking was your message. Maybe that was enough. I wanted more, but maybe that was enough.

Suddenly he stood up, flinging tears from his eyes. No, he told himself, he was not going to cry. And he was not going to patronize this—this corpse in any way whatsoever, neither with self-pity nor sentimentality. Nor lies. As far as he knew, Sidney Shaler never gave enough of himself to anyone. He was incapable of giving. Why?

Howard wanted to leave, but he forced himself to remain here in this white, nearly blank otherworld. He felt as if he too had crossed over. Could death, he wondered, be as sterile, as barren as this? And he sat down again.

He sat down in the room's pale fluorescence and saw his father standing before him as through a mist: a young man, nineteen years old or twenty or twenty-two, an athlete riding high on his youth and victory. Victory over body; victory over color, class, history; victory over self. Basketball, football, boxing, long-distance running, swimming—he had made all of them his own; inhabited them all, and in the end had used them to escape the backwoods of Kentucky. An athletic scholarship took him to Wilberforce College and another one carried him to " 'one of them big white universities way up north,' " so Sidney Shaler once quoted his mother who, proud of her only son, talked of little else after he had boarded a train for Ann Arbor to enroll at the University of Michigan. "A colored boy in 1935!" she exclaimed to her friends. "My flesh and blood! Oh yes, things are movin' on, Father Abraham."

Howard remembered that Nana, his maternal grandmother, used to say something similar whenever Marian Anderson triumphed—"Oh yes, we're climbin', Father Abraham"—whenever Joe Louis kayoed somebody white, or Adam Clayton Powell stood up and talked back, or Jackie Robinson stole home. "Oh yes, we *are* climbin'." Or whenever some little girl in the next block won a spelling bee, or when that Elam girl—what was her name?—managed somehow to outwit school authorities to become the first colored valedictorian in the history of Darby High School. "Oh yes, Father. Climbin'."

Then, aloud, in a whisper: "How far did you climb, Dad?"

It was a cruel question made more cruel by the fact that it contained its own answer: *How far? Not too far.* Fragments of some gospel song came to him from beyond the impenetrable silence; bits and pieces of old sermons. *How high? Not too high. How long? Not too long.* Then realizing how vain, how foolish such evaluations were—realizing that victory and defeat exist within us all, simultaneously—he got up again from the stool and said, "You climbed high enough, I suppose."

He got up—and this time, after rezippering the body bag, he did leave. Nothing much, he knew, had been said, and nothing at all completed. Maybe tomorrow at the laying out he could have another talk with his father. Maybe tomorrow he could be done with him.

Returning to the house on Reisinger Avenue, he greeted Jessie in the living room, as well as three of her neighbors, women from across the street, whom he didn't know. He chatted with them briefly, accepting their condolences and answering their questions about Mexico, before excusing himself. His suitcase was still in the hallway, so he took it upstairs to his old room, where he found Wade, half asleep, sitting in a rocker next to the bed. The familiarity of the room, as well as its strangeness, startled him: Everything— and nothing at all—seemed to be as it had been four years ago when he last visited Dayton.

"Hello." He nudged his friend. A copy of the *Dayton Daily News*, Wade's employer, tumbled from his lap to the floor.

"So how did it go?" Yawning, Wade stretched and sat up in the rocker.

Howard shook his head. "I don't know." He put his suitcase on the bed, opened it, and began unpacking. "I never quite said goodbye. I talked to him. And to myself. Did some remembering. Things like that." As he spoke, he threw his few socks, his underwear, and a green wool sweater into the nearly empty chest-of-drawers at the other end of the room. Finally, he hung two shirts and a pair of Levi's in the closet. Except for his shaving kit, he had completed his unpacking.

"You didn't bring much," Wade observed.

"I don't own much. I got rid of a lot of things when I left L.A." Howard put the suitcase in the closet. "I don't even own a suit anymore. I was hoping—since I knew I was gonna need a suit—I could use one of Dad's."

Wade smiled faintly. "To go to his funeral?"

"There's not gonna be a funeral, remember?"

"Okay, the 'laying out.' "

Sitting down on the side of the bed, Howard tugged at his left earlobe, chuckling. "That's got to be an irony: my having to wear one of Dad's suits to his wake."

Wade nodded, looking at his friend closely. "By the way," he said as casually as he could manage as he retrieved the newspaper and returned it to his lap, "I saw your father—oh, about three months ago. He phoned me at the office. Asked if we could meet."

"Oh?" Howard felt something—an alarm—twitch or twist in the middle of his gut. "What did he want?"

"Actually he phoned me twice, but I met him only once. He wanted to talk about you and me—that's how it went at first."

"You and me?"

"Yes. I was surprised too. We met for lunch at some restaurant downtown. As soon as we sat down in the booth, he started in. He kept talking about our 'friendship,' yours and mine—he used that word: *friendship* and *friends*. Used it several times. He wanted to know exactly when we had become 'friends' and why we were no longer 'friends.' I was puzzled by all that and told him that as far as I knew you and I were still friends. 'Are you?' he said. He seemed sort of cold. 'How can that be?' He said it like a sneer. 'You haven't seen each other in years.' It was then I realized he wasn't talking about friendship—he was talking about sex. I didn't know what to say."

Suddenly Howard found it difficult to breathe. "What *did* you say?"

"Before I could say anything, the waitress came to take our orders, and all at once your dad got real charming—you know how he could be: joking and all. Flirting. He began pointing to the menu, asking the waitress what this or that was, and what was the house specialty. I don't remember all of it. When she had gone, the charm vanished, and he turned to me—or turned *on* me, I should say—to tell me that he had always been skeptical of me, that he had distrusted me ever since I came into your life all those years ago when you and I were in high school. Since high school, for God's sake! I was nonplussed, but I did manage to ask him why he disliked me. And asking him that I got real angry, because I knew where he was heading. 'Because,' he said—and he spat the word like he was some white man saying the word *nigger*—'you were a faggot then, and I guess you're a faggot now. And you made my son one.'"

Astonished, Howard could hardly believe what he was hearing.

"At about that time the waitress came back—oh yes, something about your dad's order not being available and could he choose something else. Well, he looked at the menu again and chose, and as soon as she left I cut into something he was going to say, cut him off, and told him he was a bigot, a bigot of the worst sort, I said, because being black had taught him nothing about acceptance of others who were also despised. I was trying to be respectful. I mean, this was an old man and he was your father. But—well, my anger was getting the better of me, and I said that if it was faggotry he was talking about—"

"Jesus, Wade!"

"—that if it was faggotry he was talking about, sex between you and me—well, all that had taken place years ago when we were teenagers, and why was he bringing it up now. He said that it may indeed have taken place years ago, but as far as he was concerned it was always being repeated in his head and consequently it was taking place at that very instant, because you, *you* had never stopped being . . ." Wade tried to execute a shrug.

"A faggot?"

"Yes. You had never stopped being one, and because of that you had deliberately separated yourself from him. That seemed to be important to him, because he repeated it, with his fist hitting the table: You had willfully separated yourself from him. It sounded crazy. I didn't know what to say, but I did tell him—helplessly, I suppose, because I couldn't think of anything else to say—that it was his bigotry, his narrowmindedness which was doing the separating."

"Jesus, Wade, don't you ever . . . ?" Howard stopped.

"What?"

Howard closed his eyes. ". . . shut up?" The words sputtered out of him inaudibly. But then, staring at Wade again, he spoke up more clearly: "Don't you ever shut up?" Yet having said that, he wondered why he wished to protect his father, why he wished to defend him.

"Shut up? Look, Howard"—Wade's voice began to rise—"that man was in need of some upfront talk. And, incidentally, he was never really talking about me. He was talking about you and him and what the two of you had become to each other. He seemed to be in pain—I mean, people don't talk like that unless they are in pain. Was I supposed to hide from that?

Was I supposed to hide from *him*, like you've done all your life? And he from you?" He looked at Howard as though he expected a reply.

"All right, all right," Howard offered, twisting as he sat on the edge of the bed, impaled.

Wade went on, this time more quietly: "I gathered he was, in some curious way—I don't know—talking to you through me. Maybe he was trying to resolve something for himself or something between the two of you. He wasn't doing it very well, I admit." A laugh wheezed through his nostrils. "Maybe he knew his time was short, and he wanted to clear the slate. You weren't available. I was."

"All right. I said all right. Okay?" Howard held up his right hand. He held it up, attempting to deflect not only his friend's words but the guilt, hurt, anger, jealousy—a single sensation—that had begun throbbing in his temples. Avoiding Wade's eyes, he turned his gaze to one of the room's two windows that faced the street. Through the gathering dusk he watched the snow falling on the naked branches of the large elm in front of the house, watched it falling silently on the peaked roofs of the homes across the street and, beyond those, on the plains of the city that seemed to stretch on forever in the darkening light. He watched, but no matter how intensely he did so he couldn't distance himself from what he had just heard. Nor could he dislodge faggot, his father's epithet, that had sunk itself into him like a fishhook. "Go on," he said softly, returning his gaze to Wade at last. He unlaced his shoes, kicked them off, and sat up in bed, his back propped against the headboard. "Go on. It's okay."

With dusk turning into night, Wade got up and switched on the lamp near the window. Light, almost as subdued as candle glow, suffused the room. "Well, there's really not much more to it. I was angry, your father was angry. I finished my meal as quickly as possible and said goodbye. I left him there in the restaurant." Wade returned to the rocker. "We didn't see each other again, though we did talk. He phoned me about a month later—again at the office—to tell me he was getting a letter off to you that day. He said he hadn't written you since you'd been in Mexico. And did I want him to send you a message? I must have hesitated, because frankly I was puzzled again.

Was he phoning just to tell me that? Or was there some other motive? And why was he suddenly being so nice? Again, I didn't know what to say, but I did say, 'Tell Howard I said hello and that I'm thinking of him and I hope he comes home soon.' And he thanked me—kindly, I might add—and hung up."

"And that was the end of it?"

Wade nodded.

Like his friend, Howard didn't know what to make of it. "If he wrote me, I never got the letter. The letter never arrived."

Wade wasn't surprised. "Do you think he mailed it?" Almost immediately, however, he amended the question: "Do you think he wrote it?"

Howard, who had drawn his knees under his chin, offered Wade a bitter little laugh. "Do you think it matters?"

He didn't sleep well that night. Diarrhea woke him up once and drove him to the bathroom. Bad dreams woke him again and forced him to sit up in bed, back against the headboard in a vain attempt to defend himself against the cunning Pygmies who were now rendering him powerless as they took him out into the night and down dark pathless hills, carrying him across a deserted beach and into the baptismal waters of the night sea, the sea where breakers washed against him like whispers; where babies floated on waves that lulled him to sleep; where white corpses glowed with fluorescent fire as they bobbed up and down, drifting across the currents, singing, singing. . . .

"Dad!"

He woke again, still against the headboard of the bed. He had heard something, some voice. Yet he barely opened his eyes. Too tired to investigate it, too drugged with sleep, he slid down against the pillows only to find himself standing on the platform of a subway station. His father was beside him, thin and old—and as mute as a mannequin. He and his father had been traveling a long time together, a long distance. Now, as the subway train roared into the station, they knew they would be traveling still farther in this strange city (beneath this city), a city that seemed to have no name. They boarded the train at the last car, then moved forward three cars before sitting down amid silent men and women. The train lurched into motion and stopped abruptly, still in the station. At the same moment he remembered he had forgotten something, perhaps his suitcase or wallet—something left in the last car or on the platform. He explained to his father that he must go back three cars to retrieve what he had lost. Making an announcement to the other passengers, he asked: "Do all of you know who I am? Do all of you know my name?" The passengers tell him that his name is Howard Shaler. Satisfied (for he can now return to his rightful place in this car), he leaves his father and proceeds to walk forward—not backward—to the last car. Not finding the lost object there, he steps out onto the station platform to continue his search. Suddenly, almost as if they were waiting for him to leave, the train's sliding doors snap shut. Whirling around, he tries to pry the doors open with his hands. He shouts, but no one seems to hear him. He hammers at the doors with his fists. He shouts again, hammers again. The train begins to move, gathering speed, leaving him behind as he runs after it. "Dad!" he cries out. He feels miserable: His father is alone on the train, alone in this strange city, alone in the darkness. "Dad!"

Dad.

He jerked himself awake, frightened and baffled to find himself here in this bed. *Where am I?* He glanced around the dark room. Then he remembered. *Oh yes, Dad is dead, and I'm home.* And sank back against the bedding. *Dad is dead, and I'm glad.* The words splashed across his consciousness and, like ink spilling across a page, seeped in. If he had been fully awake, he would have been shocked, he who so often censored his thoughts and controlled his emotions. As it was, he was still half asleep. And half asleep, he was aware only of some dull ache at the back of his head: something pushing against the barricade of blood and bone. *Well, it's true. I am glad. Foolish man. He was certainly that. Foolish people don't deserve to live. They destroy; they don't deserve the beauty of green hills or islands bathed in orange mist. They destroy. He destroyed with his laughter, fooled you with it, lassoed you, strangled you. Selfish, foolish bastard! You lived long enough. Long enough to throw your piss into my face.* Now he was fully awake, his eyes staring at the blackness. *Can't take little sissy boys, huh? Not even when they're ten and eleven and twelve? Can't take 'em anywhere, can do nothin' with 'em. Yeah. You must have recognized the signs, long before I did. After all, you knew them so well. All those little sissies you taunted when you were growing up. Oh yeah, I can imagine, because I grew up with you, boys just like you. And I've heard all your stories about pussy and all your jokes about Billy or Danny or Jimmy who liked to take it up the ass. All that mindless ridicule. Now here you are saddled with such a joke forever, your own son, who has a pussy up his ass. I'd call that poetic justice. . . .* Throwing the covers back, Howard sat up abruptly. A storm had begun to ring itself around him. The barricade was beginning to break: he felt as if his brain were unraveling. Switching on the lamp, he sat on the edge of the bed, his head in his hands. *Poetic justice, yes, that's what it was, but you saw it as my revenge, my determination to separate my life from yours for—for all eternity, I guess. You guys who can't take sissy. You're the real joke. Well, I took your piss. Now take some of mine. What kind of man did you become? Answer me that. Ever since that time you left Jessie (yeah, I know you remember that summer, I know it because you could never talk about it), from that summer on, I realized you didn't know anything about yourself. Oh, I admit I wanted your—your masculinity—I admit it, and I always enjoyed watching it: your ease and the confidence. The apparent confidence. But I didn't want your manhood. No. You let your wife . . . your wives . . . me . . . You let everybody down. And all because of what? Your cock. No? Cock ruled a lot of your life. No? The shit it didn't. I've been there: I know. No, you listen, you listen to me. I know, I know.*

Then, as the storm enveloped him, Howard became aware that Jessie was in the room, that Jessie was suddenly at his side, holding him. She kept saying, "Yes, yes, it's all right. It's all right." He was coughing, nearly choking. His eyes were blinded by the storm. His cheeks were wet with tears. She put his head on her breast and held him closer, rocking him. "Yes, yes," she reassured him, fiercely, "it is all *right.*"

The following morning, Saturday, he woke up with the awareness that his diarrhea had vanished. He no longer felt the sharp cramping in his stomach. Relieved, he walked around the bedroom touching his stomach and rubbing his hand across his groin as if he were inspecting an old wound that had finally healed. Had it only been anxiety? Or had some curse been

eliminated at last from his body and his mind? He recalled
Jessie holding him in the night; he remembered the subway
train whose doors had closed against him. No, not yet, the
train seemed to say as it vanished into the void. We don't want
you yet.

His sense of relief affected his mood throughout the entire
day as he completed all the tasks Jessie had asked him to do:
He ordered flowers for the viewing that evening; he wrote the
death notice that would appear in the local newspaper; and he
sorted through the items in his father's walk-in closet crammed
to overflowing with sports coats, gabardine slacks, overcoats,
ties, shirts, shoes, and suits of a variety of materials and colors.
None of the clothes interested him, but to please Jessie he
chose a few items to take back to Mexico: some shirts, two
pairs of slacks, a tie, and the dark blue worsted suit he intended
to wear that evening.

All the while he kept remembering the previous night's conversation with Wade. He also thought about the missing letter,
the message that may or may not have been sent. He didn't
launch an all-out search for it, but he asked Jessie if she knew
anything about it. No, she replied, she knew nothing at all. "I
remember him saying not too long ago that he should write
you, but I didn't think he ever did."

At six-thirty, the letter all but forgotten, Howard and Jessie
walked into the reception area at Barrington's Funeral Home.
Subdued by the circumstances, they struggled out of their coats
and hung them in the cloakroom, before moving into the
cream-colored chapel.

Jessie was relieved to find the chapel empty—except for the
corpse that lay hidden in its bier between two tall candles in
the center of the room. She had wanted to arrive before her
friends and acquaintances descended upon the room and certainly before *his* Dayton arrived. All that day something had
been forming within her, some sense of determination, as she
recalled two long-ago moments: the night she was introduced
to Sidney Shaler at a party on Fifth Street and the Saturday
afternoon, nearly a year later, when she married him. Now,
in honor of those moments, she clasped the right hand of her
husband's son as the two of them stood over the closed casket
and conducted their own funeral for the man who had not

wanted a funeral; their own funeral for the man who, so difficult to mourn, would now be mourned, so difficult to love, would be loved.

With Howard at her side, Jessie bowed her head and spoke into the eternal stillness. "All grief is terrible," she whispered aloud in prayer, her eyes closed, "all grief is . . . hell. There's no other word for it—there *is* no word for it." Swaying, she brushed ever so lightly against Howard. "Our—our particular hell, mine and this child's, is to grieve for a man we could never hold in our arms, a man who refused to be held in anyone's arms. We"—she hesitated—"we mourn for a person we never knew. Never really touched." She began to lose command of her voice, so she waited, waited until she could make her voice go where she wanted it to go. And waiting, she held Howard's hand more tightly, her eyes still closed. "I don't know all the things that love can be," she went on, "but I do know that, at this moment, love is the grief we hold within us. It's this burning we feel at not ever being joined"—she searched for the right words—"at not having been joined by the man— this man, *this stranger*—we, Howard and I, were so often wanting." Then: "Love is mourning." She hesitated again. "Our mourning. Mourning without end." Now, shaking her head, she opened her eyes and looked up at Howard. "I can't seem to get too much beyond that."

Jessie made a move to leave the bier, but Howard held her there with the merest pressure on her arm. Listening to her lament reminded him, for some reason, of his father's old sorrow: those drowned sisters and the mother who had called for them, over and over, at the river's edge. She and her dead daughters had become a part of the mythos of his father's soul. Now, Howard understood, they had wrapped themselves around him and Jessie. Touching the casket, Howard spoke to his father: *Maybe you needed all your wives, all those women you could never love because you had lost forever those first women. Yes, I can imagine you trying endlessly in your loving, in your fucking, to fill yourself with all women, those first women, trying again and again; but you can never fill yourself enough. Never, never enough, because your cup is always emptying.*

"Maybe there's only one road out of hell," he murmured to Jessie. It wasn't a prayer, yet it was as close as he would ever come to prayer, to benediction. "Somehow we've got to love the wound he's given us, the wound he got." He thought of animals nursing their injuries, licking their maimed parts. It seemed so simple. *Loving our stink.* "We've got to love that ugliness in us, his ugliness, so that it becomes our deliverance. Our victory over him. *For* him."

Jessie didn't understand. "How do you do that?"

Howard nearly laughed. In a voice as diminutive as his stepmother's, he replied, "I don't know," and repeated it, "I don't know," and led her to the first row of gray metal folding chairs that surrounded the bier in a half-circle. "I guess you gotta work at it. Or try to."

Gotta work at it. Somehow those words (now as he sat down) got mixed up in his mind with *love is mourning*, a truth whose mystery he accepted despite his wish to reject it. Like Jessie, he didn't know all of love's expressions, but he decided, gazing at the casket, that it wasn't love which gave life its meaning. It was death. It was death that *gave* life, he reflected as he heard the rustle of people arriving behind him. Turning, he recognized several of Jessie's neighbors and some of his father's old cronies and, behind them, Wade, who immediately dislodged himself from the group and came to sit beside him. Soon, he thought, the celebration would begin—indeed, it had already begun: the tentative smiles, the light of recognition on several faces, the laughter, the embraces of friends, the reunion of saints and sinners. Returning his gaze to the casket, he watched the flames from the tall candles flicker above the bier and saw for the first time the wreath of blood-red roses perched in the distance between the flames. Death, he reflected, shapes everything around us, blinding us with its radiance, its joy, even as it deforms and defeats us. Death—now he took Wade's hand into his own and brought it to his lips—death is the enemy and the ally.

INSIDE

• DAVID VERNON •

FROM THE VIEW outside my window it appears to be a gorgeous fall day. The kind of day that you want to stroll the West Side, passing trees in transition or grab the last of the season's lemon ices in Little Italy.

The idea of being outside is seductive. But like an upstate house on sale that looks like a bargain but hides bad plumbing and rotting wood, appearances are misleading. Looking at me you can't see this greedy samurai virus that has explored, invaded, and now vacations in my blood. I picture the virus, cartoon and squat. Ziggy with an attitude. He wears Bermuda shorts that come up to his chest, slides down my bloodstream on a raft, laughing wildly and polluting as he travels on. In my mind my virus is white, fat, American and very, very Republican.

I haven't been out of my apartment in three months.

Certainly this has been problematic. But then, as the cliché goes I found a book that changed my life. It was an alternate selection of The Book-Of-The-Month Club called *New York Delivers*. There is little I need that is not covered in this book.

Near me there is the Chinese place on University, Ray's Original, New York's Only Ray's, the Homer Deli on the corner of Greenwich; they all deliver. The postal carrier comes up to my apartment. I've been buying clothes through catalogs for years. I feel like I've been preparing for this a long time.

On cable the other night there was a program on space and the universe. The host, a tower of composure, announced, as heated as a winner on "Jeopardy," that we are discovering new galaxies. No parade. No headline. This show wasn't even on one of the networks. I only caught it because I hit Channel 21 instead of 12 on my remote. So I sat back on my beige leather couch, lit another Marlboro and said, "Jesus Christ, not *another* galaxy." In all honesty I have just adjusted to the idea of leaving this one. Every morning over a bowl of Lucky Charms or Trix I chant somewhat less than half-believing, "I am the center of my universe and the universe is my apartment." Some people's galaxies expand. I feel a jerk and mine moves in closer and tighter. I vote for less space. Concentrate on what you have.

So who else delivers? Waldenbooks. The Ben and Jerry's on Fifth if they're not crowded. I call in my orders to the market on University once a week and they deliver as well.

My friend Bradley is coming over for a visit today. He is the only friend I allow up. Not that Bradley is my closest friend—he always wears solid colors and asks, "Is this too bright for you?"—but Bradley is the most tolerant person I know right now, and like an eight-year-old planning his own birthday party I feel the need to be indulged. But even Bradley is getting annoyed with me. He gravitates between love and tough love. He says he worries about doing the right thing. Sometimes he says, "Hal, you've become part of the furniture. You are filled with self-pity. So you've been sick. Lots of people in New York are. The world is a scary place, but you need to put the fear down and go on with your life." I call this Bradley's well-meaning Marriette Hartley, movie-of-the-week tone.

Last week Bradley was angry. He said, "Hal, you are a selfish fuck." (Gosh, Bradley, aren't all fucks selfish?) He says, "So you think the world should come to you. It's a risk to go outside and you were never one to take a risk." To this I take a long drag, stare him down and just say, "Glass houses, baby. Glass houses."

Bradley is partially right. I really haven't been that sick lately. I was in St. Vincent's six months ago with pneumocystis. One day after I returned home I was walking to D'Agostino's market. I stopped, out of breath. Jesus, I thought, my

65-year-old father walks two miles a day and here I am at 40, out of breath on the way to the market. I stood still in the middle of the sidewalk and lit a Marlboro. God, you would have thought that I was a stalled vehicle in the Holland Tunnel. People knocked into me, elbowed past me. Trying to bring the cigarette to my mouth I realized that my hands were trembling. I couldn't move. Like a windup toy stuck in a groove I just stood there shaking and quivering. Then, thank God, it started raining, pouring, practically a monsoon. I had to ask eight cabdrivers before I found one that would drive me home just six blocks away. I haven't been outside since.

I found a fluff-and-fold that picks up and delivers, but their work is inconsistent at best, depending on who is on shift. There is this one woman, I call her Zelda the Lunatic Starch Queen. She just loves the stuff. It is an experiment in terror. When she gets through with them the clothes could walk home by themselves. Although I've never met the woman I picture her, Elsa Lancaster hair, bloated soft-boiled egg-white eyes. Surrounded by steam and a laugh that would stop a street gang.

Bradley always tells me success stories about other HIV folk, people worse off than I am. Today he tells me a story he heard in his group therapy of some ACT UP guy with 18 T-cells who has fallen in love with some dentist who has 27 T-cells. They're giving up their Manhattan apartments and moving to Greece. I tell Bradley to spare me the "They're living life to the fullest and you can too" spiel. He frowns. In the course of ten minutes Bradley complains that my kitchen is unsanitary, that the apartment is too dark and that the living room is so filled with cigarette smoke that he can see the plants wheezing. But I can't fault Bradley today because he brought over some cannolis from my favorite Italian bakery. "Handmade," Bradley assures me, "by some hunky Italian dough-boy named Guido."

Today we watch the movie *Logan's Run* on TV and afterwards I tell Bradley that I see the film as an AIDS metaphor.

"You see everything as an AIDS metaphor," Bradley whines.

"Because everything is," I assure him. "How can you live in New York and not realize that?"

In *Logan's Run*, people live in some oversized shopping mall and they must die at the age of 30. Michael York plays Logan, who used to be a sandman and now he's running for his life. He finds an exit from the shopping mall which leads to a place they call Sanctuary, inhabited by a 60-year-old Peter Ustinov and a shitload of cats. The point is that Michael York realizes people don't have to die at 30. It was just some inexplicable plot. A whim. The point is, people don't have to die. But Bradley doesn't see it.

As he is preparing to leave Bradley announces that he won't be visiting me anymore. I feel a quick jerk; a contraction. He says that they discussed it in group therapy and agreed that visiting me at home when I'm well enough to go out is just enabling my inappropriate behavior. Bradley keeps on talking but I really don't hear a word of it. At this point he cannot disappear from my universe fast enough.

There is a place on Broadway that delivers meatball subs— thick marinara, lots of cheap processed cheese, and meatballs so round you can see them being rolled by some guy in a white tank top patting the meat gently with the centers of his palms. I order a sub and some sodas.

"Bring it over quickly," I bark.

As I hang up the receiver I hear a sinister rumble, like from the water pipes, but deeper. The rumble is followed by a subtle tremor of motion. Although the manager of the building doesn't know what I'm talking about, I notice these movements, and the teeter displayed by my plaster statuette of Hermes confirms this. I swear to God fucking Christ that this apartment is getting smaller, moving in closer from all ends like the third reel of a Charlie Chan cliffhanger.

I used to order all my subs from Pizza Palace. They have the most beautiful pizza delivery boys; jet black hair, authentic like the ones from Queens or the Bronx. And when they'd perspire I'd imagine it would be droplets of Bertoli olive oil. A month ago I received a call from the manager of Pizza Palace, one Ginger Gladworth. She said that they weren't going to deliver to me again. I made the boys nervous.

Fuck Bradley and his group.

World of Video delivers. I have an account with them and I've been watching a lot of movies lately. I figure, how many more times am I going to get to see *Dumbo*, or *A Letter to Three*

Wives? When a movie is finishing I feel like I am saying goodbye to characters that have saved many a Saturday night.
Guests in my living room. My all-time favorite movies are
Valley of the Dolls, Death in Venice, Oliver, and *Pizza Boy—He
Delivers*, directed by William Higgins. Besides the fact that I've
always been attracted to Italian men, *Pizza Boy—He Delivers* is
easily the best adult film I've ever seen. It's more than just sex,
and sex has become very boring to me lately. It's about pizza
boys: their angst, their journey to self-acceptance. It's about
taking chances, knocking on doors; delivering pizzas to lonely
blond men who have just broken up with their girlfriends and
invite you inside to have a slice then accidentally spill red wine
on your jeans and offer to wipe them off for you. It's about
youth: fleeting. It's about anchovies: always on the side. No
fee for delivering. No job too tough. I've met quite a few pizza
boys in my day—some mythically handsome—but I've never
met one who delivered. Not really.

I check the mail and there is another self-help book from a
soon-to-be-ex-friend in Los Angeles. I have a collection of them
now, *Eat Healthy, Drink Healthy*. I say fuck it. I did the macro-
biotic thing for two weeks, and let me tell you, I was not
impressed. I saw myself in the mirror, cigarette in my mouth,
cutting up sea vegetables, and I said, Hal, what do you want
to be, the healthiest corpse in the graveyard? All those books,
self-help cassettes by people who have studied the disease from
the outside. So now I only eat crap, things that I wouldn't eat
when I was healthy like Chef Boyardee Spaghetti-O's and
Cheese Whiz. I told my friend Lois that I was eating green
Jell-O. She said, "Gosh, Hal, don't you know that those are
made from horse hooves?"

I said, "Fuck 'em. What's the horse gonna do with them now
anyway?"

Another friend sent me a video called, "Hin Yin, Ancient
Secrets of Relaxation and Self-Realization." It teaches you how
not to mind having sex by yourself. It's basically three blonds
jerking off to New Age music. It does say some good things
though. It says that by loving yourself you are loving the
world, and I guess in a world fucked out of whack masturbation is the best defense.

The sub from Jerry's is on the way, so while I'm waiting I

turn on the answering machine, kneel in front of my 20-inch Zenith, push my jeans around my ankles, flick on *Pizza Boy— He Delivers*, and I start stroking myself.

In the film one pizza boy is driving another pizza boy home. They stop in the woods, drink beer and sneak glances at each other's crotch. And I'm working it. Pizza Boy #1 says, "I get so horny when I'm out here drinking."

Pizza Boy #2 looks bashfully at #1's growing bulge and says, "Yeah, me too."

First time I watched this movie I just barely touched myself before I exploded and today, countless viewings later, I'm working up a sweat, and it doesn't look like it's going to happen. I watch these two boys, neither could be over 19, having unprotected sex, shooting cum joyously into each other's faces, and I wonder where they are today. That's enough to stop me right there.

The Hin Yin tape says that having sex alone can be just as exciting as with a partner. I wonder if I should ask Bradley what his group would say about that. I can see them with their show of hands, making decisions that concern me. I grab the Vaseline Intensive Care Lotion and I start up again rubbing my soft dick. I fantasize about this dark-skinned guy who lives two floors below me. I've seen him in the laundry room teasing me with glimpses of his soiled Jockeys. He sings Springsteen songs, reads *Sports Illustrated*, and once I saw his nipple peek out from behind his tank top. And it was magic. I imagine rubbing up against him, feeling him growing harder, harder. But then I start thinking about nonoxidol-9, condoms, dental dams, no wet kissing, and I just stop. Even in my fantasies sex is not safe.

The phone rings. The machine picks up and it's the delivery guy from Jerry's calling. He's lost. I pick up and tell him that he has the wrong address, that I'm on Seventh Avenue near Greenwich right above the jewelry store with the banner EAR PIERCING WITH OR WITHOUT PAIN—YOUR CHOICE. I took the apartment mainly because of the banner, so I could remind myself daily that there was a choice in regards to pain. I always wondered if you could pay more for extra pain. Extra pain on the side. The delivery boy promises to be here soon.

I return to the TV screen where the pizza boys are at it

again. I spread more lotion onto my palms, gaze at the screen, and imagine a time before AIDS. It is 1955 and I am in an alley around Hollywood wearing ripped jeans, my right leg propped against a brick wall. I am the height of mysteriousness. Sal Mineo approaches, taking the back entrance to his apartment after a long day of shooting *Rebel Without a Cause*. He wears a T-shirt and tight black shorts that show off his basket. It's a sticky, breezeless summer night. I light a cigarette, blow smoke in his face and without a word we are all over each other, his tongue all over my chest. It is 1955 and I am healthy, my body unblemished. I can smell his hair, greasy with VO-5. Oh yeah, real good. And he's wearing Old Spice, the trademark of a true Italian-American. But then he sees the purple blotch on my side and says, "What's your HIV status?"

"What you care about my HIV status?" I ask. "It's 1955, there is no such thing."

Sal pulls up his black shorts.

"You can't reject me, this is my fantasy," I yell.

But he does. As he walks away I want to warn him to stay away from back alleys and movies where he plays Gene Kruppa. But it's too late. He's vanished.

My right arm is growing numb. My hard-on throbs, but I'm not feeling any pleasure. This just feels like work.

I travel back further, close my eyes and I'm on a boat, the *Santa Maria* navigated by Christopher Columbus. Days and barren nights go by and the ship rocks over the waves, inching our way closer. Closer. It's working. Closer. It is a night filled with stars, fresh salt air that caresses my lungs. On the deck is Columbus gazing out at the ocean. I'm wearing my white linen slacks and my navy blazer from Barney's. I light a cigarette and give Columbus the stare-down. He is magnificent, his hair unkept, a face full of moles. The ship rocks and our bodies are thrown together. Pressing. Good. Columbus invites me downstairs to his cabin to see his map collection. Rocking. Inside the plush cabin I pull my hand across the knots in his greasy hair. Columbus' hair. Good. I lick his neck and taste the salt water. He is wearing Old Spice. His frame is large, almost heroic. He wraps me in his embrace and whispers, "Before we go further I think we should share about our sexual history."

I say, "Columbus, take me, name the new world after your love for me."

Columbus sits on the bed, crosses his legs and says, "Hal, I think we should talk responsibly about this. Even though it's 1492 you never can be too careful."

And I'm soft. Jesus, I'm completely soft.

The buzzer shrieks and it's the delivery boy from Jerry's. I pull up my jeans and wipe my hands on a towel.

The delivery boy is a redhead. Hardly a proper Pizza Boy. I tip him generously and ask him what it's like outside. He brightens up, "Pretty OK, I guess." I leave the movie on while I eat my sub 'cause I don't want to turn on the TV and accidentally hear about yet another galaxy.

Bradley would ask me how I stayed home without getting bored, and I'd tell him that it's never boring. You learn about yourself by staying home. Home becomes a museum of you. A painting on my wall that I've seen a hundred times changes as I change. Why is the man in the painting embracing himself? Last month I thought it was love. Now I think that it's fear.

God, look at that, perfect, round meatballs. Perfect.

And I wonder, if like Michael York in that movie, if I found an exit from the shopping mall, if I turned the right book back and my bookshelf would revolve and I'd find a secret passageway out of my apartment that would lead to Sanctuary, to a place where people didn't have to die, I wonder, would I go?

Bradley asks me, "Wouldn't you rather be a role model, Hal, and help teach people strength?"

I've never understood the concept of role model. And why should I share what I've learned with other people? I think it's braver to stay home and face yourself than to go out and face the world. Hey, I've seen the world, fuck 'em. I've been to Europe, it's no big deal. I've seen compassion, it's overrated.

On TV, it's the last scene of the movie. Three Pizza Boys just finished having sticky-gooey sex. Now they playfully toss pillows at each other. The camera pulls back, slowly out the window, leaving them to play together for eternity in their pepperoni-induced bliss.

IF A MAN ANSWERS

• DAVID FEINBERG •

"Thou shalt not commit adultery."

I. KEN

"HELLO," SAID KEN in a voice about an octave lower than his normal range. Ken found that men were much more likely to respond when he spoke in a deep, resonant voice. He had developed an entirely distinct persona for phone sex. He suppressed his normal nasal twang that brought to mind Gilda Radner impersonating a Jewish American Princess. It was the old Marilyn Monroe trick, but not quite so breathy. His voice was virtually unrecognizable.

"Hello."

"My name's Rick, what's yours?" Even though it was a one-on-one phone-sex line, Ken didn't want to risk the wrong person finding out. He *did* have a lover. If Liverlips ever found out, there would be hell to pay. Ken had experimented with other noms de latex. Rod was the stud, first-runner-up-in-the-Mister-New-York-Leather-Contest (how he adored beauty contests). Martin was the tight-assed, anal-retentive, accountant-in-heat-about-to-explode. Rick was the straight-guy-next-door who-didn't-mind-getting-sucked-off-by-a-guy-when-his-wife-was-away-in-another-city-visiting-her-mother-for-an-operation.

"Bill."

"How are you tonight?" Ken didn't use the group line any

more. On the one hand, you could meet up to seven different people on the group line. Using the one-on-one line was like going to the cavernous Palladium at 10 P.M. on a Saturday and finding only one other guy, standing in the shadows, a drink in his hand. But the group line had its hazards too. Ken was tired of listening to crazy Artie rant and rave. Artie, a sixty-one-year-old from Westchester who claimed he looked like thirty-five, was always trampling on the group line, encouraging people who had no interest in one another to meet, playing yenta to the global village, and then cursing everyone out while bragging about the size of his legendary dick. If it wasn't Artie, there was always some other insistent crank with a bizarre kink unique to perhaps ten people on the planet Earth, interrupting the conversational flow every twenty seconds: "Anyone into chocolate enemas?" "Anyone into tattooed foreskins?" "Anyone into fisting in evening gloves?"

"Pretty horny."

"Same here. Can I call you?" Ken liked the sound of his voice. Hurry, the meter's ticking. There were times on the group line when he would find an appealing someone who was unable to give out his number, which was more or less like going to the baths a hundred million years ago with a locker and meeting a hot stud who also had a locker, when there were no empty rooms to "borrow" and neither had the predilection for the orgy room, where it was impossible to contain sex to just the two of them. The one-on-one line was his best bet.

"Sorry, I can't give out the number. I'm staying with a friend."

"I can't either. I have a roommate." Liverlips. Asleep on the couch in the study. Said he had some kind of bug, didn't want to risk giving it to Ken. Although for the life of him he couldn't imagine how, since they haven't had sex in six months. He's so fucking cold.

"Where do you live?"

"Manhattan. You?" Stay general, vague. Never give out any more information than necessary. The more you tell the more likely you're not going to fit his psychological grid. At least, get to know him first. Find out how well he fits your own criteria. Any damaging personal details can come later.

"Same."

It didn't really matter where he lived. It was impossible to invite Bill over with his "roommate." He certainly couldn't go out to Bill's. Pets were the perennial excuse. His friend David had a pair of exhausted Weimaraners, constantly woken from a sound sleep for "a walk," the alibis of adultery. But Ken couldn't very well go out to walk the goldfish. And he couldn't give the old line about running low on fags, going out for a pack of Marlboros. That's the trouble with lovers: They knew you so well, they could practically read your mind. After ten years together, Ken had a hunch that Liverlips probably knew he didn't smoke. And he could hardly say he was going out for a late night stroll in the park, not after he got rolled in the Rambles back in '82. One guy did him, pants down at the ankles, while the other fished out his wallet. Thank god he didn't take the keys too. It would have been cheaper to rent a whore. Well, let's get down to business. "What are you into?"

"I'm into body contact, oil and massage, tit play, that sort of thing. Safe stuff."

"Sounds good." Pretty vanilla. That's fine with me.

"You like to fuck?"

"Depends on the guy." Like maybe if Arnold Schwarzenegger was gay, he could get into it. In other words, not really. Did he go along? Ken didn't want to be patronizing. He could always pretend to stick some ten-inch dildo up his ass.

"So what do you look like?"

"I'm about five-ten, one-sixty-five, with brown hair and blue eyes." Ken always wanted blue eyes and a few more inches. "I go to the gym maybe four times a week." OK, so it's more like once every two weeks. "I've got a slim muscular build. I'm sure you'd like it." Liverlips didn't anymore.

"I'm six-two, two hundred pounds, with short blond hair and a goatee."

Ow! Another fashion victim.

"I've got a couple of earrings in my right ear and a tit ring."

Body mutilation. Watch out. Still, that word "tit." Somehow, just saying it got a rise out of Ken. Stimulus, response. Press the nipple-lever and be rewarded with an erection. "Wow, I go crazy for tits."

"You'd like mine."

They'd have to be better than Liverlip's. His are buried under flesh. He's gained as much weight in the past six months as Liz Taylor did to play Martha in *Who's Afraid of Virginia Woolf?* Ken might not go to the gym as often as he should, but at least he'd been able to keep the middle spread from spreading down his thighs. "And what would you like me to do to them?"

"Suck 'em, twist 'em, lick 'em, bite 'em, whatever you want, so long as you've got one hand on my dick at the same time."

Ken felt he should be wearing rubber gloves. God, did he have to have safe sex on the telephone? Did he have to whitewash his fantasies too? Wasn't it enough that he used Lysol on the receiver after he was finished?

"So what are you wearing now?" Let's get visual.

"Just a jockstrap."

"Why don't you take it off?" The oldest fantasy in the world. The stripper. He slowly takes it off, bit by bit, while Ken watches, stroking himself.

"Why don't you lick it off for me?"

Now it's getting exciting. Hard to do over the phone wires, but Ken would try his best. "What's your dick like?"

"Wouldn't you like to know."

"I think I can feel something snaking out of your strap." Ken couldn't believe he was having phone sex with Liverlips practically in the next room. He wondered if he'd be jerking off with some stranger if he hadn't had a few drinks before. OK, seven cocktails, mixed. Not that he was slurring his words or anything. Ken held his liquor well. Liverlips was out on the couch after three, a slobbering fool. Still, it was sort of risky with his lover in the study. Well, screw him. Liverlips was a horror show. Once he even counted the condoms after returning home from a business trip. Miss Priss deserves what she gets. It's a wonder she doesn't mark the phallic container of Foreplay with lipstick.

"I'm not going to let you touch it for a while. Why don't you slip out of your boxers and let that thick eight-inch dick pop out to attention?"

Flatterer. Ken was wearing jockeys and it wasn't an inch over six, but he might as well play along. "I'd like to lick the bulge through your dirty jockstrap."

"Lie down on your back. I'm towering over you. Look up at my tits."

"I'm scratching them with my toes. Do you like that?" Ken was getting into this. Fuck, Ken was so horny, it was either the sperm-line or an inanimate object. Even the cat knew he was on heat. Earlier that evening, Felix had abruptly jumped out of his lap in alarm, and been skittish ever since. It was time for release. Well, he had the security of knowing that Liverlips wouldn't pick up the extension to order a midnight pepperoni pizza from Ray's and catch him in the act. His lover had a separate line for tax purposes. Life with a consultant had its advantages.

"I'm standing over you with my big fat dick six inches above your face and my low hanging balls even closer. You want to lick it, don't you? Maybe I'll let you. You have to beg."

Liverlips wouldn't dare try this on Ken. He was the Ice Goddess of Great Neck, Long Island. He had all the sexual appeal of a bruised banana. His fantasies were all so predictable. After a decade Ken knew them all by heart: the fireman, the lifeguard, the support-hose stocking salesman. Were they ever in a rut. In a way, with his lover in the den, it was risky, even exciting. "I want it. I want it real bad. I want to lick the vein on the underside."

"I'm not giving it to you just yet. Turn over. I want you to get nice and relaxed for me. You like massage?"

Who was this man and how did he know all of Ken's buttons? He wanted to get naked with him. "Who doesn't?" Christ, he could almost hear Liverlips speaking to him. Was this guilt or what? Maybe he had had a bit too much. It couldn't be Liverlips. He would never call a jerkoff line—he was too repressed. Ken would be more likely to be talking to Mamie Eisenhower on the TOOL line than Liverlips.

"I've got you on my bed lying on your stomach. I'm rubbing oil on your shoulders, into your neck. All of your tension is at your neck. I'm getting you relaxed. You feel it? Your dick gets hard, then relaxes. You're so relaxed you're almost falling asleep. I reach over and pinch your left tit. A surge of energy goes through your cock. I rub oil into your back, down your spine. I run my thumbs up your spine. You like that, don't you? Do you want me to do more?"

Conscious thought was almost gone. What could Ken say but yes.

"I'm rubbing oil into your tight hard ass. You've got a football player's ass, two hard globes of muscle and flesh. I slip my forefinger up your ass, it contracts. I feel up to the first knuckle, just touch-typing my way up your love canal. I take it out and sniff it. It smells good. I continue rubbing your tight buns. I work my way down your left thigh and calf. I work down to your ankle. I lift your foot and rub your individual toes. You feel like you're floating on air. I press the heel of my hand into the sole of your foot. I work my way up your right leg. I press all of my weight on your ass with the heels of my hands. I work my way up your spine again. I pound your back with the sides of my hands in a gentle rapid drumming. I work on your neck again. It is less tense. There are still a few knots to untangle. I feel your tight biceps and triceps. I work down to your hands and rub your fingers individually. I go back to your neck again. I turn you over like a beached stud whale. Your dick is thick and soft. Wetness oozes from the head onto your tight stomach. I pour some oil on your chest and start working it in. You have just enough hair to get me excited."

Slow down. At this rate, they'd be finished in no time. "Oh yeah, don't stop."

"I lick my thumbs and then circle your tits with them. Then I press on them with my thumbs. Then I scratch your left nipple with my thumbnail, gently. Your dick stirs to life. How are you doing?"

Did he have to ask? "Oh man, real good."

"Do you want me to stop for a while?"

Fucking tease. "Please, don't stop."

"I cover your right nipple with my lips, I start gently sucking. I pinch your left nipple, and work my hand down to your dick. It's rock hard."

Ken traced his movements on his body. Ever since he shaved his balls last February, the sensation was somewhat dulled. Ken was getting into it. It was beginning to feel like sex. Ken wanted some sort of panty shield for the mouthpiece, a condom for the receiver. A withholding WASP, Ken usually refrained from shooting online. With phone sex, the male of the species was finally able to convincingly fake orgasm.

"I'm really close."

"Stop."

"I've got my tongue down your throat. I'm spitting. A strand of spit from my mouth to you. I'm sucking your tongue. It tastes good. It's hot."

"I can't hold it any longer."

"I'm going to shoot."

"That was the best."

"You're a very visual person." Where was a towel when you needed one?

"That was great. Maybe we can get together sometime?"

Sure, if Ken could sterilize him first. Heat him up to the flash point. Get rid of those germs! Why didn't his microwave have a setting for humans? Was it possible to eliminate all germs and bacteria from the human form? Ken doubted it. Now the guilt came. He wouldn't exactly call it cheating on a physical basis, yet, somehow, he felt he'd betrayed his lover. "I don't think so. I'm kind of involved with this guy I'm seeing now."

"That's cool. I have a lover I've been trying to break up with for the past two years. You know how it is. Manhattan apartments."

"And the AIDS crisis." That should get him off the line. The A-word an instant turn-off in any encounter. Ken felt suddenly tired.

"Yeah."

"Well, thanks." At least he didn't have to worry about catching a cab home at 3:00 in the morning. Christ, he couldn't even shower now. That would wake up his lover. He was suddenly suffused with tenderness for his lover, who had put up with all of his shit for the past ten years.

"Sleep tight."

"Pleasant dreams." Ken decided he should really give it another shot with his lover. He wasn't all that bad. Shit. When would he get the courage to tell him his test results? He couldn't go through this alone. Even if they stopped having sex, what difference would it make? They hadn't had sex for years. OK, maybe months. Ken would talk to him tomorrow. Over coffee. They'd straighten things out. They'd finally communicate. It had been such a long time. Fucking shitty world they lived in.

II. PAUL

"Hello."

Sounds nice. A deep, resonant voice. Not like Sparky, his whiny lover. "Hello."

"My name's Rick, what's yours?"

Sure, Rick. Rhymes with dick. What name would he use today? A dollar bill was on the night table. "Bill."

"How are you tonight?"

Oh, he was just bored and felt like dialing the sex line. He took another surreptitious toke on the joint. His voice was nice and raspy. No dope for Sparky. Some fucking health nut. What was the point? Nobody he knew was going to die of a heart attack at seventy-two. This fucking virus was playing Russian roulette with his friends and lovers, wiping them off the face of this earth at random. Who needed to worry about high cholesterol or secondary smoke? "Pretty horny."

"Same here. Can I call you?"

It was all pretty standard to start out, like the opening of a game of chess. Pawn to Queen-two. Knight to King's Bishop-two. Castle. Suck, fuck, shoot your load, and hang up the phone as you searched for the Kleenex to wipe up with. "Sorry, I can't give out the number. I'm staying with a friend."

"I can't either. I have a roommate."

The social etiquette of phone lines required such strict adherence to the basic script, just like an async eight-bit telecommunications protocol. One false blip and you're offline. It was just like in Goffman's book, *The Presentation of Self in Everyday Life*. Very little new information was communicated. Language itself was fifty percent redundant, which is what made two-dimensional crossword puzzles possible. "Where do you live?"

"Manhattan. You?"

Apartments were so fucking expensive in New York. Paul would have moved out six months ago, except for the rumors that the building was going co-op. He'd split the profits with his ex and then split. Things had been strained with Sparky for some time. "Same."

"So, what are you into?"

"I'm into body contact, oil and massage, tit play, that sort of thing. Safe stuff." Sometimes he lost them at this point.

Paul didn't like the group lines: The humiliation was too public. Why am I a homosexual? Because I crave rejection, he kidded himself. If Paul was dissatisfied with the current match, it was easy enough to reject him and move on to someone else. Simply press the number sign for the next contestant. He felt like he was on an endless episode of the dating game, no doubt with corporate sponsorship by Trojan condoms and Astroglide lubricant. There seemed to be an infinite supply of horny men in New York. Except, of course, when he was truly desperate. There were times, desperate times, when he'd call the group line and it would be silent. No one at all horny at 5:30 A.M. on Tuesday morning. Paul would practice Shakespearean monologs just to see if anyone was there; he would read the phone book; he would act as if his dearly departed therapist were still alive to hear his complaints and he would make them into the receiver. There was no one to complain to—the monitor was asleep, no doubt. He would play Julie London singing "Cry Me a River" into the receiver and then hang up.

"Sounds good."

"You like to fuck?" Just testing the waters. He'd play along if necessary. How much collusion was necessary for good sex? Paul didn't want to reveal himself to an absolute stranger. Yet, why not? He'd never see him or call him. Where could he possibly meet him? At the Bar on Second Avenue, with a green carnation? How could be elude his boyfriend? But what was the problem? He felt that they had broken up months ago; they just hadn't hashed it out verbally. He could have a little on the side. It was time to start dating again, he knew. But Paul was scared. Oh, fucking viruses. Life was such a bummer.

"Depends on the guy."

Pretty evasive. Was that a yes or no? Paul wished he'd be quick about it. It was like a cab. It was only with the most extreme self-control that Paul was able to ride cabs to the airport without being transfixed by the meter, unable to remove my eyes from it, ticking away in my wallet. Thirty-five dollars to JFK two weeks ago, with tip and toll. He'd never do that again. He'd sooner walk. "So what do you look like?"

"I'm about five-ten, one-sixty-five, with brown hair and blue eyes. I go to the gym maybe four times a week. I've got a slim muscular build. I'm sure you'd like it."

Who had time to go to the gym? Paul had a goddam beeper in case the new software installation failed. He was working realtime now, not in virtual. Those thirty-six-hour test periods took it out of him completely. Paul really had to stop consulting. Relax. Take a vacation once in a while. Health insurance was such a bitch. Every three months he had to scramble to make the payment to Blue Cross—he'd been working on a manual on C compilers for the past year, he didn't have time—and the publisher was chomping at the bit for the second draft. It was set for next spring. "I'm six-two, two hundred pounds, with short blond hair and a goatee." Paul would never grow a goatee, but Rick sounded like a trendoid. "I've got a couple earrings in my right ear and a tit ring."

"Wow, I go crazy for tits."

"You'd like mine." His ex used to. He didn't know what went wrong. He got his lover flowers for his birthday, sent them to his office, and Sparky called him right back, screamed at Paul for "outing" him. Paul signed with an initial. So they were pansies? Fucker can't take a joke. Sparky forgot Paul's birthday. Paul had it all programed on his laptop. Just check the calendar function every morning for anniversaries and birthdays. An alarm even went off on special occasions. Last year for their anniversary they just rented some porno and ordered in. *Asshole Buddies*, Paul thought it was. Porno movies were like Marx Brothers flicks—how could anyone remember the titles? Exactly what is Duck Soup anyway?

"And what would you like me to do to them?"

"Suck 'em, twist 'em, lick 'em, bite 'em, whatever you want, so long as you've got one hand on my dick at the same time." Paul hated talking dirty, but if it got him off. Christ. He hated when they shot and then hung up, the receiver clunking into its slot. Still not hard. Spit won't do. Paul could use some lube now. In the bedroom. He'd like to go to the bathroom and lift some hand lotion. He'd even settle for Crisco.

"So what are you wearing now?"

This guy was so imaginative, he had to be from Jersey. "Just a jockstrap." That should get him hard. He's probably the type that stays until closing at the Spike, leaning against the wall by the piss factory, right under the military red bulb dot matrix clock. Paul bet he'd look good in a harness.

"Why don't you take it off?"

"Why don't you lick it off for me?" For godsakes, the dirtier Paul talked, the hotter he got. Paul didn't understand. His voice was deep. It was a turn on. He talked nice and slow. Paul felt he was doing all of the work. They didn't have to rush. It's only fifteen cents a minute, with forty for the first. Paul could deduct it anyway. Pretend it was a modem link, and he was sending a three-hundred-page document to Tanzania. Nobody checked that closely. If Paul ever got audited, he was screwed anyway. What was one more white lie after a thousand of them?

"What's your dick like?"

"Wouldn't you like to know." Everyone was a size queen. Paul was into quantifiable figures himself, but of a more theoretical nature. What was the minimal path a traveling salesperson must make to visit all of his sites? An incredibly complex problem, much more than one would expect. Algorithms were available to approximate, make a rough guesstimate. But Paul wanted the exact answer, however irrational, however many digits past the decimal point were necessary.

"I think I can feel something snaking out of your strap."

"I'm not going to let you touch it for a while. Why don't you slip out of your boxers and let that thick eight-inch dick pop out to attention?" How did that slip out? God, that was his favorite. Some queens like dicks so big one couldn't do anything with them. Rearrange the furniture. Divine water. Clean shotgun barrels. The really big ones that never got hard. Probably from some growth hormone they took when they were kids. Paul wished he could get a hold of it. Eight inches was the ideal. Oh, fuck, everyone has eight inches on the phone lines anyway, why try to tell the truth. He read about a survey where the average American hetero male thinks an average dick is ten inches, and the average American hetero female thinks it's four. Kinsey said it was six. Fags know better. They do their own extensive research, one on one.

"I'd like to lick the bulge through your dirty jockstrap."

"Lie down on your back. I'm towering over you. Look up at my tits." Was Paul supposed to lick his finger after he stuck it up his ass? Was it OK just to smell it? He considered the consequences of having a crossed connection with a nun, a policeman, and his mother. None of these possibilities got him hard. Since deregulation, service on New York Telephone was not the best.

"I'm scratching them with my toes. Do you like that?"

"I'm standing over you with my big fat dick six inches above your face, and my low hanging balls even closer. You want to lick it, don't you? Maybe I'll let you. You have to beg." Where did this master voice come from? Not exactly p.c. these days. He swore he'd stop this dominance trip. He'd never tried it on Sparky. But let's face it, Paul wasn't good on resolutions. Paul had been calling the TOOL line far too much. He supposed that eventually he would get the phone company to block the 550 numbers. He was waiting until the monthly bill hit an even $100. But then, how would he ever know what the weather was at forty cents a minute? Paul's apartment had a view of a brick air shaft. From the bathroom, he could see the neighbor's smoked-glass shower. Suppose Paul wanted to find a government job at $3.50 a call? If Barbara Stanwyck had discovered the joys of phone sex in *Sorry, Wrong Number*, he doubted she would have nagged her husband into killing her.

"I want it. I want it real bad. I want to lick the vein on the underside."

Every week he promised himself to use the phone sex line only once a month. That usually lasted until Tuesday. Nondenominational, his weeks started on Monday. He told himself he would make the time and go to the gym three times a week, using the Stairmaster for half an hour. Whenever he thought of the Stairmaster he imagined a machine dressed in Nazi regalia, all black leather, admonishing him, "You are not stepping fast enough. You must go faster." Well, at least he never went down on anybody in the steam room. But how many unsolicited backrubs had he perpetrated? How many embarrassing stares had he committed? How many friends had turned to strangers after his careless caress? He would vow to quit the steam routine, and usually he'd be back within a week. Even after he caught crabs. He'd swear he wouldn't sit without a towel, and limit his saunas to ten minutes. Paul was drowning in his own regrets. He had no self-control. A pint of Häagen-Dazs never made it through the night in his freezer. Paul would ravage his way to the bottom of the carton at three in the morning, lit by the refrigerator bulb. A bag of m&ms would be gone in the blink of an eye. Only broccoli, like so many men in the distant past, would go limp on him after weeks in the crisper. "I'm not giving it to you just yet. Turn over. I want you to get nice and relaxed for me. You like massage?"

"Who doesn't?"

"I've got you on my bed lying on your stomach. I'm rubbing oil on your shoulders, into your neck. . . . I run my thumbs up your spine. You like that, don't you. Do you want me to do more?" Paul closed his eyes and saw nebulous spirals of equations describing muscular planes, the physiognomy of desire. Christ, computers were always on his mind, mathematical postulates, unproven theorems. The four-color map theorem was finally proven a few years ago on a computer, not very elegantly, just an enumeration of all the possible typologies of maps, a set of exhaustive possibilities. He imagined the orgiastic possibilities of all of the voices on the fiber optic network of lust.

"Yes."

"I'm rubbing oil into your tight hard ass. You've got a football player's ass, two hard globes of muscle and flesh. . . . I pour some oil on your chest and start working it in. You have just enough hair to get me excited." The minimum for adultery was three, thought Paul, two lovers in a relationship and two outside of one, where the sets intersect in the guilty party. Did both have to come? Did they both even have to been in the same room? Paul wondered whether phone sex constituted a violation of his relationship. To what degree was he cheating on his lover? Conceivably, he could be having this conversation with himself, having scripted the other's dialog into a tape recorder. In this sense, it was masturbatory. Ken would have forgotten the entire exchange. One can barely tickle oneself. Only the most self-absorbed narcissistic homosexual could stimulate himself. But wasn't that what Sparky accused him of that last argument? It was the Turing problem all over again. Imagine you are in a room with a terminal. You type a question. A response appears on your screen. You have an interactive conversation. If you can't tell whether the responses are being typed by another person in the next room, or a computer, then the computer can be said to possess artificial intelligence. Poor Turing. Another fag in distress. Alan Turing, whose ultimate destiny was a poisoned apple.

"Oh yeah, don't stop."

"I lick my thumbs and then circle your tits with them. Then I press on them with my thumbs. Then I scratch your left nipple with my thumbnail, gently. Your dick stirs to life. How are you doing?" Christ, it was all risks these days, and they were all unacceptable. Fred went to San Francisco and had his left tit pierced at the Gauntlet. He came down with hepatitis after the tit ring. OK, so maybe it *was* seafood. Sure. Some sailor he picked up at the Stud.

"Oh man, real good."

"Do you want me to stop for a while?"

"Please, don't stop."

"I cover your right nipple with my lips. I start gently sucking. I pinch your left nipple, and work my hand down to your dick. It's rock hard."

"I'm really close."

"Stop."

"I've got my tongue down your throat. I'm spitting. A strand of spit from my mouth to you. I'm sucking your tongue. It tastes good. It's hot."

"I can't hold it any longer."

Every equation held forth the possibility of singularities. An orgasm was the sexual equivalent of dividing by zero, approaching that point of infinite slope where derivatives are useless. His hyperbolic ejaculations reached their asymptotes as he climaxed. "I'm going to shoot."

Paul rarely made a noise when he came. A history of sex in bathrooms, back seats of cars, museum roofs, backrooms, elevators stuck between floors, public gardens, empty subway cars stuck in tunnels, parks, and so on had taught him the lesson of discretion. No handkerchiefs were necessary to muffle his cries.

"That was the best." Why did he feel guilty? Adultery was of the soul, not the body. Was sex all in the mind? Was it always a form of masturbation, sometimes with someone else present? No, that was the thing—they had exchanged something more intimate than fluids. They had exchanged confidences.

"You're a very visual person."

"That was great. Maybe we can get together sometime?" Paul was amazed. Out of all the randomness in the universe, the electronic sea of phone cords and remote attachments, all of the connections, n factorial over j factorial, out of the infinite number of connections, it was possible for Paul to connect.

"I don't think so. I'm kind of involved with this guy I'm seeing now."

"That's cool. I have a lover I've been trying to break up with for the past two years. You know how it is. Manhattan apartments." Of course, Paul was always looking at men, appraisingly, on the beach, in the bars, at the gym, in the steam room. But still, up until now, it was only innocent, unconnected with intention. He felt guiltier than if he had defiled his lover's bed. Why was he guilty? No bodily fluids were exchanged. That embarrassing silence after coming. Sometimes people hung up immediately. Did this constitute adultery? The postcoital conversation? The intimacy he lacked, never would regain with his lover? Paul was already thinking of Sparky in terms of an ex-lover. Something had clicked in his head. It couldn't be adultery, if they weren't even sleeping together. That's when it hit him. It was over. The relationship was over.

"And the AIDS crisis."

"Yeah."

"Well, thanks."

"Sleep tight."

"Pleasant dreams."

Paul waited a moment and then hung up the phone, turned off the light. He had made up his mind. Things had soured past repair. He didn't know it was possible to start over with someone new. But it was time to leave. The inertia of their relationship shouldn't be an excuse. Even the health crisis. Paul felt reaffirmed. There were people he could connect with, communicate with. He would start anew. Take things from scratch. Firm with resolve, Paul turned over and went to sleep on the sofa. He would leave Kenneth S. Parkington tomorrow.

PICO-UNION

• LUIS ALFARO •

ON A STREET CORNER

I think it's because I listened to too many *Lucha Villa* records when I was growing up.

I think it's because I sat through too many *espectaculos* at the Million Dollar theater on Broadway.

I think it's because I liked doing the *La Cucaracha* dance way too much in third grade.

I think it's because desire is memory and I crave it like one of the born agains in my mama's church.
And he says Amen. And he says Hallelujah.
And I want to go back to the very beginning and speak a neighborhood language like speaking in tongues.

But it's hard to be honest sometimes because I live in the shadow of the Hollywood sign. Because I live in the same town that brings you the "Alf Variety Special." Because I always want to go back to the beginning and it always begins with a street corner known as Pico-Union. My father made extra money on pool tables, my mother prayed on her knees.

A woman danced in the projects across the street. I could hear the sounds of a salsa song as her hips swayed. Each step got bigger and bigger as she thrust out her elbows and clenched her fists.

Her husband would beat the shit out of her with large big hands that looked like hammers. The punches came so fast she had little time to react. A blow would penetrate her face like slow-motion driver-training films.

Our neighbor would feed pigeons all day with a birdseed wrist that he flicked until all the birds had dropped their guard and gathered around. He would flick a birdseed wrist until he would finally snatch one, living on a diet of downtown pigeon.

A drunk from the bar at the corner staggers home, pushing people aside like a politician working a convention.

A man on the Pico bus gets slapped after this woman sat on his hand on the seat next to his. He says "If you don't like it, don't sit here."

A glue sniffer on Venice Blvd. named Sleepy watches the world in slow motion.

On 10th and Union I forced my first kiss onto Sonia Lopez in third grade. The slap she gave me felt so good, it must have been my introduction into S&M.

Bozo the clown was throwing out gifts to the kids at the May Company on Broadway, and we're all screaming and waving, hoping to catch one. And he throws this board game at this little boy and he topples over. He comes up screaming and crying with a bleeding lip and I watch in horror, afraid that Bozo will throw something at me.

People in this city used to run at the sight of a helicopter light, afraid that their sins would show through like the partition at confession.

An earthquake shook and our neighbor is running down Pico screaming that Jesus has come back, just like he promised.

A woman got slugged.
A man got slapped.
A clown threw toys.
A drunk staggered.

An earthquake shook.

A slap.
A slug.
A shove.
A kick.
A kiss.

CLARENCE

The year we had noon dances. Seventh grade. Berendo Junior High. My favorite was watching the basketball team. The Centurians. Long tall black guys with droopy sweatpants and no T-shirts. Swaying hips to the righteous sounds of the reverend when he was just a sexual thang called Al Green. Even before I heard about the *messican* rhythm. *Messican* rhythm was a nonstop tango of *salsas*, *rancheras*, and *cumbias*. You could stop in the middle of the dance and not lose the beat. 'Cause the beat was in the heart. *Messican* beat was born on street corners in downtown L.A. A rhythm hiding in alleys behind Lucy's All-Nite-Taco's and the *Habana* Bakery. *Messican* rhythm was copycat soul train with a switchblade. *Messican* rhythm was K-Day before white had soul. *Messican* rhythm was running down Broadway and ducking into Woolworth's with a ghetto blaster that was too small to show attitude or be stolen. *Messican* rhythm was hot nites and gang fights. *Messican* rhythm was our drunken fathers talking the strange language.

I always got jumped in the lunch line before I could buy my grilled cheese sandwich. But the dime. The dime I kept in my shoe. The dime I saved for Clarence. Ten cents got me into the gym before Diana Ross's part on "My mistake was to love you boy, love you boy." Clarence was always on the dance floor cause he was dating Yolanda Skipper and Yolanda Skipper was Miss Rhythm herself. Uh-huh.

If Clarence would have made it to ninth grade yearbook he would have had titles like "most likely to get stronger" or "most likely to beat you up in the hallway." A bad-ass motherfucker who worked out by lifting you from the belt loops for a round of ten. But it wasn't the muscles that won me over. It was the hair. If you had as much hair as Clarence, that means you probably stood up to your mama when she tried to drag you down to the barber by the ear. I, of course, was almost bald. But when he grabbed me and shoved me with a "Chump, move outta my way, you're taking up too much of the dance floor," a sort of electricity raced through me. Because one strong shove fueled a hundred fantasies to be used under a bedsheet quietly.

Later in the gym I imagined that I was his basketball and he grabbed me and caressed me and he ran with me like I was a part of him. A part of his body. When he paraded around the locker room in his jockstrap, you could see faint traces of pubic hair rising right above the elastic waistband. But I couldn't stare too long, 'cause it's almost like staring too long at this picture of Christ on the cross. People think you're strange.

Clarence died in the ninth grade and he left behind Yolanda Skipper and the Centurians and he left me with the memory of one strong shove. It gets me by. Even now.

One strong shove and two homeboys are my guardian angels. One strong shove and a Bruce Lee movie on Broadway is introduction into strange new worlds and cultures.
One strong shove and the sound of a helicopter or ambulance in the middle of the night lets me know I'm still alive.
One strong shove and my immigrant father with the brown *Michoacan* skin and the smell of liquor on his breath is like a warm blanket at the Floral drive-in in 1966.
One strong shove and a helicopter light has found me in downtown.

VIRGIN MARY

We used to have this Virgin Mary doll and every time you connected her to an outlet, she would turn and bless all sides of the room. We bought her on a trip to Tijuana. One of my dad's drunken surprise Tijuana trips. He'd come home from the racetrack at midnight, wake us up, get us dressed, and we'd hop into the station wagon. My mother drove and my dad lowered the seat and slept in the back with us. My grandmother lived in one of the *colonias* and she hated our 3:00 A.M.

visits. But you see, blood is thicker than water, family is greater than friends, and the Virgin Mary watches over all of us.

When I was ten, I gave the rotating Virgin doll to my Tia Ofelia. My Tia Ofelia lived across the street with my Tia Tita who lived with my Tio Tony who lived next door to my Tia Romie. Back in those days, everybody on my block was either a Tia or a Tio. They lived in a big beautiful wood-carved two-story house with a balcony overlooking the street below. We were crowded in by downtown skyscrapers, packs of roving *cholos*,* the newly built Convention Center on Figueroa, and portable tamale stands, but our families always managed to live together. Because you see, blood is thicker than water, family is greater than friends, and the Virgin Mary watches over all of us.

My Tia lived on the top floor and on the bottom lived the 18th Street gang. There was Smiley, Sleepy, Sadgirl, and a bunch of other homeboys hanging in the front yard playing Blood-stones "Natural High." Like roaches they split at the sight of a cop car slowly cruising through our neighborhood like tourists on Hollywood Boulevard. My favorite was a pee-wee who hung out on the back porch. His face was full of acne and they called him "Movie Star." All our Mexican mothers in their daily laundry line ritual would cackle like chickens, "*Oye*, Lupe, where's that Movie Star?"

My Tia Ofelia hated *cholos* and she spit down the seeds from grapes she ate just to annoy them. She was like all my relatives back then, a grape picker from Delano, California. She claims that she had dated Cesar Chavez and that she knew everyone in Tulare, Visalia, and McFarland counties. I couldn't call her a liar because she had *breast cancer*. My mom told us this in a voice reserved for nites when we didn't want to wake up my father from one of his drunken soccer celebrations. Doctors at County General took away her tits in hopes of driving away

---

*gang members

*La Bruja Maldita,** who was slowly eating at her insides. When she was feeling okay, she would tell me stories about migrant farm workers, the *huelga*† movement, and bus trips to Bakersfield.

The day I brought her the rotating Virgin Mary she was in pain. I know I should have waited, but I asked her quite innocently if I could see her chest. She slapped me hard on the face, calling me a *malcriado*.‡ While she sobbed, her hand searched for medication.

I felt so bad that day even I could feel the *Bruja Maldita* eating at my heart. I never got the nerve to go back up.

Weeks went by and my Tia Ofelia continued to rock in her chair on the porch. When the weeks turned to months, she slowly started to forget us. People would walk by and offer up a *"Buenas tardes, senora,"* but you could tell she was having trouble remembering the faces. My grandmother sent a crate of grapes to help her to remember, but nothing worked. My mom and my Tia Tita said that my Tia Ofelia was becoming a baby *otra vez*. The *Bruja Maldita* ate at her bones and she slowly began to slump forward like the G.I. Joe my brother and I melted with burning tamale leaves. Her cheeks caved in like the plaster *calaveras*§ we would buy at the border, and one day on my way home from school I looked up and she was gone.

Phones rang. Food poured in. Little cards with twenty dollar bills. Hysterical screams from distant relatives on a Mexico-to-L.A. party line. The tears of my relatives were covered by huge veils that they wore to Immaculate Conception. Dramatic uncles openly wept and even my grandmother got into the scene by attempting to jump onto the coffin at the burial. I had to sleep on the floor with dark-skinned cousins from *ranchos* in *Jalisco* and although I hated it, I had to remember that, blood

---

*the Evil Witch
†United Farm Workers
‡bad boy
§skeletons

is thicker than water, family is greater than friends, and the Virgin Mary watches over all of us.

A few weeks later the Crips drove by and said "Chump motherfuckers, greasy-assed Messicans, go back to Teehuana" and they firebombed the 18th Street gang on the bottom floor. A great ball of fire and light filled the sky. We watched my Tia escape and filled buckets of water that my dad ran across the street with.

Smiley, Sleepy, and Sadgirl died, but we couldn't go to the funeral because my relatives said they were *perros desgraciados.** So instead we rummaged through charred remains looking for usable clothes and old Vicki Carr records. My brother found what was left of the rotating Virgin Mary, and he used her head for BB gun practice. My mom cried because the memory of my Tia Ofelia would now be an empty lot where bums would piss and tires would grow. Everyday she watered a little flower that she planted on the lot until the Community Redevelopment Agency built the Pico-Union projects over the memory of my Tia Ofelia.

When I was eighteen, I met this guy with a rotating Virgin Mary. He bought it in Mexico, so, of course, I fell in love. His skin was white. He ate broccoli and spoke like actors on a TV series. It was my first love, and like the *Bruja Maldita*, he pounded on my heart. He taught me many things: how to kiss like the French, lick an earlobe, and dance in the dark. He was every Brady Bunch/Partridge Family episode rolled into one. He gave me his shirt and I told him about the fields in Delano, picking cherries one summer, and my summer in Mexico. Once my grandmother sent me a crate of grapes. We took off our clothes, smashed them all over our bodies, and ate them off each other.

When he left, the *Bruja Maldita*'s hand replaced his in my heart, and she pounded on me. And she laughed like Mexican mothers at a clothesline. And I covered my tears with a smile that was like the veils at Immaculate Conception. But my sorrow

*disgraced dogs

was so strong that relatives nearby would say, "*Aye, Mijo*, don't you see? Blood is thicker than water, family is greater than friends, and the Virgin Mary watches over all of us."

CARBURETOR MEMORY

When I was 14 my dad's illness took a turn for the worse, and I started working. He was a heavy drinker and we called it an illness then because *fucked-up* is not really a word. He's a good man really. One of those happy harmless drunks that's great for the first thirty minutes of any party. The turn for the worse was not that he was drinking more; he just decided he didn't need to come home between mixers. You know, those old low-brow socials between *El Club Jalisco* and *La Copa De Oro*. The irony of the story, which I might as well get out of the way now since we've been holding my dad's honor intact for twenty years, is this: I went to work at the same factory that he did. Almost the same job. I was spared working with chemicals because I was too young.

My brother Jaime is a year older than I. He didn't have to go work anywhere. In Latino culture the first born is like this prized cow. He was an all-star citywide basketball, football, and baseball jock who was voted most likely to succeed. In the yearbook that we shared there is a picture of me with the subtitle "Little Jaime." Everybody knew me by "Little Jaime." This whole your-brother-can't-work-cause-he's-got-to-work-out rule was further compounded by the fact that I was a little fag. "Work was good for me." "It would make a man of me." "I needed to concentrate on the things that were important."

Black exploitation films were at their peak then and I spent almost every Saturday and Sunday on Broadway in downtown Los Angeles at theaters like The State, The Tower, and The Roxy sitting through marathon bills of Pam Grier, Richard Roundtree, and Tamara Dobson movies. *Blacula*, *Coffy*, *Brown Sugar*, and *Cleopatra Jones* were but a few. Years later I saw Pam Grier in a theatrical production and I was so disappointed that she kept all her clothes on and wasn't packing a .45 in her bra. There was a faint glimmer of hope at the end of Chekov's

Three Sisters that she might cut somebody's balls off, but it never happened. Sometimes I miss those early seventies.

The factory used to be located where the Convention Center in downtown now stands. We lived a few blocks away and we used to take my dad bean burritos and have lunch with him everyday under the giant Union 76 sign. When the city bought everything up the factory moved over the bridge by the Sears on Soto. Maybe it was commuting that made my dad go bad.

It was my brother's idea that I go work at the factory. Somebody saw me holding Paul Lee's hand in sixth grade and told my brother I was queer. The isolation of a production line would give me time to think. I pleaded with my mom but Mexican moms always listen to the men in the family. If the father is not available, that position is filled by the first born, no matter that my brother was only fifteen.

I built what was called a 2–502. Four sets of fifty a day. They sold for 45 bucks each and I made $2.50 an hour. They were called carburetors. I know they go inside a car but that's about it. The foreman's name was *El Chapulin*, and he and my father spent two years at a seminary in Michoacan, Mexico, the homeland. He was a short overweight man who nobody had any respect for because 2–502's were the easiest carburetors to build. They were a domestic type that fit on Ford models from 1970–72. The things you remember! He was extremely bowlegged and sometimes they called him *Penguino*.

The shift started at seven and ended at 3:30 P.M. There was talk in my family that if my younger sister got accepted into the Marlborough School, I might have to give up a few years of high school and work for her tuition. This is another incredibly insane rule in Latino culture that I never understood. The youngest born was a girl. Now, not only would she need the resources and sacrifices that her brother, the man, would automatically get, but she would need all the protection that a private school would afford her. After all, I could walk into any job and make minimum wage. She could only walk into the garment and fish industries and work below minimum, and that simply would not do.

* * *

Sometimes I took the bus and transferred on the corner of Broadway and 7th. This would give me a chance to see what was on the marquee at The State, but most of the time *Pantera* and *Pepe* would drive by at 6:30 A.M. and pick me up on the corner of Pico and Union. These guys were bitter forty-five-year-olds with broken dreams who came over from the *Rancho* and wouldn't give me the time of day.

On Fridays we stopped at Kay's Pastrami Stand at 15th and Central and bought steak fries and cashed our paychecks. I was bringing in a whopping $84 a week after taxes and my mother let me keep $12 for the movies. I started working on Saturdays and brought carburetors home to work on at night, and I moved up to a $124 weekly.

You start with the base, move on to the gaskets, and insert all the screws. You put on safety gloves and you use the overhead power screwdriver. When you have the body assembled you oil the body and test the switches and shutter. If the base is cracked, you send it back. If the screws are bent, use them anyway.

If somebody talks to you for more than a minute, you very nicely say that you have to meet your production deadline, and you go back to work. If you feel sick, you should keep working because working is good for the body. If you don't meet your production goal, don't worry, but try harder. If the union guys try to get you to sign a card, tell them you don't believe in the mafia. If you see two employees fighting in the back by the railroad tracks, it is none of your business. If you want a prostitute, talk to the guy they call *Surdo*.

When the bell rings for morning break, sit on something and rest your feet. When the bell rings at lunch, pick a place for bean burritos where no one will bother you. If you want to drink a beer, go to the bathroom and do it. When the bell rings at the end of the day, don't wash your hands. Steal some solvent and do it at home because *Pantera* and *Pepe* will leave if they don't see you. Don't talk so much English, it gets people mad. If you get too tired, think of the saints who sacrificed so much for us. If you put up girlie posters, make sure their nipples are covered. Don't talk to the Jewish owner. Oh, and how is your dad?

This guy from Honduras had a large rat on a chain that we called the company pet.

A woman named *La Tigeresa* waited for the men outside of the gates on Fridays in a yellow van.

One time someone snuck in a ghettoblaster and I heard the same Gladys Knight song for 8 hours and a 4-hour overtime.

At Christmas time the Jewish owner went up and down the production line and shook our hands and gave us pens with the company name imprinted on them.

A shirtless dark-skinned foreman named Alberto stroked my neck and I licked the insides of his thighs.

On September 16th, Mexican Independence Day, Ranchera music was piped in over the intercom.

At the end of the year, my dad went to a Spanish-speaking A.A. (what I call aah-aah), and he became vice-president of the factory I worked at. My brother succeeded as likely as the yearbook said and gave up sports and became an executive with a large manufacturing factory. My sister got an all-paid scholarship to a school that teaches girls how to become ladies. My mom refused to listen to men and became a political organizer. At the end of that year I ran away from home and I came back five years later. Sometimes when I walk into a Chief Auto Parts store I want to blow the whole fucking place up.

FEDERAL BUILDING

The Federal Building is a big beautiful marble structure on Los Angeles Street. Across from the underground mall where we ran as kids trying to steal bottles of wine from the rack next to the immigration photo stand where my dad took his pictures. My dad says that all criminals are brought here before they're taken to the desert where big rocks are ready to be made into little rocks. He is wrong, of course. The Federal Building is the house of justice, invented by men in blue suits with badges, who drive through our streets looking for staggering downtown drunks at 3 o'clock in the morning.

We used to drive by the halls—Justice, Taxes, Records, etc.—looking for distant Mexican relatives with phony passports ready for a life in Our Lady Queen of the Angels. They stand in Pershing Square, across from the Biltmore. In front of the Woolworth's on Broadway. Uncles with shopping bags for suitcases on Wilshire. And always a lost cousin at the Federal Building. "Don't stand there. Never stand there. It's dangerous."

Because you see, justice can put up with the angry *Chicanada* at their doorstep. But *Mexicanos* with an *avenida* for an address bring illegally parked taco trucks, fake gold, and Colombian drug smugglers on their backs.

So I guess it's appropriate, since I was born at County General and live on an avenue and not an *avenida*, that I should be arrested at Her Majesty's, The Federal Building.

We have a long history together, this *ruca** and I. She has watched me grow up and play on her steps. Watched me low ride in front of her. Watched me spit at her face at an Immigration demonstration that I don't understand but comprehend enough to know that my dad can go back anytime, just never when he wants to.

I attended *Gabacho†* civil disobedience training in Santa Monica, and it sounded like we were going to war.

"That nasty ole dirty downtown is going to get a good look at us, uh-huh. We are going to run up and down her streets and when we get to Miss Federal Building we are going to spit in the old bitch's face." And we shout like a CBS news break in the sixties. "Freedom of Speech"—"AIDS funding now"—"Alto a la censura"—"Stop AIDS, ACT UP, Fight Back"—"We're here, We're queer, Get used to it."

---

*tough "broad"
†Caucasian

A man in a helmet and plastic gloves puts handcuffs on me while hundreds of people blow whistles and yell shame, shame, shame.

"You are trespassing on government property. If you do not leave the premises, you will be arrested. Do you understand?"

"Yes."

"Are you going to leave the premises?"

"No."

"Are you going to resist arrest?"

"No."

"Then you have the right to remain silent . . ."

and it all trails off like an "Adam Twelve" rerun on Channel 13.

And all I can think about is a fourth grade field trip to City Hall where I met the Mayor, Sam Yorty, got his picture and a lesson in becoming a model citizen of this great city of ours.

And I want to run my hand along her marble curves, play with her buttons, stare up at her long tall walls and admire her beauty. But these handcuffs lead me to a cell in her basement. So it isn't distant Mexican relatives from *ranchos* in *Jalisco* that get to share intimate moments with Justice deep in her bowels. It's one of her own.

Beautiful buildings like big *chingona** sharp women have secrets that can scare the shit out of you. Their looks call to you, but the hardness and coldness of her gaze can crush the little you, caught deep in the stare. The Federal Building was once a woman with long arms who reached down and touched you.

I didn't get arrested because my government wants to control the content of art money, or because a Republican from Orange County thinks that all AIDS activists are a "dying breed," or

*female gangster

because a black-and-white can stop you anytime, anywhere, for whatever reason.

I got arrested because Mayor Sam Yorty told me we were all the Mayor. Because big beautiful buildings stare down at you with a *chale* stare. Because I've lived here all my life and I've never owned anything, much less this city.

SIX-PACK MEMORY

When I was growing up my family lived next door to Lucha Villa. On a block wedged in between a burrito stand, *El Estilo Jalisco Birria*, *La Celeya* bakery, and Ceci's religious candle shop.

The first time I walked into a bar was to watch my dad play pool. Every father on Pico was required by the secret code of machismo to play pool, poker, or dominoes. I was always amazed at how well people in my neighborhood could play pool after going through dozens of beers. They seemed to get better at it. Fathers on Pico knew how to drink. I didn't learn how to do this until much later.

Sometimes when he got drunk he would put on the blue Eydie Gormé album where she sang in Spanish. We laughed as he made circles in the kitchen, dodging each other as we ran around his dancing body. Then he would reach inside of his pocket, take out all of his change, and throw it straight up in the air as we scrambled for money on the kitchen floor. That's why I like Eydie Gormé, no matter what anybody says.

About nine o'clock we'd hop into Blue Magic. The coolest Chevy Impala on Lombardy Avenue. We would speed on our three-minute track through Lincoln Park and over the railroad tracks into East L.A. She reigned over the hills that bordered Brooklyn and Gage. A plaster fortress done over by so many murals that the colors soon faded and looked like dirt.

We usually had to wait until the sun went down because we looked too young. I tried to grow a beard, pretend I had children by buying diapers, apply for fake I.D.'s, but nothing worked. Until I met Eva.

Eva was the saint of City Terrace. I was always kind of sorry that she didn't look like an Eva. You know, a graceful woman perched on a Pier-One Imports bamboo chair with knee-length hair draped in a veil that has the colors of the Mexican flag woven through it. She was a small Korean woman who never smiled and seemed to be thinking about the gun under the register. I was never nervous as I had been doing this since I was fourteen.

For Eva I simply set the bottles on the counter and offered a condescending smile while my fingers tapped the counter. She never looked at you. She understood Catholic guilt.

Eva's was every high school fuck-up's dream. A bottle of Tanqueray and tonic got you free plastic cups and a whole lime.

I used to like gin & tonic's more than any other drink. But now I get sick just smelling them. They remind me of things: gang fights, ugly barmaids making out in the alley, bums who piss on the sidewalk. But most of all they remind me of me.

This morning I woke up in the bathtub.

This has happened to me before. Usually a downtown hustler is lying next to me and the scent of our bodies is subdued by the smell of the six-pack, half-pint or frozen margarita mix that we bathed in the night before.

I raise myself up and out of the tub. My stomach and head spin while I grab at a shower curtain that I rip off a rod.

I'm waiting. Dozing and waiting. How did I get here? Whose house is this? Was I fun? Was I good?

I try to crawl to the toilet, but I lay down on the tile and thank God that it looks and smells clean.

I touch my face. I have a rash on my chin. I must have thrown up on myself last night. I wonder how I look? Is my hair okay? Do they have Aqua Net in this house?

Dozing and thinking. I'm thinking about Elvis. What did he do when he felt like this?

Later I get up and dress into someone's jeans. I open the door and see things that I never noticed much before. Cement, alleys, hoodlums, bums, and the pain.

I wonder if my father goes through this every time?

THE SEX OFFENDER

• MATTHEW STADLER •

I

WE BEGIN, STEPPING down this broken stairway, off the slippery stones of the Pellestraat, mildewed wood collapsing under foot and the drunken young boys of the trade school weaving past on bicycles imagining their happiness somewhere behind a sign advertising dancers. They shout each other's names with such volume and longing, you must imagine they fear no one ever said them loud enough before to bring them the fame or pleasure they desire. The old center of the City is filled with children such as these, who want only to rattle their voices loose at night, blessing the crisp midnight air with their sweet vigorous breathing. I could roll that one off his bicycle (that last one going past, thirteen or fourteen, with the lazy cigarette and ears stuck out like windmill blades, his black hair bristling like a dog's), tumbling together across the stones to share bruises and bless his burning cheeks with a wet tongue and kisses. *I* could shout his name, or sing it softly to him, my mouth against his belly. But I'm afraid I'd only frighten him.

So we begin, turning our backs on these children, letting them roll away into the night, and test our weight against the next step, descending below the level of the street to where the narrow cellar doorway hangs, stone walls dripping with the rains. What a fine and glorious night, this night. The clouds press down, scraping the pointed steeples of the All Saints, hiding any trace of the moon. One's eyes worry at the borders of the sky (wherever they might be) watching the anxious weather the ocean sends, hungering over our fair City. There's golden light on these walls, glimmering in tiny streams, glinting like a gilt patina, alive in the mists hanging all through the narrow streets. The Opera House is near enough to illuminate each stone in the facade of the Burlesque. Its light crawls along the sagging houses, twisting through the narrow streets, suffused throughout the luminous fog. The Opera House is golden by design and by accident sheds its light on the face of these rough stone walls.

The Clerks stand on stage at the Opera now, under bare lights in their shirts and ties. If they sing it's because they want to, and not in service of some grand illusion. The audience sits as if in a living room, adjusting their chairs and farting. If asked a question they respond and think nothing of crossing the stage to retrieve, say, a wandering child, a dropped note, or some small piece of confectionary they fancy. The Clerks present their actual lives and are not allowed to wear makeup. The Doctors/Critics/Generals call it the New Realism, Occupational Theater.

But we, we enter the Burlesque.

Through the door lanterns glow red in alcoves dug out like dwarf apses. Men are pressing at their plastic noses and piling more putty on their brows, cursing and savoring the heat that makes them sweat so. My own face is melting fast, the dark violet eyes dripping down across my rouge. If I stand on the strong edges of this cane chair I might see the line of low gas lights strung across the lip of the stage. But the chair is pushed over and lost in the tide of bodies pushing forward. Scuffling, whispers, hush and then silence, a last breath taken in and held . . .

And there is Lucrezia! The limelight upon her, cables supporting her enormous ears, her hairdo hung from above on sky hooks. She's wrapped in yards of purple silk, miles of silk, bunched up around her prosthesis, pinned to the walls by iron spikes the railroad men brought in. Within it she's dancing, dancing her timeless dance, writhing and twisting to her own muffled song. The silk bunches and grabs at her moving hips, twists round her slight ankles as she moves forward toward us. No matter that her mouth is buried behind the shimmering fabric, everyone here knows her song by heart and is singing with a lust and strength trebled by the severity of the regulations that prohibit it.

What is it like in that dark, silent bedroom where my young boy has gone? What peace is there in that empty room? The air is stirred only by his breathing. Warm, wet breath passes his ruby lips, his little nose moist with snot. The cigarette disappeared with his friends, and his clothes dropped one by one, trailing to his bedside. He lay down naked and warm on his eiderdown and put his hands together behind his head. Where was I then, lost and delirious somewhere underground, at that divine moment? What spirit hovered then above his smooth, pale body? He is asleep now, his soft belly rising and falling with each breath, his prick hard and warm, lost in its muscular dreams. When he comes will my mouth be there? Will my eyes be on his belly and my lips pushed down around him?

The Clerks stay in dormitories for the duration of their run. They go to their jobs each day and share the evening meal. Next month the Writers will be presented and I will be required to attend at least two performances, as part of the program of therapy designed for me by my Doctor. The performance will be no different from the Clerks. Five or six of them will sit in chairs or stand. Situations will be repeated. The Writer listening with care. The Writer cutting his text by a third. The Writer agreeing to terms. Two Writers collaborating on a project. Four Writers eating. Significant moments will be brightly lit, important lines printed in the handbill.

My Doctor is a four-star general. I made love with a twelve-year-old boy so I can't be a teacher anymore, but the General was so impressed by my unrepentant essay that he decided I should become a writer. I wrote about the sweetness of Dexter's skin when I licked it, the mingling of our tears when he fucked me, and my religious desire to love him more. The wise Doctor General took me under his wing, orchestrating a baffling panoply of therapeutic practices and granting me the chance of beginning this my new life. He, my Doctor General Nicholas Nicholas, set me up in the old district of the capitol and has prescribed my new career. Of course it means I've got to go see the damned Writers.

"What was the precise nature of your desire?" the Doctor General Nicholas Nicholas finally asked me, tiring of euphemisms and evasions. "What did you most want to do with him?" I was contained within a mask, a slight cotton bag really (as protection for my privacy and to insure impartiality in my treatment), but I'd let Doctor Nicholas look in once or twice to judge the sincerity of my tears. We sat in a windowless interior room with a miraculous orange flower thriving on a table between us. Its aroma penetrated my mask and colored my every response.

"I wanted to open my mouth and swallow him. I wanted to swallow us both." The Doctor jotted notes on a yellow pad and pushed at his nose with the tip of a wooden pencil. He was smooth and dry, like a little seed or a dull white pill. His forearm rippled with a river of tiny muscles whenever he tacked his tiny instrument to and fro.

"Literally swallow?"

"Yes, literally swallow."

He looked for a while at my blank mask. "Is it something you actively tried to do?"

"Swallow him?"

"Yes."

"I would put whatever part of him that would fit into my mouth."

"And would you, then, bite?"

"Well, not exactly bite. I would use my teeth, on occasion, to create a—a . . ."

"A wound?"

"An excitement, a sensation. Like you might do with your wife. Do you see?"

"No, I don't understand, exactly." He let his pencil rest and looked quizically at me imagining, I imagine, what I might mean. I took his hand in mine and put his finger in my mouth, through the bag, and sucked on it, softly, as I did with Dexter, and then I let my teeth tickle across its underside.

"Like that. Only sometimes harder and with his prick mostly."

"With his genitals?"

"Yes."

"Were you aware of the laws then?"

"What laws?"

"Concerning genital contact. The technical distinctions. Were you aware of them? Did you understand them fully?"

"I don't think so, no."

"They're quite simple really. The law applies in varying degrees depending on the nature of the sexual contact. The extremities are one thing, and then the interfemural area is another. The belly and nipples come next, then the testicles and finally the actual penis and anus."

"Like archery."

"Excuse me?"

"Like with archery, more points for hitting the bull's-eye."

"Mr., uh, uh, this is not a joke."

If you were to fly by overhead, say in a balloon, I think you would find the City is shaped like an hourglass. Dipping down out of the clouds you'd see the deep harbor carving out the western hollow, the dark green hills cutting in from the east. The noise and filth of industry might reach you depending on the winds and your nearness to the valley of the gray factories (there above the capitol's thin waist, running north like a waxy scar along the broken tracks of the national railway). The sulfurous smoke of the foundries is a permanent condition of life here, mixing obscurely with the salty sea breeze and the rich, woodsy air. The winds coming through the valley carry it down among the houses, dusting the trees and children with a soft, silky ash. Seeing this hourglass shape draining forever south with the drifting ash, you might wonder after our sense of history in this place. Does anybody feel the age of the impenetrable mountains that block our exit east? Do children remember for whom we built the railroads? And why do the factories seem to produce nothing now but capital and debt, jobs and disease? I'm no social critic and would only ask these questions of school children seconds before the ringing of the final bell; so spare me the embarrassment of spinning out an answer and return instead to the dank cellar bar, the altar at which we began, the Burlesque.

For therein lay the answer: the pure exhaustion then, when the sun crawled from out of its bed and hung like a metal disc in the eastern sky, when the long chaotic night had ended and the cellar disgorged, tumbling us out onto the empty cobble-stones, the gray light suffused throughout the filthy morning mist, our delirious breath through rasping, hoarse throats, was like the exhaustion of coming many times and never quite sleeping. The difference between coming and not coming disappears within an undifferentiated state of arousal. The body dissolves. My soul was abuzz with its own constant effusion; like when your flesh has gone numb from sex and still you keep at it until the numbness is a tingling and finally a sensation. Numbness is sensation. The costume hides you and it exposes you to the world. It imprisons you and it sets you free. Had I come last night? Had I ever stopped coming?

Know that we never stopped singing and that I slept with no one. The Burlesque is not a backroom, nor some dating bar for men without imagination to couple in. Sex is something I have hopelessly tied to the divinity of love (whatever it may be) and which doesn't compel me in the absence of that mysterious intoxicant. The magic of Lucrezia twisting in the limelight, those rolling waves of song . . . there I found this communion, this delirious ecstasy.

I said something of this sort to the lobster-man as he walked with me down the Pellestraat toward the University and the apartment building in which we both lived. He nodded, drenched and drained from the evening's revel, and mumbled back to me his few words. "I dress as her sometimes," he said. "At home."

I delighted in the thought of it. He'd pull his thick curtains shut, turning the bright sunlight dark and orange. The cat, if indeed he had a cat, would cower on the bed watching, swiveling its tiny head to and fro. The lobster-man stands naked before his secret chest of clothes. Lavender perfume is sprinkled on him like a benediction. The unholy bangs and swallowed screams of violence in the apartment above thud dully through the carpeted floor (the pulling of the organ stops, the church choir's song). The robes, the vestments. The candles are lit and the altar turned to reveal a full-length mirror of astonishing clarity.

"In silk. Not the quality and size of the actual costume, mind you."

"Certainly not."

"Just enough to create the illusion of a costume."

"And you sing?"

"No, no. Not then, not there," he rasped. The lobster-man's voice was like gravel or sawdust, or the saw that made the dust. "I imagine the song. I mouth it sometimes, but I don't take any chances."

"And her other songs, her repertoire? You've memorized her repertoire?"

The tenderness of his confession drew his eyes downward, casting glances from shoe to shoe. His fingers fumbled with each other nervously, making me feel acutely the flocculence of his little secret. He paused, as if weighing the propriety of some further revelation. "I wrote for her, in the early days. When she was still playing each night at the Opera House."

I needn't describe the depth of feeling this tender confession occasioned within me. So much of what mattered most to me had been wrapped around those halcyon days of Lucrezia's vibrance and glory, those long months of her triumph and splendor upon the Opera House stage. Such a complex tangle of yearnings had gathered, if not neatly, then at the very least, completely around that time (just as a nervous housewife might compulsively push each letter and trace of her secret lover into one small golden box, sealing the lid shut each time, hoping thereby to both save and hide every trace of her unallowable passion).

For the lobster-man to reach, with a short remark, into that hidden place and drag out before my eyes the vessel of my most secret and sincere longings—oh, the frightened housewife, the waves of confusion, desire and denial, as she stares at the golden box held there in the light of day.

How unspecific and strong that current felt. It was not that I longed to be, as Lucrezia was, glorious upon the stage. It was more a triumph of the Burlesque that I wished for. For there had been a moment, in that long ago past, an extended moment of perfection, when all was right in the Capitol and the countryside; before the banners began their rapid, almost weekly, changes, when the citizens seemed to walk with their eyes wide and sensitive to the ocean air, the liveliness of the streets, the importance, palpable as a humming, of each busy table in the cafés where we'd sit and drink chocolates. All that was best in us thrived in those lively exchanges of opinion and song, in the spontaneous expostulations of radicals or school-boys, anyone with legs strong enough to climb upon the table-top. Our vitality achieved its pinnacle in Lucrezia, in her triumph upon the stage, the Capitol abuzz with anticipation each day, and every café filled with revelers on their way to stand near the Opera House and catch any trace of sound that might drift out. She was our voice and soul, the embodiment of that insa-tiable vitality and thriving that, by some accident of history, our culture stumbled upon for its brief, shining moment.

At least she seemed so to me. I was young then, nineteen when I first saw her. Twenty-one when, a month before her removal from the official stage, I had my moment, designing for her a carapace of astonishing dimensions.

The lobster-man took my hand, watching my eyes, aswim with memories. "You knew of her then?" he asked.

"Yes," I said softly, leaning against him to steady myself. "I saw her first when I was nineteen. *Cleopatra in Winter*."

"Yes, yes. In March, a year and a half before the end. I was there."

"Inside?"

"Oh yes, I was always let in, being a writer for her."

"I'd been outside several times, before I was able to find a way in."

"Hmm," the old man sighed. "One of the many, the throngs of boys clamoring outside. I remember well."

"I suspect I saw you, arriving."

"Oh no, no. I think not. I was quite discreet. I wasn't among those in the fancy carriages with all their foofaraw."

"I made her a costume, once." This brought a shift in the lobster-man's posture, as I'd hoped it would.

"One she used?"

I noted his interest with due pride. "Yes, a carapace. She was carried off in it, at the closing of the last show."

"*Agonies of a Fly?*"

"Yes, the last week."

"But of course I saw it. I—I wept. The vaulting fans, they—they tickled the upper reaches of the light bank."

"Yes."

"And they shimmered so, the way she'd wag her head as if it were nothing."

"Neck strong as an ox, they say."

"And correctly."

We walked, dazzled by our memories, ambling along the margin of the deserted street, just as the Rugby boys walk in their afternoon exhaustion and camaraderie. I see them down my street coming in from the fields. They're golden in the warmth of the day's last sunlight. Clouds of breath dance about them and the steam rises from off their muscled bodies. Their legs, under the weight of bulky torsos, have a simple finality, a gait of resignation and peace, a giving up, as of that on the face of the Christ nailed finally to his place. There is a secret they share. The lobster-man drifted along with me in silence. The sun burned through the awful mist and shone golden against our faces.

"3. Was your crime a revolutionary act? Yes or No," I recall reading on the lengthy form given to me by the arresting Nurse. "If Yes, please explain."

I've always loved examinations. Whether as student or teacher, examiner or examined, I've always found a simple glow of friendship emanating from the neatly separated questions, an opportunity for affection in the answers or grades given. That evening it was no different. I looked at the matronly Nurse, her sweet face enclosed in its cap, the messy evidence of my sexual mingling with Dexter clutched to her breast in a little bag, and wondered just what sort of answer would best fulfill her high expectations.

"Nurse Corporal Thumb," I asked, noticing on her small

metal badge this rank and surname. "Would the Ministry prefer I go into some detail, or will a simple yes/no suffice?" She sat sternly on the bed's edge, surveying the room, still, for more signs of our interrupted passions. I heard Dexter crying in the other room and then the door closing as they took him from me.

"Detail please," she answered tersely.

"Was your crime a revolutionary act?" I read again, wanting now to at least come up with an adequate reply. Really, I had never thought about politics, nor revolution, while making love to Dexter. But that wouldn't do. I did have some small thoughts about the Criminal and Health systems, however, and the possibility of ever exceeding them, so to speak. Thinking is a hobby of mine, a little diversion I indulge in my spare time. So I put pen to paper and answered thusly:

My crime, as a crime, as a specific act, was not revolutionary. As a crime it is comprehended by the system of law and, more important, as an action it is comprehended by the system of pathology. *Any* criminal act sits happily within those systems and does not disturb them. (The complete absence of crime or illness would be, I think, more upsetting, but that's not our concern.) If it is simply action which has been made criminal, no crime can be revolutionary. But if it is my being that is my crime, maybe then my crime is revolutionary. My being recasts my actions in a wholly different light than the prevailing systems of law and pathology. My actions have entirely different meanings within the context of my being than they have when taken from that context and set as objects under scrutiny in the criminal and health systems. My being is incomprehensible and therefore revolutionary. It is upsetting in a way that simple criminal acts never can be.

Fairness procedures were followed and I was given a number and a mask (as I've said before). There were other cases like mine and we were made to wait together before seeing the Doctors for our first interviews. We wore green pyjamas and the Doctors wore white. The details of my life outside the

actual activity of child molestation (as my love affair came to
be called) were supposed to be kept out of court. I sat at a
gray metal table and took pills and a glass of orange juice.

"Your essays intrigue me," Doctor General Nicholas said as
an ice-breaker. Seven doctors sat at the raised wooden dais,
attended by nurses bearing water. Their shiny black shoes
poked out from below the false front of the wide arcing desk.
The humming of the fans was punctuated by their nervous
drumming of pencils on the table tops. Doctor General Nicholas was in the very middle, slightly higher and more lumines-
cent, I thought, than the others. "You seem to have thought a
great deal about revolution."

"Oh that," I gave back, disappointed that he'd chosen that
from among the many essays. It was hardly my favorite. "I
copied that, paraphrased it from a book I read."

"Do you read a lot?"

"I do. I read books for school."

"You're a student?"

"A teacher."

"You seem quite young to be teaching."

"I'm thirty years old. I've taught for five years now."

"Yes, I see that now, on the forms. Was the boy a student
of yours?"

I hesitated, uncertain who "the boy" was. Silly, it was Dexter of course, and he had been a student of mine. "Yes, he
was. I taught Dexter history."

"Was he aware of your thoughts concerning revolution."

"No, I—I don't really have thoughts concerning revolution."

"But your essay," a tall, Viking Doctor asked from the right
side of the Doctor General Nicholas.

"That was simply an answer to the question, the question
on the form. It's not really something I think about much."

"What *are* your thoughts concerning revolution?"

"I—as I said, I don't have any. It doesn't occur to me to
think about it."

"And your crime, have you thought much about that?"

"My love of Dexter?"

"Your molestation of him."

"Our making love?"

"Yes, your sexual contacts."

"Well, yes. I'm almost always thinking about sex with him. I was thinking of it just now, as you asked me about politics."

"About sex with him?" The line of white faces moved forward, as a wave lapping a little shore. The black shoes tucked neatly back, out of sight. "Now, during the hearing?"

"Yes, I believe so."

"You're imagining sex during the hearing?"

"Well, yes, if I understand, that is, correctly. Are you asking if I imagined sex with him now, here, or if I now, and here was imagining sex with him?"

"Either one Mr., uh, uh, either the sex now or whatever."

"Well, of course, I'm imagining all those things now, now that we're talking about it. I'm sure we're all imagining it now. Dexter and I, say, on this table, nude, the hot lights, some sort of furry rug. As I say, Doctor, all of us, sucking his sweet hard prick—"

"Thank you—"

"—here under the lights—"

"It's quite enough."

"—slick with sweat—"

"Yes, it's clear, quite clear."

"I find it hard to stop."

"You may insert your testimony at a later hearing Mr., uh, uh, in a more private setting."

"I may?"

"When there's time. The Wellness Committee has a backlog to deliver."

"With a Doctor?"

"If one is assigned."

"I must have one."

"If we so decide."

"To talk to. I still feel I misunderstand the guidelines."

"The laws are quite clear."

"Still."

According to Doctor General Nicholas, as a writer I don't go to an office to work. I organize my hours around the spirit that has possessed me, answering to my muse. I've been provided with a manual typewriter and coffee mug, notepads and clean white sheets of paper, rumpled clothing, used furniture, shelfloads of obscure, well-thumbed books, and a number of bad habits from which to choose. My mornings may be spent with painful hangovers if I wish, or they may be passed burning in the hot flame of creation. I miss the school terribly and wish to god the Ministry would restructure my new profession and construct enormous gray office flats to which every writer would report at 9 A.M. on the dot. The open interior would be filled with row upon row of linoleum desks and bulky electric typing machines waiting silently under ubiquitous white neon lights. I'd set my lunch pail by my feet, grumble terse greetings to those writers nearest, and commence. Coffee break, an hour off for lunch at noon, and a fine clear steam whistle blowing at the stroke of 5 to signal the end of another day's work. I don't think the Generals or the Ministry know what it's really like to write all day alone.

II

The Doctors Generals granted me a new life, an opportunity to find my proper place in the greater social scheme, a chance to discover the right relation of love and, I guess, politics. I would be moved, returned to the cold, northern clime of my native home, the City of my youth, with its gray factories and golden Opera House, the City of Lucrezia and the Burlesque, and now the City of this my new life. Dexter would remain in the south, where my transgressions had occurred, to be guided through his convalescence far away from my difficult embraces.

The train made the long journey without incident, rolling along the metal rails, the view out softened by the rain. After the tea service I dozed off, subdued by the train's gentle rocking and my melancholy (an inevitable feature, for me, of train travel, trebled by the nature of this particular journey) and only awoke when our forward motion ceased, the heavy steam billowing from the engine's belly out into the dusky air.

My bags had been sent with me (on the very same train, I was assured), but had disappeared from sight by the time of our arrival at what is left of the central station. I'd seen them loaded on myself, tipped up on their sturdy metal edges and pushed up the wooden ramps by the strong young men whose job it is to see to such things. Now they were gone.

I gathered my few packages and stepped out onto the platform, still sleepy. Porters tacked briskly through the crowds, wheeling trunks and luggage on their sturdy metal carts. I rubbed my eyes and looked up to see the day's last dying light, draining through the dirty glass high above me. Rain beat upon the iron lattice. I took a few breaths deep into my lungs and felt overwhelmed by the familiar smells of my native air. Where were my trunks? The porter nearest me refused my tags, evidently put off by the red Ministerial seal. I slumped against the train, burdened by my one small overnight bag, and waited for my salvation.

And there he stood, dripping in his fashionably cut trench coat, just in from the rain. My Doctor General Nicholas Nicholas, gazing at me in warm silence.

"We have your trunks," he began, with admirable calm. "You needn't bother yourself about them." I fidgeted nervously, overwhelmed by his sudden presence. He was so intact and flawless, his face was steady as the rain, and as soft and reassuring. He pointed toward the one trunk, indicating that it was mine, and took my hand to lead me out into the dusk.

The old center of the city lies like a patchwork cozy, lumped up upon its steep hills, crazy and cramped, with the central station pointing out from it into the valley of the gray factories. Even on bright days it can be enveloped in mists, and that day it was doubly so. The Doctor General had with him tram passes (one sporting my photo from the evening of my arrest) and an umbrella, and we strolled patiently across the empty plaza toward the tram lines. Everything was familiar now, the Opera House rising above the ramshackle lanes of the old city, the harbor, busy with the noise and flurry of commerce. Newspaper vendors sitting in their cramped kiosks rolled cigarettes and stared out into the evening.

Mr. Nicholas (as he asked that I call him when not engaged in an official function) offered me the tram pass and a small package of related papers: maps, guidebooks, leases, and assorted other documents. The key to my new apartment was contained therein and its address indicated on a small cardboard tag attached to the key by a string. Nicholas, or the Doctor General Mr. Nicholas, sat and watched my explorations with a fine paternal silence.

"Will I be living alone?" I asked. The tram had not yet come, and we sat by ourselves on a wooden bench by the sign saying "5," meaning the line to the University. My Doctor's silence seemed to say "wait," and so I did, not unhappily, as I knew his motivations were therapeutic and certainly not capricious. Evidently I would be told all I'd need to know in good time, probably within the sanctity of his sanctorum, or "office," as he called it.

The two of us sat together on our solitary bench, contained within the district of the Opera House, surrounded by the bustling City with its crossing trams, the seat of power directly to our north, emanating its effect, and the weather washing over us all, all of us helplessly involved with each other and each thing. The moment had about it, in my mind, all the manifold qualities of love that it was the Doctor General Nicholas Nicholas's task to unmask and unravel (or mask and re-weave, perhaps, through the woof and warp of his particular loom, the one at which he'd been trained). It was his blessing and gift.

I stared at my dumb, unyielding face in the photo, remembering the grave instructions of the clerk by whom it was taken. "Recall your crime, please," he asked, not indicating whether the exercise was meant to be silent or spoken. I kept mum, exhausted and a little puzzled, as the flash burst open and blinded me. A welcome rumbling drew me away from this memory, and I looked up to see the big number 5, rattling out of the mists and up the hill toward us. My Doctor had passed the time scribbling notes in a small book, reminders, I surmised, of things to tell me (for when the opportunity might present itself). I had only to wait one night, before I would hear them.

"Our goal is to help you organize your life in such a way that your deviant behaviors do not recur," he did indeed finally say (the next morning, after the day's bright dawn had found me boarding a northbound tram, to our rendezvous at the grand marble palace of the Criminal and Health Ministry). We were facing one another in the heavy leather chairs of his outer chamber. "This involves more than simply punishment or isolation. We hope to redirect your desires and establish a structure to your life that will help you avoid situations which might tempt you. Certain occupational and social skills will be strengthened, while the various obsessive urges that have compelled you toward deviant actions will be quelled. I rather see it as making whole what is now an incomplete person, helping you move past a stage of arrested growth."

I pardoned him the ugly language, as I knew it to be part of his job. The vastness of his outer chambers allowed me an ease of breathing I'd not felt before. Distinct from the therapeutic inner chamber (the site of our most intimate conversations) my Doctor's expansive outer chambers projected a studied informality: an opened window or two, throw rugs dotting the floor like lesions, a ramshackle scattering of curios, sweet liquers, brightly colored, green, violet, and rose, radiant in their crystal decanters, aglow in the morning sunlight. He had his feet up on his desk, the scuffed leather soles presenting their face to me. I sat in a chair rather too large and felt like the child I once was, awaiting the merciless wisdom of the Headmaster. He'd still not told me anything about my new life.

"I see Mr.—uh, Doctor, but I'm still uncertain what it is I'll be doing each day."

"Each day?"

"Yes."

"Each day will be different. This is not a program of incarceration Mr., uh, uh, rather it is therapeutic in nature. You are free to come and go, to do as you see fit."

"May I see Dexter?"

"Oh, absolutely not. There are limits."

"May I work with the children here?"

"No, no, no. You haven't listened at all to what I've said. I'll hardly be disposed to report any real progress until you *do* make an effort. Your new life will keep you clear of such temptations. No work with kids. No loitering near the schoolyards. Certain patterns must be broken if you are ever to move forward and seek self-esteem among adults."

"I'm to seek self-esteem among adults?"

"In a manner of speaking. Not actually setting out to search, rather, finding it there, as a matter of course, habitually, as it were."

"But what will I do all day?" I pried, sitting sideways on the leather easy chair. "What will I do each morning when I'm not going off to school to teach?"

"Your work, of course," he assured me, tipping slightly toward his desk. "Sessions, here, with me. And, of course, behavioural therapy."

"Alone?"

"Sometimes with the technicians."

"Will my work—"

"Be alone? Yes. You have much reflecting to do, and the committee believes your work as a writer could prove to be an essential therapeutic tool."

On that, our first full day together in this the city of my new life, we went like a whirlwind from one stop to the next, the Doctor General and myself. The day's events were dotted with occasional visitations to the Doctor General's quarters (in which were found both the outer and inner chambers) wherein rudimentary therapeutic encounters were begun or, at least, talked about (much as the dazed young freshman finds on that first thrilling day of school that classes are not so much "had" as spoken of, reviewed in anticipation by professors unwilling, too timid perhaps, to make the full plunge in without preliminaries on the first day).

We rode the trams to and fro, across the busy districts north of the center, out to the Parade Grounds on one occasion, and finally, at day's end, winding through the steep forested hills to the Vista. The freshness of the air was startling as the electric tram wound its way along the clattering metal rails. The City seemed at a great remove, though it was easily visible, through the trees to our west. The Doctor General was gazing out across it, with that certain silent smile to which I have earlier alluded. There was so much that I had not yet mentioned to him, so many fears and questions, that I felt of a sudden overwhelmed. Some small panic began in my belly and swept through me, a worry that our day had been unsuccessful, that he might right then and there pass a judgment, so to speak, deeming me unworthy of his attentions, undeserving of his help in understanding the regulations, as was my goal in this my new life.

And then, in a thought, it all passed. Silly me.

But of course. We were forever wed by his verdict. That thought, tracing through my mind as we sat then on the rattling tram ascending higher into the sparkling woodsy evening, started a warmth inside me, a glowing below my heart to which I would often return, in times of confusion or doubt. I could look to him in silence or speech and find that communion, that mingling of purpose and obsession, that I would so often need to reassure me I'd not been cast out, repudiated by the community that first taught me to love.

III

In the morning, some weeks later, I lay abed staring blankly at my empty room, as the light from the day shone brighter and brighter through my dark curtains. Normally I detest morning sloth, but I was so fagged from the previous evening's revels, I was completely unable to rise. Others in my building had never taken issue with my hours.

It was only the Burlesque that kept me so late, and that was a luxury I allowed myself but two or three evenings each week. Unlike my lobsterish neighbor and friend (and a motley gaggle of other men), I was not a nightly habitué of Lucrezia's blessed mass. I had my new life to think about, and my new profession (which demanded of me a level of self-discipline I was finding hard to muster). Lying abed, not really sleeping, I glanced at the idle black typing machine and its implicit accusations. Writing was not easy. Something about the silence, the solitary nature of the vigil, inevitably put the kibosh on my imagination. I had only a thin folder of prose to show for my two weeks' work, and most of that was paraphrased from other works.

Oh, but I had just begun. My kind Doctor General encouraged me at every turn, helping me to look upon this rocky start as evidence of my high standards and commitment. "Painful comes the motherlode," he would say, and often. I drifted away, again, into my now-forgotten dreams.

At noon, finally, I rose, with the loud ringing of the bells and my street busy with schoolchildren and workmen beginning their midday's meal. The clatter of pig's hooves echoed along the narrow lane and I knew that I'd missed the passing of the small piglet to which I'd directed so many inconsequential thoughts. His passing, in concert with the exodus of his attendant flock and the old woman whose job it was to bring them to market and then back home again at noon, normally marked the end of my first sitting at the typing machine.

I rushed to the window only to see his little pink bottom scuttling round the corner, disappearing down the hill toward a hay-strewn cart and home. On a normal day I would have called out fond greetings to the toothless hag and asked after her smallest charge, his disposition and humor, etc., etc. But I was too late, and all there was to do was sigh and lean wistfully out the window, breathing the new day's air, and watch the flocks of schoolkids wavering along the streets on bicycles, off to lunch and, God knows, a cigarette or two. True to my promise, made solemnly to the Doctor G. N. N., I spoke not a word out the window to the passing boys.

It was a sparkling fall day, the sort on which the winds blow north, relieving the old district of the cursed ash and allowing a fresh, salty fish smell to penetrate from the harbor throughout the narrow lanes of my purlieu. The noise of the Ministerial Pageant could be heard drifting on the breeze, echoed and redoubled by the distance of its traveled path from somewhere on the Parade Grounds. No matter, I'd certainly see the photos in the evening journals, and even if I didn't, the content and consequence of the day's official revel could easily be guessed by looking at the next day's faces.

Today's seemed only slightly changed from the prevailing pattern of the past weeks. A heavy Prime Ministerial brow was visible, still, on most men. Noses, I noted, had sunken—evidently in reference to the heroics of the Provincial Boxing Squad. Their victory in the International Tourney had received quite a bit of attention in this month's curriculum at the University, and had already inspired a nod from the Prime Minister, the actual pummeling of his own nose having been carried out just one week ago at the Parade Grounds. Hardly surprising, then, to find so many sunken noses now.

I was reminded of my Doctor General, whose own nose was yet unaffected by the recent fashion. He was so stable and clean. It was a luxury of his position (due in large measure to the clarity of his purpose, his role) that he could dispense with the careful deployment of fashion signals which, for most people, constituted the fundamental definition of self and function. We would be meeting in an hour, and I hurried back to my dressing table so I might be clean and ready for our morning session, to be shared, together, in the softness of his inner chamber.

The bright sun beat gaily against the tram, warming the tawdry vinyl seats. I looked out across the valley of the gray factories, gazing up into the billowing hills. The summer's green was gone, turned golden or bare by the first killing frost of the incipient fall. I'd enjoyed the haze of nostalgia those first weeks, finding lost lanes and bookstores I'd known as a student, without thinking or meaning to find them. Vistas opened up, often, that I knew well in my heart, but which my mind had forgotten. This view east, out the northbound tram to the chambers of my Doctor General, was one. It touched a sensitivity below my throat and wobbled inside my head, making a soft lump in my throat. I turned my thoughts back to the inner chamber and its promise of safety and seclusion.

I pulled the little bell meaning "stop" and got off, bounding eagerly up the broad marble steps of the Ministry's Palace. The tall doors welcomed me, turning easily on their pivots, ushering me into the echoing rotunda. The long hallway was almost empty, the many functionaries having gone off to a fine autumn lunch. Kind, thoughtful man that he was, my Doctor General always planned my sessions for midday, or the evening—a slack time in any case—to make my travels easier. My lonely footfall filled the vacant passageway. I found the Doctor's door open, and went in unannounced.

He was dressed in tweed, leaning thoughtfully over the wide mahogany desk. Sunlight poured through the windows, infusing the dusty air with a venerable glow. A book lay opened before him, an edition of Egas Moniz, in the original Portuguese. Sainted scholar, my Doctor General. I settled silently into my favorite chair, hoping not to disturb his important thoughts. How motionless, lost in calculations, as if his body were put on hold, left still and inanimate, so his mind could wander more freely. I closed my eyes, willing a similar dissolution, wondering if our minds might meet on another, distant, and unspecific plane.

"Ah, Mr., uh, uh," he exhaled when, upon looking up from the book, he saw me. "Very prompt." I glanced at the ticking clock on his bookshelf and saw that indeed I was, prompt. He strode deliberately to the door and shut it, letting the lovely room enclose us completely. The silence of the dark mahogany settled, like dust, all around us. One could feel the weight of the building, the importance of the Ministry itself, in the unwavering line of his wood paneling. The walls were even and clean, the wood unwarped. The beams that coursed across above us were true. I admired the effect, opening my eyes wide as if to let the room's geometry extend itself inside my head.

"Tea, coffee?" he offered, gesturing to the pot of water by the fire. "It's quite fresh." Slight embers glowed among the fallen ashes of an early morning fire, set, I'm sure, by the nightmaid, in preparation for my Doctor General's predawn arrival. It was part of his regimen, a part in which I sometimes joined if no other hour could be found for our day's session.

"Yes, tea please." I was fond of the ritual. His unwavering regularity was, I'm sure, largely responsible for the ease and comfort I'd come to feel about our therapeutic encounters. Had I any other Doctor, General or not, I can't imagine it would have been the same.

We reclined upon the divan, stretched out by the fire, and shared tea, a little preliminary before "going in." In the outer chamber all was informality and light. The dim gaiety of the boulevard reached in through the windows, a distant sound, and the anxious sun moved shadows through the room, visible and glorious up to the time of its setting. The dusk, here, was always spectacular, the evenings relaxed. We drained our cups, chatting, and suffered a small phial of anisette. And then the moment came.

He rose unspeaking and walked past me. The panel slid clear and he opened the door, allowing me to pass through before him. It was silent, the small chamber clean. My couch was unruffled, its coverlet tucked neatly in, just as it always was. I put the bag on my head and lay down, shifting about on the cushions to settle myself. I heard his pen touch paper, and then nothing.

His silence let us breathe, allowing a timeless hesitation, a moment, as if between heartbeats, wherein we sank further into ourselves and reached the level at which we could speak.

"What are you thinking now?" he asked, beginning. My mind drifted, released by his simple words.

"The pageants," I offered, letting go what I came to first. "The pageants and the schools. Maybe I should work with the pageants."

"What about the pageants and the schools?" he asked, shifting back to a point I'd let drift by. What about them? By what accident had I placed them together?

"People are so happy at the pageants, especially if the music is good." I'd only been to one since returning. All the people danced, though the politics baffled me. "I only ever danced at school before, when we'd chaperone the kids. Do you remember that old opposition leader, the one who fell from a balloon?"

"Do the pageants remind you of school?" he asked, directing my attention. I shifted in my place, curling up around my little fists.

"No. I miss the kids." That much was true. The Doctor's pen began its tacking. I felt my breath all warm and moist within the bag. It was pleasant inside, so soft and blind.

"Does it feel bad, missing them?" His hand paused in its labor, waiting.

"Yes." I began to feel quite small.

"What do you do, when you feel that way?" His question slipped inside me, resting in my ears, and I drifted away. I'd become invisible, nonexistent. What did I do, when I felt this way? I disappeared. Some minutes passed. The good Doctor General gave me some tissues, pressing them into my hands.

"I imagine him, almost every night," I whispered. "With me, in my bed."

"You imagine Dexter?" he guessed, rightly.

"Yes." His body swam before me, forever branded in my memory.

"What do you imagine?" His hand busied itself.

"You know, us, together. The way he—" I stopped. It was too much, too tender to be spoken. I curled in closer, wishing my Doctor's words to sweep it all away. But he wouldn't speak. His purposeful silence bore down on me, magnifying the melancholy, trebling it simply by the emptiness he left me in.

"How does it feel?" he finally asked, knowing full well my answer. I sniffled weakly in my bag, rubbing the soft cotton against my nose to clean it.

"Awful," I admitted. "It feels so sad." Again the silence, letting the implications of this insight germinate inside me.

"Wouldn't something else, some other fantasy, feel better?" I hadn't considered the option. My mind was in a rudderless drift, lost in the sea of my memories of Dexter. I had presumed it would always be so. Could there ever be anyone else?

"Maybe," I allowed. "It would depend on the fantasy." I flipped quickly through my little backlog, wondering who on this earth could possibly divert me from my blessed Dexter. There was the lovely boy in the film, the technicians' film. Indeed, already he had displaced Dexter during the occasional bath.

"It would depend on you," my Doctor General pointed out. "I can't help you, except to suggest you try. Try finding a path away from him."

Our conversation drifted on, meandering like a mountain brook in spring, its borders long since lost to the ample melt. My Doctor General's warm sun shone down, loosening the layers of ice inside my soul, enriching the prodigious flow.

At last he tapped his tiny bell, letting it sing in the listless air. I heard him slip from his bag, setting his pad and pen on the chair, and go to the door. I stayed, enbagged, and composed myself, wiping clean my tears, before removing the vestment and following him out into the open day. It was nearly three, and the technicians would be expecting me.

The technicians were a barbarous lot, silent and dry within their starched white jackets. They seemed to have been assigned to a life underground, sequestered like nuns or a jury, kept clear of the contaminating influences of daily life. I didn't know it to be so, for a fact, but I'd not yet met above ground any person who claimed or admitted to being in the technical fields, and certainly these half-dozen hadn't appeared to me outside the chamber in my brief few weeks thus far "spent," as they say, in this my new life.

I approached the daunting facade of their lair with a quickened step, fearing the grim reproaches that invariably accompanied a late arrival. The winds beat down upon the flags, buffeting them to and fro, casting undisciplined shadows across the fortified windows of the building's face. Applicants, as per normal, were gathered in bunches upon the front steps, roped in by velvet and brass, moving forward at a glacial pace. I ducked in under the steps, where the Ministerial carriage was parked, and pulled the crocheted beckoning cord, hung there for just such a need as mine.

It was Dilthy who finally answered, after peering at me through the spyglass for the customary fifteen seconds.

"Afternoon Dilthy," I said cheerfully, removing my overcoat, as was the routine. "Ponz, Flessinger," I said in turn to the two who now joined us at the entry point. They nodded, as one, but said nothing. "Fine day, eh?" A white gown was proffered and I divested myself quickly of the civilian garments in which I'd arrived. A sturdy box was opened and my garments placed inside, as Ponz and Flessinger took me across the threshold and into their laboratory.

The laboratory was in fact a small room similar in style and ambiance to the Doctor General's inner chamber. While somewhat larger than that "sanctorum," the laboratory of Flessinger and Ponz sported the same neutral wall tones and absence of an external portal, window, or door, as such. On three occasions I found the grim interior occupied, inexplicably, by some sort of tropical plant, a fecund fruit-bearing plant of astonishing color and size. Those few times, audible gasps were heard to come from Ponz and the plant was removed by a trio of assistants I had never seen perform in any other capacity.

But today the room was empty, save for my "chair," and the projection screens. Flessinger sat me down and signaled to Ponz to ready the device. I opened the flimsy white gown and saw that my little friend was feeling quite shy, all snuggled up there in his tangled nest. Ponz looked at me impatiently, not wanting to involve himself with my penis any more than was absolutely necessary.

"Should I coax it out with petting?" I asked, innocently enough. It was never clear to me exactly what state of arousal the technicians required. In point of fact, if ever I arrived "in full flower," shall we say, Ponz gave me a nasty withering glance and stood tapping his toes impatiently, waiting for the crazy thing to calm itself down. It seems there was some median point at which attachment of the phallometer was easiest, and Ponz would have no truck with anything else. He rolled his eyes at my helpful suggestion meaning, I suppose, no, and so we simply waited for the warmth of the room to unravel my little friend's length.

Thankfully, the silly twosome left the room, always, following our ritual preliminaries. Once they'd secured the device and checked to see that I was accurately positioned, a hasty retreat would be beaten to the booth, from whence they could commence with the calibrations. It was only then, through the intervention of a loudspeaker, that they would finally speak to me.

"Are you comfortable in your chair?" The voice was so tender and soft. I've no idea whether it was Ponz or Flessinger.

"Yes, quite comfortable." I could respond with as little as a whisper and they would hear me. I shifted a bit, settling down into my throne.

"You may remove the gown now, if you wish." I did. The room contained a perfect stillness. The air passed in and out, through invisible ducts in silence, caressing my skin like endless yards of silk.

"We're getting a reading Mr., uh, uh. Is that confirmed?" the soft voice inquired.

"Uh-huh," I breathed, letting loose my shoulders and neck, slumping just a little. I fear I'd disturbed the calibrations, but there was really no helping it. The first moments alone were invariably arousing; the muted tones, the circulation of the air, as I've said. Little glimpses of light, glimmering points of red and green, could be seen twinkling behind the black glass to my left. Sometimes a ghostly face would hover among them, bending close to a meter, the face revealed by its glow. When the films began the men became invisible.

"Let's find a plateau, if we can, please." I thought about history, as the Doctor General Nicholas Nicholas had earlier suggested, trying to sort out exactly how old the various signators were at the time of the First Declaration. An impressionistic landscape painting appeared in front of me on the screen. "We'd like to get a calibration here Mr., uh, uh. If you could just focus on the slide, please."

A lovely meadow sat dappled by the sun. The long, wet grass was painted a rich green, and the light seemed to indicate that it was early morning. You could see that, to the right, a small pond had collected with the spring rains. Lilac grew thick along its little shore and the rippling waves of a boy's splashings could be discerned in the disturbed face of the water. The fact that he was completely hidden from view would seem to suggest that he'd chosen to swim naked, perhaps with a little friend, the two of them, shy by nature, coyly keeping just out of the painter's line of sight. A marked stylistic break divided the painting top from bottom, just above the uppermost exposure of the pond. Evidently, the painter, a young woodsy man of twenty or twenty-five, full with life's vital sap, noting the boyish play of the little swimmers, took an extended break from his work to join them. Stripping his simple peasant garments off with a few strong tugs, he leapt with agility and grace into the pure, spring waters. The boys, naturally, seized upon him, trying their boyish strength and wiles on and against his sturdy frame, wrapping their gangly limbs around him all hither and thither.

"I'm sorry, but we seem to be getting a reading. Could you focus on the slide please?" Stupid me. I'd known for weeks now the paintings were erotically neutral, simply calibration tools.

"Excuse me, I'm very sorry." I blushed warmly and pulled the gown up over my activity. It was difficult to watch the slides, neutral or not, without looking in them for some point of interest. That this point of interest so often included a boy or two and some small degree of nudity was, I suppose, part of the reason I was here. I took several deep breaths and focused my attentions on the poorly rendered tree.

Our twice weekly sessions were such a puzzle to me. I had imagined they would involve drugs or surgery, or training of the sort a circus bear might receive. It wasn't precisely racks and vises I'd imagined, hunks of meat tossed to prone men on cement floors; but it was something of that nature. The removal of the garments, for instance, as the first practice I encountered, did then seem to presage radical methods, painful manipulations of the body, or markings of the flesh. I never thought I'd simply sit and watch dirty films, slouched in a comfy chair with my little friend dancing about in that warm, mysterious bag provided by the technicians. There were, it's true, frequent and unpleasant interruptions, sudden eruptions of noxious gas, intermittent joltings from the arms of my chair. But I tried to ignore these, focusing, instead, on the images. I'd imagine the intensity of my discomfort to be a sort of pleasure, as when Dexter grabbed and scratched at me so desperately as he did when nearing orgasm. Pain, I've found, is an attribute of intense passion.

"If you're ready Mr., uh, uh, we can proceed." It was the voice. Of course I was ready. I shifted my gown loose again, enjoying the dimming of the lights, and faced forward toward the screen. A few yards of black leader rushed by, specked and scarred by bright green scratches, their light flashing out into my chamber, playing across my bare skin. My eyes were adjusting quite quickly when a bright field of white burst open and the room seemed flooded by light. Silly, it was the cameraman's clumsiness, the soft back and bottom of an adolescent boy having achieved an arctic whiteness by inept manipulations of the shutter. The film wobbled back into focus and fixed its frame, the white darkening down into an irresistibly Arabian skin tone, as the cameraman, evidently, found his controls.

The boy lay back onto a rug and turned onto his side, letting us gaze upon the divine entirety of his naked front. One could tell from the sparkle in his eyes, the cocky grin on his devilish face, that he'd a fine and healthy awareness of his own stunning beauty. He reached down across his brown tummy and took the limber length of his erect little friend in hand. Like the clumsy feet of a Labrador puppy, it was overly large and lanky for the boy's slim frame. Its wet tip pushed up against his belly button as he, still smiling with delirious pleasure, played upon its length with his hand.

It was at this point, so soon in my revel, that the mysterious joltings began, albeit at an intensity far below that which they sometimes reached. It was a sensation that enveloped my chair, beginning in vaguely discernible points, but soon expanding like a pool of blood to warm me all over. It coarsed across and through me in waves that must have been determined by the hands of Ponz and Flessinger, spinning their powerful dials. It took me aback for a moment, distracting my attention from the screen and onto my own body.

But the boy's delightful eyes beckoned back to me, transfigured by his own pleasure, their depth and intensity increasing in concert with my own electrical sensations. It was as though the shocks were coming from him, my body wired to his pleasure centers. Each increase in voltage seemed the product of his unbearable passions. The film, Ponz and Flessinger, the chair: all of it was simply a mechanism through which he caressed me.

He was coming closer to orgasm, his legs spread out wider, his feet planted down and back arched. Yet still he looked at me, puzzled now, overcome, the muscular spasms of his body repeated in his gaze. I too was nearly there, though I couldn't touch my penis, enclosed as it was in the instrument of the Ministry, and felt myself mimicking instinctively the contortions of his flesh. Noxious fumes filled the air, as if the indescribable stink of his pleasure had burst through the screen and engulfed me, penetrating my nostrils and lungs. I felt him all over me, electrical and primitive, our mutual pleasure so heightened as to transcend into pain, awash in our mechanically multiplied effusions. God bless the Ministry that saw fit to construct this instrument of torture and divinity. The perfection of its design, collapsing this boy and I together in inseparable union within the darkened chamber, our coming so precisely orchestrated, played in concert to an impossible pitch.

It became so much more than simply me and the boy, or, rather, the image of the boy. Ponz and Flessinger, their mysterious booth and its apparatus, the Doctor General, and the Ministry that made it all possible. I felt all of their attentions, their painstaking ministrations, fulfilled in that moment of coming. The very building and its edifice, the proud soldiers marching to the Parade Grounds. It all spun around my moment, as an expression of love directed finally to me through those thin electrical wires that ran to my chair.

It was a particular and special pleasure, to have the entire apparatus of the state participate so intimately in my orgasm.

"Excuse me, Mr., uh, uh." The voice spoke. "The, uh, panel indicates that you've fouled the mechanism." The film had run out as the boy lay back exhausted, cum trailing in drops and pools from his brown chest down to his tummy. The screen had gone black again, and my chair still and silent. Indeed, I'd "spent my wad" in the cool, wired sack.

"I'm very sorry." Really I was more baffled than sorry. It was the fifth time in as many sessions that I'd "fouled the mechanism," and neither Ponz nor Flessinger had volunteered any advice as to what I might do to avoid it in the future. I was afraid to breach the topic with the Doctor General, fearing, still, his harsh judgment. The unbridled nature of my erotic enthusiasm was a feature of my being that, above all the others therapy had thus far exposed, seemed to disqualify me from continued work in the rehabilitative program.

Ponz came out from the little booth pulling on his rubber gloves, casting disapproving glances with every shake of his unamused head. He removed the mechanism and cleaned me up before attaching a second one he'd brought out with him. The "accident" rarely repeated itself, as I had not the sort of sexual stamina one reads about in the tabloids. The rest of the afternoon, typically, would be spent in a mild state of arousal, my little friend dipping and bobbing to the play of the erotic images on screen. I even fancied the various adults featured as counterpoint to the forbidden children, but the intensity of that interaction never ever matched what I felt for the boys, rarely, if ever, triggering the desired shocks and fumes.

Outside, the cool autumn night had descended over the city, drawing the day's warmth from the Capitol's stone steps. Trains rolled out of the crowded yards, shooting steam into the darkness. They let their plaintive whistles call as they left the City, going north and then east to the mountains. In front parlors children pulled on sweaters or coats to run out into the chilly night to meet, in secret, their little friends for mischief, until much later and wet with sweat they'd run back home to bed and sleep. I walked alone, emptied by the puzzling intensity of my six hours in the Ministry's chamber, observing the richness of the air and the fine twinkle of the stars up above in the cold night sky. The tram rumbled past, but I made no move to beckon it. It rattled away into the distance, light and warm, almost empty, making its patient run to the city center.

The lobster-man, no doubt, was home, perhaps before his altar, reveling in the silk. Lucrezia would be awake now, the proprietor having unlocked the Burlesque and roused her. In a few hours the show would begin again. I wasn't sure I'd be attending. Therapy had left me so fagged and dragged, I knew only that I'd go home to soak in the tub and read for a while.

The Avenue along which I walked was now empty. A few hours ago it had been full, the minions and minor functionaries of the various Ministries all clamoring to find space on the crowded trams to take them home to the residential districts on the outskirts of the City. The Prime Minister had created this broad causeway at the time of the Centennial, as a monument to the Visionaries and as a glimpse of our architectural future. Each Ministry had its building here, overlarge, cryptlike, marble boxes, each with its own facade and banners. They stretched out in two long rows toward the north, set back from the broad Avenue at a great remove, graced with wide empty plazas, and daunting shoulders of white marble steps.

Among the distant noises of the harbor and the rustle of the banners, beating about the many poles from which they hung, there, among the sounds of the old district, still a few blocks distant, I thought I could hear a thin, small voice singing. It was her song, though it was not Lucrezia who sang. And it did not come from the houses, nor from the cafés nor the plaza. The sound was borne in on the night air, as if from higher up, from above the City, perhaps from the dark hills to the east. I looked up toward the Vista, in the moonless night toward the east, searching among the indistinct faces of the heavily wooded hills, not certain what sort of sign I might find to unmask the source of this phantom.

There was something, up above the reach of the tram line, on the crest running north from the Vista. A dim glow of light from a campfire. It flickered behind the tall trees, dancing yellow and orange in the night. In its light I could see two large banners, unfurled and rustling in the wind, strange, unfamiliar banners with no Ministerial insignia, at least none that I could recognize from this great a distance. The song did seem to be coming from up above, from on high, as it were. It was soon lost amongst the growing noise of the cafés, as I came closer and closer to the District of the Opera House. But in the stillness of the empty plazas, a short distance back among the deserted buildings of the Ministries, it could be heard quite clearly. I wondered why I'd not noticed it before, walking, as I did, in the late evenings twice each week from the laboratory to my home. But I imagine I had just never stopped to listen, or thought to look up into the hills.

The Avenue ends abruptly at the northern edge of the Old District. It doesn't dissipate nor feed its traffic in along elaborate exit ramps. It simply stops like some surgical scar, some utilitarian incision, meant to run exactly so far and no farther. The trams slide off its end onto the older tracks, making the transition with an unsettling jolt. Pedestrians continue, as I did, walking gladly into the narrow lanes, leaving behind the broad, empty melancholy that the Avenue begets, a sadness as deep as the Avenue is young, as permanent as the buildings are meant to seem to be.

The Old District was fairly busy that evening. I walked now at a calmer pace, lost in vacant memories. My mind swam through that unrecoverable past, vaporous and elusive. It was Dexter, everywhere I turned my interior eye, Dexter. His slim, muscular arms and the palpitations of his heart, there, beating visibly below his sternum. How I cherished his delicate chest, sweating and vibrant, blushing with its own exertions, his heart set to racing by the infinite joy of another orgasm. I marveled at his appetite for pleasure, the long afternoons we'd spend together in his bedroom, reading out loud, inevitably pressing our books beneath us, the clothes stripped off with some impatience and force. He wanted me to read to him as he came, or recite my thoughts to his thighs and belly, touching my tongue with each word to the pulse of his unbridled erection. He was so proud, as only a boy can be, and thrilled by the new size and shape of his body. What utter confusion, that night when he was taken from me! The purity of his pain, as I heard it through the partly opened door in his sobs and crying, has no match. I hear those tears each night, fading in and out as I fall to sleep, mixing inevitably with his laughter, his groans of pleasure at coming, until it's simply a white noise of Dexter's untrammeled emotions, all of him in a numbing sound, and I fall into my dreamless sleep.

OPENING THE DOOR

• PAUL RUSSELL •

IT WAS THE summer the lesbians took over the Seven-Eleven: Candy and Denise, lovers, friends of ours who worked the afternoon shift. They'd get stoned, turn the store radio from muzak to a rock station, mop the floors like the dykes from hell they really were. They'd forget to take our money for potato chips or beer. It couldn't last—it was an open secret they were planning to raid the cash register and scoot on out of Poughkeepsie at the end of the summer to drive to San Francisco and never come back.

"The summer of hope," they called it. Their mood was terrific, and they wanted to spread it around. "Get high," they yelled at me from behind the counter. "Go party. Find a boyfriend."

I was completely immune. "The summer of 1990," I reminded them, "is not the summer of hope, thank you. Boyfriends are fatal these days."

Candy mimed a happy-face smile.

"Be glad," I told her, "you and your girlfriend are dykes."

The summer of 1990. Sean and Mike went to Istanbul and got arrested in a police raid on a gay bar; Pat bought a house in Woodstock, and a bunch of us spent Sunday afternoons helping him fix it up to the strains of Elisabeth Schwarzkopf singing Strauss' *Four Last Songs* on the boom box. It was the summer Avi and Don were diagnosed, and Rick died. And it was the summer of Jared Michelson, though when I had that conversation with Candy and Denise at the beginning of June, I didn't even know Jared existed yet.

I met him at this gay dance club called Prime Time. Even though the old days were long gone, we still headed out on Friday and Saturday nights. Like most of my friends, I'd gone cold turkey on all the fun stuff sometime in the mid-eighties. These days Prime Time was mostly an excuse not to spend the weekend sitting at home watching porn videos and jerking off.

The instant I first saw Jared I knew I'd never seen him before, because if I had—even just a glimpse—I'd never have forgotten it. He was that beautiful.

More or less. When he smiled, his teeth were too white— toothpaste-commercial white. But it was a flaw I imagined I could live with.

I never really drink anymore, so the couple of gin-and-tonics I stoked myself up with went right to my head, which I guess is why I don't really remember how I actually managed to introduce myself to him. The only thing I remember is that the deejay was playing Paula Abdul, because the first thing Jared ever said to me, leaning close as we danced face to face, was "Paula Abdul über Alles."

All I could think of to do was blurt out, "Did anybody ever tell you you look like Ted Cox?"

Jared just looked at me. We were dancing face to face, and the music was pretty loud. "Who's Ted Cox?" he shouted for everybody in Prime Time to hear.

"Just a porn star," was all I could say—shout, rather. Porn stars were about my only frame of reference these days, and cute Ted Cox was currently my favorite.

"Well, I guess I feel complimented," Jared told me. The music was so loud, I was hoping he hadn't heard the same version of the conversation I had. I thought for sure he was going to dance off to another part of the floor to get rid of me, but he didn't. We weren't really dancing together—we were just dancing next to each other. But it was like we were dancing together, and he must've thought so too, because after a few minutes he suggested we go out to the patio to cool off.

The air outside was so humid, it was almost cooler back on

the dance floor. I was completely broken out in a sweat—but then Jared was too, which I liked. It was sort of a bond between us. I couldn't believe I was actually standing out there with him—it'd all happened so quickly. I was afraid if I stopped to think about it, I'd start shaking.

I was definitely out of practice with all of this, though he didn't seem to notice—he was off at a hundred miles an hour telling me the story of his life. Which for the first couple of minutes, at least, I was all ears to hear. Anybody that beautiful, you figure they must lead a fascinating life.

He was twenty-five, he told me, and a part-time student at SUNY–New Paltz, a Libra born on the cusp and from Modena, the dullest little town in the Hudson Valley, where he lived at home with his parents and two younger brothers—there were five brothers in the family altogether but the older two had gotten married and moved away and his youngest brother drove him crazy practicing the trumpet all the time. Jared said it in a rush, like it was something he had to get out in the open from the start.

I told him I was an engineer for IBM in Poughkeepsie.

"When I grow up," he went on, talking fast and sort of swallowing his words, "I want to be an architect. That's what I've decided. You could call it my dream. I want to design cities with affordable housing. Zoos. I'd love to design zoos. Or parks. You should see the theme park I'd manage to come up with." It almost made me laugh, the way he said it—twenty-five years old, and he was talking about growing up one day. I mentioned that to him, and he sort of laughed. "I guess I don't really think of myself as an adult yet," he said. "I keep wondering when it's going to happen. Everything that happens to me, I say to myself, Jared, maybe this'll make you grow up. Get a grip on life. But it never does. So I'm still waiting."

And he sort of laughed. Whether he was just nervous, or he was sensing how absurd all this sounded, I don't know.

I'd never heard anybody run on so—not even my friend Pat, who's known behind his back as Motormouth. In my first ten minutes of knowing him, Jared had spilled all these completely personal things about himself. How the first time he ever had sex was with a black lifeguard in a swimming pool. How a couple of years ago he worked as a stripper in Washington, D.C., for six months—"Great money, plus you get felt up by two hundred different guys every night." How his roommate in D.C. was a high school football coach "with a dick this big," Jared said, marking off an impossible length between his two hands.

It didn't exactly make me want to back away, it's just that he wasn't the way I'd imagined. Shut up and keep smiling that smile of yours, I half wanted to tell him. But there was no chance. Before I knew it, he was explaining to me some scheme he had for using lasers to beam a huge pink triangle onto the face of the full moon, so everybody on earth could see it. "It'd be so ACT UP," he said. "It'd be fabulous. People would go crazy trying to blot it out. They'd probably have to blow up the moon to make it go away."

He was like some little kid you wanted to put your arms around and say, slow down. But he was already off to something else, how back in the winter he'd had this deal with some guy to cut firewood in the river bottom along the Walkill, and he'd rented a flatbed to haul the logs, the guy was going to pay him later out of the profits they made on the wood, but then Jared got sick and it turned out to be pneumonia, they had to put him in St. Francis, pneumocystis wouldn't you know, and when he got out two weeks later the guy had up and left, and took the truck too, and now Taylor Rental was saying he owed them the whole deal on what the truck cost.

It was like a thunderbolt set down in the middle of all his chatter, though he didn't seem to realize it. Nothing he said appeared to be any more important to him than anything else. I remember I got this strange feeling. I went hot and cold, and a shock spread out through me from somewhere in the middle of my chest.

I'd spent a lot of sleepless nights anguishing over whether or not to get tested. I finally did, back in '88, mainly because worrying about it was getting in the way of the rest of my life. I kept thinking myself into the symptoms, lying awake at night and wondering what I'd do if I got sick. *When* I got sick, I kept telling myself with this horrible crazy fear that gnawed and gnawed. And then three weeks of waiting, and not knowing, and not wanting to know, and diarrhea all the time I was so scared, and when I found out I was negative, it was this relief so tremendous I can't even describe it. I told myself, this is a new lease on everything, and now that you've got it, don't do anything to give it up. There were so many people, some of whom I even knew, who'd give anything to have this simple thing that I now had. This clean slate that said I could live.

It's funny how things can change. At the time, it seemed so clear—no more messing around with anybody, period. After the test, I didn't have sex with a single person. Like I said, cold turkey. I got reacquainted with my fantasy life. Safer sex! If you really want to be safe, I decided, sit at home on your sofa and watch porn movies. Let the Ted Coxes of the world take their chances so the rest of us could be saved.

I wasn't too thrilled when Jared suddenly asked me, out of the blue, "Do you have someplace we can spend the night?"

I think I just stared at him with my mouth hanging open. Insouciance is one of those words you save up, waiting for exactly the right time to use it.

"We just met," I told him, thinking the whole time, *Are you crazy? Do you think I'm crazy?*

"All this dancing really tires me out," he said. "Plus, I never take people back to my parents' house. I guess I could, but I just don't."

"Do your parents know?" I asked him gently. I wanted to steer us away from the topic of my place.

"Know what?"

I gestured round the little fenced-in garden. "This," I said. "Everything."

"If you mean Mr. Fun," he said, "they're the ones who put me in the hospital. I think I sort of passed out on the bathroom floor. Messy, messy. But they're crazy about me, my parents. They'd do anything for me. That's the one thing in life I can be sure about."

He said it so simply, I had to believe him. Sometimes, later, I wondered—but I never met his parents, so I can't say.

I didn't trust myself not to fall for this guy. As a compromise, I managed to end us up at an all-night diner in Highland. I wasn't taking any chances. For one thing, I couldn't take my eyes off him, which is always a bad sign.

"Your teeth are so white," I told him. We were sitting in

the fluorescent glare of a diner booth. He was on his second beer; I was nursing a cup of decaf.

"It's because I wear blue lipstick to make them look white," he told me, and smiled.

"No," I said. And yet I looked at his lips to see if it was true. The thought of it made me a little squeamish.

"It's a joke," he said, touching his lips, rubbing them to show me there was nothing there.

"I don't get it," I told him.

"It doesn't matter," he said. "My teeth *are* very white, aren't they?"

"It's unnatural how white they are," I joked, and we both laughed—probably a little too hard, because then he reached his hand over and covered my hand that was on the tabletop and said, "Look, I don't have any place to sleep tonight. Can I crash with you?"

"I thought you were living with your parents," I told him.

"It's complicated," he said. He kept his hand resting on mine.

I'm going to regret this in a big way, I remember thinking. I couldn't resist.

Back at my apartment he tried to kiss me the instant we were in the door.

"Forget it," I told him.

"You don't like me?" he asked.

"It's not that," I said. I didn't think I should have to tell him I didn't want to kiss him.

He sat down on the sofa—flung himself down like I'd some-how exhausted him. Putting his hand under his shirt, he massaged his stomach. "You're nervous of me, aren't you?" he said.

"No," I said, "I'm not nervous. Why do you say that?" But I knew he could see through me.

"You can sleep here on the sofa," I went on. "I'll get you some sheets."

Sometime later that night, I don't know when exactly, I woke to find him slipping into my bed. It was so hot, I was lying on top of the sheets. "No," I said.

"Don't worry," he whispered. "It's just me."

"What's wrong with the sofa?" I was groggy but not so groggy I couldn't figure out what was going on.

"Please," he said. "I get so scared sometimes. Could you just hold me for a while?" He hadn't touched me—he lay there beside me inert. "I can't seem to fall asleep these days," he said, "unless somebody's holding on to me."

His body felt cold and clammy. He was the sort of guy I used to tell my friends I could die for.

Times had changed. I wasn't about to go dying for anybody anymore.

He didn't spend the night. I woke up about an hour later and he was gone. In fact, he never spent a night with me, though later I ended up spending a number of nights with him. But he must've considered that we'd hit it off together in some offbeat way.

"I can talk to you," he told me on the phone the next day. He'd copied my number down before he left. "You were great, by the way," he said. "You were sympathetic to me, and I needed that."

All I'd done was give him a hug, but as a reward I immediately became the recipient of all the day-to-day details of his convoluted life. He'd call me up and say, "Guess what I did today?" And I never could guess, never in the least.

He had a genius for getting himself into predicaments, both real and imagined. He'd call me to ask if I thought he should write to Walt Disney or call him directly on the telephone.

"I think Walt Disney's dead," I told him. "I think I read somewhere that they're keeping his body frozen, so when they discover a cure for whatever disease he had, they'll wake him up and treat him."

I sort of wished I hadn't brought that up, but Jared didn't seem to notice.

"Well, then who do you think I should talk to?" he asked me.

"About what?"

"Oh, it's nothing," he said. "It was just an idea I had."

"What idea?" I coaxed. I tried not to let him let things drop, which he had a tendency to do.

He rekindled some enthusiasm.

"This theme park idea I had," he explained. "Pansyland. Like it? With a Judy Garland ride, and a Donna Summer ride, and a really scary Joan Crawford ride that'll make people just shriek. And, and there'll be others. I haven't thought it through all the way. But don't you think that would be great? You could make a lot of money from it."

"Forget it," I told him.

"You never know till you try an idea out on somebody. Anyway, I gotta go. I'll call you later."

Sometimes I thought Jared called me whenever he was in between two other things and bored.

Once he called to say he'd had an attack of diarrhea in a Burger King—he'd gone and shit in his pants, and could I bring him a clean pair? He'd be waiting for me in the bathroom stall.

A few days after that he bought a 1969 red Camaro from some Puerto Rican guy down in New York. Where he got the money I have no idea, but he was bursting with excitement. It'd been fitted up with a stereo system you could hear halfway to the moon. The only trouble was, the brakes were shot—you had to use the parking brakes for everything.

"What a great car," I told him.

Needless to say, he drove my friend Pat crazy, which I guess was something in Jared's favor. Pat and I'd been best friends since our Cornell days. He was the first guy I ever went out with, when he was a senior and I was a sophomore, and even after we both moved on to other things we still stayed friends.

"I mean, really!" he told me the first time Jared and I showed up for dinner in that red Camaro, stereo blasting. "Next thing I know, you'll be decked out in hightops with a baseball cap turned backwards on your head."

"You're just jealous," I said. Which he was. Pat was a control queen from day one, and most of the time I let him because it was easier than resisting. Plus I always thought it was flattering, in a way, for Pat to be so concerned with my affairs.

We had little rituals that had developed over the years— brunch on Sundays, a week in Provincetown in August. I liked the way Pat got all his friends together to help him fix up his house. Anybody else and it might've seemed like taking advantage, but with Pat you never cared. He made us drinks and put out food and turned up the stereo. Face it, sometimes it can feel like a privilege to be used.

Not that Pat and I were about to go falling out over Jared. We'd been at it too long to let anything like a stray relationship get in the way of anything. If that's what I was having with Jared—a relationship.

The friends of mine Jared got along with best were the dykes in the Seven-Eleven. Whenever we went in, he'd launch into his "When you're a Jet, you're a Jet all the way" routine. Candy and Denise, always high, would start snapping their fingers and whistling. They'd fall in formation behind him, sashaying up and down the aisles, jumping over the counters, whirling around in each other's arms while I kept watch at the door to make sure no customers were coming. If somebody did come, they'd all three stay outrageous to the last possible instant, then suddenly revert to some kind of normal behavior like nothing had happened. But they'd still be so full of "When you're a Jet" that they'd keep smirking at each other, and even burst out laughing, and if the customer looked at me I'd just look right back and shrug.

It made me a little nervous. But then I guess I could say the whole time I knew Jared, he made me more nervous than anything else.

We fell into a kind of routine with each other. On Saturdays, all through the summer, we always went and did something— "organized activity," he called it. He was passionate about organized activity, maybe because it was the only time his life wasn't in complete chaos.

He woke me up early one Saturday morning with a phone call: "Get your hairy faggot butt out of bed—I'm taking you to the most awesome place in the world."

I mustered some groggy skepticism to ask him, "What's the most awesome place in the world?" You might say I never totally trusted Jared.

"Opus Forty," he told me. "Doesn't that excite you?"

"What's Opus Forty? Sounds like a disco."

"I know what you like," Jared told me, "and I know you'll totally love this. Guaranteed. Trust me."

Trust was what it was all about, right? I let him pick me up in the red Camaro and off we went, across the river and up the Thruway to Opus Forty. It wasn't exactly a disco—it was an old bluestone quarry some lunatic art professor from

Bard had taken a bulldozer to, starting back in the 1930s, and had leveled and terraced into this odd landscape. Something between a ruin and a launching pad. "Environmental sculpture" was Jared's name for it.

"He called it Opus Forty," he explained, "because he got tired of people asking him what it was called. He figured it was going to take him forty years to finish the whole thing, so that's what he called it. And it almost did. He worked on it for thirty-eight years."

We were walking along a shelf of rock. Whatever the professor'd had in mind, it didn't look like he'd finished it. I mentioned that to Jared, who was balancing his way along a ledge, arms out, like it was a high wire act he was in the middle of— a total put-on, since the wall there was wide and to the next level was only a drop of three or four feet.

"Well," he said, "one day the bulldozer tilted over on top of him and it killed him." He smiled his dimpled smile at me. "Crushed him to death," he said. "He never knew it, but all those years he was digging his own grave."

"You've got to be kidding," I said. I didn't know whether Jared was the kind of person who made things up, but I thought he might.

"I swear," he said, pretending to teeter on the edge of the drop-off.

"What a way to go," I told him. "Under a bulldozer." I looked over at him, hoping he'd give me another smile, but suddenly he wasn't there. He'd managed to go and fall off the wall anyway. "Jared," I said.

It didn't faze him. He landed on his feet on the next ledge down.

"I'd love to do something like this with my life," he called up to me.

"You mean fall off a wall?"

"No, silly—I mean all this." He spread his arms out wide. "Isn't it great? To go and make a sculpture right out of the ground." He let his arms fall to his sides. "But then I'd be too impatient," he said. "Just think—thirty-eight years. I'd never have the patience. I can't even get through a semester."

I thought the place was pretty hideous—all those stone walls and scrubby pine trees and pools full of stagnant water. There was something lunar about it, something dead and depressing. But Jared was so enthusiastic that, giving him my hand to help pull him up out of the pit, I had to agree with him how great it was—all the time thinking to myself, he doesn't have a clue. It's not a question of patience, Jared, it's a question of time.

Jared was going to be lucky if he ever even managed to finish at New Paltz, let alone go on to architecture school somewhere. That was how little time he was going to have. But then it occurred to me that maybe the reason he was always so impatient, flitting from one thing to the next in his conversations, in his life, was because he knew he didn't have much time. And I thought, as we wandered over to the shady lawn to spread our picnic lunch, maybe he's right. Maybe he's exactly right to go on living the way he does, oblivious.

There was a conversation I wanted to have with Jared sometime, a serious conversation about life-and-death things. Things I wanted to know what he thought about. But I never had that conversation. I never got around to starting it with him.

On the way home that afternoon, the Camaro broke down on us. It just failed and died without warning. That was the first time we kissed, there on the side of the highway as we tried to figure out what could be wrong with the engine. We kept bumping into each other as we leaned over the hood, neither of us having a clue what to do with a motor, and I don't know, one thing led to another and suddenly we were in this romantic kiss.

I let go. I let my tongue slide into his mouth, all the time thinking I shouldn't be doing this, this could be fatal. But also thinking, I can't go through the rest of my life and never kiss anybody ever again. I guess you could say, right then and there I wanted to kiss Jared more than life itself. It was a feeling that passed pretty quickly, and when we got home later I washed my mouth out with Listerine, though I knew that wasn't going to do a bit of good.

But for a full three minutes, standing in plain view of everybody on the edge of the highway, we were both fired up to where nothing else mattered. We stood kissing and rubbing against each other, not caring who drove by and saw us. As it happened, a state trooper pulled up just when we were finishing that kiss. We bolted apart—I thought we'd had it. But the trooper was very nice. I don't think he'd noticed us at all—it was the car that held his eye. "A real beaut," he kept saying. "Mint condition." The whole time I was stuffing my shirttail back in my pants and Jared was combing his fingers through his mussed hair.

I guess that afternoon was the high point of something. I was right, of course, to look on the dark side of things. But I also wasn't right. Somehow the picture I have of Jared is somebody balancing right on the brink and not caring—somehow saying, nobody's ever going to be safe.

Me, I'd spent my whole life being safe, buying insurance against things that were eventually going to happen anyway.

"Get drunk," he'd say when I demurred after two beers. "Have sex. Live life, for God's sake. If you want my philosophy, that's it. What're you people waiting for, an engraved invitation?"

Another time he told me, "Some people say it's all a punishment because we had too much fun. I don't think that. I think it's because we didn't have enough."

"I don't particularly call this fun," I told him. He was in the hospital by that point, with meningitis.

"Well I'm having the time of my life," he said. He sat propped up in bed with a basket of fruit I'd brought him, and he was rummaging through it, making two piles—what he wanted, pears and apples and pieces of chocolate in tin foil—and what he didn't want. "Especially not the oranges," he said. "I hate oranges. I've always hated them. Don't you?"

That was the first time he'd been in the hospital since I'd met him, and the worst time, the scariest time. After that, I got used to the idea he really was sick. I'd known it all along, of course, but I guess Jared's enthusiasm for everything was infectious, and I'd let myself start thinking he wasn't really all that sick after all.

"I've heard this really distressing thing," Pat called me up to say. "Are you alone? Can you talk?"

I'd been annoyed at Pat all summer. Ever since he'd made it known that he was extremely skeptical about the direction my life had taken in recent weeks.

"I'm just going to launch right into it," he said. "Are you and Jared being careful? I mean, condoms and all that."

"Pat," I had to ask, "why are we having this conversation?"

"I don't want to alarm you," he said, "but I *am* your best friend. I was talking to some people who know Jared. Look, has he said anything to you about his"—he stumbled for a second while he looked for the right, delicate word—"about his condition?"

"Jared and I are completely truthful with each other," I said. But a sliver of glass had gone through my heart. "Anyway," I told Pat, "I don't see why you're calling me up to tell me this."

"It's because I care about you, honey."

"I don't want to be having this conversation," I told him.

"He's slept around, even after he got sick. Without telling people anything. You should know that about him. I'm sorry to be the one to have to tell you, but really this is something you should know. He's trouble all the way through."

"It was the first thing he told me," I said, even though that wasn't true. I remembered how he kissed me that afternoon—chances he'd taken with my life, casually, unthinkingly. And just because he'd gone and thrown his own life away.

"I have to go," I told Pat.

"You're okay?" Pat said. "You understand why I was worried, don't you?"

"No," I said, "frankly I don't," and I hung up.

Actually, I understood everything. I drove straight to the hospital.

Jared was asleep, but I shook him awake. "Who the hell do you think you are," I yelled, "dragging me into all this shit? What gave you any kind of right to do that? Can you tell me that?" I'd pulled his thin body up by the shoulders, but then I pushed him back onto the mattress hard and walked away to the window. "You're too fucking dangerous to be in the world," I told him.

From the window, you could see the hills on the other side of the Hudson, green and unruffled by anything.

Jared lay there like he was exhausted and looked up at me. I'd made him cry. Tears were running down his cheeks, but silently, and if I hadn't been looking at him, I wouldn't have known he was crying.

"I'm sorry," he said, not wiping the tears away but just letting them run down his cheeks like stains. "I know I deserve all this. I've always been so scared of it."

I was crying too, the anger and fear coming from so many different directions inside me. "No, you don't deserve it," I said, bending down to hug him, to kiss his cheeks and his tears, their salty taste. "Honey, honey, you don't deserve any of it."

I'd never called anybody "honey" before.

After we both calmed down, and I daubed his tears and mine with some Kleenex from the box beside his bed, we talked some more. I tried to be practical, optimistic. "We can beat this thing," I told him. "There're all sorts of new medicines. What does your doctor say? What about AZT? What about that mist that keeps you from getting pneumonia?"

He lay looking out the hospital room window at the hills. "I'm taking all those things already," he said in this quiet voice. "I'm taking everything they've got. But you know what? I have to tell you something I was thinking. Just before I went to sleep and you came in. It's sort of funny."

"What do you mean, 'funny'?"

"Well, what I mean is, it's odd. I think I'm looking forward to all this." He still wasn't looking at me. It was like there was something in those hills outside the window that he was interested in, that he was trying to see his way over to.

I didn't know what he was talking about, and I told him so.

"I heard it's a narrow door you have to get through," he explained.

There'd always been these moments when I thought, maybe he's crazy. Now I wondered whether the disease hadn't actually gotten into his brain.

I couldn't tell him I didn't think there was any door.

I started staying nights in the hospital room, since the nurses couldn't watch over him all the time. They put in a cot for me, but I never slept. I'd spend the whole night sitting in the chair by his bed, watching him sleep. Trying to memorize what his face looked like that was disappearing right in front of me.

Then from nine to five I had to be at IBM like nothing was

happening. But something *was* happening. I'm not sure how to explain it, how sitting there, watching Jared's face all those nights, something happened that I guess I'd been waiting to happen my whole life. Not lust or obsession or any of those other things I've always been good at. Something that got summed up in this dream I had—or maybe not a dream, just two voices I heard talking to one another when I closed my eyes in that quiet hospital room one night, exhausted, some kind of question-and-answer between these two peaceful voices, one voice asking the questions and the other voice answering them, not like they were questions that needed to be answered but just to remind themselves of something they both already knew.

Who created love? one of the voices asked.

Death created love, said the other one.

Just like that. So calm and quiet. It was like somebody had spoken it aloud there in the room.

I knew I didn't have Jared—all I could do was let him slip away from me. I remembered what he'd said about his parents, how they were crazy about him, and that was the one thing in the world he knew for sure.

Me too, I said. Me too.

As far as I could tell, his parents never actually came to see him in the hospital. I asked him if he should call them, or if he wanted me to call them. "I don't think you've told them," I told him. "I don't think you've let them know anything, and I really think you should."

"They come visit me during the day," he said, "when you're at work. Anyway, they were in California all last week, at Disneyland."

There was never any trace of visitors, no flowers except the ones I brought, and I brought a lot. Because it was September I lined the windowsill of his room with chrysanthemums, especially the dusky-colored ones, the comforting ones.

We fell into another kind of routine. I'd get to the hospital around seven in the evening, and Jared would tell me about the things that'd happened to him while I was away. His days were always a lot more eventful than mine.

"This morning a nurse came into my room with a cart," he told me, "and guess what was on the cart?"

Jared was always asking me to guess things.

"I have no idea," I told him.

"She had bunnies for sale. And so I asked her how much. Sixty-six cents, she told me. And do you know why they were so cheap?"

I just looked at him. Every day he got worse and worse, though I don't think he could tell that. He got thinner and thinner, and his stories got crazier.

"Why were they so cheap?"

"The nurse told me, these bunnies have AIDS. They used them in some experiments, and now they have to get rid of them. I thought sixty-six cents was a lot for a bunny with AIDS, so I didn't buy one. But they were cute. They were bright pink. If she comes around with that cart again, maybe I'll buy one."

Some days he was in a jokey mood.

"What's the worst thing about going into the hospital with AIDS?" he'd say.

"I can't imagine," I told him. I noticed how his eyes had gotten this shiny look to them. Maybe because his face was so thin.

"Your parents are free to look through your closet to find your porn magazines," he said.

"Did you talk to them yet?" I asked.

"Who?"

"Your parents."

I could tell he was trying to think fast. He was like a bicycle when you can't click it into gear. "Didn't I tell you?" he said. "They're in Florida. They took my little brother to Disneyworld for his birthday. But they'll be back next week."

I tried to remind myself that Modena, where they lived, was just on the other side of the river from Poughkeepsie.

"I think maybe you did tell me," I told him.

"Well, did I tell you I slept with Rob Lowe once? And Kevin Bacon. It was a three-way."

"No, you didn't tell me that one," I said.

"I was afraid I'd forget about it if I didn't tell you. I'm

getting so forgetful these days, have you noticed? I even forgot to shave this morning."

He was clean shaven. His hand shook so much, I'd been shaving him for days.

Whenever I'd actually go home, it was such a relief—just not to be there in that hospital room with him. But also, in a way, it was worse. I was horny all the time—something I hate to admit, but I'd come home from the hospital and watch porn videos. Ted Cox movies, to be specific. A month earlier, Jared had gotten a kick out of them, screaming, "Ted Cox, I can't believe you said I look like Ted Cox! He's hideous! I don't look like that, do I? Please say I don't." And he didn't, really. It used to be our version of a date, though, sitting on the sofa with our pants down around our ankles watching Southern California boys do things to each other that no sane person would dare do any more. It felt shameful and sad, but better than nothing. I remember, once, I reached my hand over to help him along and he said in this offended way, "I'm not really into the mutual masturbation thing. If I have to do it, I'll do it myself, thank you."

When I look back on it, I can see how proud I was of Jared, how I wanted to show him off to all my friends, even if they weren't really capable of understanding whatever it was I got out of him. And what *did* I get out of him? It's easy to enumerate his flaws, which if he'd been well probably would have driven me away from him in no time. As it was, I guess I felt with Jared like I'd finally arrived at something. Like finally I was an adult, that mysterious thing Jared always imagined somewhere down the line for himself. I had been notorious in my circle for not being connected to anybody. All my friends had their guys who lasted two weeks, six months—even, in rare cases, years. I always joked that I considered my relationships successful if they lasted till the morning.

But now I was finally there. When Pat called to invite me for dinner I could say, I'm bringing Jared. It sounds trivial, but after years of showing up alone it meant the world to me—never mind that whatever Jared and I had hardly even existed.

What I didn't tell anybody about was his diagnosis, the fact that, though he looked completely healthy, he was in reality very very sick the whole time I knew him. That was the secret terror I carried around with me all the time. The secret that he was lost to me. There was nobody to turn to in all that. I couldn't talk to Pat any more. I'd always thought of Pat as my best friend, but really what it was between us was a holding pattern we'd been in for ten years and that was too comfortable ever to go breaking out of. It was a lack in our friendship that I saw clearly for the first time: Our friendship got tested, and it failed the test. When it came down to it, I couldn't say to him all the things I was afraid of.

I couldn't tell him how, when Jared had diarrhea, the nurses got fed up with changing his sheets six or seven times a day, and if I didn't want him to go lying in his mess it was up to me to clean him. He'd turn over on his side and I'd wipe him with toilet paper, like you would a little baby. There were times when I got his runny shit on me—I couldn't help it. I'd wash in the scalding hot water you got from the faucet if you left it running long enough, and I'd remember that afternoon we kissed.

Jared could hardly speak any more, his mouth was so full up with white patches of thrush.

The first week he was in the hospital for the last time, he still had his summer tan. He used to lie in bed with the covers pulled off his legs because he got these sweats from time to time, and I remember looking at his legs, so brown against the white of the sheets. He had really fine legs, a jogger's legs, but somehow it was the tan that got to me. How could somebody with legs that beautifully tanned be dying? It was then that it really hit me for the first time, how there was nothing anybody in the world could do for him.

About a week after he died, I stopped by the Seven-Eleven for some soda. I hadn't been in for about a month—the hospital took pretty much all my free hours. In all that time, since our argument, I hadn't spoken to Pat again, and he didn't try to call me either. I think he also knew we were at some kind of end.

But it was more than that. I only knew Jared for three months, and for a month of that he was in the hospital and delirious, but it was enough to make me secretly know some other, important things. All I can really say is, there was some narrow door that I found. I guess I came to see some things about myself that I didn't like, things I'd managed to keep hidden from myself before. I saw how my friends, especially Pat, had allowed those things to go along in me unchanged, year after year. I'd never known I was living in that kind of desert. None of them ever told me that, and I guess I decided that if they'd really been my friends, they'd have mentioned it.

Unless they didn't know about it in themselves.

I was surprised to see Candy and Denise in full swing. I figured they'd probably gotten fired weeks ago.

"Still thinking of heading out to San Francisco?" I asked them.

"California dreamin'," Candy told me.

It seemed crazy that people were still living their lives in the world, and I felt this sudden pang of envy for Candy and Denise, the way their life together went stretching out ahead of them as far as they could see.

They asked me about Jared. I couldn't bring myself to tell them anything. "The relationship lived a full life and then it passed on into other things," I told them. I was relieved they hadn't heard anything, though eventually they'd have to—unless they'd left for San Francisco before then.

"The dogs bark," Candy said, "the caravan moves on. I liked Jared."

"I liked him too," I told her.

She thought about it for a second; then she reconsidered. "He was always a little too enthusiastic about everything," she said. "Somebody like that could wear you out." I think, in her way, she was trying to make me feel better.

"Do I look worn out?" I said.

"You didn't get hurt in the relationship or anything?" Denise asked. They were always fabulous dykes. The slogan on Denise's T-shirt said, "SO MANY MEN . . . WHO CARES?"

I thought about how I hadn't gone to the funeral. It was at St. Peter's in Highland, and I guess his family was probably there—but I wouldn't have known them. I wouldn't have known anybody there.

"I wondered," said Denise, "when I didn't see you two around. I wondered if something bad had happened."

I changed the subject.

"When you get to San Francisco," I told them, "you should go to Disneyland. You should send me a postcard from there."

"Disneyland's not in San Francisco," Candy reminded me. "It's not even near there."

"Disneyland's in Los Angeles," Denise added, putting her arms around Candy from behind and, since we were the only ones in the Seven-Eleven, giving her a big hug.

"You'll get there eventually," I told them both. "I'm sure of it. And a postcard would make me very happy."

BONE

• RANDY SANDERSON •

HE STOOD BEFORE me in shivering white bones. I fell down and watched him tremble, sway, and clatter, his eyes wide, his grin wider, he was beautiful with light shining through his rib cage. Took a shaky step toward me lifting one arm in some gesture, trying to kneel where I lay cowering but as he bent over his bones exploded apart so that I was covered with femurs, ulnas, tibias, with his skull on my side. The skull turned to me grinning and nodding and said, I've fallen apart, could you put me back together? I asked, M, is that you? and he said, Naah, it's my bones. I started reconnecting them and it was easier than I thought it would be since they kind of snapped back together, and he tried each joint as I reattached it, nodding nervously and patting my shoulder with his bony hand. I feel so connected, he joked as he strummed his ribs. I helped him up and he did a staggering dance all around me to gather some balance while I steadied him by his radius. Let's go, he said, and we went out. I told him, you'll catch your death of a cold like that, and he snickered. I had missed him, and loved him still after all that time. I said, M, what happens when you die? and he said, plenty, and I said, why did you come back here? and he said, to tell you . . . and here he paused, quaking, then said, to tell you . . . and he told me this story that happened more in outlandish noises and extravagant gestures than in words, or in lack of gravity with centrifugal force, or in feelings, or something else, but anyway it was like a party. If only you would participate, M said, swinging me around, if only you would go wild! Then a heavy fog crept around us, it shrouded his bones like a loose suit and escorted him off, and looking back at me he laughed with his teeth, a look of mischief playing about his jawbone, his dark and hollow eyes. Leaves fluttered down around me, brittle brown hands of trees, and a wind chilled me—knew how to shiver my bones. I thought about his story the way you think about a party when it's over and my chill turned warm—I was filled with a certain merriness that put a spring into my step. I heard the clatter of my own bones, and sang along with them and laughed to myself like a crazy person. I walked and walked, hoping to find him again . . . and then I woke up to the sound of his voice, cut me some slack, Action, he mumbled into the ground, big nose pressed flat in a Dutch accent because he was. He liked to use American slang at inappropriate times and for no apparent reason. It woke me.

We'd been floating, no, lying there a while I guess, I don't know, it seemed like maybe a minute but he said at least one hour, I was a poor judge of time, it had been expanding and contracting so capriciously on the beach, which was deserted except for us. He stretched and rolled his head heavily over my ribs, the bone dreams had been recurring a lot lately, filled with bone things talking and cracking jokes. I did not know what to make of them. We dove naked into the water to wash off and were battered shoreward by big waves, then sucked seaward by the undertow which made us dizzy and cold, so we staggered out and headed for the warmth of the dunes where M threw a blanket down in a hollow that incubated us and read to me from an old recipe book we had found in the beach house. His voice was boyish and husky reading off the recipe instructions, cook without stirring to 260 degrees Fahrenheit or until a little of the mixture dropped in cold water forms a hard ball, cook to 270 degrees Fahrenheit if day is cloudy, beat the egg whites, if sunny, until stiff but not dry, at high speed, now add syrup gradually, beating all the time . . . he looked at me and something in my vacant expression told him I was elsewhere. What are you thinking? he asked. Thinking? I was thinking that to be with him was easy, most of the time, to be without him was always hard, to lose him was unimaginable, and that I, who had always been a loner, had reached such a crisis of affection for him. About losing you and your bones, or me and mine, or all of ours together, I told him, and he stared for a moment then burst out laughing, which made me feel kind of embarrassed, so with my thumb and forefinger I cupped his ear into a funnel and said, I'm serious, into it, and he just rolled at that, and I said, look, I've been a monk most of my life, never been good at lovers because love is impermanent. It changes, it leaves, I said. I said I had decided that I could never suffer the misery of a broken heart again—it lingered, showing its shadowy self around the eyes and mouth on certain days. I got used to being solitary, beating off a lot. I lived alone for a long time and got acquainted with myself, got myself acquainted, then I met you and it messed everything up because now I don't want to be alone. But it seems ludicrous to give up my solitude after I've gotten so good at it, I said. M considered me seriously. Sit down on the couch and take a deep breath, Actionthing, he said. I don't even believe in monogamy and here I am being monogamous, I said. The possibility that you or I will someday lie beside a future man and tell him about way back when I loved you is too much to bear. Know what I mean? I don't know, he said as he put his hands around my head and shook it a little, but we'll be okay, he said, with his warm and dry hands.

And what he thought but did not say was that I didn't trust him. But I did. But how could I trust him? How could anyone trust anyone? I could hear faint voices in the distance and a dog barking. The effect of the mushrooms had mostly worn off, and I looked him over as if for the first time, as if we had returned to a new introduction. The day we first met was like Xmas to me. We had been in several dance classes together, and I noticed that he would spread his prehensile feet out on the floor like warm clay, then peel them off, his plié was deep and his hips were so turned out that they opened flat. He threw himself around like an absolute savage, I tell you. And he was ugly-beautiful, with a narrow head, one brown eye one blue, big nose, thick lips, and reddish bristly hair shaved to stubble. He asked me one day to go for a cup of coffee, and I felt like a kid with a present, I could not wait to open it, and when I got him naked several hours later I discovered that he had three nipples, one normal and the other like a double exposure. They seemed to call to me now—I reached out and gave him a serious titty twister which caused him to cry out in pain and shove me backward onto something hard. I dug it up and found that it was a bone. It was about two feet long and bleached white with tiny holes all over it. I grabbed it by the end and shook it at him, and he took the other end and rubbed his hands along it, smooth. Smooth, he sighed, and sniffed it. Then we leaned away in a gradual tug-of-war, two dogs and a bone, running around in a rabid circle, running around in a circle. I let go suddenly, running around, and he fell down, then rolled backward to his feet and flipped the bone into the air, up there spinning luminous white, then landing stuck upright in the sand. I said, stop flipping bones, and gave it a kiss then tossed it as far into the dunes as I could so that we were once again alone, because I was greedy. I wanted all of him for myself, all of his vital fluids and precious juices, his blood even. I was his hungry mosquito buzzing around his ear.

If it weren't for the sounds of the voices on the beach drawing nearer we might have been the only creatures on the planet, but the wind carried their voices to my ears so that they sounded as if they were just below us. I was furious, I could not believe that on the whole empty beach these people had come to us. I peeked up through the sea oats to look down at the beach, and saw that a group of a few adults, a boy, and a dog had stopped and were standing on the shore directly in front of where we were hidden, directly in front of us on this endless empty beach, directly in front of us! I slid back down to M who had been watching me from behind with that look of appreciation in his smirk, there was a magnetic attraction between us, you know, when embracing tightly we felt like puzzle pieces, his embrace was graceful and strong, and it smelled good, a sweet scent that reminded me of mowed grass. His only strong smell came from his uncut dick when he had not bathed, which at the beginning put me off, but it was an acquired taste that I soon acquired; in fact, his dick in its natural state with the whole foreskin made me wish that I had mine, and angry that I'd had no say in the matter. I held his and spoke to it admiringly, you beauty, I murmured to it, you wily charmer, and I thwacked it against his stomach and then against his thigh, and he said, hey! stop flipping boners around, then he gasped, abruptly startled by something behind me. I turned and looked up to see the man and boy from the group below, standing over us. They both stared, their hair tousled in the wind, the man's expression blank, but the boy, his features so similar to those of the man that they had to be father and son, was like an animated replica of his father. In his face the same features were recast into an open acuity, a spark of curiosity in the eyes, the mouth, not as tight, was slightly agape, the dark brows arching up slightly as if he was listening for a tiny sound. He stood transfixed, somewhere between terrified and exalted at the sight of us, and in this state of surprise he was so striking that I could not take my eyes off him. Our gaze was locked and in those moments it seemed I came to know some of him, not the periphery of his life but the very center of him. I knew he was queer, and I wondered if he had faced it in himself yet, a boy his age, twelve or thirteen, might be finding his turmoil. We stared back at them for what seemed a full minute before the man took the boy's hand without averting his gaze from us, and then with his brows slightly furrowed, turned and trudged back down to the beach. His expression was one of disdain. But I saw what passed in the boy's eyes and felt the painful need that flashed there and then softened his stomach and knees. I knew because I have felt it before myself and if I had seen a mirror at the time that is exactly what it would have looked like. What a surprise we must have been to this man and boy who thought they were on a deserted beach, to come up and find two fiercely naked men in the sand. They had to choose this particular spot, they could have gone to no other on this infinite expanse. Certainly there was something about this place that had attracted all of us, two lover men, man and boy, bringing us together by some feng shui of converging meridians in the earth, or possibly the attraction runs in the humans and not the earth, and subconsciously they felt us here and were drawn to us, that social calendar of instinct penciling us all in. Or possibly it was total, albeit stupendous, coincidence. They found us, I remarked to myself, found us disgusting, M said. No, they were startled but the reaction was a gut reaction, they did not have time to formulate the requisite disgust of two men making love, they responded to two naked bodies that were youthful and male, and had a spark of interest that possibly is bothering them just now. The man showed little, but didn't you see the boy's face? I asked, it was as if he had fallen in love, do you remember the first time you saw two men having sex? Yeah, M said, then he was quiet for a moment, hesitant to go on, yeah, I do. I caught two of the older guys in my neighborhood going at it, I must have just stared until they saw me, and then they freaked out. They beat the shit out of me and said that if I told anyone they would kill me. I remember shaking with anger that I wasn't as big as them and couldn't defend myself. I already knew I was queer, and the look of desperation in their eyes made me feel very bad about it. I hadn't known it was so terrible. It made me a nervous boy. M was for the moment a hurt, vulnerable child again, and I wished that I had big biceps, huge ones with powerful forearms and a tattoo, and that I had been there at just the right moment to grab them by the necks and smack their heads together, and then to hold them with their arms pinned back so that M could pound at their bile bellies. To pound and pound and pound like Wanda.

She joined us the next day, we drove the borrowed car which came with the borrowed beach house to the borrowed Long Island railroad train to pick her up. She was glad to be the hell out of the city. As soon as she was with us I no longer felt jealous about having to share M with her, they'd been friends before I met him. They'd met on the street one night while M was being attacked by three young thugs, Wanda saw it happen and jumped in like a wild woman, and between her and M they gave the thugs enough trouble to leave them alone. Bruised and bleeding, they'd become fast friends, with shared blood as the cement of their friendship, and I was a little jealous about this blood cement I admit. I wasn't so brave as Wanda. Faced with violence I usually became petrified and needed to pee. But I had become friends with her too, I could not help it, she was a real good hippy. No money, ragged clothes, lots of herbal remedies, I liked that, and because of a tough past she was fucked up enough to give her wisdom beyond her years, and a quiet brilliance. She lived in a spiritual world inhabited by Tarot cards, crystals, energies, a nonscientific world which she seemed to believe that everyone shared. I liked to make fun of her, any rigid system of beliefs was an irresistible target for me. But M was intrigued, he said that an alternative view was always welcome over the prevailing one if only for novelty's sake, and I said that I didn't welcome either, ha ha, and then Wanda goosed my ass really hard and I hollered. It surprised me, I expected only her usual slowness which seemed to have evolved into a way of life, because she never rushed for anything, it could wait. But she could also be quick when she wanted to be. She eased herself into the car like an old Indian woman and in her easy Southern drawl said, let's go. It was cloudy with the threat of a storm, and by the time we got to the beach it was pouring rain and the waves were heaving and the sky was churning, all was turbulence. We stood at the water's edge, three mutes deafened by the roar of ocean, wind, rain, and Wanda took some deep breaths with her eyes closed and then stripped off her wet clothes, and M, reading her mood, touched her shoulder and offered to let down her curly black hair which was balled up in the back. It unfurled and blew wild in the wind. I noticed her body was muscular, dark brown, and gleaming with water running down her back and dripping off her nipples.

Everything was liquid. The air, the land, the sea were all liquid. It was cold but I abruptly recognized that I too was stripping myself down to the skinny and leaping into the crashing waves, shocking cold, and they watching with awed expressions. But I didn't care if they thought I was silly because what I was was released. M cupped his hands and yelled, Here comes your mama! and I turned around just in time to face a wall of water that slapped my ass down. I let it batter me and drag me along the bottom for a while, then fought up for air and pounded at it with my fists, flinging myself and being tossed upside down through the air and laughing like crazy. The force of the waves was fearsome. The earth was shifting from side to side, up and down. I couldn't stand up. I glimpsed them watching me on the tilted beach, amazed at how they could stand at such an acute slant, Wanda's lips moving as the waves rose up high between us so that I lost them, animated gray and white swells as if filmed in black and white crashed down on me again and I got up laughing mutely into the roar,

saw them standing on the beach tilted in the opposite direction
this time and they seemed distant and grainy like old film foot-
age viewed for the hundredth time, M was looking at Wanda
and then hugging and bam! I was slammed down again, by
now getting a little scared. They motioned for me to come back
and I tried but got sucked backward, raking shells and sand
with my fingers, and something snapped in my head, panic
occurred there, because I was utterly at the mercy of the
waves, and was going to drown. I saw myself as liquid ab-
sorbed into the ocean, mother of liquids, my soft tissues and
muscles picked off by the tiny teeth of blenny fish, leaving
only clean bones so that eventually a skeleton was tossed there
under the dark water, waiting to be washed up on the beach
and dried. I became calm and considered the situation. I
couldn't fight my way to the beach so I decided to relax and
try to ride one in. I waited to get underneath the crest of the
next wave and surged forward, but because of some colliding
currents I was sent flipping along the bottom like a cartoon. I
ended up at the edge of the water, surprisingly with only a
few scrapes and draped in seaweed, soaked to the bone and
weirdly ecstatic from the close call. They ran over and pulled
me up and M kissed me, and took the seaweed as a necklace
for himself. Are you okay? he asked, and I said I guessed so,
because I did guess so, but I was so dazed, so so dazed that I
kissed the ground, I think, instead of M. And because of that
the storm began to clear, and we went to the car to get a sheet
to lie down on and an umbrella for shade from the emerging
sun, and we sat down beneath it watching Wanda wander in
the distance like a heron picking at shells. M found a fish skeleton and picked it up by the tail. The vertebrae and some of
the ribs were intact, along with the dried head. The shape of
it so pleasing that I got mad when he began to sing and shake
it into a shimmying bone dance because the fine bones fell
apart and the silver-gray head landed with the mouth open to
us, balking and full of tiny teeth. And with this accusation,
what had seemed a permanent grayness blew over suddenly,
with a bright sun that teased the water and air into a brilliance
of silver and white, silver water, thin white air shimmering and
blurring my vision into an intoxicating unfocus, the serene
crystal glass of vision that sees in, not out, into the lucid greater

distances of daydreams. Looking out over the dancing light of calm water my mind raced inward at hideous speeds on padded paws, and I fell into the center of stillness, with time and distance spinning outward around me in an increasing spiral, while my body lay perhaps millennia away, on some beach, the body of a young man, boyishly lanky with a slender muscularity in the legs and arms where work has made the muscles and veins stand out, a strong jaw, brown hair shaved close, the wide-set eyes of an animal. Not bad, not a bad head, not a bad body, but I was not there with that body, I was something and somewhere else. Still, I could almost feel it, the body, still, I could feel M watching me, his gaze piercing my reverie from a distance and drawing me back. Only seconds before I had not felt the weight of him next to me, so far away was I, but now through miles and decades of silence, this daydream distance, I came rushing back against my will, zooming through the expanse at light speed, aware of his face now in my corner vision, the brightness of it where sun was cut diagonally across by umbrella shadow, lighting one eye—not the brown one, the blue one—and electrifying the golden stubble of his jaw, his face perfectly still as if it were the center of a storm, the shadow creeping across the face so slowly, so much less than slowly that we have no word for it, in incremental snail paces that measure the turning of the earth away from the sun, the head turning now, this face silver and black like air and earth, turning with watering nose and moist pink lips of fire, turning, and the other fire too that glitters cold-hot in the blue eye so fierce, strong enough to summon me from a distance without a movement or sound, turning away now, though I realized it was only to lure me back. I was not a coyote. I was a man lying on my side shaded by the umbrella looking past him out over the ocean, him sitting in half-shade with the most beautiful clouds moving behind his head, him walking his hand across the water across the white distance between us across the sheet beneath us causing rich milky ripples, touching my chest and my nerve endings exclaiming this through incredulous synapses to my mind, still so numbed with distance that the reminder of a body attached to it came as a revelation, him saying in a light quiet voice that did not disturb the breeze nor the smell of seaweed, What are you thinking?

Thinking. Was I? Is that what this is? He always wants to know, it is difficult to answer, how to identify it and then put it into words, when I was really nowhere and everywhere. I was a coyote, a tree, a rock, but what was I thinking? I considered a while, until it was uncomfortable or possibly rude not to speak, and I said, I was thinking about cartoons. But I wasn't sure if this was true. For some reason his asking had reminded me of the time I was attacked. Some guys had started calling me names on an empty street. You know the story. I ignored them but they ran up and surrounded me. One of them looked me in the eye and said that even if I didn't suck cock, as far as he was concerned I was a cocksucker, then he spat in my face. It made me so mad that I wanted to break his nose, but I could not move, could only stand frozen like an idiot, and they beat me until I was unconscious. And the strange thing is that all I remember after that, the thing I saw like a television in my mind was Bullwinkle, trying to fly by fluttering his hands, with a straining neck and big turned-out feet. You see, this is where my mind went when I let it, it skipped around willy-nilly with no respect for the gravity of a situation. It was like a bad child in a shifting corner, there but not there. I would have liked to know where it would go and what it would do when I was dead, but for now it needed me, used me, yes, used me for my five senses. A voracious consumer of all stimuli, it filtered them in and sifted through them greedily, then rearranged them into a thrilling and shocking mess.

On some days I was so rattled by my preposterous dream life, by those free-wheeling nightmares and bone dreams that snatched me up and swung me around in circles, that I did not know what to do at all. They were as real as the violence that had occasionally swarmed around me, like mosquitoes, like the greedy mosquitoes we wore, when after suppertime we imposed ourselves upon the rooms, closets, and drawers of the house, slapping at our own heads, ransacking the place for sweaters or skirts or whatever. For dress-up. For the heavy blue coverall that Wanda found herself, the wool plaid skirt for M, and for me the ancient moss-colored velvet hat that looked like a lampshade with a veil. And appointed thusly we went to the beach where the fog was so thick we could only hear the sound of breaking waves, and could barely see our hands in front of our faces. And I noticed M was not his usual self when he said, Shut up, Actionthing. He always called me Action-this-or-that: Actionboy, Actiongirl, Actionman, Actionrotisseriegrill, I think he was making fun of my lack of action. But I hadn't said anything. He was hearing noises on the wind, a wailing of some kind, and he said there was a monster nearby. Wanda wrapped her scarf around his shoulders, and he went back to the car grumbling, fog nothing, this is some scary shit, and then he said, this is me leaving. I noticed how good he looked in a tube top and kilt, kind of warrior-like. And then Wanda looked at me with her big dark eyes and after a long pause quietly eased into her voice, listen here, there's something I want to tell you, she said. It always scared me when people said sentences like that, it often meant something bad. Spill it, I blurted, my voice bright and misplaced in the fog. She said, I know about the bone dreams you've been having since you were attacked. I just wanted to tell you not to be afraid of them. Dreams are powerful things that can inform you. Those bones might be speaking to you more about life than death.

She was interrupted by a terrifying shriek like the cry of an animal that pierced the fog and echoed eerily around us, we took off scrambling through the sand toward where the car might be, but it was the wrong direction. We ran in panicked circles for a while, calling to M, until I saw a faint light blinking not far away. We went to it, and I could make out the car with M leaning against it and someone else with his back to us holding a big silver flashlight, and this someone was big and muscular. What was that hideous noise? I asked, panting, was that really you? I cried, and Wanda and I fell all over each other hooting. He looked so cute, pouting in his skimpy outfit, but the guy with the flashlight cut his eyes at M with a look of disgust. M shrugged and mumbled something about cutting him some slack, Rowena. I was sitting on the hood of the car with my eyes closed when he came up and tapped the fender, holding that flashlight so it shined across his face, I thought he was an ax murderer or something, he said. I thought you were a girl, the guy said. But M handled this well. He said that all men are girls deep down, and we introduced ourselves to him,

shaking hands stiffly. His name was Carlos. M flashed me a
conspiratorial grin. But I'm sorry I scared you, Carlos said to
M in a Spanish accent, I recognized you from . . . he paused
as if he had said something wrong . . . the beach! I exclaimed,
pointing at him in recognition, you came upon us having sex.
Naah, Wanda drawled with incredulous rolling eyes. Carlos
was visibly irritated, he huffed impatiently and tapped his
flashlight against his palm. It's twoo, M said, pronouncing his
true like Tweety Bird, and beaming sweetly at Carlos. He said,
He has a problem. He has mislaid his son. I had to smile at
his choice of words. Have you seen him? Carlos asked. We
said no and asked how he had lost him, and he said that they
were staying in a house nearby, and that Eduardo had run
away. Eduardo. A strong, formal name, contrary yet comple-
mentary to his uncanny beauty. We'll help you find him, I
offered, and Carlos protested but I cut him off, nonsense, you
want to find him, don't you? You go that way and we'll go
this way and Wanda, you stay with the car lights on because
he might come if he gets lost and sees them.

I had a hunch where we might find him so I grabbed M and
we walked through the fog, which required a suspension of
disbelief because it was like walking through a wall. It was so
thick that I feared with each step that we might plunge into
an abyss, even though we were on a flat beach. My body
refused to go freely. Each blind step sent a thrill of fear up
and down my spine and I had to force my legs forward, so
that our progress was slow, our steps were those of crippled
men. It angered me not to go faster because I wanted to find
him, feeling as I did almost certain that he was in that very
same spot where we had first seen him standing on the brink
of dunes above us. There must be power to that place, that
was the attraction, we had sensed it without even knowing just
as Carlos and Eduardo had. He would be drawn there again,
it held significance for him, he had been thinking about us
since then. The fog was thinner ahead. Lightning, which had
been playing over distant water, moved to the land causing a
strange meteorological phenomenon: lightning fog. It flashed
around without thunder at first, giving silent split-second x-
rays of the surroundings. What was dark and obscured to vision
would jump out with each flash in a surprising 3-D panorama,

weirdly lit so that the sand reflected pale blue, the waves co-
balt, the fog floating in quicksilver air like diffuse clouds of
milk in electrified water. I waited for the next flash to see our
shadows, and sure enough they'd been tailing us the whole
time, now revealed by light. In darkness they followed us
along, moving faster now than we were, since the fog was less
of a wall and more a gauzy curtain. When we got to the place
I could tell we were there. Shouldn't we call for him or something? M whispered. Strange, but using our voices in all this
weather had seemed irreverent, as if we had been muted by
the fear of some kind of retribution from the elements. I
pointed silently up at the dune, this felt like the place to me.
There? Naah, M drawled. Sure, this is where he found us, I
said. M put two and two together. He looked in every direction. He said, but the dunes are identical up and down this
beach, how do you know . . . Shhh. Can't you feel it? I said.
Feel what? he said. It. It what drew us here in the first place.
He grabbed my crotch and said, I am feeling it what drew me
here. Ow, cut it out. This is serious business, I said. He said,
so is this, shaking his handful. He pulled me along a few feet
before he relinquished and took my hand instead.

We climbed up the hill of sand and could barely see, in the
same place we had been lying, Eduardo, naked on his stomach,
beating off, beating and kicking the ground and himself. He
was crying, I could hear his muffled wailing into the ground,
his whole body was shaking in waves and small trembles.
Lightning illuminated the scene followed by a growl of thunder. He was wrestling with himself, the small fine muscles of
his back and legs tensing, his ass clenching as he struggled,
and we just watched, feeling sorry and not knowing what to
do. It was embarrassing to witness something so private. I
squeezed M's hand and could see the sadness in his face. Then
Eduardo rolled over onto his back and looked straight at us, he
let out a cry of fright and then recognized us and froze in
disbelief, Ustedes, Ustedes! he cried, looking up at us as if we
were some kind of vision. I put my hands forward and said,
It's okay, it's okay, and we stepped down to kneel by him. His
face and body were gritty with sand. I pulled off my T-shirt
and began to clean his face where tears and snot had muddied
him. He realized then that he was naked and said, Ay, lo

siento, I mean I'm sorry. Don't worry about it, M said, we'll wipe the sand off you and you can put your clothes on. I brushed him off while trying not to notice the blatant fact that he was not a boy at all but quite a man, his body was thin and smooth, a boyish body without hair, which made it seem incongruous that his genitals should be so extremely developed. It was hard not to stare. I could feel him appraising my face, looking back and forth between us, will you do me a favor? he ventured shyly in an accent like his father's, his voice on the brink of change, will you kiss while I watch? This surprised us. M shrugged his eyebrows and we did as he asked, a gentle kiss which started him weeping again. Of this I have been thinking since I saw you, he said, to see you kiss and make love. My father knows this about me and he hates it. He punishes me but that will not change it. I said, I'm sorry that he's making it difficult. My heart goes out to you, I wish I could help. You can, you can make love to me, he declared, his dark eyes glowing feverishly, I never have and I need to. The offer was appealing, so genuine and needful that there was nothing of the usual coyness that accompanies seduction. He knew what he needed, and we were the redeemers. We were his redeemers. I could feel that hot tingling rise in my neck and head which meant I must be embarrassed, but M looked at Eduardo hungrily, placed his hand on the boy's thigh and my gaze passed from the hand to the growing boner. I could tell he didn't even realize what he had, the thin boyish body with the big man's parts, a fantasy in the flesh before me. But we can't, M said, we would love to, but not under these circumstances. The fool. Please, Eduardo pleaded, circumstances do not matter to me. Maybe you'll understand later, M said, but for now you'll have to settle for a kiss, and without further warning he kissed him while I watched with a stiffness in my pants that made me squirm. Eduardo's eyes closed, then fluttered open so that I could only see the whites, then they parted and he thanked M, and turned to me. Feeling foolish I took his head in my hand and pressed my lips to his gingerly, they were tender and warm, he was shy with his tongue, he took in a sharp breath and before I knew it he was shooting all over me in big pearly globs, without even touching the thing. I sat back in astonishment. M whistled long and slow in a tone that slid up, then fell down as if to say well well! We all three watched it throb, standing out of the faint nest of hair like a surprise houseguest.

Eduardo gasped, abruptly startled by something behind me. I turned to see Carlos standing over us, the lightning flashed and cast blue light on his face, showing veins and crazy shadows that made him look poisonous. Thunder rolled in a bass tremolo that seemed to come from the ground, and it grew until it became so loud that the air snapped by my ears. Carlos was impasionado, his chest heaved and he let out a strangled growling noise in a Spanish I could not translate, he glanced down at the cum dripping on my stomach and lunged at me. M and I jumped up nervously, a formidable pair in tube top and velvet hat. He had to stop and regard us venomously, with his fists shaking at his side. M said, listen here, we just found him a minute ago. He was upset so we—shut up, you, you . . . Carlos looked M up and down searching for the proper description but M helped him out—faggot? he suggested. How dare you do this to my son! Carlos bellowed and then actually began to bawl. We had been expecting a fight but not this. You filthy dogs, he sputtered. Eduardo yelled back at him that he had been alone until a minute ago when we found him, that he had asked us for sex and we had declined, and Carlos pointed at him and said through gritted teeth, no son of mine will ever become a . . . homosexual. I admired that in his excited state he had managed to remain clinical. Carlos, your son *is* a homosexual, I advised him. He is not, he is only confused, he retorted, his gaze dropped to his son's uncut cock which was still heavy with blood and standing out boisterously toward his father, he swallowed hard and told Eduardo to put on his clothes, and the boy did so, sniffling and struggling to pull his underwear on over the persistent boner which managed to capture all four of our attentions, or that is to say, managed to distract us enough from our discussion so that there were awkward pauses when the thread was lost as we each had to, out of the corner of our eyes, constantly refer back to it, bobbing there. Carlos said, the filthy things you do to each other are childish, a denial of your manhood and the continuation of your lineage, or something like that, and M said, we are just being honest with ourselves, that's all. Yeah! I agreed, and you should let your son be honest too. I became disheartened because Eduardo had gotten the pants on. But you are men! Carlos exclaimed, shaking his fist on that word. I just hated it when people said things like that. If we could all be men inside out, I suggested, if we could all get fucked just once, we would know that within the ability to yield lies the understanding. M took my hand which made me feel smart. Carlos looked at me closely, studying my face with a blank expression betrayed only by his tearful eyes, and calmly stated that if he ever caught me with his son again he would kill me. He took Eduardo's arm and pulled him away from us, the boy turned, cast an apologetic glance which wrenched my heart, and they were gone.

M took the sandy T-shirt out of my hand and shook it out, then he smeared the globs of cum around on my belly so that it would dry, and put the sticky shirt on me. I could tell he was shaken up, we fell into each other's arms and held tight for a while, then walked back to the car where Wanda was waiting for us. We told her all about it and she was mad that she had missed out because she loves a good fight, especially if she can get in it. When we drove away we saw them walking up the hill, apart from each other, toward a two-story wooden house that stood alone save for a tree beside it. Back at our place we peeled off the wet clothes and had some hot tea. We were all worried about Eduardo. M was frowning over his mug, clearly beside himself. His head was swimming, I thought, recalling that he had once told me that our bodies are nothing but excuses for liquid, that we are just more of the ocean overrunning the earth. In that case, I decided, Eduardo was all lively juice, which had flowed into us, stirring our blood with its intensity and vitality. For him I felt a kinship that lived in my blood, he was one of my tribe, and I recognized the same in the blue pulse of M's temple, which filled my field of vision and pounded like a drum. His head was so full of ideas that they sprang out his eyes like minnows, surprised and squirming around on the floor. All right! he shouted suddenly so that we all three ducked, I've been thinking hard about this and I can't just leave it there, I want to help him. I want to give him my book about great queer men and women like Walt Whitman, Gertrude Stein, and Harvey Milk, so he'll at least have some positive role models. It would have made things easier for me at that age, he said. It was a risky proposition and we all knew it but Wanda was so keen on it as well that I could hardly resist, she made us put on black like cat burglars so that we would not be seen. The plan was to get his attention through a window and leave the book, then get out of there, we weren't taking Carlos's threat lightly. But we took the bicycles for their silence and rode toward the house while I occupied myself trying to ignore the terrible cold fear in my bowels that made me shiver. When we neared the house Wanda got off her bike and lay it on the ground and we did the same, she took off her shoes and then pointed to our feet so we would too, and we did, then we crouched down and circled the house like midgets to see if we could find which room was Eduardo's. Light shined through some of the windows. Keep your heads down, the light is reflecting off your faces! she whispered impatiently, I could see only the whites of her eyes. In a second floor window we saw Eduardo silhouetted by the light of a lamp. Wanda scooped up some pebbles and put them in her pocket then scampered like a cat up the tree that stood beside the house. She motioned for us to come up and M followed. I was halfway up when my foot slipped off a toehold and I slid down the trunk scraping my shins and hitting the ground with a grunt. Shhh! they hissed, and as I gathered myself up I heard a door slam around the corner and footsteps on the porch. I was up the tree in an instant with superhuman strength, out of breath more from fright than exertion, I opened my mouth wide and gulped air as silently as possible as Carlos sauntered into the yard below us, smoking a cigarette and looking around himself in every direction. He came and stood beneath the tree, directly under me, and I pressed myself against the trunk and pretended to be invisible and there in the tree I heard my treasonous heart pounding, certain that he would hear the noise and if he didn't I would explode anyway. The cigarette smoke floated up along with the scent of him, a faint sweaty sweet tobacco smell, and passed into my mouth and nose, he was so close I could hear him suck in the smoke through puckered lips, then let it flow out relaxed, and somehow I dared to look down at the top of his head. Of his face I could see only the bridge of his nose and flaring nostrils, the orange glow of the cigarette intensifying as he put it to his lips again, then threw it on the ground and walked back to the house. I exhaled a tremendous sigh of relief, I was ready to climb down and run like hell when Wanda tossed the pebbles at Eduardo's window. He shot up from where he was sitting and warily approached the glass. Pressing a cupped hand around his eyes to block the glare of the light he saw us and grinned widely, he unlatched the window and quietly slid it open. Wanda pressed the finger of silence to her lips and he nodded, M took the book with the note we had written inside it and carefully tossed it to him, and he caught it. Good hands. Then M indicated that we had to get the hell out of there and Eduardo nodded sadly, mouthing the words thank you he leaned out the window and watched us climb down. We blew him a kiss and skulked off toward the bikes like thieves with their booty, walking along the road through webs of night, silver threads that spiders spin from stalk to stem across the path, we were giants heaving forward and snapping the filament work of an eternal spider night. With webs wrapped across the front of us in unplanned bondage, I wondered how many dismayed spiders were dangling on the ends of broken thread floating behind us, I wondered if we had done something for Eduardo without causing collateral damage as we walked close, touching hands and shoulders and looking out over the dunes that just touched this side of the road.

I heard something running behind me and whirled around to catch Eduardo, if you please. Take me with you, he cried. I told him that he shouldn't have done this, he could get in more trouble, but he assured me that he had sneaked out. Then sudden light, the ominous headlights of a car coming from the house, alerted us. The engine roared so loudly that he had to be flooring it, down the dark road the machine raced like a monster toward us. I froze in place, and then by reflex I yelled, jump! and we all dove off the road into the sand as he slammed on brakes into the spot where we'd been standing. The door flipped open and he rushed out with the big metal flashlight in his hand like a club, I heard Eduardo scream, no! and then there was no sound, only the echo of his cry as everything slowed to a crawl. I was getting to my feet with M on my left standing up, Carlos was coming at me, raising the weapon in the air so that the beam of the flashlight crossed his face, illuminating his darkened features with a silver ray that passed like the minute hand, leaving the image of his livid eye emblazoned in darkness, when Wanda jumped between us and kicked his hand, which is just like her. The flashlight went flipping in a broad arc through the black air, the silver metal reflecting available light, and standing still as if sunk into the earth, my eyes cast upward, I watched its arced trajectory while Carlos butted my chest with his shoulder and sent me crashing backwards, cracking my skull. The flipping silver light stopped in midair. I was out, way out, deep out, maybe never coming back out. If I concentrated I could feel my back on the broken asphalt, my head which had struck a rock was turned to one side, my arms were thrown open and my pants were wet where I had peed on myself. I saw Bugs Bunny shove a steel trap in his mouth, dash lipstick around his lips and suddenly he was a Tasmanian she-devil. My legs were wide open. What a sprawling chalk figure I'd make if it came to that. At age five, I could suddenly remember, I ran across the backyard and leaped high only to see that my left foot was coming down on a coiled rattlesnake. I stopped in mid-air. With an urgent stretch I inched my foot past the snake and landed safely. Strange how it changed my life: now I always looked down in the middle of a leap. I swung out on a rope over my childhood river and dropped, oh thrill in my stomach, with a delicious ploosh! into the black amber water, immersed in cool silence; Mom handed me my own Bible; Arnold the pig squealed up at Lisa who was serving hotcakes to Oliver in a frilly house-dress. I hear Wanda's voice from far away. Eduardo's face, clear and open, serious dark brows over curious eyes, M's ass running before me, speaking in tongues. I wanted out of this, I wanted to go back to him.

Good! Wanda screamed, she was standing on the beach next to me, the waves had stopped moving so that there was a strange quiet. Use the bone, use the bone, she said, poking me, and then she walked around in two small circles like a dog with her tongue out as if this was part of the story or part of the information she was imparting, and she thought for a moment before going on again carefully, use the bone, she repeated with a kind of relief as if it was a burden released. I just looked at her for a while. Bone? I can't fight, Wanda, I can't hurt a person, I told her. The hell you can't! she spat, she was impasionada. If you don't fight for yourself, then you'll have nothing. Death walks with us all the time, beside or a little behind, it follows like a shadow, if you know that shadow it's no longer so frightening. Let it come sooner or later, but not before its time, now is the time to be alive. You've got to get back to yourself, and I really mean that, she said. I asked how and she said try looking at M, but of course he wasn't there so I had to imagine him, I tried to imagine his face like the most beautiful cloud in the sky, but I couldn't remember what he looked like, not at all. I could only get Bullwinkle whom I saw very clearly, as the silver flashlight flipped through the air and landed at Wanda's feet, it stood with the beam shining up at her. See? she insisted with a wry grin, a crashing of waves, and therefore I woke up to the sound of my own blood drops dripping in the timeless tick-tock, with a squealing in my veins and out the unkind aperture, a pool of smart liquid rushing to gravity, red rush to the ground beneath my broken head. My cock was hard, the willful appendage, I know not why.

I was aroused by a sound of strangling, I turned my head painfully to see Carlos on top of M with his hands around his neck, his pelvis pressed hard against M's whose legs were open and tensed against Carlos's side. He was being raped of breath and his fists were wrapped around Carlos's wrists, trying to pull them off his throat. I heard him groaning for air and could see by his desperate jerking that he was panicked for his life and that Carlos's strength was overwhelming him. Carlos began to throttle him with maniacal strength and I could see his bones being shaken free of the muscle, I tell you, I could see his arms relax and his legs slacken open, no longer straining but vulnerable to the intrusion, and I felt a stab of jealousy and terror which here I am not afraid to admit. He's killing him, I heard myself moan, killinghim killinghim. I staggered to my feet and saw red spots before my eyes, found that I had to concentrate very hard not to black out, I searched the ground for a weapon, saw Wanda on her side gasping for breath and Eduardo next to her getting up to his knees, clutching his stomach. He rushed at his father as I found the bone sticking up out of the sand. I picked it up, it was about two feet long and

thick, the bone that the day before I had respectfully kissed
and sent flipping away from myself, I had caught in my own
hands tonight. Of this I had been thinking for some time now,
the gravity of this bone, the weight of it in my hands, the
perfection of it in its naked simplicity. It spoke to me in the
language of the bone which speaks not only of structure but of
the nature of the animal that surrounded it, that gloved it, this
bone gloved by my hands, by my nature, by my pumping
dripping heart, by my muscle and disposition, by my
queerness and rage. I stood over them with it, Eduardo saw
what I was about to do and letting go of his father he rolled
away and covered his face. M's arms fell wide on the ground,
the palms open in supplication, I couldn't see his face, only
the back of Carlos's killinghim head as he continued to strangle.
I raised the bone in the air, my eyes all pupil-less blood. Do
it! Wanda shouted, he's killinghim! And for a moment I froze,
dreading the impact, afraid to injure even at the cost of my
lover's life. But the bone took over, it whispered, kiss me,
skull, and suddenly hissed downward, making its stern impression. Carlos collapsed on top of M, they were both still. I sank
down beside them and rolled Carlos off. M was still breathing,
his breath coming in short gasps. I sat him up and rested him
against me. Wanda crawled to us, her face yellow, bastard
knocked the wind outa me, she said. We pulled Eduardo to us
and wrapped our arms around him, M's breathing became
deeper as his throat opened. He looked at me wildly, touched
the back of my hand and his hand came away bloody, deluxe
vermillion. A spell of lightheadedness overcame me, followed
by an earthy urge from the pit of my stomach which sent vomit
gushing out of my mouth. I fell forward onto my hands and
knees, undulating, and retched until nothing was left. Then
the wave of fast sick left just as fast and I felt a woozy ecstasy
like my head was going to float away from my body.

Carlos was groaning back to consciousness, I wondered what
he would do or say, and I worried the bone in my hand just
in case. The air was full of excellent smells, the sound of the
waves crashing was music, so much better than when they
stood still. M rubbed my neck, his touch was warmth that
melted my anger and fear, I was so surrounded by the love of
friends that I wept, their sweetness was stronger than the

meanest shove. I felt drunk, I was drunk, I was intoxicated by
the language of this bone but the words were stuck in my
throat, bone words you might say, but I could not let them
out, could only grasp tightly this bone like the happy warrior
I was. When Carlos came to he staggered to his feet, and without saying a word—his were stuck too—made his way to the
car. Eduardo helped him into it and then got in himself, clearly
concerned about his father, and we took our bikes and fled.
But once at home we were too shaken up to get any sleep. We
were somnambulists, addressing our wounds and reenacting the
crime all night long, even embellishing with surprise twists of
plot and absurd endings. Wanda had to return to the city in
the morning so we drove her to the train, and as we hugged
goodbye she said I'd done good, that I'd done what I had to.
And that was true. As the train pulled away I noticed the dark
bruises on M's neck, I grabbed him and held him tightly, and
kissed him deeply right there on the train platform, daring
anyone to make it any of his business. And walking me backward against a high sky along the long platform, walking me
backward on the beach with the glare of sunrise to our east
blowing him hot and freckled, I try not to stumble, but to
trust, because he says, walking backwards is good for you,
makes you trust me even just a little, Action. The fear that
rises up with walking backwards, because I could step into a
hole or some object and fall, ebbs and flows with his steering
instructions, simple one word commands like left, right, dip,
slow, down, up. He says, today—right—you are seeing the
world in—left—a new way. I can count the fine hairs on his
chest and—dip—just allow myself to be steered. But then I
step into some vacancy he hasn't seen and fall down. We are
lighthearted and we laugh, then take off running like two glad
dogs into the wind. And when I fall behind him I can see the
work of nature, the work of his surly ass pumping, pounding
pouting appallingly powerful, please just let me put my hand
in your blue speedo, not to grab or grope but to cup lightly a
pounding buttock for percussion sake. I make that my new
goal, just to get my hand on that there, the right one even
though he's kicking up his heels causing sand to fly in my face,
my chest, my belly, my groin, my thighs, my breath grows
sharp and I'm gulping sand and air. I huff, I puff, I want to

blow his house down. I in- I ex-hale . . . put . . . my . . . hand . . . in . . . your . . . speed . . . o . . . hell, he's fast he's more than fast he's pushing bones through the sand but I am catch . . . ing . . . up, and ah! with a fanatical grab I get my hand in that blue and tug hard enough to tear enough to pull his genteel parts flat against his belly of heavenly salty grit, and grind we do to a halt swinging down in a crazy helix to the earth way below, his sweet blue speedo yanked crooked down to thigh and knee, we laugh with our teeth, so hard I can't see, roll in sand all full of forceful wind rip-pumping in then out of lungs where absorbing membranes perform their oxygenating duties as our bodies pound each other with each breath and I roll on him feeling the crush of my self against his in painful anguish and a tearing sadness that I cannot have him, eat him, be him, know him in his depth and expanse, his blond cock and pink balls lolling confused this way and that way over his thighs. Oh, contain me because I am just about to explode buddy, what will you do with me then, who will clean up, who will bury me in the sand to leave a bone exposed for you to fall upon, to crack open and taste the marrow juice, who will remember we were here to defy death, who will know that today I learned to defend you and live defiantly, and that we made love out here in the open, pouring ourselves into each other, our liquids into the sand, our arms and mouths open, your jaw relaxed, you tilt your head slowly as if asking a question and I can almost feel the earth rotating on its axis in crooked yaw, in your face the concentration required to orbit a heavenly body around the sun, and the quick then extravagant slow earth shaking tremors of muscle, and oh boy, we come in canon, your jaw is locked your back is arched and muscles are rippling within you that scientists fear to name. You (exhale) are a singular (inhale) expression of wonder (exhale) to me. Twisted into a knot are we, watching the sand swirl.

EVERYMAN

• ROBERT GLÜCK •

FOR GEORGE STAMBOLIAN

MAC

I WAS ALREADY twenty minutes late. I had *made* myself late, following the minute hand in a loose reverie while my breath fanned mint aftertaste into my head. I was shaved and dressed, longing for some memory or plan. I rose from the twisted sheets and looked out. Mac's window was empty and so was the sidewalk on both sides of Clipper. Lily and I ran down-stairs; we dashed to the corner and onto the strip that divides Dolores. She sniffed the grass a moment, then dropped into the gentle curtsy female dogs make when they piss. We crossed back; Mac stood on the sidewalk in front of my house. "C'mere Bob." Lily ran ahead to greet him.

Mac was trembling. All winter he'd postponed going in for tests. "I'm going in but am I coming out?" He wet his lips and stared up Clipper at the rosy horizon; for a moment his face inhabited the light and the peaceful air. I consoled myself— yes, yes, half an hour late, so what? Cars passed and continued up into the sunset where each driver lost definition and the cars seemed to lurch and decide by themselves.

"Ed's sick too."

"That so?" Mac raised his hand to the back of his neck in sympathy, the gesture's small wind laden with Witch Hazel. When I say his face inhabited the sky, I scoop out space so my drama has its theater. Mac couldn't be distracted from the sky's larger court. Lily sat in front of him so alert she drew closer without changing position; big apricot ears tipped forward, beige tale broadly sweeping the sidewalk behind.

He lowered himself painfully to my porch step. I was late: for a long moment the sky without sun remained pure blue, then it subsided. "Aw, don't give me that you're too busy." Lily reseated herself directly in front of Mac, eyes beseeching, big tongue lolling. He absentmindedly drew dog biscuit after dog biscuit from a jacket pocket crammed with them. His joints were swollen so he lifted the biscuits lightly with two fingers. He held each one up; it drew Lily's eyes upward prayerfully. Half the cars had their headlights on.

Mac looked up with raised eyebrows and open mouth as though I'd interrupted him with startling news. When I remained silent he said, "I'll tell you something, Bob. I went to the Castro Theater last night and I did not even recognize myself in the mirror in the lobby till I moved." Now I was surprised, as though Mac existed in the present for the first time. His sudden arrival pushed me backwards. I became so tired I actually heard voices squabbling in my dream.

He emptied one pocket and started on the other. The biscuits were shaped like a cross-section of bone, the marrow a dark maroon. "I could see myself move," he added, "I'm not that far gone." Mac despised the drama that makes unique gestures, but he was wavering, losing bearings. I wondered if he had ever recognized his body. It retained an applicable quality from his younger days. Short and nimble, it climbed a ladder to fix a window or paint his garage door white. Now it was a foreign vehicle, Saab or Toyota. Lily tenderly freed each biscuit from his fingertips with the tips of her front teeth, then chewed with her head lowered and lips drawn back as though concentrating; she looked rather isolated on the sidewalk.

Actually, Mac was completely recognizable to me—his white hair and stiff part and shiny black shoes and his street and his biscuits. His sidewalk was still wet—he'd hosed it down. An old man with bright blue eyes. Lily wouldn't budge until she was certain his pockets were empty; she glanced back with disbelief when I prodded her. They united against me, the White Rabbit whose schedules and appointments diminished life. When the party was over Mac got to his feet and Lily climbed the first stair. It was as far as she could go on her own. I clasped my hands under her belly to lift her rump and we started up together. "Hey Bob, hope someone carries *my* hind end upstairs when I'm as old as your daughter."

I ran Lily up and threw a handful of kibble in her bowl. She disregarded it, her senses pitched upwards in anticipation; she nudged the air towards the door with her snout to increase her chances. When I avoided her eye, her joy faded and she dropped into a corner. She brought her bushy tail around so she could smell her fur and declined to raise her eyes when I said goodbye.

"C'mere Bob. I got a shirt in my trunk for you."

"I'm in a hurry Mac." But he was already on his way. I followed him into the dusk pleading, "Why don't you wear it?"

He looked over his shoulder, but not as far as my face. "Oh, I can't use it now."

He put the package in my hands. By the light in his trunk I saw a blue dress shirt folded inside its cardboard and plastic box. "—from Sears." He turned back to his trunk. "And these pajamas. Now wait a minute, you don't wear pajamas." We looked over at my bright window, then up at his dark one. I lowered my gaze to the spectator who cried in dismay, "I don't understand what you and Denny got going between you!" He actually waited for me to reply. I was gearing up when he continued, "You both leave the garbage cans on the street. You walk right by them. It's happened a dozen times. Let me tell you that might be fine when there's no wind to speak of—I've seen lids roll clear down to Church when it's rainy and windy outside."

Mac closed his trunk, closing the subject of the garbage and my nakedness. He waved me on in disgust.

Mac had a waking dream that his body was hiding from him in the red lobby of the Castro. A few days later his wife Nonie told me Mac was in the hospital with cancer in both lungs. Still, I looked for him when I stepped outside. He'd sat on an aluminum tube chair on the sidewalk, weed killer in the cracks, uniting in himself our corner of the world. The garage behind him stood for economy and conservation; it smelled of paint and clean cement. On the back wall he'd built a shelf for the orderly toolchest, a stack of yellow Penzoil cans, and a green hose coiled around itself; on the floor sand soaked up a blue-brown oil stain at its own pace. Elsewhere a city exploded and fire rained down, but here on hot days Lily sat with Mac in the shade of his overhead door, and neighbors stopped and talked as though his garage were the courthouse. I felt the romance of accord between a municipality and its citizens. The courthouse makes citizens and they like to sit, consider, and mingle their stories with the present.

A few weeks before, Mac dialed me a wakeup call at eight. I rolled out of bed. "Thank you Mac." I'd set the alarm for eight-thirty; I think Mac was afraid I'd miss my eleven o'clock flight and blow his trip to the airport. He provided such insistent Samaritanship that I felt exploited. What if you don't want someone to phone you when the mail arrives, your tire is low, the police are ticketing, or garbage day comes? We drove in his perfect blue Dodge, in its small climate of Witch Hazel. It was Mac, not Nonie, who wore scent, who needed response to make himself present. Mac related a number of highway disasters witnessed by Nonie and himself. This was a strangely reassuring lullaby—his belief that the exact circumstances of death have value. We were driving down San Jose Boulevard where it becomes a delicious canyon whose sides are retaining walls higher than the sketchy eucalyptus, the canyon bridged by walkways across the narrow sky with its bright clouds.

His landlord had just changed all the old double-hung wood windows to aluminum, and in the car Mac rejoiced. He praised the ugly new windows as unselfconsciously as a Greek chorus—thrift, conservation, he spoke from the darkness of these qualities. Then Mac asked, "Notice anything different?"

His face tipped back with sly expectation. Small men often seem flirtatious. I had an uncomfortable sexual moment. A black asphalt road curved upward, a light gray cement curb, a white metal railing, a few agapanthus, a few mock orange trees fallen out of bureaucracy's arboretum: the definition of nothing to see. I felt slightly hysterical to be considering it. "Mac, it's the San Bruno on-ramp to 280."

"They trimmed the trees. Things seem different, you don't know what it is—sure enough, they trimmed the trees." I'd say it was his ability to tame the impersonal by training on it the ecstasy of his surprise. He'd rescued Clipper Street—myself with the others—by willing our lives into meaning, however incomplete. The corner market, the neighborhood *Progress*: the meagerness of these gods only revealed the intensity of his faith. I was not in his league.

On 280 we dropped into valleys of white fog and emerged in broad daylight. Mac needed some information to purvey back on Clipper. On the way I told him where I was going and when I would return, and about Denny's trip to Denver for his grandmother's birthday, Stanley's visit, and Lily's trip to the Russian River.

His comb raked dull blond furrows from his sharp part.

He sat on my steps when the sun left his side of the street.

His big neck stood sore and naked.

Lily languished by the window as though she were calling his name; when he appeared in his window she moaned.

He had a limp—he'd worked at the docks and had taken a bad fall. Ed sees an old man falling off a ladder because Mac was on one so often, but I think he fell from the deck of a freighter.

I asked him if he was in the union. "Aw, they were just troublemakers."

He disliked the boyfriends of our women neighbors. "That Frank is a real Jew."

I lowered the trunk on my Toyota. "Mac, you know I'm Jewish." I found that hard to say. I was barred from the moment, no longer one with the day and the street. His insult was homegrown but it also seemed exotic, like Fascist demons in movies. Had Mac despised me all along? Had I provoked him?—by condescending from the vantage of class?—by forcing him to represent the past? Was he asking for more attention?

"Aw, that's not what I mean." He shrugged with exasperation. We saw each other as unwilling and limited. I'd thought of Mac as a master of ephemera, a novelist like me who worked outside the medium; he was bigoted, meddlesome and loose-tongued, with a gossip's contempt for his neighbors. And myself? I wanted my community romance intact. I wanted nothing new from Mac. *Good fences make good neighbors*—could describe our inner lives. So Mac and Nonie make idle chitchat of racial insult over dinner in their yellow kitchen. I didn't want to witness the disjunction between Mac's speech, his actual life, and the romance I invented for us.

It took me a week to visit Mac in the hospital. During that time Gorbachev pushed to win control of the Ukraine and seven people died in a fire in Harlem. A strike closed San Francisco ports, the dollar plunged against the yen, and the FDA approved AZT. Dean Martin's son was missing in a plane crash. Twenty thousand people in China perished in a chemical spill, Jessica Hahn admitted to a sexual liaison with evangelist Jim Bakker, and a restaurant was caught serving alligator.

France began to put its abortion pill in use. The body of Dean Martin's son was found and an Atlas rocket costing $161 million blew up as it was taking off. Reagan pondered a move against the Japanese and Afghan warplanes killed eighty-five people in raids on Pakistani villages. Nonie said I would have to sneak past the nurses to visit Mac. I was creeping along a lime-green wall by the second nurses' station, averting my eyes, when I realized they didn't care at all. A Chinese nurse leaned against the counter, a jolly audience for the seated women who laughed with excitement and called, "Ireeen . . . Ireeen. . . ." They were some impediment Nonie had invented; without remorse she had pretty much stopped going.

Mac's room was dim. He was naked; I stopped in my tracks. Two nurses, young Chicanas, stood on either side of him. One cradled his head against her shoulder and moved a white cloth over his arm. The other gazed at his IV with a solemn expression. I was shocked by his blunt nakedness, his smooth wiry body and by how fresh his legs and thighs looked. His hands lay open on either side of his luminous torso; his eyes were fixed, but when he caught sight of me he modestly averted them. I had not meant to see anything so personal, and I felt a pang of anxiety as the borders of our friendship shifted. I retreated to the hall.

One nurse asked, "Mr. McMillin, are you comfortable now?"

"I know where I'd be more comfortable."

"Just a little while longer."

The other nurse echoed, "Just a little while."

I drew a chair up to his bed. A knot or splinter on the

inseam of my jeans irritated the skin of my inner thigh with every move. "You look good, Mac." I sided with the stupid philodendron in its bid for normalcy, undermined by stainless steal buttons, C and D, on the wall behind it. Mac was hooked up to an IV, only that, no tubes, blood, or respirators. He received no therapy, yet we treated him as though he were recovering. In the hall someone whistled within the echo of his own whistling, someone with soft shoes walked down the corridor calling "Jackie, Jackie, Jackie. . . ." The air was empty to breathe and papery, but crowded with dings of elevator arrivals, squeaks of carts and gurneys, deep coughing and clatter of dishes, doctors' names paged, names that never could be understood, summarizing the anxiety of illness, the lack of stimulation that made me sleepy and hungry for sensation. When I closed my eyes a slice of pecan pie bled amber syrup on a Melmac plate.

Mac rose to the challenge: faced with the annihilation of particulars he organized his part of the abyss. He pointed to the nurses' station across the hall. "See that gal, Bob, that's Maria, she's got a sister in Fresno who . . ." I realized that the trouble was not on my pants but on my leg, a pimple or rash or ingrown hair—I longed to go home and see what had appeared on my skin.

Mac was telling me about Maria's sister. His rambling story replaced the subject of his death. Mac believed in the value of Maria's sister's experience in Fresno because he gained knowledge as an end in itself. His solidarity was consoling because it was faith in the value of everyone's personal history. Then again, maybe I was consoled by Mac's inability to locate a frantic loneliness in himself.

You go along and something's different. The second time I visited, it was apparent he was dying. He had already started, his body was stuttering, losing integrity. It scared me. I had seen this stuttering once before but had forgotten. I held his hand and he covered mine with his other, then held up all three hands to show how swollen his fingers were. I couldn't make out what he was saying. I could tell he was loaded by the way his irises dropped to the corners of his eyes when he rolled his head. There was a sense of dangerous speeding, time as space, like speeding over the ground as the airplane descends

when just a moment before in the air we seemed motionless.
Mac was out of time, whispering. Then with perfect composure he asked, "Bob, do you know my mother's number?"
When I didn't reply he said, "Why don't you let me drive you
home?" His blue eyes were bright; he cocked his head on the
pillow of the deathbed with conspiratorial irony.

"I'll come visit you again."

"Hope you find me here." Then he frowned at the ceiling
and asked, "Is that your luggage?" When I turned to go he
added, "Take care of yourself, Bob."

I doubt they did "everything they could." Mac didn't expect
that kind of care. He followed the prescribed behavior with a
conviction that resembled faith in an afterlife, which doesn't
give much to the dying except structure for the experience of
their death. Mac's illness existed for the hospital, his death
belonged to the nurses and doctors and the world beyond.

Mac's service was held at Reilly Company Funeral Directors,
a neighborhood mortuary at the bottom of Dolores. The gray
building was vaguely Italianate with ponderous brackets and
"rusticated" stucco. Two plump businessmen stood chatting in
the sunlight on the corner with all the time in the world. On
either side of the grand doorway small cypresses grew in stone
tubs. The space for death was a parlor—framed mirrors, green
drapes, a floral tapestry couch, two torchiers with candelabras
of electric bulbs, and a grandfather clock. A man in a black
and blue uniform stood inside the door; he was so fat and
pigeon-toed that his arms circled around him when he waded
the few steps to point the way.

I entered the funeral chapel just as Mac's service ended. It
was a small gathering although Mac knew at least a hundred
of his neighbors and his works of mercy took him to other
parts of town. "Bob, c'mere," and we'd be hauling scrap wood
for the potbellied stove of an ancient couple who lived on a
hill in a tiny earthquake cabin. The chapel emptied; Nonie
approached, hunched forward in grief. She cried "Oh Bob"
and her small body fell against mine like a slight breeze. We
had never touched. I wasn't embarrassed; I felt tremendous
latitude, that anything short of dying would be appropriate. I

laughed as though we were meeting at a party. Nonie looked
confused, then fell into other arms.

I was stopped short by Mac in his big casket. Now I felt
like an intruder. Mac was always so prim; he never broke the
social contract except by dying. His cheeks were apple red as
though he were ashamed to be in that position.

DENNY

"Look at this, Sweetie." I showed him a forgotten document
I'd found while hunting for checks in my top desk drawer. It
was an agenda we had drawn up for a Sunday night long ago.
Our days and nights were still full of meetings. The agenda
was printed in pencil on typing paper soft with age; it proposed
categories and subcategories, beginning *Item One: Warm Up
Kisses and Music a) Denny wants 20th C. b) Bob wants 18th C.*,
and ending, *Item Twelve: Pillow Talk.* "Look at all the things we
used to do," I marveled. We read silently the amazing access to
all the body blocked off for the duration. "I forgot we did
them." We glimpsed a lost horizon.

"Oh Bob," Denny said, a modest virgin. He reorganized us
on the sofa. He sat face forward, his body so slight his limbs
resembled the clothed emptiness of a marionette. I reclined
with my feet on his lap; I considered his bony eloquent profile.
On the carpet Lily slept deep in the big blond nest of her
body, dazed by extreme age and arthritis medicine. Denny
sipped clear liquid which broke into metallic greenness on his
tongue and juniper in his nostrils. He furrowed his square
brow and cocked his head in an ironic attitude of considering
and raised his glass, an outsized triangle on a stem, a shape so
simple it might have been neon above a bar, "Nectar of the
Gods, mon ami."

I raised my glass to the Martini maker. "The modernist cocktail." We drank from that utopian wellspring and browsed
through *Architectural Digest.* The cost of the magazine was an
extravagance, but we considered entire homes that were stylish
blunders or myths of habitation, tried them on for a moment
like new hats. A glazed chintz, silver peonies drifting on grassy
green—the brief entertainment of lifting a flower to your

nose—would it be right for this room? We saw ourselves against a panorama, climbing to the true global village. The flagstone terraces, heavy pages and paneled bedrooms were a voluptuous garden without soil, the only home we ever pictured sharing. Image is a spring of lasting passion. The gin gave the future we assembled a certain credence.

Our game was so retro. Above our acted-out feelings—retro, neo, and pseudo—arched a rainbow of pleasure. Denny curbed my taste for the ornate. Our love was predicated on convivial sex and the gift of validation, the luxury of shared assumptions and an urge to corrupt by creating new desires in each other. I wanted a Pompeian frieze around the top of the room. I looked up prayerfully but Denny cautioned, "Pure of line, Bob. Look at this." He showed me a transom window, a fan of glass above a paneled mahogany door. "Clarity above an obstacle."

"You know, I'm worried about Ed."

"What's wrong?"

"Intestinal things."

"Oh Bob, Ed always thinks he's sick."

"Ed says, 'The pain is under my fifth rib and feels orange' and the doctor starts shouting."

"He creates suspicion. Is he worried about AIDS?"

"Ugh. He stopped long before I did. Isn't it strange that you and I gave up all the unsafe sex on our agenda, even though the viral horse would have already left our barn?"

"It's your cow and your barn and your horse and your stable door. That's sexual ideology for you, mon ami. When is Mac's funeral?"

"Last Thursday. The service wasn't announced and Nonie kept it to herself. It started at twelve on the dot and lasted till twelve fifteen. A third of the mourners missed it trying to park. I came in at the tail end and you know—there was Mac. He still looked interested." We sat with our drinks. I thought, No, it's Ed's awareness of death in the midst of life that aroused me and that doctors recoil from, negating them as it does. But the sudden friendship with a corpse shocked me, the fear that I might be dead—that Mac's a ledge and I jump. I hadn't meant to see anything so alien. Nothing is more unlikely—hell or rising from the dead or Bardo states or the Isle of the Blessed— nothing is more fantastic than for someone you love to stop, just stop, and be lowered into a hole and covered with cement and actual dirt.

"Cremation's the revenge," Denny said, "but you don't have the sense the person died. All these memorials and no body. I miss Mac. I wish I'd visited him in the hospital."

"He died in three weeks. Lily still waits by his gate." Lily's ears tipped forward though her eyes didn't open. Then she slowly climbed onto her legs. Denny called, "Lily?"

I said, "Hey baby, where you been all night, your hair's all mussed up and your clothes don't fit you right." She licked her chops thickly and surveyed us without interest. Then she walked away and a moment later we heard lapping water in the kitchen.

"It took Mary-Madeleine two years to die of lung cancer. Her daughters chose a beach north of Santa Cruz."

Denny leaned back miming boredom. "Beaches are like corridors in office buildings."

"She was in a box wrapped in gold foil. The ashes were actually thick flakes and bonemeal. I took a handful and walked down."

Mary-Madeleine was as new to her mid-seventies as I was to my mid-thirties; she had already scattered unfinished poems, unraised children, and their dads. "I threw her out to sea, but the wind caught the ashes and threw them back in my face, and Mary-Madeleine went right up my nose and in my eyes. I was so blinded I had to kneel. I probably still have some of her lodged in my lungs."

"A walking urn," Denny said.

As an epitaph for Mary-Madeleine I keep a motto she wrote out for herself on a scrap of unruled note paper: Luck is when Opportunity meets Preparation. The t's aren't crossed, but the script is bold and the sentence is circled in red. It records an imaginary encounter; she had no Opportunity and, except for her death, she was never Prepared. I held my breath by a bank of wheelchairs outside her door, listening to her doctor. We've done everything we can, You waged a good fight, It's time to just make you comfortable. Which meant, Pump you full of morphine and let you die. She said, "I see." See what?—a short man with huge eyebrows and chalky skin.

In the hall he took my elbow and said in a whisper, "Make sure she understands." He was discouraged: He'd been forced to renounce for a moment the lie that everyone gets well, that death is weak, merely an unsuccessfully treated illness.

So I changed from bystander to the herald of death, carrying a coffin into the sick room. Beige drapes with abstract leaf patterns held the daylight back. I sat next to her. Her head rolled and pain sort of pushed her tongue out of her mouth in slow motion. I waited with my question until the spasm subsided, one expression on my face as though no time passed.

"Now it's time for Mighty Mouse." She was referring to a little blue pill.

"Mary-Madeleine, do you understand what your doctor said?"

She replied wistfully, "I guess everyone has to die sometime." With that she divorced her rambling life from the medical marvels and aligned herself with the dying of the ages—with them she met her destiny. Had she pretended to herself for our sake that she was recovering? The farce was over and her solitude was complete. Her large body began to dwindle; one dawn a month later she faded away.

I think of Mary-Madeleine's death in contrast to the death of Kelly, a very sweet man, my dad's best friend. Kelly died when I was sixteen. He checked into the hospital for nothing special, some tests, and quickly fell apart; he didn't want to live. My mom told me he died gasping for air, his mouth gaping, his eyes bulging, his head rearing up. She said it was heartless of the staff to let Elinore see him like that, but now I see him that way and always will. He struggles for breath, the terror of that suffocation, a surprise forever protracted, rising. While Mary-Madeleine subsides, her vital signs lose tension. She falls through veils of morphine to a second sleep. Kelly's spasm lasts through eternity like the end of a story where he gains or loses everything. I see him clearly though I'm absent, the cords standing out from his neck. After his funeral, leaving the church, those tendons become the elastic band in Elinore's red panties; it snapped and the priest thought her laughter was convulsed sorrow.

* * *

On this stage I have constructed for my soliloquy, I *can't speak* about my death or bid you to look in my grave. As for ordering my tomb, over the two dates put an image of men fucking—to show what made me happy. Do the following stories belong here? They don't "come to mind" but intrude themselves. The first is more resonant but simple to tell. It's just the pleasure my mother took in four eggs she brought seven hundred miles to my house. "See, it has a blue shell." She held out the egg for me to look at though not to hold. "Bob, look at this." She was submitting a new piece of evidence, asking me to reconsider, but the problem was beyond articulation. She tipped back her elegant face, a conclusive gesture, and for a moment she occupied the sixty-eight years of her life. It was a moment, breathless and possible. I asked for her best maternal advice. She replied without hesitation, "You are alone and you have only yourself to depend on, emotionally and financially." My cousin's black hen laid the eggs. They did have a blue cast and thick, sturdy shells, and my mother took an urgent pride in the rich orange of their yolks.

My friend Kathleen said of her husband, "Art's a lucky man." I asked what made him lucky—what is luck in general? She said, "His parents are both alive." Art was fifty-seven. Kathleen is not simple; she didn't mean his parents were pure joy, but that Art is still a child, his body still given to him. My mom's advice was chilling because it eliminated her own presence from my life. She gave her son exactly what he asked for, her best survival kit. I should have asked for comfort.

Last week my dad told me this story. Forty years ago on Buckeye Road a traffic cop beckons my dad into an intersection where another cop tags him. At traffic court there are eighty people, all tagged at the same place. Judge O'Connell is a lush and a wild card. He raises a pistol and points it around the court. Everyone jumps and ducks for cover. He explains that a car driven by a drunk is as dangerous as his loaded gun. Defendants plead guilty, except for my dad, who pleads "guilty with reservations." The judge calls him into chambers. My dad says, "O'Connell, don't you wonder why eighty people got tickets at one intersection? Doesn't that seem a little strange to you?"

The judge thinks a moment and says, "Why don't you call me Your Honor?"

My dad was sitting in a Mission chair in the bay window of my living room. He lowered his face—the fierce eyebrows and heavy pouches I seem to be inheriting. He studied the legal situation. A bunch of yellow and lavender stock emitted obvious perfume. I was suddenly aware of the southern sky behind him, not cloudy but flat gray, and that I had acknowledged the day by wearing an old green cardigan.

My father replied to me as though I'd asked the question, "O'Connell, I'm supposed to be judged by my peers—if I call you Your Honor, you'd have to call me Your Highness." My dad triumphed over corruption and hypocrisy with the small weapon of language, a weapon that guarantees happy endings, that is, endings where truth is completely expressed. "Anyway," my father confided as though turning away from the judge, "he wasn't so full of honor. Chuck knew him. Chuck was my helper on the truck. Chuck was a nonperson: no driver's license, no Social Security number. No draft card. He beat O'Connell for ten dollars an hour in some flop house. His Honor used to shout, 'Not in the head, anywhere but the head.' "

"So Chuck was gay?" I felt a restless mirth verging on anger. What was my dad saying with this fragment from the mid-fifties—was he helplessly following the path of association?—as his son is doing in this chapter?

He looked surprised. "Naw, they met outside some bar. Chuck was a drunk—ten dollars was a lot of money in those days." So a man without identity was my father's helper and Judge O'Connell's helper too, and both Chuck and my dad beat the authority out of the Judge. With authority there are always spectators, with spectators always mirth.

My dad thinks it's easy for me to visit O'Connell's court with him; he doesn't realize how easy it is for me to visit O'Connell's hotel room. The child without name or home beats the father with his own paternal staff, lust turning their roles upside down. When there's a child in the family there's always a lesson to learn. Today's lesson is: Pleasure has performed another miracle—the lucky child will never die. Chuck is handsome as sin, sandy brown hair, drowsy eyes, a few freckles, the narrow chest and gleaming skin of the Prodigal Son. Don't spare the rod. The sweet must of the red floral carpet, the dusty blinds covering an airwell, the pine furniture.

Antique authority sheds his robes to become the baby, Naked Lust. On his knees, torso across the bed, the child-martyr inhales the sour breath of old chenille while the torturer proceeds with lazy goodwill, not angry or fierce. Devils and angels debate on either side of the mattress, the debate of the urge for more life against the urge to break life's tension. "Congratulations to your soul," one of them says officially. "Welcome to some heaven of love." Another replies, "Not a very permanent heaven this love affair," and as if to confirm this, another voice says, "Back on the bus, everyone." Deliverance for the camera—memory constructed of film clips and pages from grainy porn magazines. The judge makes a moaning noise that replaces *his* memory. It's like an old daguerrotype, the image of a golden age always disappearing into mirror. Chuck rises to the occasion: He beats the judge with joyous destructive energy.

The beating sets the judge in his own soft body, but his intensity stands for the thrill Chuck might be experiencing. Do Not Disturb hangs from the doorknob. The judge will base his orgasm on his mental reconstruction of the pleasure in a patch of silky skin on Chuck's erect cock. I admit I'm attracted to their reassuring failure, their aura of the already-known. It's easy to back away from the two men. They shrink as the screen diminishes and descends, their actions cartoonish, hyper, the young man writhing, the judge throwing a tantrum, a frantic child.

I am intrigued by the specificity of my dad's memory, though he lacks the sheer disinterestedness and solidarity of Mac.

When I was young the uncanny took the form of Abraham Lincoln. I had forgotten Lincoln's part in my childhood, writing this story brought it to mind. A magazine spread shaped my fear—*Life* I think—on his disinterment—in the nineteenth century? Is that possible? The article described nails grown long and the handkerchief-covering-nose smell, and the disconcerting fact that the corpse was well preserved rather than a decent skeleton. In the grave it continued to be Lincoln. With his Frankenstein height and his long hands, Lincoln embodied a bleak solemnity which made his benign gestures especially intolerable. There was some kindness to a little girl; he wrote to her after he had been murdered. He spooked me in grainy photos where even the light is decayed and rotten—the wound at the back of his head, his boogeyman clothes, the intolerable resemblance of his body in the coffin to his photos and statues, a face from a waxworks whose expression is wax.

I confused Lincoln with a comic cover of Frankenstein bashing through a brick wall, and I feared for my safety and the continuation of my being. Yes, I am lying in bed and the closet door stands half open. I make out a few empty hangers and the shoulders and sleeves of my shirts, red and black, blue and white, forest green, white Oxford cloth, allies whose value derives from fidelity to me rather than their worth as clothes. A dark wind from the closet pushes the door, touches my face. First the dreary fear, then the lanky monster gives it shape. His body pitches forward, his eyes are dead, his huge arm is raised and wildly foreshortened. In confusion any feeling is an acceptable distraction—even terror, even nostalgia for the tolling bell. In the bathroom he bashes through the wall of white brick tiles, a force nothing can stop which comes for me in its own time, but surely at night when I am defenseless, fat, larval, without a reason to launch a self-defense—what is there to defend?

This monster was further conflated with Muscle Man, a zombie casually invented by my older brother and then forgotten by him, reanimation not worth considering, and it was in part his casual existence and the shabby materials of the story that frightened me, alerting me as they did to the random danger of becoming a living corpse. Intolerable the dead whose state partakes of life rather than the negation of all states. Muscle Man starts off as a kindly elementary school teacher who loves children (lots of examples of fatherly love), but one bright rainy night his car skids off a cliff and crashes on rocks far below and explodes into flames, and all that's left for the doctors to put together are muscles, so he only drinks one drop of water a year and only eats one crumb of bread. He has no stomach but his muscles retain their vitality. He is heroically muscular; I don't think he wears clothes but I am not free to look at his crotch. Physical commotion has a sexual dimension, and the depth of perspective of the live body in the abyss generates the violence of the sexuality. A commotion—a man hangs by his neck from a rope, his cock erect, an impure reversed death. How can I appease Muscle Man's energetic spirit? In his search for children he crashes through walls—to do what? He calls, "Bob . . . Bob . . ." Why do the dead want my body?—to relive their solitude? When he annihilates me I am his child or childish lover.

I never got that far in the confusion of living and dead, and perhaps all this has little to do with the death of actual people. The image of lovers on my tomb was a promise of possession to keep the argument of my life open, if just rhetorically, in the fact of death. The image of my parents was again a guarantee of possession, an incomplete abstruse document of possession to read forward and backward endlessly like romantic love. So it's no surprise that when I was younger death seemed a matter of possession of the body. I dreamt my mother died: I put her in my wagon and wheeled her to our temple—they didn't want her—then to my dad—he didn't want her—no one else seemed to want her—so I kept her for myself on my toy chest. I never told the rabbi or my dad about my dream; I couldn't count on them to remain indifferent. If they *discussed* the dream or even reacted the image would be partly theirs, it would be correctly taken as a challenge, and I did want to keep my mother with me.

Her skin begins to peel so I remove her clothes and place my toy on the hallway floor, on the green carpet, and smooth her skin back. I don't exactly see my toy's body, it remains a blindspot, but my confusion distills into tremulous pleasure. Then I sit by my bedroom window and look out; instead of the despicable houses and front lawns, I am surprised to see my small life staged in a sweeping pastoral vista. I am conscious of the disjunction between the absolute visual stillness—intense blue through the firs, the meadow's gold sheen, the slight motion of cattails by a fence—and the terrible rattle and cough of the old lawnmower unseen somewhere down below.

NONIE

Nonie tries to keep her weight up to eighty. She is entirely white, entirely wrinkled, with fragile arms and legs and the pan face and nasal drawl of the Midwest. She is as reclusive as Mac was gregarious, though entirely united with Mac in keeping an eye on the street from the outlook of their top floor apartment. Only after sunset did their blue curtains draw together, lit within by the TV's quavering. Why make this portrait of Mac and Nonie? I'm trying too hard to recover—what? Mourning is appropriate for separation, in this case divorce between Image and Feeling, the antique parting of ways, the wound that leaks meaning. Without reason Mac died, Nonie mourns. They pass so quickly through story into metaphor and explanation. It's not much of a story, just reruns of cozy programs like, "Murder, She Wrote" with actors who do not portray people—incomplete expressions of destiny and nature—but the more recognizable character actors of yesteryear. Recognition is everything: Feeling agrees to be DESOLATE LONELINESS, glad that it has a part however low, and at the same time it is TOWERING INDIGNATION to be so rejected. Bob, this is Nonie 'cross the street, your front door is open. Bob, this is Nonie, your lights are on. I run downstairs and sure enough my actual headlights glow feebly in the dusk. Any story underwrites its experience with the value of experience itself. Any language wants to be total, pathless yearning. Bob, do you eat tomatoes? Mac packs them in a brown paper bag. When he steps out of his door he is aware for the first time of the day. When he closes his eyes a slice of pecan pie bleeds amber syrup on a Melmac plate.

When he opens them he's aware of "the day" and the gem-incrusted gold sky without point of view above and around him. He waits to cross the street. I relish his energetic relation to the everyday as I do the daily horoscope's, his confidence that unwittingly supports doubt and emptiness, yet always coincides with reality *on some level*. At my door Mac raises the tomatoes towards me in a fixed gesture of offering. Embarrassed by his own generosity (a stiff eloquence) he counters my thanks with a gruff order: Now share those with Denny. His face tips back as though in combat. Realistic portraits began with death masks and praying tomb figures in the thirteenth century. The paper bag has surprising weight, suggesting moral gravity. The tomatoes are silky, fragrant; an increment of blue in their skin adds density to the bright red. The nephew's backyard in Stockton, the slow ripening in his dusty garden, the vines climbing, their somber scraggly life in the full sun.

Three weeks after Mac died Nonie called me over. The weather was springlike in its extremes, robust and still. It had rained at night; the sidewalk was damp, the air was clear and calm, the sky held a few gray clouds traveling fast and low. Nonie opened her door a crack and looked out, then backed away, leaving the rest to me. I gave it a push. Nonie stood in a blue quilted housecoat a few yards down the hall. She had a flu that first constricted her chest, then gave her sinus headaches and a sore throat, then descended again four inches to her chest. She led me into her yellow kitchen and offered me a brown and gray Harris tweed sports coat, an electric razor pristine in its square plastic case, and a brown bag full of TV dinners. As a group they had the thwarted quality of dead people's things. I examined them for signs of loyalty to Mac.

"The sleeves are too long for me Nonie."

"If you don't give it to a friend, I'll just throw it out."

"I shave with a blade."

"Couldn't Denny use it?"

"Why don't you eat this Nonie?"

"This is Mac's food," she explained to a child, the sentence trailing up an edge of exasperation. She sat down on one of the two kitchen chairs. Maybe she couldn't swallow what was his, but I bet she just didn't like it, it didn't suit her. So I guess they didn't share food when they shared a meal. Why did she think it would suit me?—did she view the food as male? What has that got to do with Fish Almondine? Or pizza chips filled with shrimp meat? I understood that she wanted me to take it all. I found a new owner for the shaver. Phyllis liked the jacket, and the exotic food remained stacked in my freezer.

I didn't know how to feel about Mac. By this I mean I was lost and didn't know how to align feeling and event. I didn't know how to make surrogates to embody the various voids. I had missed most of his funeral because I was watching the clock, frozen in my bed, held in check by loud voices I couldn't interrupt or understand. I located no memorial service for Mac inside me. Meanwhile I was depressed and teary imagining that I was remembering Ed's death; that is, I could respond to Ed's misfortune only as an episode from the past. Lily waited for Mac's amazing abundance, refusing to budge from his gate, nose pointed up the stairway. She responded to my calls with quick glances of reproach.

"Look up Bob." Nonie's white head appeared three stories above. She threw down a baggie of biscuits to console Lily, so I guess dog biscuits remained an item on Nonie's shopping list. The baggie, wrapped in a rubber band, dropped from a terrible height and stung my palms. I doled them out on the spot. Lily ate them intently, but they were not enough or not what she wanted because she returned to her station by Mac's gate. Maybe I had underestimated her? Meanwhile, Mac's food remained stacked in the deep freeze eternally, a testimonial tidy and contained as his garage.

From April to September Mac's death remained in my freezer—skeleton, death's-head, hourglass—the sad and spooky food so fraught and at the same time so generic it was hard to see. I thought it was Mac's monument, a pure, solitary burial. Then I became busy, really too busy to shop or cook. I examined the Fish Almondine. The cover showed the meal as it was and would be, like the image of the man alive on Pharaoh's coffin. It was understood the first resting place was temporary. Just directions to cook in a microwave. The odor of Mac's dinner: the fixed air in its plastic bubble, then break the sack and it floats past my face like a balloon of savory smell. (Hold your nose before the searching odor of a corpse, fan it away with the word Evocative.) It was not bad at all, lacking individuality but tasty, the kind of fish we Americans like, without a suggestion of alien existence or regret for the sea. But Mac was able to confer distinctions. You could say in my dinner Mac's blue eyes were open. Every night the monument turned into a ritual by entering my body. I consumed his distinctions where before I had seen none, just an unknown expanse of bright utopian images to appeal to the stranger passing the frozen food compartment. To make wild assertions: to say I prefer Stouffer's Pizza Chips to Birdseye's Pizza Wraps. To eat Mac's food which was anyone's food—a generic confrontation with salt, oil, too sweet, pumped up with flavor, empty and exciting, a little sensational. I was not anguished. Perhaps I ate his food with a greater awareness of the moment, a curiosity that floated on the moment, an expectation that deepened the silence (I say silence although the TV was on, was on, was on). In that way I mourned for Mac.

ED

Ed asked me to take him to get his HIV results.

In 1975, at a couples' workshop, the group asked Ed what he wanted from me. Ed replied, "For Bob to be a home I can always return to." The group turned and asked what I thought of that.

"Yes, that's beautiful." It took years to understand their downcast expressions. All day they'd guided me towards a healthy response: You can't assume love, you can't have affairs, you can't ignore me.

I'm still glad Ed regards me as a haven, though I'm finally suspicious of that model. My relationship with Denny also seemed necessary, as though he needed some kind of help. Is this true if both lovers believe it? Now I believe I was the one who needed help—of course!—who greedily helped myself to it, help that was given without expectation.

Ed is a presence who returns. He became a gardener in the Flower Conservatory. He lives with Daniel in a meticulous Victorian cottage. They earn plenty of money; they built Ed a studio to paint in. Daniel happens to occupy the first-lover position in Denny's past that Ed has in mine. Daniel and Ed met in the Fuchsia Dell in Golden Gate Park.

Ed was a translucent Japanese beauty when we lived together, his bones hollow as a bird's. He grew robust during his gardener years, but he retains a floating quality. It was in Ed's life with me rather than in my life by itself that I experienced isolation most keenly, a solitude that terrified and aroused me, granting me faith in the existence of my body, so that love of life came to equal excited desperation. When we separated I took into myself some of his glamorous solitude— I don't think that's unusual. I practiced narcissism and unconsciousness until they became second nature. If Mac is the spirit of conservation, Ed is the face that daydreams, and you can't look squarely enough at that face to speak of ownership. His solitude retreats through thresholds to the unspeakable, yet I bring him into this story because he's capable of a talkative grief that can still be trusted. Ed is in real trouble. Terror makes him clumsy—he feels a sickening animation in inert objects, some rhythm lifelike in its rudimentary pulse.

Slow pinwheels, looming walls. I judge myself and Bob judges me. The day is sunny, windy, strong autumn wind. I wear gray jeans that seem extra tight, especially in the waist. I've lost so much weight I don't wear my coat, it hangs, making me teeter. Walking from the car to Dr. Parmer's office, my spirit races ahead only to wait for my body to catch up.

I must be hyperventilating because everything's in a slow spin, time seems its own. On "Star Trek" an advanced civilization is invisible to the *Enterprise* crew because they live at hyperspeed detectable only by shrill insect squeaks caused by moving so fast. Spock accelerates to see them, but then the crew appears frozen.

I avoid Ed's face; I have no reply to the rigid features there: invention paralyzed by the thought of death. I touch his shoulder. He says the mirror stopped returning an image he recognized. He told himself, Everyone feels this way, everyone feels shattering fatigue, internal collapsing akin to grief. At night he arched, ascended, woke up drenched, then dragged himself out of bed to dry off, laid towels over the wet sheet in dreary terror. He kept the nightsweats secret even from Daniel sleeping inches away. Ed said, Everyone gets nightsweats sometimes.

How amazing, I think, his secrecy and this disclosure. Ed's not giving his story, he's taking it from me. I lose consistency, I give Ed the theater of my unconscious and my faith in his images. Faith is still a means of understanding. Mac taught me that. I help Ed restage his trouble in his own symbolic world and in the dreamlife of others so he can benefit from the promise made by life-as-it-is. In the fifteenth-century play, Everyman pleads with Discretion, "Look into my grave once piteously." Everyman wants to bring his death to life by giving it a biography, but Discretion rejects him. Everyman tries to place the image of his fate in Discretion's mind in order to create one moment of promise.

Bob says he'll be surprised if my tests come back negative. That enrages me, as if he wishes it. Part of me is resigned to being HIV positive, a great burden would be lifted. All the months—one and a half years of diarrhea, colitis, the abdominal cramping that passes from one side of my belly to the other taking my breath away. The anal operation that finally cured the fistula that took me through two lances to drain the infection and how my body shape changed after that. The fear and blood. If I'm positive it will be over, in some odd way I'll be cured. I almost want it. I don't want anything to stop, but positive means medication, some action I can take. These are my thoughts as we walk down the long hall to Dr. Parmer's office.

We wait on a burnt orange couch. Daniel arrives and we all sit facing the same direction like on a bus. My years with Bob confer an element of safety on what we are about to do. He's my past, he'll walk me through this judgment and somehow things will still go on. Across the room a woman lowers her magazine and stares at the orange cushion on the chair next to her. Her eyes open too wide—she calls someone's name—she's furious in her dream—huge quarrels dwarf our voices and the weak office music.

Daniel and I wait for Dr. Parmer in a small examining room. Sweat drops from my nose and forehead, my scalp is damp. The pile of a dingy rug spreads across the walls. Daniel rotates on the small black stool. We hold hands. He looks numb. He has great love and warmth. I am overcome by loneliness. I lean back against the wall.

Normally Dr. Parmer meets my eye but today he hides his face, turns to close the door. Daniel scoots back and rises to give the stool to the Doctor. Dr. Parmer looks at me and I begin to cry. My feelings seem artificial. He sits erect, rambles on. The room disappears in the same dark gray. Crying is all that exists.

I am ludicrous, I am crying for nothing because this is a mistake, my results are negative. I almost laugh so I step out of myself like leaving a noisy room and turn back to the commotion. Dr. Parmer and Daniel look shocked, I'm *jeering* at them— In disbelief my mind races back and forth to my death and the exact time of infection, which sex act, with who. . . .

Ed shrinks the space of contraries till he can't move. I also want to know where he got the virus, as though we can settle this by withdrawing it from chance, as though danger can be organized and set aside. I also am too tired to continue believing in chance. I want to find some tiny inherent reason for Ed to die—well, he *would* contract the virus. This is naive writing, the hope for each sentence naive, that it release awareness like the sudden clamor at the beginning of a storm. Ed's desolation is so intense it sheds a contradictory stillness, a moment elongating under a huge burden, like the long vanishing point of an annunciation.

My death floats before me in the small dark room. I cry as it gives me numbers, lab results. Death doesn't offer anything else, no hand holding, no apologies, no plan for the future. It knows me in smaller and smaller fractions—it doesn't know what to do. Now these feelings are me.

I stand and my knees give way. Daniel holds me as we walk. Roz the receptionist looks up as we pass, sadness and confusion on her face, and I think maybe I'm overreacting.

Bob stands as we enter the waiting room. We look at each other and he knows. We embrace and some of my fear leaves as he absorbs it. Bob says, "Now you can figure out what you're going to do." He speaks firmly. These words bring us back. Daniel and I are caught up, but these words locate our feelings in time and space. We are three standing together.

Daniel drives me to Bob's. Daniel has to return to work and I don't want to be alone. Bob takes me upstairs. As we sit down he says "Eat," but it's a pointless act.

I make a comforting gesture to Ed—it contains the thrown open hands of exasperation. I reject him for threatening to die—and leave me—why doesn't he get on with it? I stop believing in his story, not just the "outcome" but the basic tenet, the pitiful urge for more life. There was an old woman who swallowed a fly. Like the old woman I take inside me the disloyal sound of typing. The conflict ceases to be real, I have to retell myself the facts of the epidemic, I can't believe this. . . .

We sit across from each other. Bob says read and I agree that's my ammunition. Bob says dump Dr. Parmer. He suggests calling his mother—the thought of Dorothy is reassuring. I call Daniel's doctor and say I have AIDS.

We leave for Dr. Owens's. Sitting on the exam table makes the room seem floorless. It's painful to focus my eyes. It's like I never left a doctor's office, the exasperation where such a small part of life has meaning. I must be hyperventilating—the air is gray, tiny black veins crawl over the walls and I'm tumbling forwards.

Dr. Owens holds me as I begin to cry. He lifts his hand to the back of my neck; for a second he believes I'm his child even though we're the same age. He apologizes for my bad news. He says, Get on AZT as soon as possible and have the P24 Antigen test done, it's only been out a few weeks. He suggests Valium to calm me down and with that I want it badly. I don't want to continue the same feelings. As he and Bob talk, I'm already backing away, the scene before me is animated but two-dimensional.

Bob drives me back to his house. My future is determined, a passenger in a car. Crying eases the pain, so I keep crying. The air is heavy with fog. The windshield's a glass that magnifies me larger than life. Bob's terrified of my fear, he's wearing his face. I cover my eyes as I cry as though shielding them from glare. I feel the world needs me. I won't get to do all the paintings I have ideas for. Bob tells me in a sharp voice that I'm not going to die. I regret having a low opinion of myself for so long. I caused this whole mess, if only . . .

Bob's so much in control. His life looks simple because it is going to go on. All he has to do or think about is drive the car, get us home, very simple.

I tell Ed I'm writing about Mac's dinners. Ed says, "Maybe they weren't Mac's food—they probably collected in his freezer because he hated them. Did you notice that Mac's hair went from white to dirty yellow, depending on when he bleached it?" He laughs, surprised by what he said, but he doesn't want to be distracted from his fear. His life is suspended—its small increments give way to the intolerable coincidence of mind and the world. The questions that lead him forward with their small answers become one question. He slowly rotates over a wild stasis while I try to domesticate his terror with language.

Bob wants me to merge my self and my medical existence. He's telling me that people have made something normal here. "This is going to be like a job, Ed—something that takes planning, lots of time." His voice is rising. I think, let me grieve, let me indulge.

Lily greets us at the top of the stairs, wagging and huffing, shining black eyes. I'll die before her. I sit down next to her and she methodically licks my face with her rough tongue.

Things in Bob's house feel either old or new. The old is good because it's familiar, but the new dares me to live, as if I will age before it. I look at the huge cedar bed Bob and I constructed and see years stacked up in it. I stand in the hall judging things by degrees of safety.

Bob brings me a Valium and goes to run errands.

Ed in the bathroom, the reassuring heat from his crack when he wipes himself, as though he really is a factory burning calories. He considers his face, puffy and sallow. His hands rest on the sink and one foot is poised behind the other. He always felt he could escape as a woman or become someone else if a situation demanded, maybe because his Japanese features already belong to "someone else." Now he's trapped in a prison that allows no leaching into otherness. He lies down on my bed, feels agreeably fragile, abandoned, aware of the action of his breath, its regularity—he's made of flesh and witness to this fact. The charm of extreme grief is that it gives way to marveling tremulous reverie. Ed drifts then focuses, drifts then focuses. He's on his side, looking absently at his hand, his eyes drifting and then refreshing themselves on the image, each finger's expressive curl, distinct ecstatic wave, as a Bernini is hyperflesh though marble. Each image is an increment of promise. Every so often a cat walks across the roof making a sound of rain beginning. The Valium is delivering its calming message. Then the dark dart of a splinter comes into focus beneath the skin on the side of his forefinger, so he becomes aware of the small hurt that must have been there all along. How did he experience the pain until now? Redwood infects, he informs himself. It pops out rather easily. A red bead forms on the small wound. Ed feels a thrill of self-love and validation when he sees his own blood. He brings the finger to his mouth, hesitates—afraid of infection? He considers his polluted blood with pride and fear. Mac's illness belonged to the world, even in the hospital he was weaving together a collective destiny, while Ed's illness is his own possession.

I wake and feel very relaxed. Daniel's on his way over and Bob's in the kitchen cooking and shuffling papers. The more alert I become the more startled I feel. No matter how hard I run I only move an inch at a time.

My nap is a border. I fell asleep leaving one realm behind, and wake to a weight and substance the old never had. I was never so entirely my physical being.

I leave Daniel and Ed alone on the couch. In all the efficient friendship there isn't much room for emotion. I interrupt them, brightly enough to include myself in their union, but not enough to take up squatter's rights in their suffering.

We three eat dinner. We watch a comedy video—the actors numbed by the sadness of their effort. I doze off halfway through. It's late. We say goodbye. We step down into the night. The door swings on its hinges, the wind, the wooden stairs. All my feelings before seem limited.

NONIE'S MAP

I called Nonie every few weeks to see if there was anything I could do. It was only a gesture, but I was surprised by how little she needed. Mac had been the world; Nonie, a navy blue cowboy scarf over her head, dark glasses, black leather jacket, white face, beer on her breath, had sometimes darted to 24th Street to buy an aspirin. Since Mac's death the blue curtains had been drawn.

I was lonely to the point of fear and I couldn't reconcile Denny's good will with his lack of intention. I called friends but no one answered. Finally a friend who was jealous picked up his phone and in gratitude I listed my disappointments and grievances to cheer him up. While we talked I looked at Nonie's window for a sign of life. Nonie had continued to look out, but secretly, as her temperament dictated. Two beats after I put the phone down it rang.

"Bob, this is Nonie 'cross the street. Can you fill a prescription for me?" I looked up in time to see her curtain fall back. "You know the Sunshine Shopping Center?" She was surprised I'd never heard of it.

"It's in Colma, Bob." Colma is two cities away—a city of

stone cutters and miles of suburban cemeteries, a city of the dead where Mac was buried five months before.

"Nonie, maybe it's time to change to one on Twenty-fourth Street?" Nonie was silent till the conflict ceased to be real.

"Okay Nonie, but come ride with me so you can show me where it is."

"Oh Bob, I can't do that." One would have to know Nonie a long while to tell if she is shrewd or simple.

I regrouped. "Okay, make me a map. Make a map so I can find it without any trouble. A map a child could use."

I crossed the street to collect the prescription and map. It was Indian summer; the heat softened the asphalt, banked against the stucco wall of her building and blistered the paint. I climbed the stairs, the bolt turned before I could knock and after a moment I pushed the door open. The apartment emitted waves of Pine Sol. No more Witch Hazel. The photos were gone, as well as Ed's painting of their old cat. I felt a helpless loss of scale in this apartment stripped of personal markers—the fulfillment of a blunt loneliness. Nonie stood halfway down the hall. She looked weak. She had remained in her quilted blue housecoat and fuzzy blue slippers since the funeral, had remained in the familiar with determination. The white buttons on her housecoat, the view from her window.

The map was ready, folded on the yellow Formica in the generic kitchen. An envelope contained some money and the prescription. I looked at the map. It was just a jagged line with another line branching off. I couldn't read it at all. At the top of the second line she had printed Sunshine Pharmacy. We stood gazing at it, then flatly at each other. She waited for it to sink in that I would really be going to Colma. When it did I asked, "Nonie, on this map, where are we?" She pointed to the bottom of the first line. "So what is this turn?"

"It's where you turn." The map was drawn on a torn square of lined paper in quavering pencil.

"But where is it?" I was glimpsing Nonie's horizon. Her map had no scale. It was a crooked line to the Garden of Eden, a freeway through elastic interior space to the fountain where

Life blazes—the sum total coiling slowly on itself, rising up as an obstacle, greeting the traveler with the sound of *s*.

Nonie grew impatient. "The Sunshine Pharmacy, before the last cemetery." To prove her point she took the pencil and capped the top line with an arrow pointing to the word Sunshine.

Silence and change began a slow spin around us. "How do I know it's the right cemetery?" The problem was too simple to utter. It made me long for indirection.

"You just go along the line, then you turn here," she said to a child for the last time.

EVERYMAN

What can I write for Ed? The question puts Utopia on the café table with the mealy apple and chopped orange, meager allegory garden. I reply, To die and return from the grave. Scale falls off the page, a map that goes beyond decay and orderly renewal.

A prayer begins: Inside me a handful of valleys, a dozen winds, flat, impending as an old *Life* cover. Our junky Chevy zig-zags up a mountain face and the horizon grows blue and heavy as it's left behind. Climb out. Legs wobble. Chill air, moist as a peach. My senses fall towards yellow lights clus-tering on the desolate shell. An inhabited landscape, forest and meadow. A joyous readiness: Again and again I revive the visible to give eyes and a sunset to readiness which does not abate, whose fulfillment is not in sight.

I'm a longing that goes with Ed's longing—longing as precision, a gesture forward— Stepped-forward words bow as their performance ends. He's pressed to his bed by the volume of voices he can't interrupt or understand. Then, as though remembering the "moral," Ed lives forever, dies and revives, keeps returning. What is the *circumstance* of his death, the *agency* of renewal?

I rewrite so a pratfall makes Ed lie down in green pastures. Bees are bees or crosses of the dead—skin sore, tongue thick, sour. The earth's surface. I touch my face, pale worms swallow each other in the soil of my apartment. I dream for Ed, lending my unconscious, a commons producing images. The dark air somehow noisy.

An age of monuments is coming. Let me be battlements so chance can overwhelm me but long ago. "Something happened to me." Ed returns to himself appeased; he climbs as stones crumble backwards under his feet—the harsh path lit by torches and reaching music. Let death be noted in the guidebook. An age of monuments, nonsolutions that last through eternity.

I order sadness and fatigue like pop songs—Parsifal melodic in his hymnal; singing, he's a note. In the next glade Ed's nose lifts to the scorched symbols. Terrified paper birds unfold in the blast. Don't leave me this way. I'm safe in heaven, somehow. St. Sebastian raising his eyes, the cunning expression of Houdini.

Timelessness leads Ed by still waters in the travelog. I believe in the visible and invisible but so what?—the latter a fallen tower in a steel engraving, the former light as a toy.

The reader's expectation may be the faith to restore, the anticipation you enter and become. To answer your question answers every question; you move your arms and legs in the world's unfinished blue. Time sputters, catches like an outboard motor; the jolt towards yourself. Ed can never be done. He turns from side to side on the axis of his spine, radiant; sits forward, alert. The odd moment has authority. Ed never sees or hears enough; he can't include himself; the next breath revises ardently.

Burning isolation. From each red window his outstretched arms. His anxiety is a prayer. When it consumes he falls into a mystery. He covers his face, takes the form of lost bearings. Now more than ever his loss spills over, filled too high with the water of opposites.

"A formal feeling comes." Irreversible caravan, fretful and deep. Each image a leaf fallen far from the Tree. Ed safe in its pattern. But his longing will be open, add zero to the integers of the world (we alive dimly sense a god). HIV attacked what I meant to say (god shaped as regression, god of interruption confirmed by lab results). It had the tender physicality of a nursery, odor of talk and urine, like a nursery open to the future.

Let Ed sail past the coordinates. Let him be Sinbad, someone like that, fast clouds over slow clouds. He tips forward to meet data that does not contain his image. Bark of a neighbor's dog—wind shifts, a trumpet of deep distance. He returns from the hospital as dark transcendence in sunny seas. "C'mere Bob, you're looking sharp." Let Mac return, god of deliberate fantasy. "Hey Bob, you like the sky?" Mac cranes forward as he reels back from a city with traffic. "Up the hill an earthquake cabin, no heat, she can't move, pills on a wood shelf—he's—aw, don't give me that you're too busy. Here's a fact I'm not using—"

You name the forces used in prayer or any magic. Ed's solitude, Mac's fact (a faith I almost believe in): Let Ed rise from the grave. Let him live forever. Let him live while the origami world unfolds into pages, Glass on the sill, Wind in the flue. Now I part my hands. Now I've said my prayer.

AFTERWORD

• ANDREW HOLLERAN •

GEORGE STAMBOLIAN DIED in his sleep the Sunday before Christmas, 1991—at 8:30 that morning. His companion Michael Hampton called to say he'd awakened in their bed in New York City around 6 A.M. and discovered that George was "gone." Earlier that week, Felice Picano talked with George about the introduction George was planning to write to this fourth edition of *Men on Men*; but George, he could see, would not be able to complete it. Toward the end, his illness affected his brain. He would sit up in the middle of the night and say he wanted to get dressed; he would talk reasonably and then talk nonsense. Yet he kept going right to the end. A few days before he died, he and his lover even went to the Met for the premiere of a new opera, *The Ghosts of Versailles*. George went to a lot of concerts and plays; I recall him complaining about some other event he'd attended this past autumn; having lost a lot of weight, he said it was hard to sit through a play on what little flesh was left on his buttocks.

A disappearing ass was not the only aspect of his illness that plagued George: A year or so ago, he was operated on for a rectal fissure and it took a very long time to heal. One day he told me about a conversation with his doctor during which George went on at length about his concern over the appearance of this particular part of his body. "I'll bet you've never met a man so vain about his rectum," George finally said. The astonished doctor said: "You're right."

He was proud of his body, you might say, with reason. *The Persian Boy* came to mind when I thought of George Stambolian. Not because he was Persian—he was of Armenian descent, a matter of some pride and emotion for him—but because he looked, I thought, like the Persian Boy, even though I forget the specific characteristics Mary Renault gave to her hero. George had the most beautiful, perfectly shaped eyes, under two perfectly shaped black eyebrows, and a face that was handsome in the way faces were handsome hundreds of years ago in Byzantium—though George was born and brought up in Bridgeport, Connecticut. Haunted by the massacre of the Armenians at the hands of the Turks earlier in this century, George was filled with stories of his relatives and forebears he heard as a child—stories he wanted someday to put into a book. That he did not is our loss, though some of that growing up is beautifully rendered in the only story George himself ever contributed to the anthologies he edited, the one in *Men on Men 3* called "In My Father's Car."

George cared so much about writing, about language itself, that it may have been difficult for him to write more fiction himself. What was not difficult for him was to praise writers he admired. His first book was on Proust; he was one of those people who could discuss *Remembrance of Things Past* in the way one talked about real friends, living people—he knew the novel so completely. He also loved Beckett. His literary taste was wide-ranging. Reluctant to feature only New York writers in the first volume of *Men on Men*, he searched out a group of California writers, like Robert Glück and Kevin Killian, to introduce. He was always looking for new writers, new work; his last book would be, in fact, this fourth edition of *Men on Men*.

For someone who went to Dartmouth (known at the time for its sex-starved heterosexuals who would drive miles to meet women unavailable in their cold forest) it was ironic that he paved the way for gay male fiction in academia; it was doubly ironic, perhaps, that he taught women at Wellesley College, where he was a tenured professor of French language and literature. George's books include *Marcel Proust and the Creative En-*

counter (1972), *Homosexualities and French Literature* (1979), and *Twentieth-Century French Fiction* (1975). Besides the courses on French writers, he taught a seminar on the nude, and another on gay fiction. He often described to me scenes in the latter class: the shock of some young woman encountering novels depicting gay sex. But that was part of George's persona, I thought: the civilized connoisseur to whom nothing human is foreign. Though in the matter of gay fiction the humanity was his own: He himself had brought it to the classroom.

I'm not sure who else could have done it as well or as dis-cerningly as he: George led a double life. I'm not sure when he began going to Flamingo. George's earlier years—how he got from Dartmouth to Wellesley—were an earlier adventure. When I met him, he was living part of the year in Boston, teaching, and part of the year in New York. In New York he lived partly in Manhattan and on eastern Long Island, with his lover of many years. He also traveled a great deal all his life. He'd been to Egypt and Greece; had lived in Paris. (The last trip he made was shortly before he died, to Dr. Roka's clinic near Zurich.) But at some point he began going to Flamingo, and the baths. George prized dancing and sex. One of my most visual memories of him occurred when I glanced across Second Avenue one afternoon and saw him walking to the Saint on the opposite sidewalk to pick up tickets for some party: Silver-haired, slender, in the harsh sunlight, he looked rather like a monk—devoted to a religion of eros, a devotee of Bacchus, a professor of desire.

George's passionate appreciation of sex, and the senses, and the body, was as wide-ranging as his taste in literature: He loved the natural odor of skin, he loved the way the body smelled. The last time we met, he described how he was edu-cating a beautiful young man in making the body present-able. He cherished the body not only in the flesh, but in all its representations: sculpture, painting, literature, photogra-phy. He took sex seriously. He wrote a book consisting of interviews with a voyeur, an exhibitionist, and a masochist (*Male Fantasies/Gay Realities*). He also had a sense of humor about what we do to obtain sex—the tales he told of his adventures on the sex-phone lines, into the night in Boston and New York, cars towed, the occasional find who loved the body's scent as much as he, were hilarious. He lived life in a good-natured way. There was no rancor when he told me, toward the end of his struggle, "Life is madness. Madness." In fact, the word I keep wanting to describe him with is "civilized"—except that word has become devalued of late to convey something merely snobbish, aloof. Not so with George. He had his snobberies, no doubt—he was La Duchesse in the letters we wrote; I was the Baroness Putbus's Maid—but to me he was civilized in the sense of believing in the art of life, in having tact, intelligence, and very good manners, not to mention *joie de vivre*, in knowing how to behave so as to give other human beings pleasure.

This included, in a way, the series he is known for—the *Men on Men* anthologies. As an editor, George was scrupulous, thorough, completely attentive. He kept contributors notified of every important stage in the book. He worried about the cover, organized the participation of other writers and himself in readings, went on tour (and met new writers for his anthology on such trips); he read every review, sometimes responded personally to comments he thought unfair, inaccurate. An editor who worked with George on the first *Men on Men* tells me he simply ignored all her comments—which fits my impression of him: confident, perhaps imperious, in his own judgment, taste, selection. The *Men on Men* series proved a success; George kept assembling successive volumes, and became a scout for his publisher for other gay books worthy of publication.

During my last visit with George, in his apartment in Cambridge, Massachusetts, one of these was on the table—a British book he'd "discovered" for his American publisher: Neil Bartlett's *Ready to Catch Him Should He Fall*. (It's testament to George's energy that on the day I write this, the *Christopher Street* bestseller list has two books he "sponsored": Bartlett's novel, and the third *Men on Men*.) We'd already discussed that morning—after George's return from a night with his young friend at a Pet Shop Boys concert—the recent academic studies of gender and homosexuality in fiction, and the story by Balzac, and an essay by Barthes, on which Bartlett had based his play *Sarassine*—and then, as I sat there, marveling at this man's energy, he began to praise Bartlett's novel. He praised it with so much conviction I felt I had to read it at once, on the plane home that day, and begged him to lend me the galleys. Cynical and bored with toiling in the field of fiction—this field that had sprouted bumper crops since the day it was first encountered as a new, exotic forest—I was awestruck by his enthusiasm for this new writer. How could he get so excited, still? And not only over Bartlett. He then began reading aloud one of the stories he had accepted for the fourth *Men on Men*—a particular favorite of his. And I marveled that anyone could retain so much enthusiasm and excitement not only in the face of a debilitating illness, but also despite the familiarity, the banality, of something that was no longer being done for the first time. To George, however, it was still exciting.

But then the energy he brought to introducing new gay writers to the public had always been intense. He founded the gay caucus of the Modern Language Association. George went to all the conferences that have sprung up in recent years, the Out/Write in San Francisco (this year in Boston), the conference at Harvard two years ago, Rutgers this last, the annual Lambda Literary Awards at the ABA, and, most particularly, the awarding of the Ferro-Grumley Award. This award was George's doing—George's determined carrying out of the wishes of two men he became very fond of before they died. After their deaths, George set up the Ferro-Grumley Foundation: took care of the legal details; prompted the Ferro family for support; raised money wherever he could, including from his own pocket; chose the panel of readers and judges; brought to reality an idea that—except for his loyalty—would almost certainly have died aborning. And it was George—and Allen Barnett—who left the Foundation money in their wills so that it would become even more firmly established after they died. It was George—in this and so many other cases—who furthered a cause he believed in: that of gay literature.

When Robert Ferro was alive, he used to refer to this genre in letters as "gaylitter" and joked that the only prize he could aspire to would be a photograph on the wall above the jukebox in a gay bar on West Street. But in fact, since his death, gaylitter had become much more respectable—thanks in no small part to George. You may think what you will about the odd, symbiotic relationship between literature and the university. You may wonder why books must be taught in college courses before acquiring a certain prestige, why the artist and teacher move together like the shark and the sucker-fish that swims on its back. You may ask if there should be such a thing as "gay lit" in the best of all possible worlds. As Ed White points out, in France there is no category for these writers. You may wonder what the meaning is of this explosion in gay studies, conferences and criticism; whether it's not just a way for gay scholars, grad students, publishers, to be gay at work; whether it has any significance beyond that to the culture at large. You may even ask if these awards do not create an atmosphere that gay-litter was blissfully *free* of when it began.

Whatever you decide, it seems that in George Stambolian we have not only an example, but a cause, of the whole remarkable boom. He was the link, the interface, between two heretofore unrelated places: the University and the Saint. In his own life, and work, he brought a new subject into the forum. Because of him, gaylitter is now a subject taught in school, and disseminated to people who might not otherwise have had access to this particular form of vicarious life.

Indeed, something George wrote, about the reasons for accepting the challenge of putting together his first anthology of gay writing, expresses his credo with startling clarity in the first paragraph of his introduction to *Men on Men 1*: "In matters of gay writing I confess to having the zeal of a missionary for whom nothing is more tempting than a chance to reach new audiences." Or the chance to dispel "the notion so often repeated by hostile critics that gay fiction must inevitably be second-rate because homosexuality itself is somehow incomplete."

Reading George's introductions to the first three *Men on Men* volumes is fascinating. One is struck not only by the fact that AIDS was present, both as subject and killer of the very writers he was publishing, from the very start, but that George kept refining his belief in the importance of this writing. In *Men on Men 2*, he astutely described the paradox of gay people's refusal "to be denied one's history and identity as a member of the community, and the equally adamant refusal to have one's individuality reduced to being nothing more than a reflection of that community." (In other words, the gay writer is saying: "I'm gay, yes, but not *just* gay; I'm also an individual person.") "What is being sought" in gay fiction, he wrote, "is a balance between one's need for self-definition and a wariness of all definitions. What is being expressed is a protest against all forms of cultural isolation."

This last sums up a very deep strain in American life, it seems to me; one that has fairly dominated our history in the past three decades. "The history of any culture is a history of change," George wrote in *Men on Men 2*, "and of struggle. Throughout its own history, American culture has been repeatedly enriched by artists from different regions of the country and from different minorities—Jews after World War II, then blacks and women. . . . Gay fiction is providing access to language for an ever more diverse community and producing writers whose . . . language can no longer be ignored. Above all, it is revitalizing American literature by contesting its social and literary assumptions." Because, from *Men on Men 3*: "Gay fiction . . . can question all decisions about what art is and what it is not, what can be represented and what cannot, what is private and what is not. These are ultimately moral questions, and as surprising as it may seem to some, gay fiction today is a moral art." As was George—among other things—deeply, passionately moral.

ABOUT THE AUTHORS

GEORGE STAMBOLIAN was professor of French and Inter-disciplinary Studies at Wellesley College, a trustee of the Ferro-Grumley Foundation, and a member of the Advisory Board of the Lesbian and Gay Studies Center at Yale University. He attended Dartmouth College and received his Ph.D. from the University of Wisconsin. In addition to editing all four *Men on Men* anthologies, he was the author of *Marcel Proust and the Creative Encounter* and *Homosexualities and French Literature* (with Elaine Marks) and the editor of *Twentieth Century French Fiction* and *Male Fantasies/Gay Realities: Interviews with Ten Men*. He wrote and lectured extensively about gay literature. He died in December 1991.

FELICE PICANO is co-publisher of the Gay Presses of New York and lives in New York City. He is the author of eight novels, *Smart As the Devil, Eyes, The Mesmerist, The Lure, An Asian Minor, Late in the Season, House of Cards,* and *To the Seventh Power*; two books of poetry, *The Deformity Lover* and *Window Elegies*; a collection of stories, *Slashed to Ribbons in Defense of Love*; and two volumes of memoirs, *Ambidextrous* and *Men Who Loved Me*. He edited an anthology of gay fiction, *A True Likeness*, and his poems, reviews, and stories have appeared widely. He is the author of *The New Joy of Gay Sex* (with Charles Silverstein), which will be published by HarperCollins, and is at work on a new novel.

ANDREW HOLLERAN is the author of two novels, *Dancer from the Dance* and *Nights in Aruba*, and a collection of essays, *Ground Zero*. His "New York Notebook" column in *Christopher Street* received a Gay Press Association Award, and his stories and articles have also appeared in *New York*, *The New York Native*, and *Wigwag*. He divides his time between New York City and Florida, where he is writing a novel.

LUIS ALFARO lives in Los Angeles and attended the Mentor Playwrights Program. He has written and performed in two performance pieces, "Bitter Homes and Gardens" and "Downtown," and has been published in *Blood Whispers: L.A. Writers on Aids*, edited by Terry Wolverton. He is currently at work on a new performance piece.

DAVID B. FEINBERG is the author of *Eighty-Sixed*, winner of a Lambda Literary Award, and *Spontaneous Combustion*. His stories, essays, and reviews have appeared in *The New York Times Book Review*, *The Adovocate*, *The James White Review*, *Christopher Street*, *Outweek*, *Diseased Pariah News*, and *NYQ*, as well as in the anthologies *Men on Men 2* and *The Gay Nineties*. He lives in New York City and is now at work on a new novel and a play.

ROBERT GLÜCK is the author of a narrative poem, *Andy*; three volumes of poems and prose pieces, *Family Poems*, *Metaphysics*, and *Reader*; a collection of altered translations, *La Fontaine* (with Bruce Boone); a collection of stories, *Elements of a Coffee Service*; and a novel, *Jack the Modernist*. His poems, stories, and articles have appeared in *Ironwood*, *Poetics Journal*, *Semiotext(e)*, *Christopher Street*, and *The Advocate* and have been anthologized in *The Faber Book of Gay Short Fiction*, *New Directions Anthology*, *Personal Dispatches: Writers Confront AIDS*, and *Discontents*, edited by Dennis Cooper. Born in Cleveland, he holds an MFA in writing from San Francisco State University, where he was the Director of the Poetry Center from 1988–1991. He received an Academy of American Poets Award and a Browning Award, and lives in San Francisco. His short story "Everyman" is one in a forthcoming collection of the same title.

RICHARD HOUSE was born in Cyprus and lives in Chicago. He is a graduate from the Falmouth School of Art (in England) and the Art Institute of Chicago. His work has appeared in *The Village Voice Literary Supplement* and the anthology *Discontents*. He is at work on a novel, tentatively titled *Hush*.

MANUEL IGREJAS was born in Newark and now lives in Montclair, New Jersey. His fiction and poetry have appeared in *Maelstrom*, *Win*, *Gaysweek*, and *A Shout in the Street*, and his poem "Herois do Mar" will appear in the anthology *A New Geography of Poets*. The recipient of a fellowship from the New Jersey Council of the Arts, he is at work on a play, *Hell on the Hudson*.

GREG JOHNSON is associate professor of English at Kennesaw State College in Atlanta, where he lives. He holds a Ph.D. in English Literature from Emory and is the author of two books of criticism, *Understanding Joyce Carol Oates* and *Emily Dickinson: Perception and the Poet's Quest*; two story collections, *A Friendly Deceit* and *Distant Friends*; and a book of poetry, *Aid and Comfort*. His fiction has appeared in *The Southern Review*, *Virginia Quarterly Review*, *Southwest Review*, *Ontario Review*, and the anthologies *Prize Stories: The O. Henry Awards* and *New Stories from the South: The Year's Best*, and his reviews have appeared in *The New York Times Book Review*, *The Atlanta Journal-Constitution*, and *The Chicago Tribune*. The 1991 winner in the PEN Syndicated Fiction Project, he is at work on a new collection of stories and a novel, *Pagan Babies*, from which his narrative "The Valentine" was drawn. *Pagan Babies* will be published in 1993 by Dutton.

RAYMOND LUCZAK, a native of Michigan, became deaf at the age of seven months due to double pneumonia. After graduating from Gallaudet University, he moved to New York City, where his play *Snooty* won the New York Deaf Theater's 1990

Samuel Edwards Deaf Playwrights Competition. His poetry and essays have appeared in *Christopher Street*, *Art & Understanding*, and *The New York Native*. The story included in this anthology was taken from his novel *A Collage of Hands*. He has completed seven screenplays, and is editing an anthology of deaf lesbian and gay voices for Alyson Publications.

DALE PECK was born in Bay Shore, New York, and lives in Manhattan. He attended Drew University, and his fiction, essays, and reviews have appeared in *NYQ*, *Outweek*, *Amethyst*, and the anthology *Discontents*. "Fucking Martin" is from a novel, *Martin & John*, which will be published in 1993 by Farrar, Straus & Giroux.

JOHN RECHY divides his time between Los Angeles and New York City. He is the author of nine novels, *City of Night*, *Numbers*, *This Day's Death*, *The Vampires*, *The Fourth Angel*, *Rushes*, *Bodies and Souls*, *Marilyn's Daughter*, and *The Miraculous Day of Amalia Gomez*, and a documentary, *The Sexual Outlaw*. His fiction and articles have appeared in many periodicals, including *The Los Angeles Times Book Review*, *Saturday Review*, *The New York Times Book Review*, *Mother Jones*, *The Nation*, and *The Advocate*. He has received the Longview Foundation Award and a National Endowment for the Arts Award. His new novel, *Autobiography: A Novel*, of which "Love in the Backrooms" is a part, is both a sequel and a prequel to *City of Night* and will be published in 1993.

PAUL RUSSELL is the author of *The Salt Point* and *Boys of Life*. His poetry and short stories have appeared in *Epoch*, *The Carolina Quarterly*, and *The Crescent Review*. A professor of English at Vassar College, he lives outside Poughkeepsie, New York, where he is at work on a new novel.

DOUGLAS SADOWNICK was born in New York City and lives in Venice, California. A graduate of Columbia, his fiction, essays, and reviews have appeared in *L.A. Weekly*, *The Los Angeles Times*, *The Advocate*, *The Village Voice*, *High Performance*, *NYQ*, *American Film*, as well as in the anthologies *Blood Whis-*

pers: L.A. *Writers on AIDS, Sundays at Seven*, edited by Jim Picket, and *Positively Gay*, edited by Betty Berzon. "Sacred Lips of the Bronx" is part of a forthcoming novel of the same title.

RANDY SANDERSON was born in Miami and lives in New York City. He is a member of the Merce Cunningham Dance Company. "Bone" is his first published work, and is part of a forthcoming novel, *Stand Backwards*.

MICHAEL WADE SIMPSON was born in San Diego and lives in Newburyport, Massachusetts. He attended the University of Southern California, and his fiction has appeared in *The Crescent Review, Western Humanities Review, South Carolina Review, Black River Review*, and *The Sun*. He has completed one novel, *Three-Quarter Time*, and is now at work on a second, tentatively titled *Tree of Life*.

JACK SLATER was born in Dayton, Ohio, and divides his time between Los Angeles and a small town in the central mountains of Mexico. His articles have appeared in *The Los Angeles Times, Ebony, The New York Times Magazine, The New York Times Book Review, California, Essence, Emmy*, and *Rolling Stone*, and he is at work on a novel titled *His Own*.

MATTHEW STADLER is the author of *Landscape: Memory*, which was nominated for a Lambda Literary Award. He was born in Seattle, where he now lives, and attended Oberlin College, the London School of Economics, and the Columbia University Writing Program. His work has appeared in *The New York Times Book Review* and *Grand Street*, and he is at work on two new novels, *The Dissolution of Nicholas Dee* and *The Sex Offender: A Moral Tale*, which develops the narrative in this anthology, and a book-length essay about the paintings of Denton Welch.

DAVID VERNON was born in New York City and lives in Los Angeles. He attended New York University, and his short stories have appeared in two anthologies, *Blood Whispers: L.A. Writers on AIDS* and *Indivisible: New Short Fiction by West Coast*

Gay and Lesbian Writers. He is currently at work on a novel and a collection of stories, *Absence*, which will include "Inside."

PETER WELTNER holds a Ph.D. from Indiana University and is a professor of English at San Francisco State University. He is the author of a novel, *Identity and Difference*, a collection of stories, *Beachside Entries/Specific Ghosts*, and three novellas, *In a Time of Combat for the Angel*. His stories and articles have appeared in *ELR*, *The Ohio Review*, *Ironwood*, *American Short Fiction*, *Five Fingers Review* and *The James White Review*. He lives in San Francisco, where he is at work on a new collection of stories, *The Risk of His Music*, which will include "The Greek Head," a short novel, *The Truth of a Life Can Never Be Free*, and a novel, *The Long Walk Back Down*.

NORMAN WONG was born in Honolulu and lives in New York City. He attended the University of Chicago and the Johns Hopkins Writing Seminars, and his fiction has appeared in *The Kenyon Review* and *The Three Penny Review*. He is currently working on a novel.

PUBLICATIONS OF INTEREST

Fiction with gay themes has appeared in many mainstream periodicals in recent years. The following is a selective list of journals and magazines that *regularly* publish gay fiction. Contributors should inform themselves of the editorial policy of each publication before submitting manuscripts.

ADVOCATE MEN. Box 4371, Los Angeles, CA 90078

AMETHYST: A JOURNAL FOR LESBIANS AND GAY MEN. Southeastern Arts, Media and Education Project, Inc., Box 54719, Atlanta, GA 30308

BGM (black gay men). The Blackside Press, Box 9391, Washington, D.C. 20013

BLACK/OUT. The National Coalition of Black Gay Women and Men, Box 19248, Washington, DC 20013

CHRISTOPHER STREET. That New Magazine, Inc. Box 1475, Church Street Station, New York, NY 10008

THE EVERGREEN CHRONICLES. Box 8939, Minneapolis, MN 55408

FAG RAG. Box 331, Kenmore Station, Boston, MA 02215

THE JAMES WHITE REVIEW: A GAY MEN'S LITER-ARY QUARTERLY. Box 3356, Traffic Station, Minneapolis, MN 55403

MANDATE. Mavety Media Group, 462 Broadway, 4th Floor, New York, NY 10013

OUT/LOOK: NATIONAL GAY AND LESBIAN QUAR-TERLY. Box 460430, San Francisco, CA 94146

THE PYRAMID PUBLICATION: THE PROVOCATIVE JOURNAL FOR LESBIANS AND GAY MEN OF COLOR. Box 1111, Canal Street Station, New York, NY 10013

RFD: A COUNTRY JOURNAL FOR GAY MEN EVERY-WHERE. Box 68, Liberty, TN 37095

TORSO. Mavety Media Group, 462 Broadway, 4th Floor, New York, NY 10013

TRIBE: AN AMERICAN GAY JOURNAL. Columbia Publishing Company, 234 East 25th Street, Baltimore, MD 21218